Maggie Furey was born i[...] qualified teacher, but has [...] Radio Newcastle, been an advisor in the Durham Reading Resources Centre and organized children's book fairs. She now lives in County Wicklow, Ireland with her husband and six cats.

ALSO BY MAGGIE FUREY IN LEGEND

Aurian
Harp of Winds
The Sword of Flame

DHIAMMARA

Maggie Furey

LEGEND

First published by Legend Books in 1997
20 Vauxhall Bridge Road, London SW1 2SA

1 3 5 7 9 10 8 6 4 2

Copyright © Maggie Furey 1997

The right of Maggie Furey to be identified as the author
of this work has been asserted by her in accordance
with the Copyright, Designs and Patents Act, 1988.

This book is sold subject to the condition that it shall not,
by way of trade or otherwise, be lent, resold, hired out, or
otherwise circulated without the publisher's prior consent in
any form of binding or cover other than that in which it is
published and without a similar condition including this
condition being imposed on the subsequent purchaser.

An imprint of Random House UK Limited

Random House Australia (Pty) Limited
20 Alfred Street, Milsons Point, Sydney,
New South Wales 2061, Australia

Random House New Zealand Limited
18 Poland Road, Glenfield
Auckland 10, New Zealand

Random House South Africa (Pty) Limited
Endulini, 5a Jubilee Road, Parktown 2193, South Africa

Random House UK Limited Reg. No. 954009

A CIP catalogue record for this book is available from the
British Library

Papers used by Random House UK Limited are natural,
recyclable products made from wood grown in sustainable
forests. The manufacturing processes conform to the
environmental regulations of the country of origin

Typeset by SX Composing DTP, Rayleigh, Essex
Printed and bound in Great Britain by
Cox & Wyman Ltd, Reading, Berkshire

ISBN 0 09 968111 0

Dedication:

This one is for those special friends who have given their unstinting help and support to Eric and myself over the last twelve, hair-raising months:

Sheila Mawer and Geoff Green, for putting us up and putting up with us during the homeless months of the house move.

Diane Duane and Peter Morwood, for taking us by the hand and leading us safely through the minefield of the move to Ireland.

Philomena and Michael O'Connor – whose warm and wonderful company is a joy and an inspiration.

And Dónal Cunningham, computer-Mage without peer, who, among many other kindnesses, was instrumental in getting this manuscript delivered on time. (He makes a mean chocolate truffle, too!)

Thanks, guys – for everything.

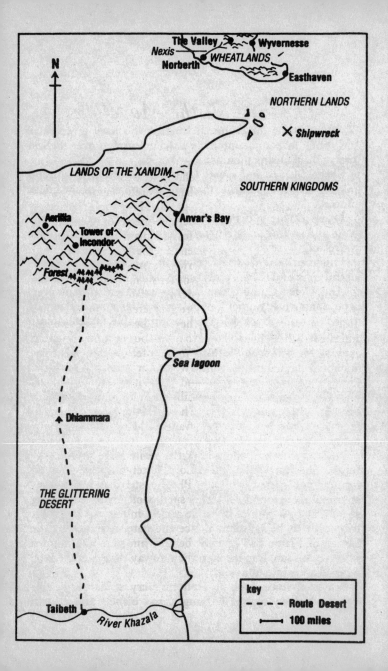

1

The Last of the Magefolk

When Aurian failed to master the Sword of Flame, the Phaerie were free at last. To Hellorin, it was a stroke of good fortune beyond belief that the flame-haired Magewoman had not only, through her weakness, granted his people the liberty they had craved, but had also been the means of restoring the Phaerie steeds, which had lived for so long in human guise, far across the sea. 'Ride, my children,' he roared exultantly. 'Let the world tremble, for the Phaerie ride once more!'

'No,' Eilin shouted. 'Lord, you must not do this. Let the Xandim go. These are intelligent beings!'

For an instant, the Forest Lord hesitated. While the Mage had been trapped in his realm they had become close friends, and she had meant a good deal to him – but now that he could exercise his will again nothing must interfere with his freedom. The days of the Magefolk were over, and once again the Phaerie could take the world and shake it to its foundations. Hellorin shrugged, dismissing Eilin from his mind along with his soft-hearted son, who would have left the Phaerie steeds in their useless human form. D'arvan would be taught to know better in times to come.

With a spine-wrenching leap, the white mare sprang skywards. The heart of the Forest Lord, fettered and earthbound for so long, soared with his Phaerie steed as her hooves spurned the ground and she sped aloft, with stretching strides, along a path of invisible air. So intent was he on his triumph that he failed to notice the gate in time that the Sword of Flame had opened behind him. He did not see D'arvan, his son, leap through the gateway after Aurian, to be whirled away into oblivion.

Scores of voices took up Hellorin's cry as his people followed; shadowy figures no longer, but comely and clad in

1

radiant flesh: soaring behind him on their own mounts, who but moments before had worn the guise, and held the consciousness and intelligence, of mortal men. Higher and higher the Phaerie climbed, swarming upward like a drift of dark smoke as they followed their lord into the heavens. Those who remained earthbound, through lack of sufficient horses, scattered into the forest as though they planned to follow the hunt on foot.

The Forest Lord glanced proudly back at his followers, his triumph marred only by the fact that this gathering was but a pallid reflection of the great ridings of old, for little more than fivescore of the Phaerie steeds had come with the strangers to the Vale, and only so many of his folk could take to the skies. Firmly, he shrugged the thought aside, determined not to let such comparisons mar this great and triumphal moment. If the missing horses were on this side of the ocean they would be found – and if they were still lost across the seas, beyond the powerful reach of the Phaerie, then others could easily be bred from the stock that had been recovered today.

Casting such mundane matters from his mind, Hellorin revelled in his new freedom, breathing in great draughts of the icy wind that stung his face and burned thinly in his lungs. Glancing down, he gloried in the power of his Phaerie mount as the white mare leapt from cloud to cloud, striking thunderbolts earthwards with her silver hooves.

Far below, Hellorin's keen eyes spied human shapes: a throng of fleeing Mortals who were swarming like ants through the smouldering trees near the rim of the Vale. Though such creatures had their uses, they must first be taught a lesson – that the Phaerie were their masters now. With a triumphant howl, the Forest Lord called up his pack of great hounds and spurred the white mare, sending her hurtling downwards, towards the invaders. His people followed, curving down out of the sky like shooting stars, their eyes ablaze with the thirsting lust for Mortal blood, their voices upraised in a shrill, discordant song of battle that sliced the air like blades. One by one, the mercenaries who had followed Eliseth on her ill-fated raid were hunted down like deer amid the trees, and like deer were slaughtered while the earth

2

amid the roots of the tortured forest drank deeply of their blood. Only when all the Mortals had been slain did the Phaerie look around them for other prey.

In the centre of the Vale's great bowl, on the shores of the lake, the Earth-Mage Eilin shuddered to hear the death-screams of the slaughtered Mortals. The Phaerie Lord's treachery was a minor matter when compared to the loss of her daughter, but the betrayal hurt none the less. Eilin, almost crushed beneath the weight of her grief, stood numb and irresolute. Only her stubborn pride kept her on her feet. For the second time in her life, she beheld the destruction of all she held dear – her daughter, her home, her hopes. The first time, when Geraint had died and her life had fallen apart in ruin, she had risen above grief and disaster to build a productive and purposeful life from the rubble of her dreams – but she was older now: crushed, bewildered and alone. How could she ever find the strength and courage to pick up the pieces a second time?

Beside her, her daughter's erstwhile companions, Vannor and Parric stood at the forefront of the band of rebels who had sheltered in her Valley during her absence in the otherworldly Phaerie realm. Through her constant vigil at Hellorin's magic window that had looked out on her own world, she had come to know all these folk over the last months – with the exception of one, a stranger; by his colouring and facial structure a foreigner from across the seas, where the magic of the Forest Lord's window did not reach.

None of these Mortals meant anything to Eilin – save that she couldn't wait for them to leave. The Mage wanted her Valley to herself again – she wanted time to repair the devastation that had been visited upon her by the Weather-Mage Eliseth, and solitude in which to assimilate the horror of losing a daughter and the pain of her betrayal by the Phaerie Lord. There was no help for it, however. These people had been Aurian's friends and companions. They were as stunned as Eilin by the horrors of the day, and she knew they would need to rest and collect themselves before she could be rid of them at last. They would find no support from her, though –

she had nothing left to give. Let the Mortals shift for themselves!

Of all the folk who had survived the dreadful events of that day, Dulsina, who had scarcely known the Lady Aurian, seemed best equipped to cope. As she looked around at her devastated companions, the woman realized that if they were to spend the night in a comparative degree of comfort it must be up to her. Parric had wandered away from the others and was standing with his back to them, his head bowed, his shoulders slumped in grief and defeat. Even at this distance Dulsina could hear the bloodcurdling sound of his ceaseless cursing. Sangra was struggling valiantly, with little success, to stifle her tears. She was grasping the hilt of her sword so tightly that her hands were a knot of bones, as if by force of arms she could defeat the sense of dread and desolation that had overtaken her.

Fional, though distraught at the loss of his friend D'arvan, was with the stranger – the exotic man with a tanned face, long dark hair and the lithe, muscled body of a dancer. The archer was trying his best to calm the stranger as he cried out loudly in rage and anguish, in some foreign tongue, while Vannor – dear, good-hearted Vannor, who up to a moment ago seemed so calm and collected – had sat down on the ground so abruptly that it looked as though his knees had turned to water, and covered his face with his hands. Worst of all, the Lady Eilin stood unmoving, a little apart from the others, her eyes blazing with a bleak and terrible light in a face that had been turned to stone.

Someone would have to take care of them all – that much was plain. Perhaps, Dulsina thought, it might be better if they could leave this unhappy place with its tragic associations, and return to what remained of the rebel camp – if, as she hoped, their sanctuary had escaped the flames. Her companions, however, seemed unable to rouse themselves from their shocked and grieving lassitude – and when she tried to persuade the Lady Eilin, she was repulsed by an impenetrable wall of ice and, behind it, a blaze of suppressed rage that seared like fire.

4

There was little in life that daunted Dulsina, but the way the Mage's eyes looked straight through her chilled her to the heart. For her very life, she dared not push Eilin further – for she was certain that the next time the Lady's dreadful gaze turned upon her, it would be not chill with indifference, but burning with wrath. Dulsina, no fool, changed her plans with alacrity. We can move what's left of the encampment here, she decided briskly. The gods only know, we'll need some comforts about us, after the terrible things we've seen and suffered today. The sun will be setting before much longer, and we must have food and shelter organized before it gets dark.

Already the sun was sinking into the wrack of smoke that hung over the Vale like a grim, grey pall. Dulsina sighed. Surely there must be someone here who could help her? Someone sensible, and capable, who was still in possession of his wits? It was with a sense of profound thankfulness that she noticed Hargorn, standing a short distance away on the shore of the lake. The veteran was looking out across the water at the island, leaning heavily on his sword, which he had planted, point down, in the muddy bank of the lake. As she approached him, Dulsina's relief vanished abruptly. For the first time since she had met him, Hargorn looked like an old man. But as he heard her footsteps he straightened, and though there were telltale glints of moisture on his seamed face as he turned towards her, he was dry-eyed and seemed in full possession of his wits – save for the dread, bitter emptiness that lurked behind his gaze.

'Maya's gone,' he said softly, before Dulsina could speak. 'The poor lass was here in the Vale all the time and I never knew it – and now she's gone again.' His voice sank to a whisper. 'I was always so proud of her – what she made of herself. She didn't know it, but she was like the daughter I never had.' Then he shook himself, and his eyes became alert once more. 'But there's no sense in mourning her as if she's dead when we don't know for sure,' he added decisively. 'Maya would have a thing or two to say about that – she's got more balls than most men put together – sorry, lovey,' he apologized to Dulsina, remembering, belatedly, that he was not talking to

5

one of his men. 'What can I do for you, anyway?'

Dulsina had to swallow back her own sadness before she could reply. His words had reminded her of the Solstice Eve when she had lost Vannor's daughter in the crowded Grand Arcade. Maya and the Lady Aurian had rescued Zanna from the throng and brought her back safely to the carriage. The two young women, warrior and Mage but the fastest of friends, so full of the courage and promise of youth, had been through so much hardship and suffering since then – and now both of them were gone.

'Come on, now,' Hargorn gently interrupted her thoughts. 'It doesn't do to dwell on it – I shouldn't have set you off. The gods help anyone who dares to tangle with Maya and Aurian – and standing around here like a bunch of wet hens won't get *us* anywhere, either. Thank goodness the two of us are here – *some*body's got to have their wits about them.'

Dulsina smiled, comforted by the warm sense of comradeship that existed between them. She and the ageing warrior had shared a soft spot for each other ever since he had smuggled her to the Valley with the rest of the rebels, after Vannor had forbidden her to come.

Taking a grip on herself, the woman explained her predicament to Hargorn. 'The Lady Eilin won't shift from this spot, poor thing, and the rest of them are more like headless chickens than wet hens. We need to get a camp together before nightfall . . .'

'Don't worry,' the veteran assured her. 'I'll round up our folk and get them busy. I'll set some of them to building shelters, if you can come back to the camp with the rest of us and choose what you want us to bring. We can be back here with food and blankets in no time.'

As he hurried off, Dulsina noticed that his sword was still where he had left it – planted in the mud of the lakeside. Hargorn wasn't usually so absent-minded. Was age catching up with the veteran at last? She called him back. 'Hargorn – you've forgotten your sword.'

He looked at her bleakly, and shook his head. 'It was a sword that was responsible for this disaster in the first place. I'm finished with fighting, Dulsina – I haven't the heart for it

6

any more – not after today. I'll never touch a sword again.'

After a time, Parric pulled himself out of his dazed reverie, and realized with dismay that dusk had fallen. He was aghast to discover how long he had been simply standing there, lost in anguish and horror – and thoroughly ashamed to find that Dulsina and Hargorn had been forced to cope alone. They had managed very well without him, the cavalry master admitted – but it shouldn't have been necessary.

'Don't worry about it,' Dulsina told him. 'Once we got our belongings moved from the old camp, the rest was easy. There's dry wood enough for burning now, on the edge of the fires where the trees are still just smouldering – and there was no need to hunt. Lots of animals were killed by the smoke – if you look in the woods there are bodies all over the place.' A slight catch in her voice and her pale, strained face were the only things about her that hinted to Parric of the carnage she had witnessed in the forest.

Now that Dulsina had mentioned it, the cavalry master became aware, for the first time, of the mouthwatering aromas of roasting meat. A short distance away from him, a rough camp was taking shape, with primitive shelters constructed from wooden frameworks draped with blankets, cloaks, and hides. A huge fire blazed like a beacon on the shores of the lake, with a cluster of smaller cooking fires close by.

'Is there anything I can do to help?' Parric asked guiltily.

'Yes,' Dulsina told him. 'You can go and comfort your friend Sangra and that poor young man you brought with you from foreign parts.'

The cavalry master looked through the gathering darkness, across the sward to where Sangra and Yazour were sitting close to the fire, deep in talk and holding tightly to one another's hands.

'It looks like the two of them are managing well enough without me,' he grumbled. 'Where's Vannor?'

The deep line of a frown appeared between Dulsina's dark brows. 'Never you mind about him,' she retorted firmly. 'You go and help your young friends over there. I've dealt with Vannor myself – instead of letting him sit there and brood,

7

I've sent him to talk to the Lady Eilin. The gods only know, someone ought to do it.'

Eilin cursed and clenched her fists at her sides in annoyance as she saw the Mortal approaching. Once her unwelcome guests had begun to set up their camp – near the very beech-grove where Forral had first made his shelter, she thought, with a flash of old pain that she'd believed to be long behind her – the Mage, seeking solitude, had retreated across the charred and splintered wooden bridge to the sanctuary of her island. No one, she'd been certain, would dare to follow her there. How wrong she had been – but when Eilin's unwelcome visitor came close enough to be recognized, she found that she was not in the least surprised.

Over the years the Mage had heard a great deal about Vannor from Aurian, during her daughter's summer visits. More recently she had observed him through Hellorin's magical window, until his rash return to Nexis in search of his daughter, and had been impressed by the compassionate, level-headed way in which he'd ruled his band of rebels who had taken sanctuary in her Valley. He had been the first to recognize that his folk were being helped, albeit by some mysterious, invisible entity – D'arvan – and he had made his followers obey the strictures and limitations that the Forest Lord's son had set about the rebel camp.

Nevertheless, despite her respect for the former rebel leader, Eilin was still irritated by his unwelcome intrusion upon her peace. No doubt he would be wanting to discuss the details and possible repercussions of Eliseth's attack and disappearance – and what of Miathan? What part had the Archmage played in the drama that had occurred? What would *he* do next? The Mage sighed. May the gods forgive me – I just can't face this, she thought. She knew that these matters were important, and would eventually have to be addressed – but not just yet. She was too heartsick and weary right now to worry about the future.

In the blood-red light of the setting sun, Eilin stepped back from the bridge and deliberately turned away from the approaching Mortal to regard the ruins of her old home.

8

Following the vanishment of the Sword of Flame, the tower had returned to the Lady's island – after a fashion. The damage by wind and weather, the scarred black stone and twisted ironwork, the fallen ceilings and gaping windows with their drifts of shattered crystal, the sense of desolation and abandonment – these sights were painful beyond all bearing. How will I ever build it up again? she thought desperately. Where should I even start?

'We – your Mortal friends – would be more than happy to assist you, my Lady, if help you need. It's a daunting task to be faced alone.'

The Mage swung round with a gasp. Had the wretched man been reading her mind? 'I need no help from the Mortals,' she snarled. How dared he suggest that she was not capable of rebuilding her own home? Vannor bowed low, but said nothing. Eilin let the silence stretch out between them until it became a gaping chasm. The Mortal waited until the suspense tautened to breaking point, but the Mage proudly refused to acknowledge him further.

Eventually Vannor spoke, his voice very gentle, just as though her previous angry words had never been uttered. 'Lady, there's food and fire and companionship on the other shore. Will you not cross your bridge, and join us?'

Eilin could not meet his eyes. It had been bad enough to hear the kindness in his voice – if she saw the sympathy and concern that she knew would be written on his face, the brittle citadel of pride she had constructed around herself would shatter. She could not countenance the idea of breaking down into tears in front of this wretched man.

'I need no charity from *your* kind,' she snapped at Vannor, biting off each word with savage emphasis. 'A plague on your food and fires and company! You have no business here, and I want you all gone by noon tomorrow, or you must face the consequences.' She turned, at last, to glare at him. 'This Vale is my place, Mortal. *Mine!*'

Vannor, clearly unimpressed by her threat, looked at her long and appraisingly. 'As you wish,' he said at last. 'No one would dispute your right to this place, Lady. But if we can ever assist you . . .' he stopped himself, and shook his head.

'No,' he muttered softly, as if to himself. 'You wouldn't, would you? In your stupid, stiff-necked pride you could never bring yourself to ask for, or accept, Mortal help – not supposing you were to perish here, of hunger and cold and loneliness.'

At his words, Eilin's anger boiled over at last. She flew at him like a harpy, shrieking curses at the top of her voice. It was a relief to have a target for the rage that had been building within her. Vannor faced her, unintimidated, with steady calmness – and yes, there it was – the pity that she had so dreaded to see was clearly written in his face. It stopped her dead. Suddenly the Mage realized what a spectacle she must be making of herself – a distraught, dishevelled harridan, pathetic and ridiculous in the tattered remnants of her pride. Her curses spluttered into silence, and she closed her mouth abruptly.

Vannor inclined his head respectfully. 'Lady,' he told her, 'Aurian taught me everything I need to know about both the stubborn Magefolk pride and the stormy Magefolk temper – but it didn't make me love, or respect, her any less.'

Unexpectedly, Eilin found her mouth twisting in a wry smile. 'Your friendship with my daughter has given you a rare insight into our character,' she admitted.

Vannor grinned back at her. 'Indeed,' he agreed, 'but Aurian taught me far more about the good side of the Magefolk character than the bad. Courage, loyalty, a rare honesty . . .'

His words were interrupted as the air above him was split asunder by the belling of the hounds, the clamour of horns, and the wild, triumphant hunting cries of the Phaerie, who came hurtling out of the sky like thunderbolts, bearing with them the ghastly trophies of their hunt. The Forest Lord had returned to the Valley.

Though Parric and Sangra had been arguing with him for some time now, Yazour refused to be browbeaten, intimidated, or persuaded into changing his mind. He was determined to head back to the Southern Lands, in search of his friend and mentor Eliizar, and admit to the older man that he had made a mistake. He should never have come north with the Magefolk – this was not his land, and now there was nothing left for him here.

Following the disappearance of Aurian, Anvar, and his friends among the Horsefolk, Yazour was finding himself very much adrift and alone in a land of strangers. Of the companions who had set out with the Mages from the Khazalim city of Taibeth, only he remained. Harihn, the young warrior's former prince, had betrayed the Mages twice and formed an unholy alliance with the Archmage Miathan. As a consequence, he had been slain in the Tower of Incondor. Shia had followed Aurian and Anvar through the rift in time, to meet some unknown fate. The winged girl Raven was now Queen of the Skyfolk, and when Yazour had last seen her she had been well on her way to finding a new maturity, and beginning to atone for her former mistakes.

Poor Bohan, the gigantic eunuch who had been so devoted to Aurian, had perished at the Xandim stronghold, and even Schiannath, Chiamh and Iscalda, Yazour's newfound friends among the Horsefolk, had met with an uncertain fate when the Phaerie, freed by Aurian's failure to master the Sword, had reclaimed their horses back from human form. In one lethal stroke the Xandim had lost their leaders. Schiannath the Herdlord, and the Windeye Chiamh, had been saved from the Phaerie but had followed Aurian in their equine form. Along with the remainder of the Xandim, Iscalda, Schiannath's sister who had befriended Yazour, had been transformed irrevocably into the shape of a white mare and claimed by Hellorin, the Phaerie Lord.

Yazour had looked on, helpless, as the humanity of his friends had been ripped away. Aurian and Anvar had vanished, and the young warrior had been forced to remain behind, alone, because he had not been quick enough to follow them through the rift in time. And now he must live with the guilt of his failure. Though his fellow warriors Parric and Sangra were doing their best to be kind to him and make him welcome in their midst, the Khazalim soldier knew himself for an alien and an outsider. Without Aurian, without *some* point to his existence here, he could feel neither at home nor at ease.

11

'Yazour, don't leave us. You're our friend – we need you here.' Sangra returned to the attack. 'There's so much to do – so much to put right.'

Yazour sighed wearily and shook his head. 'I want to go back to the south, to my own people,' he insisted. 'I can be of far more use to Eliizar and Nereni, now that Aurian is gone and her quest has failed . . .'

'Failed! Don't you dare say that, you bastard!' Parric snarled. Yazour ducked reflexively as a fist whistled past his face. The cavalry master, beside himself with rage, pulled his arm back for another try, but Sangra, just as swift, caught his wrist before the second blow had time to descend. 'Parric, no!' she cried. 'That's not going to help matters.'

The cavalry master subsided, but glowered at Yazour with a look that mingled coldness and misery. 'Don't you *ever* say she's failed,' he muttered. 'It isn't over yet.' He jumped to his feet and walked stiffly away.

Yazour realized, too late, that his careless remark had wounded Parric deeply. He was sorry – he liked and respected the little man. Not knowing how to take back his words without making matters worse, he mumbled an awkward apology to Sangra and scanned the encampment, desperately seeking a diversion that would take their talk in a less painful direction. His attention was drawn by the sound of shouted imprecations on the island across the lake. 'Who is the woman yelling at Vannor over there?' he asked.

'Why, that's Aurian's mother, the Lady Eilin,' Sangra told him. 'She lives alone here in the Vale. The poor soul – I don't blame her for sounding so angry. How can she bear it? Her daughter is gone, her Valley burned and her tower in ruins. She'll be lonely now for sure – in fact, depending on what's happened to Miathan, she could be the last of her kind.' The warrior shook her head. 'The death of the Magefolk – who would have thought *that* would happen in our lifetime?'

Poor woman! thought Yazour. The only one here of all her kind – just like me. He looked again at the slender figure, his heart aching in sympathy. She seemed so isolated, so vulnerable . . . And she was Aurian's mother . . . An idea began to take shape in Yazour's mind, but before it could resolve itself

12

the voice of the Forest Lord thundered down from far above: 'See your prey, my warriors. Take them now!'

'Take cover,' Vannor yelled. 'The Phaerie are attacking!

How dared they! Eilin's anger, so recently directed at the hapless Mortals, now found its true and fitting target. 'No!' she cried. She ran back across the bridge towards the fires, Vannor a stride behind her, even as the Phaerie came arcing down out of the sky. Eilin reached the great campfire ahead of the Forest Lord. All around her people were drawing swords, shouting, running, crazed with panic.

'Stay by the fires!' The Mage augmented her voice by magic, until it rang out clearly above the noise. 'Stay close to me – it's your only chance!' As the terrified Mortals began to collect around the great bonfire, Eilin looked wildly about her. A staff – she needed her staff! But she had relinquished her own to D'arvan, long ago, and now it had gone with him to some unknown fate. But all she really needed was something through which to focus her power . . . Then, through a gap in the gathering crowd, she saw Hargorn's abandoned sword, still planted upright in the mud by the edge of the lake. The Earth-Mage ran and snatched up the unclaimed blade. She poured her power into the weapon and felt a shock run through her as her magic took on a sharp, raw, aggressive edge far different from the nurturing forces concentrated by her staff.

Closer and closer the Phaerie came, sounding their silver horns and singing their eerie songs of death as they rode. Already they had descended to the level of the treetops. They were an awe-inspiring sight, terrifying in their beauty. Freed from that amorphous otherworld in which they had been imprisoned, they had cast off their grey and shadowy forms, and now were clothed in robes of shimmering, many-hued luminescence that trailed behind them in sparkling drifts like comet tails. The Phaerie rode bareback, but the horses, with their streaming manes and tails, were controlled with bridles and reins of pure white light, and sparks flew from their hooves as they raced through the air. As the riders reached the tops of the trees, everything that their trailing vestments

13

touched took on the same mysterious radiance, to be limned in frosty rainbow sparkles that spread from branch to branch, outlining the boughs and leaves in delicate traceries of light.

Eilin forced herself to ignore the beauty, remembered the cold, cruel hearts and minds that concealed themselves behind such glorious magic. She cried out once, to focus her powers, and struck the ground hard with the point of the sword. A dome of glimmering green force sprang into being over the entire encampment to shield the helpless Mortals, just as Hellorin came charging down heedlessly, on the heels of his hounds and in advance of his followers, heading straight into the midst of the camp. As the shield sprang up in front of him he tore at the white mare's mouth, trying to divert her from her headlong course, but it was too late. As one by one his hounds came within range of the magical barrier, they were stung by sizzling bolts of green lightning. Yelping, they recoiled and retreated. Terrified by the roaring wall of light that had appeared almost beneath her hooves, Iscalda reared and shied to one side. The Forest Lord, caught off balance, lurched forward across one snowy shoulder and fell. Striking Eilin's barrier in an explosion of emerald light, he slid down the shield's curving hemisphere in a spray of spitting green sparks, crying out in agony as he slithered inexorably and ignominiously to the ground. The mare gave a shrill scream of triumph and bolted, vanishing into the trees.

Hellorin clambered painfully to his feet. The rebels broke into cheers and hoots of derision, but there was a deathly silence from the Phaerie as they landed close to their ruler. The Lord of the Phaerie, backed by a menacing phalanx of his followers, faced the Earth-Mage through her translucent shield of energy.

The Forest Lord was the first to break the silence. His tones, at first, were conciliatory, belying the glint of anger in his eyes. 'Lady, you are an Immortal, like myself. You dwelt in my realm for some time, and I almost began to think of you as one of the Phaerie. Surely you cannot be siding with the Mortals against me?' He shrugged. 'No, it is impossible. Are you angered because I rode off and forgot you? Now that the Phaerie are free, do you wish to strike a bargain or obtain some

14

favour from me, that you use these pathetic creatures as bait?'

'I want nothing from you but your absence.' Eilin spoke through gritted teeth.

Hellorin seemed taken aback. 'Is this how you repay me, Lady, for the healing and sanctuary you received in my realm, and for the kindness that was shown you by my people?' Now he no longer troubled to hide his anger.

'I have not forgotten that I was succoured and sheltered by the Phaerie – but the contrast between your compassionate behaviour then and your brutal activities now is more than I will tolerate.' Eilin clenched her hands round the hilt of Hargorn's sword, to still their trembling. 'This is *my* Valley.' Her words rang out in challenge like the clash of steel on steel. 'We are in *my* realm now, and these Mortals are here under my protection. How dare you attack them?'

The Forest Lord's face turned dark with anger. 'Do not cross me, Mage, I warn you,' he snarled. In his wrath his form expanded, growing larger and larger until it towered over the Mage, higher than the treetops, blotting out the stars.

Eilin forced herself to face him without flinching. 'Will you really try to match your powers with mine?' she demanded. 'I think not. On your own ground, you could probably defeat me – but here? You are new in the mundane world – you have not had time to become accustomed to the workings of the magic here. Over many years, my power has *created* this place. The very bones of the earth will reach out to protect me! Perhaps you could prevail – but at what cost, to one so newly free? Is it worth the risk, for a handful of Mortals?'

'Curse you, Lady. Your kind were ever false and faithless,' Hellorin hissed.

'As yours are pitiless and perfidious,' Eilin shot back with equal venom.

Hellorin shrugged. 'And your people, of course, have practised only kindness and consideration towards your Mortal brethren down all the ages? Come, Eilin – surely this is a jest at my expense. What interest can you have in such lowly creatures as these? Since when did the Magefolk care about Mortals, save where they might be used as servitors, or to further some scheme of conquest?'

15

The Earth-Mage tilted her head and looked him in the eyes. 'Since one of those lowly creatures became the father of my daughter's child. And since *you* have earned my undying contempt, by using and betraying Aurian – not to mention the Xandim – in pursuit of your own ends.'

The Phaerie Lord gave a booming laugh. 'The Xandim are our property. And as for Aurian . . . Surely you did not expect us to swear fealty to a failure and a weakling – to bend our knees to one of the hated race that put us out of the world – when we had an opportunity to slip the Magefolk leash for good? You must think a great deal of your daughter, Lady, if you consider that she is worth the freedom of an entire race.'

Eilin, inwardly raging, struck her sword against the ground in a thunderclap detonation of power. 'I think a great deal more of my daughter, evidently, than you think of your son,' she cried in a clear, cold voice.

Hellorin's mocking laughter ceased abruptly. 'Weigh your words carefully, Mage. I have destroyed beings of greater power than you, and for lesser insults.'

'And did you destroy them for telling the truth? That would be like the Phaerie indeed! You fool – you have no idea, do you?' The edge of Eilin's voice was whetted with scorn. 'In your insatiable lust for revenge on those who occupied the world while you were excluded from it, you seized the poor Xandim and went charging off before the matter of the Sword of Flame could be resolved. Haven't you even *noticed* D'arvan's absence? While Aurian and Anvar were distracted by *your* perfidy, Eliseth tried to steal the Sword and created a rift in time. The Mages vanished into it – as did Maya and your son!'

Hellorin blanched. 'This cannot be true,' he whispered.

'It can and it is,' Eilin replied remorselessly, 'and you might have been able to prevent it.'

The Phaerie Lord's gigantic form thinned to vapour and vanished as he dwindled back to human size. 'But how did it happen?' All trace of his former anger had fled from his voice. 'Where have they gone?'

'Beyond our help, I fear,' Eilin told him grimly. 'You are free to seek your son wherever you will – but you must search

16

elsewhere. You Phaerie are masters of bargains and debts, are you not? Though you did not swear fealty to her, you are still in debt to my daughter, because she has given you and your despicable kind your freedom. As Aurian cannot be here to state her terms, I will give you mine, in her place. This Vale belongs to me. Get you gone from here – and never return.'

'Is that really what you want?' Hellorin demanded in amazement. 'To end our friendship thus?'

Eilin regarded him stonily. 'Friendship, indeed! Never again do I wish to hear that word debased by your lips! I saw little evidence of friendship when the Sword was found. The Phaerie idea of friendship seems to begin and end with their own convenience – and their Lord is the worst offender. I cannot end what no longer exists, my Lord.'

Hellorin sighed. 'Very well. It shall be as you wish.' The gathered forms of the Phaerie thinned like wind-blown vapour, and vanished like a dream.

Suddenly, Eilin's knees began to shake. The Mortals began to crowd around her, offering their thanks and congratulations. Roughly she pushed her way through them. 'That goes for you Mortals, too! Get away from me! I want you out of here by tomorrow!'

With a curt, angry gesture she brought down her shields and, turning her back on them all, went back across the bridge to the solitude of her island. When no one dared to follow her, it proved to be a hollow victory.

2

A Peculiar Quartet

Blind with terror, Iscalda fled headlong through the forest, bursting through the bushes and twisting between the trees, oblivious of the leg-breaking tangles of roots beneath her feet, the thorny twigs that pulled painfully at her mane and tail and scored her white hide, or the springy branches that rebounded to lash at her with bruising force and snatch dangerously at her eyes. Her mind was blank, save that it screamed one thought over and over: *escape!* Her attention was all behind her, straining to detect any sounds of pursuit. The Phaerie Lord must not recapture her – she would sooner die than be his slave again – or go once more through the horrors of the last few hours.

Iscalda was a warrior, no stranger to bloodshed, and Hellorin's quarry had been no friends of hers, yet she had been unprepared for the carnage when the Phaerie had descended from the skies upon their helpless prey. Not a single one of the human mercenaries had survived. One by one, the Phaerie had hunted them down with relentless thoroughness and hacked them to pieces in some savage ritual where points were scored by the taking of trinkets such as a neck chain, a weapon, an earring or a belt buckle from the corpse of the unfortunate victim. Sometimes a severed head would be seized by the hair and borne aloft when the Phaerie took to the skies again, and thrown or snatched from one rider to another in the fashion of some macabre child's game.

The callous, cold-hearted cruelty of her new masters filled Iscalda with fear. It was abundantly clear that they held no respect for any living being save themselves – and that might well include their steeds. The Phaerie had snuffed out the human component of the Xandim race without a single thought – what might they do to her? On she ran, unseeing, unthinking, pursued by terror; her mind clouded by the ghastly images of her own people turned into mindless beasts of burden, and the remorseless savagery of the Phaerie hunt. This one opportunity had been sent by the gods, and would never come again. Iscalda only knew that she must flee far and fast. She must lose herself completely, hide herself so well in the forest's depths that Hellorin would never find her.

The magical trappings fashioned of light, through which the Phaerie Lord had controlled her, had fallen away from her head when Iscalda had shed him from her back, so she was free to run unencumbered. And run she did, until the forest itself stopped her flight. All at once a narrow stream, screened until the last second by the low branches of the trees, appeared in front of her. Unprepared, Iscalda gathered herself in a clumsy half-leap.

Something hit her across the forehead with stunning force. There was a sharp, wrenching pain and her vision exploded into light as hot blood poured down her face. Blinded by the salty fluid streaming into her eyes, she hit the ground hard on the other side and her foot plunged down into a hidden space between two roots, twisting beneath her with an agonizing jerk. Her momentum threw her forward and she went crashing to her knees, to flail to a floundering halt with her forelegs scrabbling for purchase in the soft mud of the stream bank and her hindquarters in the water.

The white mare lay there spent, until thought began to seep gradually back through the panic that had clouded her mind. The shock of the fall had brought her back to herself. Though Iscalda was trapped within her equine form, a vestige of her human consciousness still remained: sufficient for her to recognize her danger. What had she done to her face? What if she had broken a leg? Iscalda tried to blink the blood out of her eyes until she had achieved blurred and bleary vision. With considerable difficulty she managed to struggle to her feet on the fourth attempt, and stood there panting and trembling with her head hanging low. There was a stabbing pain around the fetlock of her near foreleg where she had landed awry. Was it broken? Iscalda had no idea, but she could not put her foot to the ground.

19

Feeling sick with pain, the mare turned awkwardly on three legs and hobbled into the stream. She stood there impatiently until the icy water had numbed some of the throbbing agony from her lame foreleg, and wondered what to do next. Hellorin would still be looking for her, she was sure. In her human form, she had known such men as he. His wounded vanity would never allow him to let her go free – no more than her own pride would ever permit her recapture. Whatever happened, Iscalda would not give in. If she could no longer run, at least she could still hide. If she could only get under cover before the Phaerie found her . . .

Not without regret, Iscalda hauled herself stiffly out of the soothing water and headed into the shadowy world beneath the trees, seeking a safe place to rest. It seemed to take for ever as she blundered, three-legged, through the bushes, attempting to hold her injured limb up out of the way. She made painfully slow progress: racing the threat of discovery; racing her exhaustion and the increasing agony in her leg; racing the growing terror that threatened to expunge her reason; racing the sinking moon that was plunging all too quickly towards the horizon. She must reach a place of safety before the absolute darkness that would follow moonset, or she stood little chance of finding a haven at all.

When she finally reached a suitable location, she was so spent that she scarcely recognized it for what it was. Save where she had entered, the narrow clearing was protected on three sides by a thicket of thorny brambles and overshadowed by the sweeping boughs of trees. For the first time that night, Iscalda knew she could stop running and could rest at last, if only for a little while. Gratefully, the mare folded her aching legs beneath her and let the deep, deep waters of exhausted slumber close over her.

Iscalda woke in the darkness, smelling wolf. With all her instincts screaming an alarm, she scrambled to her feet, only to fall heavily to one side as her injured leg, forgotten in sleep, collapsed beneath her. Frantically she struggled upright once more, pitting the agony in her foreleg against the more urgent imperative of survival. There was a movement in the bushes, and she was drowning in the smell of wolf, wolf, wolf . . .

Iscalda reared, smashing down her good foreleg to maim and kill – and threw herself to one side with a bone-wrenching jerk, almost falling again but pulling herself upright at the last second with a tremendous effort of will. Her heart was racing like the hooves of a runaway horse. Lowering her head, she peered down at her adversary and exhaled on a snort of disgust at her own stupidity. Wolf indeed! Had she been in her human form she would have laughed at herself.

The deadly predator that had scared her out of her wits was a cub so tiny that she had almost blown him away with one snort. The pathetic little creature was shivering violently with cold, and as it noticed her it began to whimper with hunger. Iscalda's ears flicked forward curiously. She wondered where its parents were – a question that also concerned her own survival. Nowhere near, that was for certain – not when the poor cub was crying like that. Had they been killed in the fire? Or had they survived, and were they searching even now for their lost offspring? Her first impulse, to kill the creature, had been the most sensible – so what had made her pull aside at the last moment? Despite her natural equine aversion to the carnivore, Iscalda couldn't help feeling sorry for the lost baby. It reminded her of Aurian's son, little Wolf . . .

Iscalda stiffened, and looked closer. But no – it couldn't be! Wolf had been left safely behind at Wyvernesse, with his lupine foster-parents and the Nightrunners to protect him. What had happened to Aurian's adult wolves? Why would they have brought him here, into danger? Why had they left him alone and helpless? No – it *must* be some other cub. But even as the denial went through her head, she knew it was Wolf indeed – she remembered the flash of white beneath his chin, and the way that one pointed little ear turned up, and the other down. Also Iscalda recognized him deep within herself, in a way that would have been almost impossible for a non-shape-shifter to understand. Somewhere behind the appearance of the animal, a human personality was concealed, and Iscalda could recognize it as a calling of like to like.

Extending her nose, the mare nudged the cub closer to the warmth of her body. She was forced to admire his courage.

21

Weak though he was, Wolf snarled at her, and snapped at her face with his minuscule puppy teeth with no regard for the difference in their sizes. He was cold and hungry and alone, however, and at length he seemed to decide to trust her. If only she could feed him – that was his greatest need – but at least she could keep him warm. Iscalda was too tired to think of anything beyond that. When it grew light and she had rested, she would decide what to do next. She stretched out beside the cub, shielding him with the warmth of her body, and within minutes they were both asleep.

After the departure of the Phaerie, the rebels – still discussing what had happened in tones of relief and amazement – went off to busy themselves with the details of supper and shelter, and the packing of their few possessions for tomorrow's departure. One member of their group, however, had eyes for nothing but Eilin's retreating figure. Because Mages no longer existed in the Southern Lands, Yazour's people stood even more in awe of magic and its wielders than the northern Mortals. The young warrior was lost in admiration at the way in which the Lady Eilin had faced down the terrifying Phaerie Lord, and had driven him away. He recognized and under-stood her loneliness and isolation – was he not in a similar position, with his loved ones dead or far away?

The shadowy figure in the gloom bowed her head, her shoulders slumping wearily. Though it was hard to tell at such a distance, it seemed to Yazour that she was wiping her face on her sleeve, as though she were weeping. How he wished he could do something to comfort her . . . Suddenly, he felt a shiver run through him. Who could anticipate the mysterious workings of the gods? It was obvious, now, that he had been brought here for a reason after all. Yazour smiled to himself. Though he was too late to follow her, there *was* a way in which he could help Aurian, after all. What better way to assist the Mage, in her absence, then by helping and caring for her mother?

Full of his plan, he almost set off across the bridge to inform the Lady. Then he remembered her harsh words and the look of cold, hard anger in her eyes when she had left them. Yazour swallowed hard. Perhaps he would wait a while, until she had had a chance to calm herself after her confrontation with the Phaerie. She needed him, that much was certain – unfortunately, he might have a good deal of trouble convincing her of it.

His companions, when he spoke to them over a belated supper that night, were far from encouraging. To Yazour's indignation, Vannor made no effort whatsoever to master his laughter. 'You want to *protect* the Lady Eilin?' he chuckled. 'Yazour, you're an incorrigible romantic. What are you going to defend her from, that she can't manage very well on her own? Why don't you ask the Lord of the Phaerie whether she's in need of protection?'

'Nonsense.' Dulsina defended Yazour. 'You're a dear man, Vannor, but sometimes you can be an idiot. The poor Lady has just lost her daughter and her home is in ruins. Of *course* she needs someone to be with her. We're all grieving over the fate of the Mages, but it must be much worse for Eilin. She'll need solitude in which to mourn, it's true – but not all the time, for goodness' sake!'

'It's not a matter of power, or strength,' Yazour agreed. 'Often our greatest foes are those that creep upon us unseen: loneliness, anxiety, sorrow and hopelessness. No one can battle those enemies alone. She needs someone to be with her, to distract her mind and cheer her . . .'

Clearly, these subtleties were lost on Parric. 'Suit yourself.' He shrugged. 'If it'll put you off racing back to the south all on your own, then I'm all for it. Just remember, though, that these Magewomen are different from your protected, secluded southern girls. Never forget whose mother the Lady Eilin is. If you start even hinting that she's some kind of help-less female, she'll have your balls for breakfast. They're very touchy, are Magefolk – you should know that by now. You're a braver man than I am, Yazour, to even attempt to defy her, when she's so determined to be left alone.'

Yazour sighed. It looks as though this will be even more difficult than I imagined, he thought. I don't care. Aurian's mother needs me, and I will persuade her to accept me some-how. For Parric, he put on his bravest face. 'I don't care how

23

stubborn she is. When I talk to her tomorrow, she'll find that I can be stubborn too.'

In the cold, dark dead of night, the mundane world was an inhospitable place. Hellorin looked out across the bleak stretches of wind-scoured moorland and cursed softly to himself. He had been so long away from the world, he had forgotten how unpleasant its climate could be. Though the Phaerie, with their magic, were unaffected by the cold, they had been accustomed, for many a long age, to more congenial surroundings – yet to Hellorin, having newly won his liberty, it seemed out of the question to go slinking tamely back to the comfort of his palace in the Elsewhere of his long exile.

'My Lord, this is ridiculous.'

Hellorin looked around to see Lethas, his chamberlain. The Lord of the Phaerie sighed. Lethas did not usually tend to complain – he had run Hellorin's palace with effortless ease for centuries, and little was beyond the scope of his administrative or, failing that, his magical abilities.

Tonight, however, the chamberlain was frowning. He pushed his dark, wind-tousled hair out of his eyes with the brusque, exasperated air of one who has repeated the selfsame gesture far too many times. 'Lord, our people should be feasting now to celebrate the success of our hunt. What comfort can be gained out here in this forsaken place?'

Hellorin could not help but agree. The Valley had groves of trees that could be formed by magic into temporary walls and roofs, and would have been the perfect place to recreate the great woodland feasts of old, within the natural shelter of the crater's towering walls. Those insolent, invading Mortals should have been expunged from Phaerie lands – except, of course, that those lands did *not* belong to the Phaerie.

The Forest Lord frowned. The Vale was Eilin's realm. The Mage had paid for it with the death of her beloved soulmate. She had taken that barren crater and with her own Earth-magic and endless years of toil had created a verdant haven of peace and beauty in these harsh northern moors – and she had made it abundantly clear to him that she would, if necessary, fight for her home to her very last breath – or his.

All around him in the gloom, Hellorin could hear the restless rise and fall of muttered complaints. He ground his teeth. He had lost his precious white mare somewhere in the Vale, and worse than that, in the wake of his confrontation with Eilin, his authority among his people had suffered a telling blow. Something would have to be done, he knew. He was aware that the Mortals were leaving on the morrow – perhaps that wretched, stubborn Magewoman would be more amenable to reason if she had no one to protect. Relieved at the thought of taking some action at last, he turned to his chamberlain. 'Tell my people to be patient,' he ordered. 'The tempers of the Magefolk can cool as quickly as they ignite. Tomorrow, we will return to the Vale and talk to the Lady Eilin again.'

'Your will, my Lord.' Lethas turned away, then turned back again. 'Lord, have you forgotten that the Lady Eilin owes you a debt for the saving of her life?' he blurted. 'If this is not the perfect time to make a claim on her, then I'm a Mortal! If you ask me, it's not talk that female needs. Anyone else who dared show such blatant disrespect to the Lord of the Phaerie would be punished. You ought to –'

'Be silent,' Hellorin roared, 'or I will punish *you*!' Taking a deep breath, he went on coldly. 'When I need your advice, be sure that I will ask you. In the meantime, I advise you follow your orders – ere I find myself a chamberlain fonder of his duty and less fond of his own opinions.' The Forest Lord strode away, fuming, leaving the unfortunate Lethas to babble his apologies to the empty air. In his heart, however, Hellorin was forced to concede that his chamberlain was probably right. That wretched, mule-headed Magewoman! This ridiculous, impossible situation was all her fault! She was making a laughing stock of him in front of his people. Hellorin imagined her, in the shelter of her Vale, gloating over the memory of his ignominious defeat. When tomorrow came, he promised himself grimly, they would see who gloated *then*.

While the sun was just waking, the world breathed stillness through every pore. The only sound, the trilling of the birds, merely served to accentuate the expectant hush, as though the

25

Valley had put on a cloak of silence stitched with the silver tapestries of their songs. The low, angled rays of the early sun stretched long fingers into the Vale, making blue, attenuated shadows that lifted the textures of the trees and plants into vivid relief against a backdrop of silken amber light. Each gnarl of bark, each blade of grass, stood out distinctly, silhouetted against its own small shadow.

The scintillant hues of the fragrant, dew-drenched earth were echoed by the light that sparked from the glittering crystal in Eilin's cupped hands.

'I just can't see him anywhere.' Frowning, the Mage straightened her back and looked up at Vannor and Parric from her kneeling position on a folded blanket. 'I always had a fair talent for scrying,' she went on in a puzzled voice, 'and I learned a thing or two about it from the Phaerie while I lived with them. But this time I'm beaten. I've tried the bowl, the mirror and the crystal this morning, and every method tells me the same thing. Miathan is not in Nexis – he's not even on this side of the ocean. I just don't understand it, Vannor. All the crystal shows me is darkness – yet, had he died, I would have felt his passing.'

She threw down her crystal in irritation, and it bounced into the grass to rest beside the tiny silver-backed mirror borrowed from Dulsina, and the pewter bowl filled to the brim with clear water, both of which had produced similarly unsatisfactory results. 'By the Goddess Iriana – he must be *somewhere*! And until we discover his whereabouts, there will be no certainty in anything we do.'

Vannor tried not to betray his own concern, lest the Lady misconstrue it as a slight on her abilities. Though she was still adamant that they must leave the Valley, her attitude to the intruding Mortals seemed to have softened a good deal during the night, and he did not want to jeopardize this fragile new accord. The former head of the Merchants' Guild looked towards the campsite, and saw one or two figures awake now, crouched sleepily over the fires or tending pots, while other folk were busy rolling up their bedding and dismantling the makeshift shelters. There was a lot of yawning, but little talk at this time of day; only the occasional drowsy murmur broke

26

the peace of the morning. Vannor rubbed thoughtfully at his short, bristly beard. These were *his* people now. He was responsible for their survival, and they were counting on him to make the right decision.

'Well, I reckon we'll have to risk it anyway,' he said at last. 'Wherever that old bastard Miathan – begging your pardon, ma'am – is hiding himself, he doesn't appear to be in Nexis, or even in the north – so we'd better make the most of his absence.'

He looked across at Parric and grinned. 'Just think, my friend – there's an entire city out there with no one in charge of it. We can't have that now, can we?'

'I should say not,' agreed the cavalry master with a completely straight face. 'Why, we have a *responsibility* to go back and take care of those poor, lost folk.'

'You're absolutely right – but first, I think we should go back to Wyvernesse and talk to the Nightrunners. For one thing, I want to see Zanna –' For a moment, Vannor's front of determined cheerfulness faltered. He couldn't bear to think of bringing his daughter the news that Aurian was gone. Breathing deeply, he took a firm grip on his emotions. 'And also,' he went on, 'this time I definitely want to take up Yanis's offer of men and ships – just in case anyone in Nexis has been harbouring similar ideas to our own. Once we control the river, the rest should be easy.'

Parric nodded. 'Good idea, that – after all, we want the Nexians to have the best possible leadership, don't we?'

Perfect! The cavalry master had fallen right into his hands! Vannor chuckled to himself, and sprang his trap. 'I'm glad you feel that way, Parric old friend – because when we get back to Nexis, I'm putting you in charge of the garrison.'

'What, me?' Parric's face fell. 'Oh bugger it, Vannor – you can't be serious. I hate that kind of responsibility – you know I'm not cut out for it.'

'Oh aren't you?' Vannor retorted mercilessly. 'After you arrived back at Wyvernesse on that whale, Chiamh told me you had been masquerading as ruler of the Xandim.'

Parric groaned. 'Masquerading is about right,' he grumbled. 'Why couldn't that Windeye have kept his damn mouth

27

shut? It was only for a month – and the Xandim would never have accepted me if Chiamh, the poor bastard, hadn't forced them to.'

'Nonsense.' Vannor was determined to brook no argument. 'Chiamh said you did a fine job as Herdlord of the Xandim – and you'll be just as successful as commander of the garrison.'

'You'd better bloody hope not,' Parric muttered gloomily. 'When I was Herdlord, they were so desperate to get rid of me that I had a revolt on my hands before the month was out . . .'

The two men were so engrossed in their plans that they had forgotten her, so Eilin took the opportunity to pocket her crystal and slip silently away. The Mage had intended to pass by the camp without drawing attention to herself, but the ever thoughtful Dulsina, who seemed to notice everything, had spotted her, and intercepted her with a mug of fragrant tea. 'Here you are, Lady – it's the last of the rosehips from before the winter. I'm sorry we have no honey, but though it's a bitter brew at least it'll warm you. It's a fine enough morning, but there's a bit of a chill off that dew.'

Eilin accepted the mug gratefully. 'That's kind of you, Dulsina – it's been a long time since I tasted rosehip tea.'

'There's another thing I wanted to mention,' Dulsina added, blushing awkwardly. 'Back in our old camp, Lady, we have a flock of chickens and a small herd of goats. We found them in the forest when we came – I expect they must have been yours in the first place. I thought I'd better tell you – you'll be wanting them again now. I did my best to look after them.'

'Why, thank you Dulsina – and thank you for telling me.' The Mage found herself smiling in pure relief. She had forgotten about the well-tended livestock in the rebel encampment, and had been wondering how she would manage to feed herself once the Mortals had gone.

Reluctant to enter the muted bustle of the camp, she took her leave and wandered away, mug in hand, towards the lake. 'If only they were all like Dulsina,' she muttered to herself, 'I wouldn't mind them staying here.' She knew it wasn't true, though. She had slept little the previous night, but had done

28

a lot of hard thinking. Her feelings towards the rebels had mellowed to the point where she no longer wished to strike out at them in her grief – but she still had no wish to share her home with them, and would view their departure with considerable relief.

When her unwelcome guests were ready to go, however, Eilin discovered that Vannor and Parric were still so deep in their discussion that they scarcely even took the time to say goodbye to her. So full of anticipation and a certain amount of apprehension were they, at the thought of returning home, that everyone seemed to have forgotten her already. The Mage, who was standing near the end of the bridge ready to say her farewells, found it difficult to dismiss a pang of hurt at the slight. Typical Mortals, she thought as she watched the knot of ragged figures diminish into the distance. Selfish, thoughtless and ungrateful! She had given them sanctuary and saved them from the Phaerie – and they lacked even the consideration to thank her, or say a proper farewell. Well, good riddance to them all. Thanks be to the gods that they were gone at last, and she had her Valley to herself again!

She had no idea that she was wrong. Enjoying the tranquillity, Eilin made her way along the shores of the lake, completely unaware of the eyes that observed her from the nearby forest fringe.

How could he break the news to Eilin that he would be staying? Up to this point, Yazour's plan had been simple enough – just make himself scarce and find a comfortable hiding place until the others had gone. Vannor had agreed, albeit reluctantly, to make a hasty departure, in the hope that the Lady wouldn't notice that one person was missing from the group. Once they were safely gone, Yazour had only to wait for a while (Dulsina's plan, this) to give the solitude time to take its toll on the Mage . . .

Which was all very well, of course, but Yazour was still extremely doubtful of his welcome, and now that the time had come he was finding it very easy to put off that initial moment of confrontation. It was important to both of them that Eilin accept him – he felt very strongly that he owed it to Aurian to

29

take care of her mother in her absence. Perhaps he should wait a little longer, just to be on the safe side . . .

As the sun reached its zenith he ate the food Dulsina had left for him – cold venison and hard biscuits of flour and water that she had baked on hot stones at the edge of the fire. Afterwards, Yazour decided to explore his surroundings a little. He could come back later – there was no hurry, after all. He already knew that the Lady Eilin was very perceptive – it wouldn't do to linger too close and have her discover him before he was ready. Keeping low to the ground, he slipped stealthily away from his hiding place in the bushes and headed for the depths of the woods, taking great care not to betray his presence by any telltale movement of branches or snapping of twigs.

Time passed quickly for the warrior. He enjoyed exploring this northern forest – it was unlike any place he had ever known. Woodlands were completely unknown in the desiccated climate of his own land, and both the great forest on the desert's edge and the high, sweeping pinewoods of the Xandim mountains had lacked the lush verdancy of the broadleaf trees that graced these rainy, temperate lands. Everything was so very different here: he savoured the aromatic scents of the grass and the tiny plants that he crushed underfoot with each step; he revelled in the endless, restless sway of twig and bough and the swirling dance of light and dappled shade as the sun flashed against the pale surfaces of the leaves. Best of all, though, Yazour loved the sounds: the incessant susurration of the wind in the trees mingled with a torrent of birdsong that drenched him in a downpour of glorious bright notes.

After the terror of yesterday's fire, the birds and animals who had fled for protection to the lakeside were beginning to creep back to their former territories. Yazour the hunter could observe them with ease – he knew how to move soundlessly and melt into the background, and the wild creatures, protected as they had always been in Eilin's Vale, were still in too much of a state of turmoil and confusion to take much note of one unaggressive human. An uneasy truce seemed to exist between predators and prey – for the present. There was food

30

in abundance for the carnivores close to the area of the fire's destruction, for here lay carcasses aplenty, killed by smoke and untouched by flame. The survivors of yesterday's inferno were currently preoccupied with seeking lost mates and offspring, or attempting to establish new territories or defend their former ranges against homeless interlopers from the Valley's immolated, uninhabitable outer reaches. There were tracks everywhere, crossing and re-crossing one another, and the young warrior followed them with interest, finding an endless fascination in the various struggles for supremacy.

Suddenly Yazour stopped, a startled exclamation on his lips, and bent low to touch the ground. There, cut into the moss, were the sharp indentations left by a horse's unshod hooves, galloping at breakneck speed. Iscalda! He had forgotten all about her in the fear of the Forest Lord's attack, and his relief at Hellorin's dismissal. Had she managed to escape the Phaerie completely? Could she still be free?

There was one way to find out. Yazour was an accomplished tracker, and in her breakneck flight the mare had left ample evidence of her passing in the form of scattered leaf-mould, churned soil and broken twigs and branches. The tracks circled in a wide arc through the broad band of woodland, gradually heading back towards the centre of the Vale. With his heart in his mouth, Yazour pieced together what had happened on the churned-up stream bank, and frowned with concern as the pattern of hoofprints changed to an awkward, three-legged gait.

Eventually, drawn by the frenetic buzzing of flies, he found Iscalda in a shadowy clearing that was overhung by the branches of the surrounding trees. She was a heartbreaking sight. Afraid to startle her, he remained hidden downwind of her while he tried to work out the best way to approach a creature that was clearly at the very limit of her endurance.

The mare was in a sorry state. Her head drooped and her body sagged with weariness. One foreleg was swollen and held up at an awkward angle so that the hoof barely touched the ground. Iscalda's long, silken mane and tail hung in tangled strings all snarled with twigs and leaves. Her once white coat, caked with sweat and clinging patches of brown mud, was stained with smears of green where she had crashed into trees during what must have been a headlong flight. Her legs were cut and scraped and her hide was striped with streaks of blood where thorns had gouged their deep and stinging tracks. A ragged wound, presumably from the sharp end of a branch, was torn across her face, narrowly missing one eye.

Then Iscalda lifted her head and saw him, and let out a loud, joyous whinny. Yazour smiled with pure relief. She had retained enough of her human wits to recognize him. Only when he stepped forward did he notice the wolf cub that lay on the ground within the mare's protective shadow. What in the name of the Reaper was Iscalda doing with a *wolf*, of all things? Yazour bent down to examine the little creature, which by now was too enfeebled by hunger even to lift its head. It took him longer than it had taken Iscalda to realize the cub's identity, since he refused to believe the evidence of his own eyes, but its markings were too distinct for there to be any mistake. Yazour was horrified. Wolf must already be dreadfully weak – and here he was, tarrying like a moonstruck idiot when he should be getting Aurian's son to safety. If she ever found out, she would have his hide!

Yazour scooped up the cub and buttoned it inside his tunic for warmth. Not without a pang of guilt for increasing her pain, he grabbed a handful of Iscalda's mane to hurry her along as best he could. 'I'm sorry,' he told the mare, 'but we must get Wolf back to Eilin as soon as possible.'

The Mage wandered down to the side of the lake and seated herself on a large rock that overlooked the water. The lake was deep blue and tranquil, spangled with quicksilver flashes where ripples caught the sunlight. What few sounds could be heard were all very much a part of the scene: a whispering breeze in the reed beds, the piping of birds in the nearby grove, and the gentle, rhythmic sigh of wavelets lapping against the rounded stones that edged the shoreline.

Eilin sat there for a long time, soaking up the blessed solitude and letting the peace and beauty of the scene soothe her abraded feelings – her irritation at the unmannerly Mortals, her smouldering anger against the Phaerie and especially their

Lord, and her deep, abiding anguish over the uncertain fate of her daughter. Eventually, however, she realized that it wasn't working. With no human company to distract her, she found her mind returning again and again to the very subjects she wished to escape. Sighing, she looked out across the lake towards the ruins of her tower. She ought not be sitting here brooding in any case. She should be out there working on her island, building temporary shelters for herself and for her livestock, which must be rounded up and brought from the rebel camp. She ought to be making a start at clearing the debris from the tower site, thinking about the beginnings of a new garden and generally beginning to put together a new life from the wreckage of the old. After all these years, she had it all to do again. The Mage hid her face in her hands and rubbed her tired eyes. She had not even started yet, but already the sheer immensity of the task ahead seemed too much for her.

As he approached the island, Yazour watched the oblivious Mage in pity. Surely now, the Lady would forgive him, and accept his assistance? She looked so desolate, how could she help but want his company? It was only common sense. But the Khazalim warrior had already had a taste of Magefolk stubbornness from Aurian, and knew how little sense of any kind entered into the picture. Lonely or not, Eilin was just as likely to throw him out of the Vale, simply in order to maintain the splendour of her solitude. That way, she could weep unseen as much as she wanted, and her pride would remain inviolate.

That accursed stiff-necked pride! Yazour thought. It won't get her anywhere. For her own good, I must persuade her. In any case, Iscalda needs her help – and when I explain the situation to her, she won't turn away someone in such dire need of healing. Besides . . . he looked down at the wolf cub he carried. She must owe me a favour for finding her grandson. He turned to the white mare, who was waiting patiently at his side. It had taken a long time for them to get this far with her slow, halting gait, but she had refused to stay behind and wait for her friend to return with the Lady. In any case, he certainly couldn't stand here any longer. Little Wolf was desperately in need of care and attention. Yazour took a deep breath. 'I'm counting on you to help me with this,' he told the horse – though the Reaper knows how you could, he added in the privacy of his thoughts. Taking a firmer grip on the wolf club, he stepped out into the sunlight.

Eilin started violently at the sound of his approach. 'You! What are you doing here? Why in the name of all the gods didn't you leave with the others?'

All Yazour's carefully prepared speeches flew out of his head. 'I . . .' He cleared his throat and held up the wolf cub. 'Lady, I have found your grandson.'

'*What?* That wolf – my grandson? How dare you make sport with me, Mortal!' Eilin leapt to her feet, her face crimson with rage.

Yazour felt his own anger blaze up inside him at such an unfair accusation. 'I do *not* make sport with you. For Aurian's sake I would never do such a thing,' he shouted at her. 'Look!' Again, he held the cub out towards her. 'Just *look* at him, you stubborn woman. He was cursed into this shape by Aurian's enemy. She had no chance to tell you herself, but despite his outward appearance Wolf is your own flesh and blood, and he needs your help. For his sake and the sake of your daughter, learn to look at him with your heart, and see him as he truly is.'

Eilin opened her mouth, then closed it again. Slowly, she reached out and took the cub into her arms. As Yazour watched, her eyes filled, and tears went streaking down her cheeks. 'It *is* my grandson,' she whispered. 'It is . . .'

Suddenly, the Mage became all briskness. 'By the Gods, this won't do! Yazour, find some dead wood and make a fire. And we'll need a shelter – we can't expect the poor little thing to sleep out in the open tonight. And you, you poor creature . . .' she turned to Iscalda, addressing her just as though she were still human. 'Poor child, be welcome. Only be patient a little while longer, and I will see what I can do to ease you . . .'

Her words tailed away into silence as Yazour rushed off to do her bidding. He was glad of a chance to get away quickly, before she could notice the smile on his face.

3

The King Beneath the Hill

It was wonderful, Eilin reflected, how a person's life and prospects could change so dramatically within the brief span of an hour. Her new responsibilities left her no time to brood. Yazour had cleared the old fireplace in what remained of the kitchen of her ruined tower. Now he was building a rough lean-to shelter against the only portion of the wall that was left standing. Though she had sent out her strongest thoughts, she had been unable to find the wolves that had come so far with Aurian from the southern mountains. Sadly, it seemed that they had perished in the fire. Instead, the Mage had located and summoned a pair of the Valley's wolves, who were nursing a family of their own. These were the descendants of Aurian's childhood companions – and wolves have long memories among their own kind. They were happy and honoured to foster the Mage's son, the grandson of the Lady.

Iscalda was looking much better now. Though she lacked the specialized healing abilities of her daughter, Eilin had cleaned the mare's lesser wounds made by bough and thorn, and used her powers to ease Iscalda's aches and pains and accelerate the knitting of her flesh. Thanks be to the gods, the injured foreleg had not been broken, though the muscle had been cruelly wrenched and strained. Eilin had done all she could, but despite her best efforts Iscalda would probably be lame for some time to come. In the end, on Yazour's advice, the Mage had resorted to Mortal remedies, and the injured limb was now swathed in a hot compress of moss and herbs.

Eilin was glad she had listened to Yazour after all. When he had first suggested to her that he stay, she had given him a short – and negative – reply. But on reflection she had changed her mind, and it was proving to be one of the best

35

decisions she had ever made. This capable young man had been Aurian's friend, and he certainly had his wits about him. Gratefully, Eilin sniffed the savory aroma of the venison that Yazour had spitted over the fire. *Not only can he hunt and track, and build a shelter just as well as he can use a sword, but he can cook, too,* she thought with a smile. *When I see my daughter again – and I must keep on believing that I* will *see her again – I must compliment her on her choice of companions.* The Mage no longer wanted to drive the young man away. The discovery of Wolf had altered everything. Eilin still had her home to rebuild and her Valley to restore to life, but the additional responsibility of her grandson had made her rethink her ideas rapidly. One thing poor Forral had taught her was that there was no disgrace in accepting an honest offer of help – nor in admitting that she couldn't do everything alone. She knew from bitter experience that if she tried to overstretch herself Wolf would be the one to suffer, and the poor child had sufficient burdens already. She had no intention of making the same mistakes with him as she had with Aurian.

Despite the humiliations she had dealt him, Hellorin could no longer find it in him to be angry with the Mage. When he thought of her all alone in her Vale, her home gone, her daughter gone as was his son, he pitied her. None the less, she had brought much of her solitude upon herself – and he had a horde of angry and impatient Phaerie to answer to. Eilin must not be permitted to thwart the will of the Forest Lord. He had planned to appear before her and say: *'See? Already you are missing the luxuries that only I can provide.'* It was just as well he had decided to assess the situation first, otherwise he'd have made a complete fool of himself.

Hellorin ground his teeth as he glowered across at the island, and its scenes of bustling domesticity. What had the wretched woman been up to in his absence? Who was that accursed Mortal? He had expected to find Eilin alone, grieving, desolate – and vulnerable. He had intended to bargain with her, to offer his help with the rebuilding of her tower if she would welcome the Phaerie back into the Vale. Now, when he saw the Mage so busy, so purposeful and no longer alone, his heart misgave him.

The Phaerie Lord continued to watch until the long blue shadows that pursued the sunset had stretched out their arms to embrace the Vale. For the first time, he asked himself why he kept hounding this woman – and to his utter astonishment, he discovered that he missed her demanding company and acerbic tongue more than he would ever have thought possible. She reminded him of Adrina, D'arvan's mother, also a Mage and until now his only love.

Also, for the first time in an incredibly long existence, Hellorin had discovered that he could not always have his own way – that here was an indomitable personality who, if it suited her, would continue to defy and thwart him until her dying breath. And while he was aware that he could force his will upon her by claiming the debt she owed him, he didn't want to incur her outright enmity. He had enjoyed their sparring, their regular battles of will, far too much for that. Besides, though conscience and contrition had previously been unknown to him, he realized that yesterday his behaviour had appalled and disgusted the Mage, and he had no wish to put himself further into the wrong with her.

For the first time, Hellorin admitted a hard and painful truth – that despite all the power of his rule, he could not escape the consequences of his own actions. If he had not ignored Eilin's desperate pleas the previous day, she would not be shunning him now – and he might still have his son. The recovery of the Xandim was too high a price to pay for what he had lost – yet now, the horses were all he had to show for his return to the mundane world, and he would continue to cling fiercely to his possession of them.

Well, so be it. Hellorin straightened his spine. It would be a bitter dose to swallow, but it seemed that he must face up to his own mistakes – and then see what he could do about recovering lost ground. Forcing himself on the Mage would bring him nothing but trouble. Sooner or later, Eilin would need his help, and until then he must be patient. In the meantime, who needed her precious Vale? Instead he would build a city – a marvellous and magnificent home for the Phaerie.

It was an idea that had been born the previous night on the bleak, inhospitable moors, and had been growing at the back of his mind ever since. Hellorin felt his heart stir within him in excitement as he began to formulate his plans. Why, he had not enjoyed such a challenge in aeons! He remembered a place, far to the north of the Vale in the high, windblown mountains where humans rarely ventured. There was a deep, broad cleft between the arms of one such mountain, with steep, pine-clad slopes on either side that cradled a grey and misty lake – Flying Horse Tarn, it had been called in the old days, for it was virtually inaccessible to any but the Phaerie and their magical steeds. At the mouth of the valley a high green hill arose from the foot of the tarn – Flying Horse Tor. That would be the perfect place for his city.

Hellorin's lips stretched wide in a smile. Even with magical help, it would take a great deal of labour to construct such a place from nothing. He would need many Mortal slaves to build on so grand a scale. What entertainment his Phaerie would have, raiding Nexis and the lesser human habitations for slaves, so that they could build a city of their own. It would be just like the old days!

The uneasy thought crossed his mind that Eilin wasn't going to like this in the least; then he shrugged. Hellorin reminded himself that he was Lord of the Phaerie. He had no intention of letting a Magewoman's whims rule his life – and besides, it would teach her a valuable lesson. If she had not crossed him in the first place, he would simply have settled his people in the Vale, and never even thought of building a city. Hellorin turned away, and prepared to take his leave of the Valley. So be it. Let Eilin think she had won for now. Hard though it was, he would even sacrifice the white mare to keep up the pretence that he was vanquished. Soon enough, she would find out what she had done.

Hellorin smiled, envisaging the havoc he would wreak in the city of the hated Magefolk. Ah, but now there were no Mages left, save Eilin. Would it be better simply to occupy Nexis, and save much time and trouble? No: it was useful as a breeding ground for human slaves, but the leavings of their former foes were not good enough for his folk – not initially,

38

at least. Yet when his son returned to the world, as Hellorin was certain he would, Nexis would make a princely gift for him.

The Lord of the Phaerie smiled at the notion. Two great cities, one in the north and one in the south – and all the lands between ruled by the Phaerie, released from their imprisonment at last. He would build his own city first, he decided, and one of the first things he'd create would be another magic window – one tuned, this time, specifically to D'arvan so that as soon as he returned to the world Hellorin could send warriors to bring him home. Though they had not parted on good terms, the whelp could be brought to reason, the Forest Lord was certain. There were ways and means. Once D'arvan had joined his father's ranks, Nexis could be taken at their leisure.

Had Hellorin, in that moment, been able to look as far as Nexis, he might have felt less sanguine. With the departure of Eliseth, the last magic-wielder had gone from the city, and unclean forces no longer fettered by the presence of the power that fuelled the ancient spells, were stirring in the depths beneath the earth.

Once, he had walked the earth in giant form. Once he had been more than this broken, raving creature left imprisoned in a tomb of stone down all the long ages; wits scattered, lost . . . lost. Bound and fettered under the iron control of minds hard and brilliant as diamonds, sharp and merciless as steel. Aeons he had waited, helpless, hopeless. Then, long after all hope had gone, there came a feeling, a stirring – almost imperceptible – a lifting of pressure, a faint promise of hope. A glimmer of light in his eternal darkness – a slender crack in the walls of his tomb. The Moldan's hatred stirred, and began to expand as slowly, slowly, thought returned, and strength. The spells of control were decaying – the endless night of his imprisonment was drawing to its close. And, after all this time, there was still such a thing as vengeance.

Little by little, Ghabal began to stretch forth his will, pushing with all his might against the strait constriction of lifeless rock that surrounded him. His searching tendrils of thought encountered a fissure, a hairline fault in the rock that widened to a narrow chink. Concentrating all his powers into that one spot, the Moldan pushed with all his might. The rock creaked in protest, then the chink expanded with a loud, reverberating crack as the widening fissure snaked like a jagged lightning bolt through what once had been a solid mass of stone.

The Moldan rested, spent. A trickle of ancient dust slithered down through the new crevice, whispering secrets in a soft, sibilant little voice as it fell. When he had regained his strength, Ghabal pushed again, widening and extending the fissure a little further. Once more, he paused to recover. With freedom in sight – and after so long – it was difficult to be patient, yet he knew he must take whatever time he needed. It could prove a fatal mistake to overextend himself at this point – he might be trapped down here for ever.

After a while, the Moldan's efforts settled into a rhythmic pattern of exertion and rest. His thoughts sank into a drowsy blankness, taking him no further than his next gargantuan effort to expand his fissure by another fraction. Hopes and plans he must put aside for the present – they would only distract him from his essential task. When he finally freed himself from this stony prison – ah, then there would be time for plans and more! Then at last he could find some pawn, some vessel, who could bear his spirit home across the seas to his beloved mountain, where he could become himself again, healed and whole.

Ghabal had lost all track of time. He might have been testing and stretching his bonds for hours – or aeons. He had crushed down his impatience and was measuring his strength carefully, trying to conserve as much energy as possible. He could go on like this indefinitely if he wished – had it been necessary. Instead, with a sudden shock like falling from some massive height, he encountered space. The Moldan's will, concentrated to thrust against the stony barrier, abruptly found itself unfettered, and the force of his power, with nothing upon which to impact, snapped back to him with a fearful, explosive recoil that sent his senses reeling down into a spiral of darkness.

Free – he was *free*! The thought pierced Ghabal's dark unconsciousness like a single, blazing sunbeam, guiding his fragile spirit safely back up into the light. He pulled the tatters of his torn and tender consciousness around himself and rested a moment, taking stock. Though he had hurt himself when his will had exploded outwards, there was no damage that would not mend in time. The powerful energies of the elemental earth would renew him, feed him, heal him. And while that was happening, it would not hurt him to explore a little, just a little . . .

By the Mother-Earth that spawned him, but there had been some changes since he had first been locked away beneath this hill! Tentatively, Ghabal extended his consciousness into the tangle of tunnels, passages and chambers that honeycombed the promontory beneath the Magefolk dwellings. Incredible! Those accursed Mages must have been as busy as a band of moles for centuries to have accomplished all this. Then the Moldan found the place where the web of underground passages joined the Nexian sewer system, and was astounded all over again. Why, he thought gleefully, those arrogant fools have created a vulnerable network of hidden paths that run beneath their entire city. How I should like to bring it down around them, send it crashing into ruin . . .

Alas, Ghabal was no longer what he had been before the Magefolk had defeated and broken him. He no longer had the power, and would not possess it for some considerable time to come, when the deep energies of the earth should have nourished and renewed him. Besides, what would be the point in annihilating the city? Accomplishing destruction on such a scale would only waste his remaining powers for nothing – for the Magefolk themselves were gone. His very return to consciousness and freedom was clear proof of that. What had happened to them? he wondered. He hoped that their fall had involved the greatest possible torment and suffering.

Curious, the Moldan withdrew from the widespread area of the sewers and probed a little more carefully through the catacombs beneath the Academy itself. Perhaps there were clues hidden there, to explain the demise of so powerful a race. But to his disappointment, there were no memories encoded in the structure of the stone, such as the Moldai left to record their deeds. The vast collection of volumes and scrolls meant nothing to him – it was simply heaps of mouldering, desiccated plant and animal remains, and he wondered why the Mages had left such a clutter of rubbish beneath their home.

Ghabal's tendrils of thought reached the chamber of the Death-Wraiths and recoiled in horror, withdrawing back into the core of his awareness like a sea-beast's tentacles. The time spell he recognized all too well, to his dismay. It had been used against him to great effect in the past. But what else was here? Something that reeked of evil magic – some horror beyond the darkest imaginings of a Moldan. If the Magefolk had dared to meddle with such malevolent atrocities, then their fall was well deserved, and must come as no surprise.

Tentatively, the Moldan began to explore again, taking the greatest care to shun the chamber of the dreaded Wraiths, and staying alert for any further unpleasant surprises. More and more chambers, more debris and trash – and suddenly, once again, he encountered the cold, metallic tingle of a time spell. Ghabal stopped abruptly. A Mage was here! One of the accursed, detested Magefolk. Had the Moldan possessed an embodied voice he would have howled in fury. As it was, the whole of the city shook with the force of his wrath.

Finally, Ghabal calmed himself. So one of their unholy brood had survived the destruction of the Mages. At least one of them was left, then, to suffer the vengeance of the Moldai. Putting forth a single, slender filament of his awareness, Ghabal approached the periphery of the spell with caution, seeking a weak spot from which he could turn the spell into something far more deadly. He was extremely circumspect – it was not advisable to interrupt the field of a time spell when the original creator was no longer present to renew the magic. Occasionally the victim could break loose . . .

Too late. A bolt of magic came sizzling out of nowhere, scorched its way along the Moldan's thought-thread and drove straight into the core of his awareness. Suddenly Ghabal found himself utterly paralysed, all his external senses shut down dead.

'Got you!' The cracked old voice reverberated, grim and cruel, within the dark, sequestered core of Ghabal's consciousness.

'You have *nothing*, Mage!' the Moldan snarled, though his words were nothing but an empty boast. As he spoke he tried to writhe quickly away from the fetters of the iron will that bound him, but his foe's hold simply tightened, preventing his escape. Then he could do nothing but shriek in soundless agony as the other rent his mind asunder with power that stripped bare his innermost thoughts like talons of steel. Ghabal could only cower, screaming, as his entire existence, his dearest hopes and deepest fears, were all laid open to the searing gaze of the dreadful Mage.

After an endless, excruciating age, it was over. The Moldan, cowed and whimpering, cringed away from his tormentor and tried to pull together the pathetic remnants of his thoughts like the shreds of some torn and tattered garment.

'Good,' grated the terrible grim voice. 'Very good indeed. A Moldan – one of the ancient Earth-elementals from across the ocean, eh?' The voice dropped in intensity, became gentle and almost mild, like some grisly caress. 'Well, Moldan – I feel certain that you and I can reach some kind of understanding.'

Miathan smiled to himself as he twisted the chains of his will more tightly around the Moldan's consciousness. He had conquered the elemental by means of surprise, using the remnants of the ancient Magefolk spells that had bound it, and he counted himself fortunate indeed to have done so. Now his very survival depended on keeping it cowed, off balance – and under his control, for it could prove to be a much-needed weapon in his hand. He knew now what the creature wanted above life itself: someone to take it home. And, by the laws of its kind, it would owe an incalculable debt to anyone who could assist it.

So Eliseth had dared to betray him? Well, somehow, somewhere, she had met her match, according to the Moldan's thoughts. The weakening of the spells which had imprisoned them both was proof that no Magefolk existed anywhere near Nexis – save himself, of course. But though it would be easy enough to return to the Academy and take the reins of his city once more, simply picking up where he had left off, caution made him hesitate. He could not be the only remaining Mage – even if Aurian and Eliseth had come to a confrontation, surely one of them must have survived. And how many Artefacts of Power did the victor hold?

No, whichever of the Magewomen had conquered, if the Archmage stayed in Nexis he would be a sitting target. He needed to be somewhere else, somewhere hidden – somewhere completely unexpected – until he could find out what had happened and formulate his plans accordingly. A powerful ally wouldn't come amiss at this point, either – and Miathan suspected that, with a little ingenuity and the assistance of a time spell and the Moldan's particular powers, he could lay a deadly trap for any wielder of the Artefacts who might dare return to Nexis.

The Moldan's capacity for destruction was tremendous, and the Archmage had divined that its powers could be unleashed in its absence, simply by means of imprinting its will upon the rocks in a spell that could be released at a time of its choosing. Miathan's time spell could delay this until the appropriate moment, and the use of one of the Artefacts within the precincts of the Academy would provide the trigger.

The Archmage's thoughtful frown vanished, to be replaced by a cold and calculating smile. 'Moldan,' he said in a wheedling voice that dripped with false solicitude. 'How would you like to go home?'

4

The Silence of Years

The Sword of Flame spun away, clattering over smooth white stone. The blackened chalice that was said to be a fragment of the Cauldron of Rebirth fell ringing to the floor, rolled in a circle on its rim and came to a trembling halt. Eliseth stumbled forward and fell to her knees, downed by her own unexpected momentum and by a sickening swirl of disorientation as reality wrenched itself back on to its normal course. She touched the paving beneath her and bit back a shriek as pain exploded through blackened, blistered hands that had been burned by the Sword, following her theft of the Artefact from Aurian. Instinctively, the Magewoman concentrated her powers to block the pain. Further healing could wait – at the moment it was the least of her concerns.

When had it come to be night? As her vision gradually cleared and the whirling in her head steadied, Eliseth looked about her, expecting to see the same Valley she had left – only moments ago, it seemed. Instead she saw a low, white wall sculpted in the familiar, nacreous marble that still, despite the surrounding darkness, held its own faint glimmer. The Weather-Mage, amazed and disbelieving, pulled herself unsteadily to her feet and looked over the low parapet. Nexis lay sprawled in the valley below, and she could discern the dark, swelling humps of the hills beyond, black against the cloudy sky.

The city looked different somehow – the contours of its streets and buildings seemed subtly altered from the shapes she remembered – but Eliseth gave the matter little thought as her heart leapt with joy at the sight before her. She uttered a soft, triumphant cry of relief. By some miracle, the grail had returned her to the Academy and placed her on the flat roof that topped the Mages' Tower. Though she did not look to any gods, it seemed that this time her unvoiced prayers had been answered. Not only had she survived her horrifying fall through the rent in reality – but she was safely home.

The Weather-Mage, shivering a little in the cool breeze and still very shaky from the shock of her recent experience, leant against the parapet in the silken darkness, and took deep breaths of blessed, smoke-tinged Nexian air. Her narrow escape from the tumultuous events in the Valley had left her feeling light-headed and inordinately pleased with herself, as though she had been responsible for her own good fortune. Once her plan to defeat Aurian had recoiled with such dramatic and deadly consequences, snatching Eliseth away out of the world, survival had been her only concern. She could only recall an incandescent blaze of multicoloured light – a sensation of being sucked, swirling, into a darkly gleaming vortex. She remembered wishing with a desperate wild yearning to be back at the Academy – but who would have suspected that the Artefacts would take her desire so literally? Clearly, the strength of her own will had saved her.

Her gloating was interrupted by the faintest whisper of sound and a flicker of movement at the very edge of her vision. Eliseth spun round with a startled curse. Behind her, a long, dark form was inching weakly across the roof. A pale hand stretched out, reaching for the precious Sword. Anvar! Eliseth exhaled with a hiss. In the panic of her fall through time and the subsequent relief at finding herself back in Nexis, the Weather-Mage had forgotten, briefly, that Aurian's lover had also been drawn into the vortex.

The Magewoman saw Anvar freeze as he realised that he had been discovered. In the shadowed gloom of the rooftop his eyes met hers and for an instant Eliseth saw fear, determination – and the icy steel of implacable loathing. Then with unexpected speed he lurched forward, his outstretched hand snatching desperately at the Sword. Eliseth reacted instantaneously, gathering her powers and lashing them out towards the recumbent form in a coil of smoky blackness laced with threads of searing blue-white light. Anvar jerked once, convulsively, as the spell hit him, pouring over him in a writhing mass of dark vapour webbed with crawling strands of blue.

Then he was utterly still, unbreathing, locked away in an instant and stranded outside the stream of time – until Eliseth should choose to bring him back again.

The Weather-Mage laughed aloud in triumph as she walked over to her prey. For a moment she stood there, looking down at him with a sneer. How easy it had been to defeat him! Without Aurian to protect him, the former Academy drudge had soon betrayed his lowly half-Mortal origins. Following the capture of Miathan, taking another Mage out of time had been a simpler matter – and one that put Anvar into her power while she decided his future at her leisure. The possibilities of the situation were now beginning to dawn on Eliseth. With her enemy's paramour enmeshed and isolated within the crawling blue shimmer of the spell, she knew she had some time to ponder the considerable advantage his capture would give her over Aurian – who, judging from her absence, plainly lacked the courage to follow her so-called love to his fate. But she would turn up eventually; of that Eliseth was absolutely certain. And when she did . . . The Weather-Mage smiled coldly. Aurian was a pathetic fool in her soft-hearted devotion to this half-Mortal scum with his tainted blood. Eliseth knew that she could use Anvar as bait to rid herself of her foe for good.

Without a backward glance, she left her victim where he lay on the cold stone of the roof – isolated as he was in her time spell, he should be safe enough up there – and strode across to the door that led down into the tower. Eliseth's eyebrows rose in surprise then drew down in a frown as she tugged at the latch and nothing happened. This door was never locked! A closer examination showed that the latch was stiff with rust.

'I was up here only five or six days ago,' the Magewoman muttered to herself. 'How could the wretched thing get into this condition in so short a time?' Reluctant to actually damage the door that kept the weather out of the tower, she stepped back and unleashed several brief, successive bursts of pure force at the recalcitrant latch, until the metal was shaken loose from its coating of corrosion and the bar rattled loosely in its socket. Even with the latch free, however, the door, its swollen panels cracked and weathered to a faded silver, stubbornly resisted Eliseth's attempts to push it open.

Eventually, as her patience was reaching breaking point, the door groaned open reluctantly on stiff, rust-caked hinges, allowing her sufficient space to shoulder her way inside. She leapt backwards with an involuntary gasp as dank, clinging trailers of cobwebs swept across her face. Colliding with the wall, she found it slick and slimy to the touch. 'What the blazes?' With a grimace, she scrubbed her hands against her skirts, then illuminated the stairwell with a bolt of searing lightning.

It was unbelievable. Long after the incandescence had faded back to darkness and the dazzle had left her eyes, Eliseth stood transfixed with shock, unable to accept what she had seen. The clean white stone of the staircase had vanished beneath a thick layer of dust and grime, and it was clear from the lack of footprints that no living soul had passed that way for many a long age. The ceiling was festooned with webs, and the curving walls glistened black with slimy mould. The air within the passage was stale and fetid with neglect and decay.

Dumbfounded, the Weather-Mage sat down on the top of the staircase, oblivious of the dirt and the chilly dampness that immediately began to seep through her skirts. How could this have happened? The upper reaches of the Mages' Tower had clearly not been used in years. But that was impossible – or it ought to be. Eliseth's mind went back to her terrifying fall through the gap in creation. She had passed through space, from the Vale to Nexis. Had she also travelled through time? And if so, how many years was she adrift? Had she journeyed to the future or the past?

'Use your brain!' the Magewoman muttered to herself. 'It must be the future. Had I travelled into the past, the Academy wouldn't be deserted like this.' But how far into the future had she come? Eliseth remembered her uneasy feeling that Nexis had somehow altered from the city she remembered and, scrambling hurriedly to her feet, she left the stairwell and rushed back to the low wall that looked out across the undulating landscape of rooftops. In the darkness, however, and from this great height, she could make out no details to help her gauge the passage of time. Though a scattering of lamps glittered on the darkened streets of the city, there were no lights or other signs of life among the Academy buildings, and no soldiers manned the guardroom at the gate. Eliseth might have been the only person alive in all the world. For the first time since she had vanquished Miathan, she felt the cold touch of true fear. Without warning, she had been wrenched away from everything that was familiar and secure. She shivered as an unaccustomed sense of loneliness swept through her.

This was useless. With an effort, the Weather-Mage thrust aside the insidious feelings of fear and desolation that were threatening to swamp her good sense. Straightening her shoulders, she turned and strode resolutely back towards the tower stairs. As she went, her foot caught on something that rolled away with a metallic rattle and a flash that sent rippling waves of power right across the rooftop. With a start, Eliseth recognized the grail that had been partly responsible for bringing her here. Stooping to pick it up, she stowed it safely in a deep pocket in her robe. The Sword, however, would have to remain where it was for the time being. She knew better now than to try to handle it. It had already injured her – indeed, she had been lucky to survive her first encounter with the Artefact. Until she could discover a way to master, or at least endure, its wild and lethal powers, it would be no use to her.

Eliseth descended the staircase with difficulty. Since she had little skill with Fire-magic, her wispy attempts at Magelight were dim and of short duration. They had an annoying – and dangerous – tendency to flicker into oblivion at the slightest wavering of her concentration, plunging the treacherously slippery steps beneath her feet into utter darkness. She passed by Miathan's chambers on the upper landing and Aurian's door on the next floor without a second glance and headed directly for her own rooms, for by this time the Mage felt a desperate need for the reassurance of familiar surroundings. There was little comfort to be found, however, in the decay and ruin that met her eyes as she let herself into her chambers. Her suite was unrecognizable as its former, pristine self.

Eliseth wandered from room to room, recoiling in disgust as her feet sank almost to the ankles into the oozing remains of a rotting carpet whose hue, once snowy white, was grey now, and stained with black mildew and greenish mould. The discovery of her jewels, still safely locked in their dusty box, cheered her, however. She pocketed them clumsily, wincing and cursing at the stiffness of her burned hands, but her hopes of finding anything else that was salvageable soon withered, for her precious possessions, amassed over many years for their beauty and priceless value, had long ago been lost under a thick blanket of rot and dust. Her numerous clothes, made from rich, luxurious furs and fabrics and carefully stored in closets and chests, had also succumbed to the ravages of time. A thin, cold wind blew in through the broken windows, stirring the shredded rags of curtain that still hung there and adding to the atmosphere of abandonment and dissolution.

This devastation of her quarters was too horrible to contemplate, and Eliseth could not bear to remain and investigate further. Though she had too much pride to break into a run, she turned abruptly on her heel and descended the remainder of the staircase recklessly in darkness, not bothering to waste time on an attempt at Magelight, and not pausing until she had reached the door at the bottom, which she blew into splinters with a single lightning bolt. Stepping carefully over the smouldering debris, she hurried out into the courtyard. Only when she had regained the open air at last did she feel that she could breathe again.

Eliseth's sense of relief, however, was short-lived. The silence of years weighed down on the Academy like a dense, muffling blanket, adding to the eerie sense of desolation. Memories of treachery and violence thronged about her like the Death-Wraiths that Miathan had once manifested, to his cost, from the grail. The shivers that ran up her spine were not entirely due to the cold wind that swirled around the Magewoman's shoulders. 'Enough of this nonsense!' she muttered to herself. 'Just because you're tired and hungry, there's no need to carry on in such a spineless fashion.' After all, she thought, with a grim smile, she had not eaten in years. Suddenly she remembered the food that the Archmage had taken out of time and stockpiled in the storerooms behind the kitchen. Could it still be there? Hunger lent fresh impetus to her steps as she hurried across the courtyard to find out.

At least there were candles in the kitchen. No longer did Eliseth have to concern herself with the vagaries of Magelight, once she had ignited the first wick. As her flame took hold and the amber glow of candlelight swelled to encompass the room, she was startled by the pattering and scuffling of a multitude of small feet. Shadows moved and scattered into corners and under benches as cockroaches and rats, so long the undisputed kings of this domain, scrambled for cover. The Magewoman wrinkled her nose in disgust, but pressed on undeterred, heading for the storerooms. Any food that had been taken out of time would have escaped the attentions of the scavengers.

Her hopes were confounded. Miathan had spent too long out of the world, a victim of her magic. In his absence, the time spells had gradually decayed, and the provisions that had not been accessible to the vermin had rotted down into a stinking black sludge that set Eliseth retching. She beat a hasty retreat, mopping at streaming eyes as she stumbled out of the kitchen.

Irritation was fast overcoming the Weather-Mage's hunger and dismay. Plainly, there was nothing for her here at the Academy. As she searched for alternatives, her mind turned to the Mortals of the city. Down in Nexis there was one person, at least – if he was still alive – who owed her. She drew her cloak across her face and set off down the hill.

Bern felt the blood drain from his face as he opened the door and saw the Lady Eliseth. His knees sagged, forcing him to cling to the edge of the door for support, and his mouth opened and closed wordlessly as he gasped for breath. I'm dreaming, he thought. I must be. This is a dreadful nightmare – I'll wake up in a minute and she'll be gone . . .

The Mage showed no signs of going anywhere. A malicious smile appeared on her flawless face. 'What's wrong, Bern?' she asked him in poisonously sweet tones. 'Why, you look as though you've seen a ghost.'

'But I . . .' The baker managed to find his voice at last. 'Lady, I thought you were dead. When you vanished in that flash . . . I was sure you'd been killed. We – everyone – thought *all* the Magefolk were dead.'

Eliseth shrugged. 'You were wrong, then.' Without waiting to be invited, she pushed roughly past the baker and swept into the room. Bern followed her on shaky legs. By this time, he had sufficiently gathered his wits to notice the lines of strain and weariness on Eliseth's face, and the charring and blistering that disfigured her hands. Apart from that, she looked just as she had when last he had seen her. Her silvery hair, normally so smooth and immaculate, was snarled like a crone's and reeked of wood smoke as though she had only just come from the burning of the Valley's trees. Where in the name of the gods had she been all these years? he wondered. And what had she been doing there?

'Clearly you have profited from the absence of the Magefolk.' The Weather-Mage was raking the newly refurbished bakery with her eyes. 'As I came up the lane, I noticed that you've purchased the building next door to expand your premises.' She turned her cold and penetrating gaze full upon him. 'I find myself wondering, can all this newfound prosperity be due to the grain that was supplied by me some time ago?'

'Indeed, Lady – I'm a man of some substance now.' Bern saw no point in denying it. He was well aware that she would be taking careful note of all the repairs and additions to his property. Everywhere she looked, there would be signs of his increased affluence, from his rich, expensive clothing to the gleaming new ovens and counters. Against all logic, he prayed that she would not discern the many subtle, decorative touches that could only denote the presence of a woman – but it was not to be.

The Mage raised an eyebrow. 'Well, well. And have you been wed, Bern, in my absence? Are congratulations in order?'

'Why, Lady – what makes you say that?' he asked, a shade too quickly.

Just then a voice rang out from the back room. 'Who is it, Bern?'

The baker cursed under his breath as a short woman with sleek brown hair scraped tightly back into a knot appeared from the back room. She was well advanced in pregnancy, and two young children, a boy and a girl, peeped shyly at the visitor from behind her skirts. Before the baker could send her back, Eliseth stepped forward and held out a hand to her. 'Why, you must be Bern's wife,' she said brightly. 'I'm delighted that he has found such a charming and lovely helpmate – and such sweet little children!'

As Eliseth had deigned to speak to her, Bern had no choice but to introduce his woman. 'This is my wife, Alissana,' he mumbled. The woman, plainly flustered, had recognized one of the Magefolk. Bern saw her shudder as she took Eliseth's hand with its blackened flesh, and noted the terror in her eyes as the Magewoman spoke of the children. Alissana tried to curtsey but was unbalanced by the ungainliness of her pregnant body. She would have fallen, dragging the Mage with her, had Eliseth not held them both upright.

'Clumsy bitch!' snapped Bern, and raised his hand threateningly. The woman blanched, her hands moving quickly across her body as if to shield her unborn child. Flinching away from her husband she scurried into the other room, followed by the younger child, the boy. The other, a girl of about five or six, hovered in the doorway, watching the Magewoman with huge, round eyes.

Eliseth shrugged, and turned back to Bern. 'I presume you keep a chamber for guests somewhere on these expanded premises of yours. Show it to me at once, and then I will require a hot bath and a good meal – and in the morning, your wife can arrange to have some new clothes made for me.'

Bern's eyes bulged. Oh dear gods, she couldn't be wanting to *stay*! 'Why, Lady,' he gasped, 'you do us great honour, but . . .'

Striking out like a serpent, the Magewoman gripped his wrist in a blackened claw. 'Listen, you despicable little turd – you owe me, and never forget it,' she snarled, gesturing around the refurbished bakery, to the comfortably appointed living quarters in the room beyond. 'Without my gift of that grain, you'd have none of this.'

Despite his fear of her, Bern's grasping, mercenary nature revolted at such a claim. 'Lady, with all respect, you seem to have forgotten that the grain was not a gift but payment, for infiltrating the rebel camp and —'

'And luring them out of their lurking place so that I could deal with them — a task which you singularly failed to accomplish.' There was steel in Eliseth's voice. 'You thieving Mortal scum! Having failed to keep your side of our bargain, how *dared* you appropriate that grain? You had no right to it whatsoever!'

Bern wrenched himself from her grasp and fell grovelling to the floor. 'Forgive me, Lady — I didn't mean to steal your grain,' he wailed. 'But what was I to do? It would have been a crime to waste it. Although it rightly belonged to the Magefolk, I thought all the Mages were gone!'

'Evidently,' the Mage said flatly. 'But you were wrong — and now you must atone for your mistake. Unless, that is, you would prefer your wife and children to pay for it in your stead.' Her voice was as cold and deadly as a steel-jawed trap.

Bern shuddered to think what she might do to his unborn child. Having no other choice, he throttled his anger, and subsided in defeat. 'Very well, my Lady,' he whispered.

Alissana barely had time to leap back from the door at which she'd been listening as Bern burst into the room.

'The Lady will be staying with us.' He spat out the words as though each one tasted vile. 'She's demanding a hot bath and food,' he added with a scowl, 'so I'll stoke up the fire and start the water heating, while you start cooking — and for both our sakes, you'd better make it the best meal you've ever produced in your life. Well go on — don't just stand there gaping, you brainless baggage. Get to the stove, and get busy!'

His wife scurried to obey him, suppressing a chill of trepidation at the thunderous expression on his face. During the years of their marriage, she had become all too well accustomed to her husband's temper, for he had a tendency to take it out on his family whenever anything went wrong. As she assembled the meal, Alissana fretted. She was a sensible, even-tempered woman, who had been well aware of the baker's failings when she wed him but had chosen him in any

54

case; in the aftermath of the Magefolk vanishment, he was the only man of any substance among the impoverished labouring folk of Nexis. She had learned perforce to shield herself and the children from the worst of his rages, and this time she understood his anger, fully sharing his anxiety.

It had stunned Alissana to discover that their prosperity had stemmed from some unholy bargain made with the Magefolk in the past. Difficult and sometimes brutal as Bern could be, he represented security and even luxury for herself and her children. Alissana shuddered at the memory of the twisted black claw that the Mage had held out to her, and Eliseth's ice-cold eyes. The Lady terrified her. Alissana feared for the safety of her children – and now the Mage had accused Bern of stealing . . . Her hands trembled as she rolled pastry for a pie. What if Eliseth should slay him in a fit of pique, or turn him into something unnatural? What would become of his family then?

Grumbling and swearing all the while, Bern was testing the temperature of the water in the big copper that was built into the side of the fireplace. His back was turned towards his wife. Almost of their own accord, Alissana's eyes went to the metal box with the tight-fitting lid that was placed safely up on a high shelf, out of the children's way. Rats and mice were a frequent problem in the bakery and recently Bern had gone to the local herbwife and purchased a new batch of poison. Swiftly, Alissana reached up for the box. Bern's back was still safely turned as she sprinkled the white crystals between the layers of apple in her pie. Before her husband had time to turn round, the deed was done, the box replaced on its shelf, and the crust clapped into place, hiding the evidence of her deadly handiwork. Only when Alissana came to put the pie into the oven, did she notice that her hands had stopped shaking.

Some time later, Eliseth, clean and refreshed now, sat before a blazing fire in what was evidently the best bedchamber in the house. The fact that Bern and his pregnant wife had given up their room to her caused her not the slightest qualm. It had been most uncomfortable and inconvenient to have no servants around to tend to her needs, but now, for the first time since her precipitate return to Nexis, she was filled with a soothing sense of life returning to its proper course. She savoured the thought of the baker staggering up and down the stairs with his buckets to fill, and later empty, her bath. At least Mortals were useful for something.

The Magewoman had been immeasurably relieved to see that, though he had aged, the baker did not seem to be so very many years older than she remembered, and the expression on his face as he'd answered the door had afforded her a good deal of malicious amusement – enough, perhaps, for her to overlook the fact that he had appeared anything but pleased to see her.

Now she had found that she was not too far astray in time, Eliseth's chief concern was the condition of her hands, which had been so badly seared by the Sword of Flame. She wished that she had bothered to learn more than just the most basic of healing arts from Meiriel. Though she had tried everything at her disposal, all her best efforts could buy only freedom from pain and a certain amount of sensation and flexibility in her clawlike fingers – sufficient to allow her to use her hands again except for very delicate or complex tasks. The skin remained seared and blackened, and nothing seemed to change that. She had an ominous feeling that nothing ever would. The Weather-Mage bit her lip and swallowed against a tightness in her throat. Demons take the accursed Sword of Flame! What had it done to her?

The arrival of Bern with a tray of food interrupted Eliseth's brooding. She was surprised to see him, for she had expected that he would feel himself above such menial service when there was a woman around to do the work. He had certainly been surly enough about filling her bath. But Alissana might be too frightened to approach a Mage – or, in all probability, Bern was trying to keep his wife away from her.

As he put the tray down in front of her, Eliseth laid her other worries aside for the moment. 'Sit down here, Bern, and keep me company while I eat,' she said. 'I want to know exactly what has been happening in the city while I've been away.'

Little by little, Eliseth extracted a picture of what had taken place in Nexis during her absence. She had, she discovered, been missing for over seven years – easily enough time for the foolish, gullible Mortals to convince themselves that the Magefolk were all safely dead and gone. None the less, it was fear of Miathan's restless ghost that had kept the Nexians from sacking the Academy – a fact that Eliseth noted with interest. It was difficult to contain her shock and anger, however, when she discovered that the Council of Three had been abolished and that upstart Vannor, of all people, now ruled the city. Since the night she had tried to fuel her magic through the pain of his mangled hand, and having first defied her he had gone on to escape her grasp entirely, Eliseth's hatred of the merchant had been virulent, and her grudge against him deeply personal. She could allow no mere Mortal to make an idiot out of *her* and go unpunished.

The same went for Vannor's daughter. The Mage's supper lost all its savour as she remembered how the little bitch had infiltrated the Academy in the guise of a maidservant and succeeded in worming her way into the position of Eliseth's personal maid. No one had ever been able to work out just how Zanna had managed to rescue her father and then vanish with him so effectively, but, since the girl had been Eliseth's servant, Miathan had always blamed the Weather-Mage for the escape – completely overlooking the fact that *he* had been the one who'd entrusted the girl with the prisoner's care.

Her stomach churning with anger at the thought of Zanna, Eliseth pushed her plate of roast fowl aside. 'Do you know what became of Vannor's daughter?' she asked Bern, trying to keep the sharpness from her voice.

Bern shook his head. 'She married, Lady, I think.' He shrugged. 'I don't know where she's living – it's not in Nexis, though. I think she stayed away for safety's sake, when the Phaerie started raiding. She comes to visit her father from time to time, and brings her children.'

The Magewoman sighed. Ah well – there'd be time enough to discover the whereabouts of Zanna. First of all she would concentrate on the girl's father, the self-styled Lord of Nexis. She had no idea, yet, how she would take her revenge on him. Then something that Bern had said broke through her thoughts of revenge to come into the forefront of her mind. 'What did you say about the Phaerie?' she demanded.

Eliseth listened with dismay as he told her the sorry tale. In the turmoil of events that were taking place around her when she'd been snatched from the world, she had forgotten about the Forest Lord and his subjects. But it seemed that, in the absence of the Magefolk, the accursed Phaerie had been getting out of hand. In the first three or four years of his reign, Vannor had had endless trouble from the skyborne raiders. On nights when the moon was bright and the north wind rode the heavens, the citizens of Nexis and the surrounding countryside had soon learned to lock up their livestock and bar and bolt their doors when the Phaerie, on their great strong horses that trod the air, came hurtling down from the skies. At first, only strong men were taken, but later specific craftsmen began to vanish, masons, tilers, builders, carpenters and smiths. All were borne northward, too fast to be followed, never to return.

Later, farmers and shepherds also began to vanish – always those from the bleakest holdings, who knew how to get the best from the tough vegetation and thin soil of the upland farms. A different pattern was emerging here, however. The farms were discovered abandoned, with entire families gone, and the barns and fields stripped bare of livestock, implements and crops alike. Vannor, Eliseth was maliciously pleased to hear, had almost driven himself demented trying to get to the bottom of the mysterious abductions, but he had failed to discover the reason behind them, as abjectly as he had failed to put a stop to them. Soon farms were being deserted for another reason, as many of the outlying families fled their land to seek sanctuary with relatives who lived in the city.

Not that Nexis was really any safer. The Phaerie struck when they pleased, and snatched whomsoever they wanted. Young girls were often abducted now, and sometimes even children. Women were being stolen away from home and family to suffer who knew what fate. Spinners and weavers were being targeted, as were seamstresses and lacemakers – not to mention bakers, brewers, and the members of the oldest profession of all. The garrison seemed to be helpless – after so many failures to keep matters under control the commander had given up, and was occupied instead in drinking himself into an early grave. Though Nexis had prospered, by and large, under Vannor's rule, there could be no true peace or prosperity until the problem of the Phaerie had been dealt with once and for all.

Bern was a frightened man, that much was plain, thought Eliseth. He had escaped the Phaerie once, that day long ago in the Vale, by plunging into the lake and hiding beneath the overhanging bushes at the water's edge until they were safely gone before creeping away and finding one of the loose mercenary horses to make his way home. He had never forgotten, however, the horror of their attack when they had slain Eliseth's force of hired soldiers to the last man. He had fortified the bakery as well as he could, but still lived in fear that one night he, too, might be seized – and what if the Phaerie took his family?

It was all the same to Eliseth if they did – save that Bern himself might prove useful to her in the days to come. The Mage was more preoccupied with the threat that the Phaerie posed to her plans. She intended to take up the reins of power in Nexis, and it might prove difficult if the blasted Phaerie were still rampaging through the city. On the other hand, if she could get rid of them she would win the admiration and respect of the populace. She wouldn't have to lift a finger to oust Vannor – the stupid Nexians would be begging her to rule them. Scarcely listening to Bern's ceaseless tirade of whining complaints, she continued to make her plans as she pulled the apple pie towards her, and began to eat.

Eliseth's eyes flew open wide with shock as the first pain lanced through her innards. As she toppled from her chair, clutching at her stomach, she could already feel the poison seeping into her blood like an insidious black tide. She clawed at her throat as she thrashed helplessly on the carpet, choking on a corrosive mixture of bile and gore.

There were only seconds in which to save herself. Thrusting back her panic, striving her utmost to ignore the pain, Eliseth turned her will inwards, to slow her labouring heart. She reached, as though with invisible fingers, into her veins, to break down the deadly poison into its harmless constituents, which could be flushed out of her system.

Gradually, the agony and distress diminished. To her relief, the Mage felt the rhythms and functions of her body returning to normal. The receding waves of pain washed her back to the shores of consciousness. Feeling weak, nauseated and dizzy, aching dully as though she had been beaten both inside and out, Eliseth opened her eyes.

Where was Bern? Where was that two-faced, sneaking, back-stabbing lump of Mortal offal? Behind her, the Magewoman heard the soft snick and creak of the door being opened. Having discovered that she was about to survive his craven attack after all, the treacherous bastard was making a hasty escape.

'No!' Eliseth snarled, rolling over. She had had enough of Mortals slipping from her clutches. There was time for a fleeting glimpse of the terror in Bern's eyes – then a bolt of sizzling lightning left her hand in a swift, fluent motion. The baker's body crumpled, smoking, to the floor.

Cursing horribly, the Mage grabbed the edge of the table and pulled herself upright. A swift gulp of wine from the flask on the table helped to restore her. When she had steadied herself a little, she staggered across the room to the baker and looked down at his smouldering corpse with a frown, wrinkling her nose in disgust at the stench of charred flesh. 'Damn the snivelling little rat to perdition – I would never have thought he'd have the nerve,' she muttered to herself. All the same, now that the first fierce blast of her anger had dissipated, she began to regret killing him so quickly. She'd had plans for Bern and his family, and now he was useless to her. And she'd have to kill the wife and children, too, or the news of her return would be all over Nexis in no time, putting Vannor immediately on his guard. Eliseth cursed again. Bloody Mortals! It was all very inconvenient.

Well, at least the baker had given her the information she needed before she died. She could leave now and return to the safety of the Academy, dealing with the remainder of Bern's family on the way. The Weather-Mage reached for her cloak, carelessly draped over the back of a chair. As she lifted it, she felt an unaccustomed weight, and touched a hard, lumpy shape hidden in the deep pocket that was sewn into the lining.

Eliseth stopped breathing and stood utterly still for a moment, the cloak forgotten in her hands. An incredible idea had suddenly occurred to her. What if the chalice she carried still had the power to perform the original function of the Cauldron of Rebirth? If it did, the possibilities were staggering!

With hands that shook a little from excitement, Eliseth took the grail from her pocket and filled it with water from the jug on the table. As the liquid filled the cup, it seemed to take on the properties of the tarnished interior, turning a deep, viscous black without sparkle or reflection. A dark steam rose, curling, from the light-devouring surface. Holding the chalice very carefully, so as not to spill any of its contents over her hands, the Mage returned to the corpse of Bern and sprinkled a few drops over the still-smoking body.

At first, nothing seemed to be happening. There was no sign of life nor movement from the scorched, recumbent form. But then, just as Eliseth was about to turn away in disgust, she blinked, and looked again. The surface of Bern's body was covered in a dark, moving cloud that looked, from a distance, like a swarm of tiny, glittering black bees. The Magewoman noticed that the charred shell of his peeling skin seemed to be softening a little, and gradually turning to the paler hue of healthy flesh. Within minutes, he was recognizable as human again but, to her disgust, neither breathing nor moving.

Acting on impulse, Eliseth lifted his head and trickled a few drops of dark water from the grail into his slack mouth. A tense moment passed, and then another, while the Mage held her breath in anticipation. Without warning, Bern inhaled sharply with a strangled gasp, and leapt clumsily to his feet. 'Lady, I didn't! It wasn't me,' he screamed. Then he blinked, and recognition returned to his eyes. 'What happened?' he demanded, forgetting, in his confusion, to address the Mage with any mark of respect. 'What was I doing?'

Eliseth, already framing an angry response, bit off her half-formed reply. Her eyes widened with shock as she realized that Bern, after his first, shrieked protest of innocence, had not spoken a word aloud. *She could see into his mind!*

She could see much more clearly once she realized what was happening, and began to focus all her powers of concentration. There, through the murky roil that constituted Mortal thoughts, was the baker's intense bafflement as he puzzled in vain to retrieve what had happened during the weird blank spell which had left him unconscious on the floor. She saw his horror and fear, as he cast his mind back to realize that someone had tried to murder the Mage – and that only one person could have been responsible.

Alissana! Eliseth took the image straight out of the Mortal's mind. So it was Bern's accursed woman who'd had the temerity to make an attempt on her life! The Mage's wrath boiled over beyond all controlling – and suddenly, with a wrenching change of perspective, she found herself looking at herself. Eliseth gasped, and flung her hands up to her face – but they were not her hands, nor was it her own features that she could feel beneath her fingers. She was seeing the room through Bern's eyes!

Acting instinctively, Eliseth clamped her will down upon Bern's weak and cowardly Mortal thoughts, and felt them streaming through her mental grasp like grains of sand through an hourglass. She discovered that the sensation differed from that of occupying another's body, where the victim's individuality was thrust aside and the personality of the intruder took over. In this case, the baker's thoughts were still his own – the Mage simply controlled them, as though his mind was a restless horse that she could restrain and guide with the reins of her will. With a thrill of delight, she realized that he was actually unaware of her presence within him. The sensation of control was exhilarating, and Eliseth wondered just how far her hold extended. Tentatively at first, she began to probe the limits of her newfound power.

There was no risk of damage or danger to Eliseth's own body – she seated it carefully in a chair out of harm's way. Soon, she discovered that all she needed to control were the so-called higher functions of the baker's mind, and the automatic processes of his body took care of themselves. For a time

62

she amused herself by making him move around the room and perform simple tasks. Then, when she felt ready, she decided to put her hold over her puppet to the test. Riding the web of Bern's thoughts like a lurking spider, she turned him towards the stairs – and the rooms where his family slept.

5

The Undead

Little Alissa, named after her mother, awoke in the darkness. She had slept uneasily that night, her dreams disturbed by the presence of the cold-eyed woman with the silver hair who had come to stay. Though she was not usually a timid child (she was a big girl now – six years old – and had to look after her little brother Tolan) there was something about the stranger that made Alissa want to run away and hide. She was grateful for the reassuring presence of her mother who, as the visitor had taken over the best bedchamber, was sleeping on a pallet on the floor of the children's room.

The noise that had awakened Alissa came again – the stealthy shuffle of a furtive footfall on the stairs. Trembling, the girl huddled deeper beneath her blankets, and hugged her rag doll tightly. She heard the harsh, repetitive hiss of ragged breathing outside the door. Feeling slightly foolish, Alissa relaxed her stranglehold on the doll. It was only dad, coming to bed. How could she have forgotten him? But as she listened to his fumbling efforts with the door latch, she shuddered, and tensed again with fear. He must have been drinking too much wine again – and she knew all too well, with a sad wisdom that belied her brief span of years, what the result would be.

Most of the time, Alissa's father was just the strict, stern master of the little household. He worked hard and expected his family, children included, to do their share, or woe betide them. Occasionally, however, he would spend the evening in a tavern, or sit up late on his own drinking wine, and then there would be trouble. On too many nights Alissa had crept out of bed, disturbed by the sound of blows and muffled cries, to watch or listen unseen, her heart hammering with fear, as he beat her mother. Too many times in her short life she had been thrashed during his drunken rages, or clouted as a result of his savage temper in the mornings that followed. Usually, the children's room was a sanctuary when he was drunk. If they were out of his sight, he often didn't bother them. Tonight, however, there would be no escaping him, unless . . . The door swung open, spilling a wedge of light into the room, but Alissa, shivering in her thin nightdress, was already under the bed, rag doll and all.

It was very dusty under the bed. Alissa put her hand over her face and breathed shallowly, hoping to subdue the tickling in her nose. Peeping out from her hiding place, she saw a pair of feet in sturdy boots shuffling unsteadily towards the pallet on the wall, where her mother, tired out from a hard day's work, slept on, oblivious. Hoping against hope that her father would be in one of his better moods and just go right to sleep, the child inched her way nearer the edge of the bed and craned her neck to see better.

Dad put the lantern down on the floor beside the pallet. He stooped, and as the golden wash of lamplight illuminated his features Alissa thought he looked *strange*, somehow. His expression was preoccupied and distant, as though he listened to some faint sound, far away. Her mother stirred, disturbed by the light, and rolled over on to her back. Something glittered in dad's hand. Alissa muffled a shriek as the knife flashed down, burying itself to the hilt in mother's chest. With an odd, gurgling noise, the woman convulsed, then went limp. Alissa, numb with horrified disbelief, desperately wanted to look away, but could not. It was as though she had been turned to stone. This couldn't be happening – it couldn't be her father who was doing this dreadful thing! The blood – the blood was everywhere, reeking, darkly gleaming in the lamp-light.

With a jerk, dad wrenched the knife out from between mother's ribs and turned towards her little brother, who was awake now, and howling in his cot. Only then was the spell of horror broken. Alissa realized, with a shock that sent a bolt of ice shearing down her spine, that she would be next. Dad turned his back on her, the knife raised high to strike. Alissa rolled out from underneath the bed. Little Tolan's high, thin scream drowned her footsteps as she raced towards the door, and then the sound cut off abruptly. Dad, whirling, lunged towards her with an incoherent shout, but Alissa was out and hurtling down the stairs before he could reach her. She reached the outer door a scant few strides ahead of him and pulled frantically at the handle – but the door was locked, and the big key turned too stiffly for a child to manage.

Alissa shrieked as the wild-eyed figure she had known as her father loomed over her, eyes wild and vacant in his spattered face, his knife, dripping gore, held high in one clenched and bloody fist. As he swooped down on her she ducked beneath his clutching hands and dodged away, taking the only route left open to her – the short passageway that led into the bakery – though she knew that that outside door would be locked too. Bern, hot in pursuit, tried to turn too quickly and his blood-soaked boots slipped on the polished tiles of the hallway. Alissa heard him curse, and recognized the thud as he fell. It would give her a moment – a single moment – in which to hide herself.

Gasping for breath, the child ran into the bakery and looked wildly around for a place of concealment. The only place that seemed to offer a refuge was the big oven, cold now that the fire had gone out. Without another thought, Alissa ran across the room and climbed into the bread-scented interior. She slammed the door behind her just in time and huddled in the darkness, still clutching her rag doll and scarcely daring to breathe.

Eliseth, her awareness ensconced like a parasite within Bern's mind, used the baker's eyes to scan the room and scowled in vexation. Curse the child! Where in perdition had it gone? She made Bern try the door. Still locked. Well, in that case the misbegotten little brat couldn't be far away. At first she thought of the closets until she gleaned from Bern's memory that they were too well stocked to provide enough space for a hiding place – then his eye fell on the ovens. One of them wasn't large enough to hold a child, but surely the other . . .

The baker moved as though he were sleepwalking: conscious, but with no volition of his own. He made no effort to fight the Mage as she guided him across the room to the oven and had him wedge the heavy door shut with the shank of a broom. The ashes of the fire were still warm, and it took no time at all to rekindle a blaze. As Bern piled on more wood, Eliseth heard Alissa shrieking. Testing her control of the baker, she forced him to stand there and listen to the death of his daughter. It took a long time for the screams to stop.

Leaving instructions in Bern's mind that rendered him immobile for a time, Eliseth rummaged through the house, picking out items she thought might be of use to her. Bern's small hoard of gold she took, and blankets, quilts, provisions, candles and anything else that could be found in the bakery to make her life more comfortable in the decaying Academy. The baker's wife had been much shorter than the Mage, so her clothes were useless, but Eliseth helped herself to several pairs of stockings, some gloves, and a thick woollen cloak. Although it only reached her knees, it would keep out the worst of the cold until she could get another.

Eliseth heaped her selections on the floor by the back door and returned to the Academy, unencumbered and unseen, by the swiftest route. Once there, she extended her consciousness towards Bern, for she could not control her own body and someone else's at the same time, and had been forced to leave him down in the city. It was far easier to find the baker than she had expected. In the dank squalor of the Academy kitchens, she lit a fire, then filled the chalice with water and squatted down by the hearth to look into the cup by the light of the flickering flames. Their link, through the Mage's control of the grail, was such that she seemed almost to be drawn to him. As soon as she thought of the baker, she saw him in the water, lifting the body of his son out of a tangle of blood-soaked blankets.

Bern bowed his head over the little corpse, and wept. 'Gods, how could this have happened?' he cried in anguish. 'How could you let this happen?'

Eliseth shrugged, and insinuated herself into the baker's mind once more. She forced him to leave the bodies of his family, and sent him downstairs to harness up the horse and load her looted implements and provisions on to the cart. Then she sent him back indoors with a bottle of lamp oil and a long stick from the woodpile that would serve as a torch. For many reasons, it would be best to get rid of the evidence.

With his will under the Mage's iron control, Bern drove his horse and cart up the hill to the Academy, laden with goods that had once been his own hard-won possessions and were now Eliseth's spoils. Behind him, the flames of the burning bakery roared up into the night, sending a swirl of sparks drifting towards the sky like lost, searching souls.

Eliseth made herself as comfortable as she could in the hard wooden chair, and watched the flames licking the sooty stones of the fireplace as the twilight deepened outside the window in the Archmage's suite. She suspected that, long ago, Miathan must have set some kind of self-activating spell upon his chambers to seal them, for though the traces of his magic had eventually faded in his absence, his rooms, located high above the damp lower storeys of the tower, were in by far the most habitable condition. It was just as well, since the Mage was exhausted. Throughout the daylight hours she had been concentrating hard to control the mind of her puppet as he swept and scrubbed the rooms, throwing out anything that was soiled or decayed beyond saving. Eliseth sighed and stretched. By the gods – it had been almost as wearying as doing the work herself.

The Mage poured herself another glass of wine, and picked fastidiously at a platter of bread and cheese. It had been worth all her effort to create this haven. None of the Mortals would dare come near the Academy – they were afraid of the place, and she would make sure they stayed that way. For the first time since she had come into this strange future, Eliseth relaxed. She was safe here, and now she could be reasonably comfortable while she worked out the best way to restore the Magefolk rule to Nexis.

Her possession of Bern was an excellent beginning, and boded well for the future. Eliseth could get into his mind at any time without his being aware of her presence. She could see through his eyes and manipulate his actions from a safe distance, and afterwards, she had discovered, the baker had no recollection that his will had been under the control of another. A slow smile of triumph spread itself over Eliseth's face. What a weapon this chalice had turned out to be. Miathan had been an utter fool not to discover the potential that lay within it – but thank the gods he had not. It was the solution to all her problems. Not only would she gain her revenge on Vannor and his wretched daughter, but she would rule Nexis, and those stupid Mortals wouldn't even know it.

This led to a further thought, and the Mage felt pleasurable excitement stir within her. Aurian would arrive eventually – that much was certain. What if Eliseth were to possess Anvar in the same fashion? Then she could spy on her enemy's movements, and influence her plans from afar. What if she could kill Aurian without a confrontation, either physical or magical – without, indeed, endangering herself in the slightest way? And wouldn't it be marvellous to bring about the ultimate betrayal – a fitting fate for the Mortal-loving bitch, and the one thing that would hurt Aurian more than anything else in the world – before she put an end to Eilin's daughter once and for all?

Eliseth laughed aloud. I'm going to enjoy this, she thought. But she knew her pleasure must be postponed for a while. After all, Aurian was not here yet – but Vannor was, and it was through him that she intended to carry out her conquest of Nexis. And what better time to start than tonight?

Somehow, however, the Mage could not settle down in the Archmage's chambers. Perhaps it was because she would be spending the night in what had once been his bed that she was consumed with uneasy thoughts of Miathan, and remembered the last expression of fury and loathing that had been stamped indelibly on his face in the instant she had betrayed him, and taken him out of time. Disquiet began to stir within her. Supposing her time spell had weakened in her absence – what then?

What utter nonsense! Eliseth tried to laugh at herself for entertaining such foolish fancies, but somehow the laughter had a hollow ring. It would be a simple matter to put her mind at rest, she told herself firmly – she need only go down into the catacombs where she had stowed Miathan's immobile form in one of the archive chambers, out of harm's way. She would see that he was still there, safely in her power, and that would be that. Yet Eliseth paced the chamber uneasily, putting off the moment when she must venture down into that dark labyrinth of abandoned tunnels. There were more unpleasant things than Miathan down there. She remembered the Death-Wraiths, and wished that she had not.

By this time, Eliseth was becoming increasingly annoyed with herself – so much so that her anger finally outweighed her trepidation. Snatching up a lamp from the table, she clattered swiftly down the spiral stone staircase and, slamming the door of the Mages' Tower loudly behind her, marched across the courtyard and into the library without a backward look.

As soon as she entered the cold, damp archives, Eliseth remembered why she had hated spending so much time in this place whilst researching the powers of the grail. Her footsteps, sounding far less swift and certain now, echoed hollowly in the narrow tunnels, on sloping floors with a smooth depression down the centre where the stone had been worn away by the feet of generations of archivists who had passed and re-passed through the catacombs. Trails of moisture gleamed on the wall, reflecting the light of her lamp, and the Weather-Mage shivered in the damp, chill air. She wished she had thought to bring her cloak with her. Still, she thought, I won't be down here for long. I just need to check on Miathan and leave. If I remember rightly, the room where I left him is just along this passage . . .

He was gone. She couldn't believe it. *Miathan had escaped her.* At first she thought she must have lost her way and come to the wrong chamber – but there was no mistaking it. To be absolutely sure, she had marked the door, and when she stepped back she could see the runes shimmering in the lamplight. Eliseth looked into the empty room, and dread went through her like a bolt of ice-cold lightning. *Where was he?* Suddenly, the Mage remembered what Bern had told her – that the Mortals were afraid to come near the Academy because of Miathan's ghost. Could he still be here? Could he,

70

even now, be lurking in these dark tunnels? Creeping up on her? With a gasp of horror, Eliseth turned and fled.

The wine that she had taken from Bern's home was of poorer quality than she was accustomed to, but for once Eliseth didn't care. Once she had regained the sanctuary of her chambers – Miathan's chambers, she thought with a shudder – she had barred and bolted the door, and reinforced the lock with every warding spell that she could dredge from her panic-fuddled mind. The Weather-Mage was badly shaken. She took another long draught from the cup that she held in trembling hands and tried to assemble her scattered wits. Her plan to stay here and rule the city from the Academy was in ruins now. One thing was for sure, she thought grimly – until she had discovered Miathan's whereabouts, it would not be safe to remain in Nexis at all. Should the Archmage come up on her unawares, she could measure her life in minutes – if she was lucky.

Once the initial shock had faded, Eliseth began to think more calmly. It seemed doubtful, she decided, that Miathan could be here at present. Surely he would have discovered her by now? Her emergence through the rift in time had caused a backwash of power that he must certainly have sensed, had he been lurking in or beneath the Academy. Perhaps there would be time after all to deal with Vannor and Anvar – then, once her pawns were in place, it wouldn't matter if she had to leave the city and hide in safety elsewhere. Everything hinged on Vannor. If she could only act quickly enough . . .

Unfortunately, swift action was impossible. In reality, three or four anxious days – she was so busy that she almost lost count – were to pass before the Mage was ready.

At last! Eliseth thought with relief. After tonight I can find somewhere safe. The night was old, but an hour or so still remained before the sky would begin to grow light. Unseen in the darkness, Eliseth glided along the mossy path that led up from the river and through the gardens of Vannor's mansion. She approached within an arm's length of the sentry, and still he did not notice her. Dear gods, however had these pathetic creatures ever ended up ruling her city? Eliseth reached out a

71

hand in passing and touched the man's face.

'Shit!' The guard started and spun round, his sword leaping out of its scabbard in a single fluid motion as he turned. He saw nothing. By that time, the Mage was gone. From several yards away, she heard his companion's voice.

'Thara's titties! What in perdition do you think you're doing, waving that sword around?'

'But I felt something touch me,' the other protested. 'Something brushed my face.'

'Oh for pity's sake, don't be so bloody feeble – it was probably just a moth. It's bad enough being stuck out here on duty in all this wet, without you seeing sodding fairies . . .'

Their faces faded in the distance as Eliseth left them and made her way up through the shrubbery, heading for the great house itself. She was glad of the drizzling overcast that deepened the gloom of the night. She was using an air spell to diffuse the light around her silhouette, and as long as the moon did not show itself from behind the low clouds she was fairly confident that she would not be seen.

Eliseth had given careful thought to this plan. Vannor was too well guarded to be approached directly – she would never be able to get him alone, as Bern had been, so that she could slay him by magical means. Besides, she did not want the Mortals to know that she had returned to their world, and if she used her powers against the upstart ruler of Nexis her secret would be out. She had more sense than to try a physical attack against Vannor. Even one-handed, he was stronger and more experienced with weaponry than she. There was just too much that could go wrong.

There was more than one way, however, to kill a Mortal – and in fact it was Bern's late and unlamented wife who had given her the idea. In the Mage's pocket was a small vial containing poison made according to instructions from one of the scrolls in the library, and concocted from ingredients found in Meiriel's infirmary. The last days had been spent in experimentation on the rats and other vermin that infested the Academy, until she was sure she had it right. According to the records there was no antidote. Of course, in order to make sure that her poison reached its intended victim, she would probably have to kill everyone in the merchant's household — but then, they were only Mortals, after all. The lethal liquid was colourless and tasteless, and much to Eliseth's satisfaction it was slow-acting, so that Vannor would take a long and painful time to die. At last he would suffer the death his perfidious daughter had prevented so long ago – but Zanna would not be able to save him this time.

The Mage had reached the rear of the house, and found the back door that led into the kitchen. Carefully, so as not to make a sound, she tested the latch. Locked. She put forth her powers, and after a moment heard a satisfying click as the mechanism of the lock sprang open. A faint glow of lamplight outlined the kitchen window. Edging alongside the wall, Eliseth flattened herself against the brickwork and peered around the side of the frame. The kitchen fires, banked for the night, had been revived, and a solitary man was working at the long wooden table. As she had expected, Vannor's head cook was up well before the dawn, setting the dough for the day's bread before the rest of the kitchen helpers were awake.

The man seemed surprisingly young to be a head cook, and, most unusual for one in his profession, he was very thin and gangling. Eliseth dismissed these details with barely a glance. To her, one Mortal was much the same as another. There was no sense in waiting. Taking a deep breath, she gathered her will to manipulate the air within the kitchen. A glowing patch of greenish mist appeared close to the feet of the unsuspecting cook. Slowly it elongated and solidified in form, until it had taken on the appearance of a small green serpent. Then the Mage paused. This was her favourite illusion and it would distract the cook sure enough – but what if he was afraid of snakes, as were so many of these ridiculous Mortals? He would yell and wake the rest of the household, and that was the last thing she wanted. Eliseth cursed under her breath and dissolved her illusion of the reptile. What could she use instead? A more complex creature would tax both her powers and stretch her ingenuity to the utmost – but she could do it. For the chance of revenging herself on Vannor at last, she could certainly do it.

The Mage narrowed her eyes and concentrated with all her

might. The patch of mist turned pale and opaque. It shimmered and twisted in upon itself, until, after several minutes, an outline began to emerge. 'Come on, come *on*,' Eliseth muttered impatiently to herself as slowly, one by one, the details of the creature began to solidify from the amorphous background. When the cook glanced down, a small white cat was sitting at his feet.

'Now, wherever did *you* come from?' Smiling, the man stooped down and reached out to stroke the creature. Eliseth, concentrating so hard that drops of sweat broke out on her forehead, shifted her illusion away from his outstretched hand.

'Frightened, are you, little one? Has someone been mistreating you?'

Eliseth grimaced and cast her eyes up to the heavens. She had never been able to work out why some Mortals actually spoke to animals as if they could understand. Still, if it served her purpose . . . Though she was unable to reproduce sound in her illusion, she opened the kitten's mouth in a silent mew.

'Poor little thing – are you hungry? Just you wait here a moment, and we'll see what we can find for you.'

As the cook vanished into the pantry, Eliseth moved like lightning. She slipped through the back door, sprinkled her deadly liquid over the bread dough on the table, and was out again before the cook emerged. As she slipped soundlessly down through the gardens, she glanced back to see him silhouetted in the open doorway, a plate in his hand, calling out to the cat that was no longer there – and never had been.

Between the Worlds was a lonely place. Forral had no notion of the time that had passed in the Mortal world while he had been trapped here, for time held no sway in the realms of Death, and the silvery, misty landscape of rolling hills and starry sky remained unchanging, never altering their aspect to mark the passing hours or changing seasons. Now that the Reaper of Souls had forbidden him access to the sacred hilltop grove and the portal it contained, the swordsman's only contacts with the world he had departed were the spirits who would pass through this limbo, singly or severally, on their way from the Door Between the Worlds to the Well of Souls, where they would be reborn. All of these, however, were guarded and guided by the Spectre of Death, in his guise of the old hermit with the lamp, and the Reaper would not permit Forral to approach the shades too closely, or delay them with his questions.

Increasingly, it seemed to the swordsman that *he* was becoming the ghost in this landscape of the dead, for the longer he lingered here, the more insubstantial he seemed to become to the shades of the once living who passed through swiftly on their way to a new existence. When he had first come to this place, the others had noticed him at least, or heard his voice, though when this happened they were always sped quickly on their way by their grisly guardian. Now, however, his fellow spirits seemed not to see the form of the lonely swordsman who hovered anxiously nearby, desperate for news of Aurian. It was most painful when a familiar form appeared, whether the shade was that of an old friend or even an enemy. To see someone he had once known in the Mortal world pass him by without the slightest trace of recognition – it was almost like dying all over again.

Forral had become increasingly frustrated and wretched as the relentless isolation gnawed away at his confidence and his nerve. There was no way to help this timeless imprisonment pass more easily – he could not eat, or drink, or sleep, and there was nothing to do or to make, and nothing new to see. He could touch nothing, feel nothing – not even his own body. Occasionally Forral would begin to walk, or even run frenziedly, endlessly, in an attempt to escape this dim and dreary landscape, but he never tired, and his hurrying steps only led him among the rounded hills, back to the place where he had started – the valley below the sacred grove. The way to the Well of Souls was barred to him now by a barrier of some invisible force, as was the Door Between the Worlds. Even Death himself would no longer converse with Forral, for the Spectre simply vanished every time the furious and embittered swordsman attempted to confront him. Forral knew that the Reaper was waiting him out, hoping that sooner or later he would tire of this miserable half-existence, and volunteer to be reborn.

Had he not been so afraid for Aurian and her child – his child – Forral would have capitulated gladly. How could he leave, knowing that he might be losing a chance – a single chance to help them? Even so, he was alarmed to find that his memory of the Mage was fading, eroded by the endless changelessness and solitude of his surroundings. How long, he wondered, would it be before she vanished completely in the mists of forgetfulness? How long did he have left, before he lost even his sense of his own identity – and what would become of him then? As Forral waited – for what, he could not say – it took every shred of courage in the warrior's heart not to give way to despair.

The swordsman sat on the silvery hillside, brooding upon his unhappy thoughts. Recently, a whole stream of people had passed through the door, singly or in groups of two or three – about a dozen altogether. What was going on? Some catastrophe had struck, he was sure, to bring so many through at once – and what was worse, he felt certain that he ought to recognize some of the faces, but the memories lurked tauntingly just out of his reach. Am I losing my mind? he thought despairingly – and if I do, what will remain of me? Will my spirit cease to exist completely? Forral shook his head. Perhaps Death had been right all along. He should have listened to the Spectre. Maybe he should find him, admit defeat, and consent to be reborn before it was too late . . .

Forral sensed that the Door Between the Worlds was opening once more. He could feel it, like a stirring of the tides of energy within his incorporeal form; like the subtle, almost imperceptible change of atmosphere between a worldly night and morning. Even as he cursed himself for a fool, the swordsman leapt to his feet and ran, as he had run so many times before, racing down the valley in a fruitless attempt to beat the Spectre of Death to the already widening portal.

As always, he was too late. Before he had reached the narrow mouth of the valley, Forral could feel the change within him as the Door closed again upon the mundane world. Still he kept going, fighting his disappointment, anxious to catch a glimpse of the new arrival in the Reaper's realm, and hoping that for once – just this once – he might be perceived. The ground mist swept aside from the valley's dark mouth, to reveal the familiar sight of two figures, the bewildered newcomer led by the spectral figure of the old hermit with the lamp.

Memory struck Forral like a physical blow. Grief and a raging sense of injustice swept through the swordsman like an inferno as he beheld the familiar, stocky figure that followed in Death's wake. He started forward eagerly. 'Vannor! Vannor, you old fox!'

'What? Who is that?' The merchant peered through the swirling mist. For the first time that Forral could remember, his old friend looked confused and uncertain. Well, it was hardly surprising, was it? Suddenly he realized that Vannor probably would not understand, as yet, what had happened to him. I had better tread very carefully, the swordsman thought, but it was already too late.

'Forral?' Vannor's voice, usually so gruff, rose in an unsteady squeak. His eyes wide with horror, he began to back away through the mist. 'It – it can't be you,' he stammered. 'Forral is *dead*.'

The swordsman sighed. Clearly, there would be no gentle way to do this. He strode after the retreating figure. 'So are you, Vannor old friend,' he said bluntly. 'Why else would I be here?'

'You are here because you are recalcitrant and foolish.'

Forral and Vannor swung round with a gasp. They had forgotten the presence of Death. The Spectre was wearing the hooded guise of the old hermit who conducted those who had passed through the Door to their final rest. He beckoned to Vannor. 'Come, Mortal. Pay no attention to this renegade – he will do your own cause no good whatsoever. You must accompany me to the Well of Souls, and be reborn.'

Vannor scowled. 'Now just a minute,' he protested. 'This renegade, as you call him, happens to be a friend of mine. I'm not going anywhere until I find out what is going on here.' His frown grew deeper. 'What in perdition happened to me, anyway? I don't remember how I got to be here. How is it that I'm dead?'

Death sighed. 'If it matters at all, you were poisoned, as were most of your household.'

'*What?*' Vannor yelled. 'Who did this? Who else was poi-soned? All of them? Was Dulsina killed? What about Antor, my son?'

'Your son has already passed this way.' Death shrugged. 'The one you call Dulsina, no. It may be that her time is yet to come. As for the murderer's identity – well, this is not the first occasion that your enemy has made a good deal of work for me.' He smiled grimly. 'I look forward to the day I welcome that one into my realm.'

'Who?' Both men spoke simultaneously.

'The Magewoman Eliseth.' Death said.

'She's back?' Vannor gasped. 'But –'

Forral wondered at his friend's shocked response, but Death held up his hand, forestalling any further questions. 'The manner of your coming here is of little import. You must come with me now, Vannor – and try, if you can, to persuade your friend to join you, for he refuses to listen to reason. Too long has he lingered Between the Worlds.'

Vannor gave the Spectre a hard look. 'I'll accompany you if Forral will, but if he wants to stay here I won't leave him. He's my friend.'

Forral felt relief wash over him in a flood of warmth. He had never realized just how desperately he had missed a com-panion in this dismal place. 'Vannor, what about Aurian? I know she must be alive, because she hasn't passed this way, but is she well? Is she safe? Is Anvar taking care of her? What about our child?' So anxious was he that the questions poured out of him, tumbling over one another without waiting for an answer.

A chill went through Forral when he saw the grave expres-sion on the merchant's face. 'I'm sorry, Forral – I can't answer you.' Vannor sighed. 'About seven years ago, she and Anvar were attacked by Eliseth in the Vale. Aurian had found the Sword of Flame, but Eliseth stole it from her. Then the three of them disappeared – they literally vanished into nothing-ness.' He shook his head. 'I wish I . . .'

Suddenly an odd expression swept across his face. To the swordsman, it looked like stark fear. Forral blinked, and rubbed his eyes. Light was deceptive in this place, but it looked to him as though Vannor was *fading* . . .

'Forral – help me,' the merchant cried. 'I feel strange – there's something pulling at me . . . Oh gods, I can't see you . . .' His voice diminished to a despairing wail that was drowned out by a roar from Death.

'Stop! This soul is *mine*!'

Forral was brushed aside as the Spectre lurched forward, but it was too late. Vannor was gone.

6

Metamorphosis

According to the messenger, Vannor's life hung in the balance. There was no time to lose. Yanis had put the fastest of the Nightrunner ships at Tarnal's disposal and the winds were fair for Nexis, but to Zanna the vessel seemed frozen in time, as though it were trapped in the same ice that gripped her heart. She stood in the prow, grasping the rail until her fingers ached, trying to will the ship forward with every ounce of her formidable strength and her desperate need. Every second might make a difference. Her younger brother Antor was already dead – she had been given no chance to say her farewells to him. Zanna felt her heart constrict with pain. It was so unfair! Antor had been little more than a child – he had scarcely begun to live, and now he never would.

Zanna swallowed back her tears, determined to stay in command of her emotions in this crisis. If only Tarnal were by her side to reassure her – but, as usual, he had assumed command. She could hear his voice in the background, giving orders to the men as he strove to plot the fastest course and adjust the sails so that every last scrap of speed could be coaxed from the boisterous wind. His zeal was unnecessary – this crew had been together for a long time and knew what was needed – but Zanna understood Tarnal's need for occupation to prevent his thoughts from dwelling upon what might await them in Nexis. She, alas, was without such means of distraction, and she missed her husband desperately, wanting the comfort and support of his loving presence.

On the vessel flew, a grey shadow in the night-black sea, with the wind singing in the sheets and a high curl of creamy foam where the bows carved a path through the tossing waves. Unable to contain her impatience, Zanna left the prow and began to pace the slanting deck, oblivious of the risk. *Hurry*.

Her thoughts urged the vessel on. *Oh, hurry. We must get there in time!*

How could this happen now, when everything had been going so well? The seven years since the Battle of the Vale had been good ones. Is this our fault? Zanna wondered as she paced. Did we let ourselves become complacent? When Vannor returned to the Nightrunners with the news that both Aurian and Anvar had vanished from the world, it had seemed a catastrophe beyond all understanding. Zanna and the Mages' other friends and companions had grieved long and hard for them both, and Parric had been inconsolable. It had taken several days for Vannor to persuade them that not only their friends had been lost, but their enemies, too. Eliseth had gone the same way as Aurian and Anvar; then news arrived from Yanis's contacts in Nexis that the Archmage had also disappeared.

Zanna remembered with shame how she had berated her father for his pursuit of power when Aurian had so lately been lost. He had been right, though. With Nexis leaderless, the people had been desperate for someone to supply the lack. With Sangra's assistance, Vannor had sobered up the grieving Parric with brutal efficiency and enlisted the cavalry master's help, and that of the rebel and exiled communities. Yanis had provided ships and the armed support of the Nightrunners – and within a month, the former head of the Merchant's Guild had become High Lord of Nexis.

Then the changes had begun. With the Magefolk gone, the shadows of awe and fear had been lifted from the Nexians, and a new age had blossomed under Vannor's beneficent rule. The accessible items from Miathan's hoarded supplies had been released from the Academy, and new recruits for the garrison had been trained hastily by Parric and Sangra. Robbers and footpads had been dealt with, making the night safer for folk to walk abroad. The merchants who exploited the Nexians had been persuaded to mend their ways by the disciplined troops backing Vannor's authority. Homes were rebuilt for the poor and dispossessed, and the wretched beggars vanished from the streets. Jarvas's sanctuary was rebuilt as a shelter for the old and needy, and a school for healers had been established there, under the auspices of an unusually sober Benziorn.

Vannor had given the citizens of Nexis years of peace and plenty, yet Zanna was aware that not everyone favoured the new High Lord of Nexis, and what he had wrought. The one great disaster of Vannor's reign had been his failure to deal with the sporadic attacks by the Phaerie, and people who had lost family and friends blamed him for the disappearance of their loved ones. The merchants, also, were incensed by the decimation of their profits, and what they saw as unwarranted interference in their affairs. The fact that Vannor had once been head of the Merchant's Guild added insult to injury. In the fulfilment of a long-cherished dream, he had overridden their objections and outlawed the practice of bonding, and that, Zanna knew, might well have been the final outrage that had precipitated this attack.

As the darkness began to give way in the east, the ship turned into the estuary. Soon the docks of Norberth, grey and indistinct in the ghostly morning light, loomed into sight and passed like slowly moving shadows as the ship continued upriver. Zanna closed her eyes in pain. It seemed that everything was conspiring to remind her of her father today, for the river passage was another of Vannor's innovations. In consultation with Yanis and the other merchant captains, he had had the river dredged, the weir removed and a series of locks installed to allow the passage of ships all the way to Nexis itself. Today, Zanna blessed her father's foresight. It would allow her to reach his side all the quicker.

Zanna and Tarnal wasted no time waiting for the ship to dock at Nexis. Instead, they had themselves put ashore where the gardens of Vannor's mansion stretched right down to the river. Zanna was shocked by the number of armed soldiers guarding the flimsy jetty and patrolling the grounds, but to her relief Sangra was commanding them and allowed herself and Tarnal to pass immediately, without delaying them with unnecessary talk. Running hand in hand up the steep gravelled paths they arrived breathless at the house. Dulsina opened the door to them, her face white and her eyes red from weeping and bruised beneath from sleeplessness and strain.

Without a word, the two women fell into one another's arms.

'Is he . . .?' Zanna was the first to pull away. Whatever the nature of the news, she could bear the suspense no longer.

'No – not yet. He's still fighting, but . . .' Dulsina shook her head as she guided Zanna and Tarnal across the hall and into Vannor's study. Parric was already there, pacing restlessly back and forth in front of the fire.

'Zanna . . .' The cavalry master's voice was choked as he held out his arms to her. 'I'm sorry, love,' he said hoarsely. 'I blame myself. If the garrison had guarded him better . . .'

'Nonsense,' Dulsina interrupted crisply. 'Don't be so daft, Parric. Things are bad enough here without that kind of stupid self-recrimination. Make yourself useful instead, and get Zanna and Tarnal a glass of wine.' She turned to Zanna. 'The gods only know how someone could have got into the house to do this terrible thing. It seems to have been the bread that was poisoned, but we've lost the cook along with the rest of the servants, so I don't suppose we'll ever find out. I only escaped because I was staying overnight in the city with Hebba – she hasn't been too well of late.' Dulsina bit her lip. 'We have to face it, Zanna – this is a cruel poison. Your poor father is suffering so greatly that death would be a merciful release.' Fresh tears shone in her eyes. 'I'm sorry, my dear. Even Benziorn says that nothing can be done. He can only give soporifics to Vannor, to ease his passing from this world.'

Dulsina's face shimmered into a blur as Zanna's eyes too filled with tears. Her breath caught in her throat to become a convulsive sob. Tarnal, visibly mastering his own grief to support his wife, put his arms around her, and Zanna drew strength from the embrace. 'Can I see him now?' she asked in a small voice that she scarcely recognized as her own.

Zanna had no idea how many hours she had sat at her father's bedside, but darkness had fallen outside the window long ago, and her eyes felt like burning coals in her head. Dulsina sat opposite, shivering with weariness, and Benziorn would come in from time to time to check on his patient, shake his head, and leave again with a sigh. Vannor lay cold and still, as though he were a corpse already, his eyes half open but glazed and unseeing, and his breathing so shallow as to be barely perceptible. His limp hand felt chill and clammy in Zanna's grasp. The waiting was unbearable – this knowing that it could only be a matter of time. Almost, Zanna wished that it could be over, to spare both her father and herself – yet while he lived, how could she help but hope for a miracle? She remembered the time she had rescued him from the clutches of the Magefolk, and led him to safety through the pitch-black maze of the library archives, and the dreadful, stinking sewers. Now Vannor was embarking on a darker road still, and this time there seemed to be no way that she could bring him home.

She must have dozed a little, for she jumped guiltily awake as her sleep was disturbed. Faint grey daylight glimmered at the window, and there was a low hubbub of voices coming from the hall downstairs. Now what? She scowled. Why were Tarnal and Parric allowing this to happen? There was a sick man up here – he shouldn't be disturbed. After a few moments the door opened, and Tarnal put his head into the room, beckoning Zanna and Dulsina away from Vannor's bedside and out into the upstairs hall. 'I thought you should know,' he whispered. 'There's someone at the door – an old crone by the look – she's all muffled up in shawls and stuff. She says she's a herbwife, and swears she has an ancient remedy handed down from her grandmother that can save Vannor's life. It's probably a lot of nonsense, but . . .' he held out his hands and shrugged. 'What is there to lose? The only thing is, Benziorn is furious – he says she's a fraud and there is no cure, but she's after a reward for trying. He's insisting that we send her away.'

Zanna and Dulsina looked at each other. 'Send her up,' they replied in unison.

The crone insisted on being alone in the room while she worked. This gave Zanna a shiver of unease, then she thought: let her. What harm can she do at this stage? Then the old woman went inside, the door closed firmly behind her, and there was nothing to do but wait – and pray. Dulsina, Zanna and Tarnal gathered in an uneasy knot outside the door, and after a short time Parric, looking pale and strained, came up to join them, carrying a tray with cups and a bottle of spirits that he put down on a little table by the wall. They waited, saying little, sipping sparingly at the warming brandy while Benziorn paced below in the hall, muttering and cursing under his breath, and occasionally casting black looks up at Vannor's closed door.

Eliseth emerged from Vannor's chamber, clutching the basket that contained the grail hidden beneath a cloth, and laughing inwardly to see the circle of anxious faces that waited to greet her. Thanks to her illusion of an ancient hag, these fools had no idea of her true identity. All had gone according to plan. She had dispatched the merchant with another dose of poison, and brought him back to life again using the grail. He had no memory of what she had done. Though he did not know it yet, Vannor now belonged to her.

The Mage risked a sidelong, venomous glance at Zanna as the woman stepped forward anxiously. 'What happened, goodwife? How is my father?'

Collecting herself quickly, Eliseth composed her features into the illusion of a toothless smile. 'Be at ease, my lady, all is well. Your father was far gone indeed, but my skills have drawn him back. Even now, he is recovering –' She was talking to empty air. With a joyous cry, Zanna had flown into her father's room, with Dulsina close at her heels.

Tarnal stepped forward with a smile. 'You must forgive them, old mother – they aren't really ungrateful. This family owes you a debt beyond all paying, but we will do our best, for you've brought us a miracle tonight. I'm sure they will be back directly, once they see for themselves that Vannor is all right. In the meantime, would you like to come downstairs and refresh yourself?'

Eliseth shook her head. 'Thank you, but I will wait here,' she replied firmly. She did not have long to wait, however. After a short time Zanna emerged, her glowing face transfigured with delight. 'He was awake! He knew me! He's going to get well again!' Collecting herself, she turned to Eliseth. 'Good mother, how can I thank you? Whatever is in my power to give you is yours – you only have to say the word.' She waited expectantly.

The Mage shook her head. 'My lady, I ask for nothing. To see our dear Lord Vannor restored to health is reward enough for me.'

'But there must be some way to repay you,' Zanna protested.

'Truly, I want nothing. By your leave, I will go now,' Eliseth replied. Leaving the Mortals open-mouthed behind her, she went downstairs and scurried out of the house, remembering that she was meant to be an old woman, and therefore must not stride. No one attempted to stop her, which was just as well for them.

You'll repay me, Zanna, never fear, Eliseth thought as she took the river road back towards the Academy. I'll receive my reward when your precious father kills your husband and children before your eyes, leaving you to be dealt with by *me*. The Mage smiled grimly. Vannor's escape from the Academy seven years ago had cost her a good deal of embarrassment and inconvenience, and Zanna was to blame. But she had made a grave mistake in crossing Eliseth. Revenge would be sweet – but it must be postponed for a time. If she wanted to rule the city through Vannor, it was vital that he act as he usually did, or suspicions would be aroused. Besides, when Aurian came back into the world Vannor would be among the first people she contacted. Eliseth would have the earliest possible news of her enemy's movements and plans, and that would give her an inestimable advantage.

Eliseth made the most of the fact that it was early morning, and few people were up and about, to slip back unnoticed into the Academy. On entering her chambers, she freed Bern from the time spell that had held him immobile in her absence. Over the last few days, she had convinced the baker that it had been he who had murdered his wife and children, and that the guards were combing the city for him. In return for her sheltering him in the safety of the Academy, he had sworn to serve her, but she did not trust him enough to go out and leave him unattended. Bern had been sunk deep in guilt and misery since the deaths of his family and she would not put it past him to go down into the city and turn himself in, betraying her presence in the process. That would be a catastrophe, but even if he were simply to take his own life out of guilt it would be an inconvenience. It was beneath her, as one of the Magefolk, to take care of herself.

Having sent Bern to make some breakfast, Eliseth took the grail from her basket and filled it with water from the jug on the table. Before she ate, she would check on Vannor, and see how his so-called recovery was progressing. She wanted to make quite sure she could control him, for she could think of many tasks for him to perform, to secure the city for her return and bring the recalcitrant Mortals under her control. And one of the first of his tasks, she thought grimly, would be to mount an attack on those accursed Phaerie! Though she knew that Vannor stood little chance of defeating the Forest Lord and his subjects, he might at least weaken them sufficiently for Eliseth to succeed where he had failed. And what if a few hundred Mortals were lost in the process? They bred like rabbits anyway – there would soon be more.

The Mage looked into the depths of the chalice and concentrated on summoning the image of Vannor. She found the merchant sitting up in bed and eating soup, surrounded by his family who were watching the progress of every spoonful from plate to mouth.

Tentatively, Eliseth wormed her way into Vannor's mind, reading his thoughts like an open book as she sifted through hopes, dreams, fears and plans. As an interesting bonus, she found out what had happened to Aurian during her enemy's travels across the sea, for the Mage and Anvar had told the entire tale to Vannor on their return. Eliseth committed the details to memory – they might very well come in useful one day. Then she turned her attention back to her victim. She wanted a test of her control that would not alert or alarm Vannor's loved ones. After a moment's thought, she exerted her will, and made him drop the spoon into his bowl, splashing hot soup on the coverlet.

Dulsina started up with an anxious cry. 'What happened? Are you all right? Do you feel ill again?'

Vannor shook his head, mopping ineffectually at the soup stains on the quilt. 'I'm all right, love, don't fuss. I can't think

87

what came over me – my attention just wandered for a minute.
I must still be tired, I expect.'

Smiling smugly, Eliseth withdrew from his mind and
returned to her own body. Her triumph lent extra savour to
her food. She had dealt successfully with Vannor – and now it
was time to deal with Anvar. To a Mage, knowledge was
power, and her appetite had been whetted by the information
she had picked up from Vannor's mind about Aurian's adventures. She wanted to know more about the Southern Lands –
and Anvar had actually been there. Still smiling, she went
downstairs and selected a long, keen dagger from the guardroom armoury. Then she returned to her room, filled the grail
to the brim with water and, carrying it carefully in both hands,
made her way up to the rooftop where Aurian's lover lay.

The air outside was thick and oppressive, almost humming
with tension. Heavy towers of black cloud had massed across
the city, and Eliseth could hear the low, menacing growl of
distant thunder. She felt a shudder of ecstasy run through
her. As the raw, wild power of the storm drew closer, so the
strength of her magic would increase. Through the viscous,
copper-tinged gloom she could make out the faint blue glimmer of her time spell across the roof and hurried towards it,
walking carefully so as not to spill the water from the grail.
Anvar lay face down on the roof where she had left him, a long
dark form whose identity was indistinguishable beneath the
crawling, flickering blue web of the spell. Eliseth set down the
chalice with a decisive click on the roof's smooth paving, and
laid down the dagger close to her hand. 'At last,' she breathed.
'It will take more than Aurian to save you now.' Then, gathering her powers, she arrowed them towards him, and dissolved her spell.

The victim of a time spell experienced a few moments of
disorientation as the binding magic was removed. It was an
easy matter for Eliseth to remove the spell and replace it with
one of simple sleep, before Anvar had time to struggle or even
realize what was happening to him. Once she had him helpless
she began to tear into his mind, raping it of information,
wrenching his thoughts apart without a care for the suffering
she caused him and revelling in the soundless screams of his

88

trapped and tortured spirit as his body convulsed in agony. Eliseth was enjoying herself. In hurting Anvar she was striking out at Aurian – and though she could have obtained the knowledge she needed far more easily had she killed her victim and taken control as she had done with Bern, she wanted to impose her will upon him, and make him suffer.

The entire story of her enemy's long journey spun into Eliseth's mind too fast for her to follow, but that did not concern her. As long as she had the information in her memory, she could peruse the details later, at her leisure. When at last she was certain that she had taken all she wanted from Anvar's mind she withdrew, picked up her dagger, and looked down upon the last spasms of his agonized writhing with icy scorn. She put a knee into his back, dragged his head up by the hair and removed her spell. She felt his body tense as he regained consciousness. Down came her hand, and her sharp blade hissed across his throat, laying it open in a burst of crimson gore. As Anvar's lifeblood pumped across her hands, Eliseth threw back her head and laughed triumphantly.

This time, Anvar went hurtling through Death's grey doorway so fast that he barely had time to notice the intricate carvings. Before he truly had time to take in what had happened to him he found himself, stunned, outraged and aghast, in the silvery half-light of the world beyond the portal, with the path to eternity at his feet.

'No!' Even as he howled his protest, the Door slammed shut behind him with a low, concussive boom that carried dreadful overtones of finality. Spitting out curses, Anvar hurled himself again and again at the unyielding wood, but to no avail. Suddenly, the memory returned to him of agony and helplessness, with Eliseth's thoughts raking through his mind like searing talons, and Eliseth's knife at his throat. Anvar stopped hammering at the Door. His hands fell limply to his sides as cold dread congealed deep within him. With growing horror he realized that while last time he had entered this place voluntarily and been permitted to leave again, he was here for good this time. He thought of Aurian, saw a vivid image of her strong-boned, serious face and flaming hair in his mind's eye. A pang went through him like a dagger piercing his heart at the thought of losing her. This can't be happening! His thoughts churned aimlessly in panic. *I can't be dead!*

Suddenly Anvar felt the touch of a hand on his shoulder 'Get away from me,' he snarled, his voice cracking in fear.

Even as he spun, a voice cried out: 'Anvar? Lad – it *is* you!'

To his utter astonishment, Anvar found himself looking into the face of Forral.

'What happened?' the swordsman demanded. 'How did you die? Where's Aurian?' In his anxiety for answers he reached out and grabbed Anvar by the shoulders, shaking him impatiently while the Mage tried in vain to settle the jumbled upheaval of his thoughts.

'Forral – leave him be.'

Anvar remembered that ominous, chilling voice all too well. He looked up and shuddered. Death seemed to think his hermit guise unnecessary for someone who had passed through his realm before, and his dark, shrouded figure loomed over the two men at the gate. But the Spectre's attention seemed all to be fixed on Forral. 'This has gone far enough,' he snapped. 'Mortal, will you never learn? I had a certain respect for your courage and strength of will. While you interfered with no one but yourself, I was willing to permit you your folly, but twice now you have accosted the souls within my care. Last time, your interference robbed a man of his natural passing and allowed him to be snatched into an unnatural slavery.'

Death's voice was stern and implacable. 'Forral, I cannot – dare not – permit you to linger here any longer. I had never thought to see these times again, but there is a power in the mundane world that is misusing the Cauldron of Rebirth, and it is no longer safe for you to remain in the vicinity of the gate. You must come with me now – both of you – and enter the Well of Souls to be reborn before it is too late.'

Forral's hands were still clamped around Anvar's shoulders like bands of iron, but the Mage paid them little heed. At the Spectre's words, he finally understood what Eliseth was doing – and why. Even as he opened his mouth to warn the others, he felt a *wrongness* beginning – the first stirrings of an arcane, invisible force that reached through the closed Door of Death like the turning of an unclean tide. The misty scene around him flickered and began to grow dim as he felt himself caught, as though in the grip of a giant hand, and pulled back towards the portal that separated the living from the dead.

'No!' Death roared. 'I will not permit this!'

For an instant all was confusion. Anvar felt one of Forral's hands slip from his shoulder, through the swordsman's grip with the other hand tightened. The force from beyond the Door continued to tug at the Mage, harder and harder, its pull becoming painful as the intensity increased. Then Anvar felt, for the first time, the numbing non-touch of Death as the Spectre's fingers clamped tightly around his arms. There came a cry from Forral – of horror and triumph mixed – and then only two figures stood where three had stood before.

On the roof of the Academy, the Weather-Mage finished applying water from the grail to the gaping wound in Anvar's throat, and watched with satisfaction as the blood stopped pumping from the severed arteries and the sundered flesh began to knit itself back together. Eliseth waited tensely. It seemed to be taking a long time to bring her victim back to life – far longer than it had taken for the restoration of Bern. She glowered down at the lifeless body, clenching her fists so tightly that her fingernails dug into the skin of her palms. If this didn't work . . .

Anvar convulsed once, arching his spine like a stranded fish as his chest heaved with a wheezing, gasping breath. Eliseth acted instantly, striking out at him with another time spell. She sat back, feeling immensely relieved. For a moment she thought of removing the spell again to test her control as she had done with Bern and Vannor – but then again, why take the risk? The grail had worked perfectly well with the first two victims, and it was far more powerful than any magic this thin-blooded halfbreed might possess to resist it.

Besides, Eliseth was in a hurry. She had done what she'd set out to do – and the information she'd gleaned from Anvar's mind was even more useful than she had hoped. Until now, she had never thought beyond Nexis – but why limit her ambitions to the north? With Vannor in her power she had control here, and Anvar was in place, ready for Aurian's return. If she travelled south now and sought other races to dominate, she could increase her strength a thousandfold before her enemies – Aurian or Miathan, wherever he should be – could find her. Besides, she would be safely out of the way when she instructed Vannor to make an attack on the Phaerie. If they should strike back at the city, as well they might, she wanted to be nowhere in the vicinity. Furthermore, the Magewoman had discovered in Anvar's mind the details of an invincible stronghold from which she could eventually hold the reins of the world in safety and security. It was as well that there were no more dragons in the city of Dhiammara, for Eliseth intended to use the place herself.

In that instant, the Mage's smug thoughts were cut off by a searing crack of thunder. Beneath her feet, the foundations of the tower began to shake. Eliseth sensed that some alien, unrecognizable variety of magic had triggered the earthquake, but had no idea that, in using the grail's powers in the Academy, she had sprung a trap that had been laid for her long ago. As the tower rocked and vibrated her mind went blank with panic. She could do nothing but stay where she was – the tower, protected from destruction by many spells, was as safe a place as any – and watch in horror as the city crumbled around her.

A piece of the stone balustrade that bounded the edges of the roof cracked and broke loose, vanishing into the depths below. Eliseth crouched down low for stability, clinging tightly to the precious grail, and looked out through the gap at the collapse of the city.

From somewhere in the centre of Nexis the Mage heard the tearing crack of stone as the garrison plateau with its large walled complex of buildings fractured right across the centre. The high, protective walls that Miathan had built around the townlands broke apart and toppled in a hail of stones, and a surging wave of earth was shrugged loose from the southern slopes upstream from the city to fill the valley bottom with debris. A long fissure appeared in the riverbed below the Academy promontory and the gathered waters went swirling and boiling down into the bowels of the earth in a burgeoning cloud of dust and steam.

At last it was over. The tortured landscape ceased to quake, and the dust began to settle. The only sounds were the groans and screams of the injured and bereaved. Throughout the city dozens of fires had sprung up, spreading the destruction further. Eliseth shuddered, paying no heed to the suffering of the Mortals below. Her thoughts were all for herself. She had no idea what, exactly, had happened, but she had a very bad feeling that it had been aimed at her, and that the missing Archmage was behind it, somehow. It was high time she got out of here.

Some three days later, Yanis was surprised to receive a message from Vannor asking for a swift ship to ferry some unknown person and a manservant to the Southern Kingdoms. He was very surprised that Zanna's father had time to concern himself with such trifles right now, for after the mysterious earthquake the Lord of Nexis, only just recovering from his illness, had his work cut out to keep order and deal with the crisis. It made little difference to Yanis, however. Considering the amount of gold that Vannor was offering, the Nightrunner was only too happy to oblige in person, though for some reason the mysterious traveller, who had spent the whole journey heavily hooded and cloaked, made him very uneasy. But by the time he had dropped off his passenger in a secluded cove on the southern coast, and made the return journey through seas that were still unstable and storm-tossed after the quake, all traces of his earlier curiosity had vanished from his mind, along with all memory of the unknown voyager.

7

The Wild Hunt

Aurian stood shivering in the deserted courtyard, alone save for the ghosts. In the pallid moonlight, the buildings of the Academy took on the ivory gleam of old bone. The void black apertures of its doors and windows held a travesty of remembered life, like the vacant features of a skull that contained a half-familiar echo of loved features now decayed to dust; the abandoned receptacle for a consciousness that had long since fled.

A thin, cold wind snivelled and whined among the abandoned buildings, stirring shadowy movements in dark corners and tainting the air with whispered ghostly voices. Miathan and Eliseth, the arch-plotters; Davorshan and the Fire-Mage Bragar, whose ambitions had exceeded their abilities; the healer Meiriel, lost in her insanity, who had fallen to Aurian's sword in a faraway land . . . All were here tonight, thronging the shadows, awaiting their revenge upon the one Mage who had dared oppose them . . .

'Balls!' Aurian snorted. 'Ghosts, indeed!' Taking a firm hold on her runaway imagination, she put her shoulder to the door of the Mages' Tower and thrust her way inside.

Once round the first curve, the pitch-black stairwell presented a challenge even to her Mage's sight. Raising her hand, Aurian called a ball of sizzling blue Magelight to hover above her head. The shallow marble steps spiralled upwards before her, slick with a film of icy condensation. Shadows from the sphere of cold fire leapt and lurched across the weatherstained walls and web-hung ceiling, causing flickers of movement at the edges of her vision that froze her in her tracks and sent her whirling, hand on the Staff of Earth, to face a nonexistent threat.

'Don't be a bloody fool,' Aurian told herself disgustedly.

'There's no point in going on, if you're seeing ghosts in every shadow.' The only trouble was, she knew perfectly well that ghosts could – and did – exist.

Gritting her teeth, the Mage continued up the staircase. The twins' chambers, Bragar's rooms, Eliseth's suite – room after room she found abandoned and empty, all trace of its former occupant erased. Unease pricked her, an icy finger drawn up her backbone. Surely this could not be right? Even if the Academy had been abandoned, and all the Magefolk were dead, the mouldering remnants of their furnishings and belongings should still be here!

When she reached the familiar door to her own quarters, Aurian hesitated, reluctant to discover what lay within. These rooms had been her home for so many happy years – they held precious memories of Forral, and Anvar, and dear Finbarr, her friend the archivist who had perished to save her life, on the Night of the Wraiths. Ridiculously, she felt that to see her chambers vacant and abandoned would wipe away so much of her former existence . . .

'Ridiculous is right,' Aurian told herself firmly. Possessions, after all, were not so important, and nothing – *nothing* – could erase the memories of people she had loved so well. None the less, it hurt to enter those bleak, dank, echoing rooms. What had happened, she wondered, to the moss-green carpets and drapes; to her cosy bed with the heavy, brocaded hangings that could be pulled close against the night, to create a secluded haven for the joy that she and Forral shared? What had become of the bright clothes the swordsman had persuaded her to buy as they wandered the booths of the Grand Arcade? What had happened to her summoning and scrying crystals, to her irreplaceable collection of books and scrolls, and to Anvar's precious guitar, which she had bought him as a gift on that happy Solstice he had spent with Forral and herself? A wave of unbearable loneliness and longing swept over her, so intense that it almost sent her to her knees. Where were they now, the two she had loved above life itself? Forral dead, and Anvar – where? *Where?* Aurian shivered, and fled the sad, abandoned chambers, her Magelight hovering above her, always one step ahead of her hurrying feet.

Up, then – and up once more, round another curve of the staircase. Only one set of rooms left to search. Despite her determination, Aurian's feet began to slow of their own accord. If she had hesitated to enter her own chambers, how much more did she fear to trespass within Miathan's domain? The last time she had set foot in the Archmage's lair, she had felt the menace of the dreaded Death-Wraiths, and seen her beloved Forral slain by the deadly creatures called up through the profane, perverted use of the Cauldron of Rebirth. As she approached the door, memories came swarming unbidden into her mind, just as those hideous, malevolent abominations of Miathan's summoning had thronged the chamber where her love lay slain. Dread froze her, shaking in every limb, on the topmost landing of the staircase.

It took more courage than Aurian had known she possessed to open that door, but in her heart she was certain that she must. Knowing that if she hesitated another instant she would never find the strength to do it, she lifted her hand to the latch, every sense alert for the betraying signs of a magical trap, or a wardspell. There was nothing – and that in itself was enough to put the Mage upon her guard. Alive or dead, it would be most unlike Miathan to leave his private chambers open to the prying of any stray wanderer – let alone another Mage. And if he *had* done so, there was sure to be a reason.

Cautiously, Aurian took the serpent-carved Staff of Earth from her belt and, reversing it, used the heel to push the door ajar. Out of the darkness beyond rushed a fetid reek of carrion. The Mage took a hasty step backwards, choking and retching, slipping off the topmost step and only just saving herself from a fall with a frantic clutch at the handrail.

'Seven bloody demons!' Thick darkness surrounded her – her light had gone out when she fell. Beyond the sound of her own, involuntary exclamation, nothing stirred. The silence lay heavy, dead, and thick as the noxious, cloying stench that clogged the air. Yet in Aurian's mind, a familiar sound began to grow – the snarling, rasping hum of raw magical power. In her hand, the Staff of Earth began to vibrate in response, and glow with emerald light as it answered its counterpart. The Mage's heart beat fast. The Sword! The Sword of Flame was within! Clinging tightly to the smooth wooden rail, Aurian pulled herself upright, ignoring the throb of bruised ankle and shin and a nagging ache in her left arm which had briefly supported all her weight. Blotting her watering eyes on her sleeve, she cast another ball of Magelight – as bright as she could manage – and transferred the Staff from her right hand to her left. Drawing her sword, the Mage crept cautiously into Miathan's lair – and halted, transfixed with horror and despair.

The Magelight blazed up, highlighting every stark, inescapable detail of the ghastly sight that met her eyes. Aurian took in the entire scene in one single, frozen moment of horror. The floor, the walls – even the ceiling of the chamber were spattered with blood. A headless corpse was spread-eagled, limbs askew, before the fire, pierced through the heart and pinned to the floor by the Sword of Flame, which was glowing all along its length with a blinding crimson blaze. And set upright upon the hilt of the Sword, the severed neck impaled upon the grip to rest on the crossguard, was the head of Anvar.

A cry of grief wrenched itself free from Aurian's soul, yet no sound escaped her lips. She could not bear to look, yet she could not look away. Her lover's face was twisted in a rictus of agony, yet her gaze traced every beloved feature. Then, her heartbeat stumbled, faltered, and began to race as the eyes of the corpse slowly opened, weeping blood, and turned to fix her with a glazed and sightless stare. The Mage's grasp grew white-knuckle tight around the Staff of Earth, as the grey lips parted. Anvar's corpse began to speak, but it was not his voice that issued forth, but the strident, mocking tones of Eliseth.

'You should thank me, Aurian – I've done you a favour. I have performed the very sacrifice that you were too feeble-minded and faint of heart to make yourself. And here is the Sword of Flame, ready and waiting, marked and bonded to you with the blood of your beloved. It only waits for you to stretch out your hand and claim it, then victory will be yours, and the power to rule the entire world. Go on – take it. Take it if you dare. Pick up the Sword, and take the world into your hand – if you can pass my Guardians!'

97

Beyond Anvar, beyond the reach of the fading Magelight, there was a stir of movement. From the mouth of Anvar's corpse, from the dead and staring eyes, strands of dark vapour began to pour, coalescing and growing and forming into a legion of vast and shifting shapes with malevolent gargoyle faces that pulsed and flickered, ever-changing, in a swirling vortex of cold evil. Eliseth had summoned the Nihilim. The Death-Wraiths had returned to claim Aurian's life, as they had claimed the life of Forral.

Someone was screaming. After a moment, Aurian realized it was herself. Wrenching herself free at last from the macabre spell of Anvar's mutilated corpse, she turned and fled head-long down the tower stairs, pursued by the sound of Eliseth's laughter, the Death-Wraiths at her heels.

Sobbing, gasping for breath, the Mage burst out of the tower door and into the courtyard, and swung round at the sound of another voice.

'Aurian? Aurian!' Faint and ghostly, it seemed to be calling from the library, which lay across the courtyard to her left – and that was only natural, after all, for it was Finbarr who was calling her. Finbarr, who had saved her once before. Without a thought, Aurian turned and ran towards the sound – through the great portal, through the echoing, empty library, and through the scrolled iron door at the far end that led into the archives. The branching catacombs rang to the sound of her running footsteps as the Mage fled downwards, still following the thread of Finbarr's faint, elusive call, constantly aware of the pursuing Wraiths that thronged ever closer behind her.

'Aurian . . .' The voice was coming from her left now, from a dark, narrow, musty passage that Aurian had no recollection of ever seeing before. Though she didn't like the look of it, there was no time for hesitation – the Nihilim were right on her heels. Sending her faltering Magelight before her, Aurian plunged desperately into the dark maw of the tunnel – and ran right into the arms of Miathan.

'I knew you would return to me at last!' The dead gems of the Archmage's eyes were alight with a gleam of triumph. Though her mind screamed out in protest, Aurian's body was limp in his grasp, her will rendered powerless by the hypnotic glitter of those dreadful jewels. Miathan plucked the Staff of Earth from her feeble grasp. His gaunt and haggard face was scant inches from her own, his noisome breath like the air from an opened tomb. Gathering every scrap of her will, Aurian spat into his face. It was all that she could do. Cold and cruel, the Archmage smiled. Slowly, he turned the Mage round, until she could see the swarm of Nihilim that hung in the shadows, waiting.

'I give you a choice, my dear.' Miathan's voice was an obscene croon. 'Submit your body, your will, and your powers to me – or submit yourself to the Death-Wraiths, as their prey. Choose, Aurian. Choose now!'

'Never! I will *never* submit to you!'

And then suddenly Shia was there, between the Mage and the hovering Wraiths. 'Aurian! Wake up – you're dreaming! Wake up!'

As the voice penetrated the sound of her screams, Aurian felt a stinging blow on her face. She tried to fight, but something heavy pressed down on her, preventing her from moving. She opened her eyes to see Maya, sitting over her with one hand raised, ready to strike again. D'arvan knelt nearby, looking grave, and beyond him Aurian could make out a pair of horses watching her quietly, their outlines blurred by the early-morning mist that drifted among the shadowy trees. The scent of moist earth and the rustling whisper of leaves told of a forest. The warm breeze and the thick, heady fragrance of full-grown greenery hinted at summer.

'Where the bloody blazes am I?' the Mage muttered.

'Don't worry,' Maya soothed her. 'You're safe.' She helped the Mage sit up. 'But that was some nightmare, my friend!'

'Nightmare?' Aurian echoed blankly. 'I don't remember . . .'

'Well, *I* do!' A huge black shape emerged from the bushes.

'Shia!' Aurian cried.

Another great cat, with heavier bones and its ebony coat patterned with dapples of gold, followed Shia from the bushes, but though Aurian was glad to see that he had come in safety through the gate in time, her attention at first was all for her dear friend.

Shia was purring fit to rattle Aurian's bones. 'I came to awaken you.' Her mental voice echoed oddly in Aurian's mind. 'I was in contact with your mind throughout your wretched dream – and it was *not* a pleasant experience.' She rubbed her head against Aurian's face as the Mage knelt to embrace her. 'Never fear, my friend. It was only a dream. We'll get Anvar back safely.'

'Anvar . . .' As the memory of the dream came flooding back to her in all its vivid and ghastly detail, Aurian began to shake uncontrollably. Never, as long as she lived, would she forget that dreadful vision of Anvar, impaled upon the Sword of Flame . . .

Maya put a comforting hand on the Mage's arm. 'It's all right, Aurian. No matter how terrible it was, it was just a dream.' She glanced up at D'arvan. 'Get her a drink of water, would you?'

When D'arvan had disappeared among the trees, she turned back to the Mage. 'I already know about the dream. Your thoughts were so intense – probably because you were distressed – that D'arvan was picking up the details from your mind, and passing them on to me.' She frowned. 'I'm sorry, Aurian – we should probably have wakened you sooner, but considering where we've ended up, we thought the dream might mean something. When we came out of that – whatever it was – we were in such a sorry state that we all slept for a while. When you didn't wake, D'arvan said you were suffering from the effects of your struggle with the Sword, and we should let you rest, so the cats went off to keep watch, while we stayed here –'

But Aurian was listening no longer. Maya's words had been enough to drive the horrors of her dream to the back of her mind. She was remembering, instead, the final battle in the Vale, and her discovery of the Sword of Flame. Scalding shame fled over her as she recalled her failure to master the Artefact, and the catastrophic consequences. Those horses, grazing quietly among the trees, she had also known as men – Schiannath the Xandim Herdlord, and the Windeye Chiamh, Seer of the Xandim and a close friend. Her failure to claim the Sword had unleashed the dangerous, unpredictable Phaerie upon the world once more, and they had used their powers to reclaim their legendary horses, turning the shape-shifting Xandim into simple beasts.

That was not the worst of it, however. Aurian remembered pursuing Eliseth and the wounded, captive Anvar into the gap that had opened up in reality, and trying to follow them through an endless, viscous grey nothingness interspersed with flashes of lurid colour. She remembered nausea and disorientation, and helpless panic when her prey had disappeared at last. She recalled the last desperate, wrenching effort that had brought her – with these dear and loyal friends who had followed her – back to the real world. And with a sick, sinking feeling in the pit of her stomach, Aurian realized that, thanks to her own failure, Eliseth had not only Anvar, but two of the Artefacts – the Cauldron of Rebirth, and the all-powerful Sword of Flame . . . Aurian gasped, and frantically groped around her in the thick bed of leaves. She found the Staff of Earth first, safe and sound, and then, as her hand fell on the Harp of Winds, it responded with a plangent cascade of shivering notes, as though the Artefact itself was mourning for Anvar, who had made it his own.

D'arvan returned at that moment, and sat down beside her, placing a dripping cone of folded birch bark in her hands. 'Here, you'll feel better for this,' he told her. 'I'm sorry we have nothing stronger – you look as though you could do with it.'

'You can say that again,' Aurian muttered. But, though her nerves were still unstrung and her worries ever-pressing, the sight of the makeshift cup soothed her with its happy memories. She caught Maya's eye. 'I see you've been teaching him some of Forral's wilderness survival techniques . . .' Her words tailed off. The warrior had mentioned something earlier, about . . .

'Maya?' The Mage gripped the fragile birch cup so tightly that it crumpled in her fist. '*Considering where we've ended up*, you said. Just where *have* we ended up?'

The small, dark-haired warrior sighed. 'We're in the woods, above the southern side of Nexis.'

Aurian dropped the ruined cup, barely noticing that she

had done so. 'What does Nexis look like?' she asked softly.

Maya bit her lip, plainly reluctant to answer, and finally it was D'arvan who replied.

'It has changed, Aurian. Nexis has altered beyond any accounting for the one year of our absence.'

The Mage frowned, trying to put her thoughts in order, despite the throbbing in her head. 'So we travelled . . . Clearly, we moved between places – but have we also moved between *times*?'

D'arvan nodded. 'It's a difficult notion to accept – but what else could explain such a difference in the city?'

A coldness settled in the pit of Aurian's stomach. 'Show me,' she demanded.

'Indeed, Mage. Look upon your city. See that the Phaerie have not been idle in your absence.' Hellorin smiled bleakly and drew back from his Window of Seeing. Though his face remained impassive, as befitted the Lord of the Phaerie, he could scarcely contain his excitement. Oh, he had waited long for this day! He had always known that his son would return one day – and as a bonus, D'arvan had brought the missing Xandim horses with him.

From his high tower in the delicately constructed palace, Hellorin sent out a mental summons that reverberated to the furthest reaches of his new city. This time, there was no need to wait for moonlight. The Phaerie hunt must ride at once. Not a moment must be lost, lest the Forest Lord's quarry should escape him once again.

As the cats, the Mages and Maya stole through the woodland, moving with as little noise as possible over the soft blanket of living moss, Aurian could feel the dew of dawn striking right through her cloak and the Xandim leather tunic and breeches that she still wore. She felt lost and anchorless, lightheaded and drifting. This change in time and place had happened far too fast. For the Mage, it was as though the dreadful battle in the Vale and her disastrous confrontation with the Sword of Flame had taken place but an hour ago. She could still smell the smoke on her hair from Eliseth's burning of the wildwood, and the leather of her garments was stained and stiffened in places with Cygnus's blood. When she reached the edge of the forest and looked out between the last trees, Aurian felt her stomach lurch. Nexis it was – so much was still familiar – but how the city had changed!

The companions had come out of the woods above a steep fall of land where an earthslide had stripped the slope of its trees as far as the river. Beneath the eminence where Aurian stood, the verdant forest ended abruptly and below it lay a wilderness of boulders, mud and naked earth, strewn with the snapped and splintered trunks of trees. The river, dammed by the rubble that had swept down the hillside, had swollen above the obstruction to fill the upper valley with a long, narrow lake. Below the choking mass of earth and trees, the river had dwindled to little more than a stagnant thread that trickled haphazardly through the bottom of the muddy trench that had once been the river bed.

Now that the river, the lifeblood of the city, had vanished, Nexis had begun to die. The wharves on the northern bank rose high and dry on stilt-legged pilings above the abandoned watercourse. It looked as though many of the warehouses had been destroyed by fire. Miathan's great new walls, which had been described to the Mage by Zanna during her brief stay in the Nightrunner stronghold, were cracked throughout their length and in places had collapsed completely. The Academy, however, still stood high on its promontory in the loop of the dried-up river bed. As far as Aurian could see at this distance, the library and the Mages' Tower were still intact, though the weather-dome had been broken open like the shell of a shattered egg. Was Anvar somewhere down there, as she had dreamed? Aurian could scarcely bear to think of it.

The Mage wrenched her attention from the Academy and forced herself to examine the remainder of Nexis. What had happened to the houses on the northern slopes of the valley? The outlines of the streets, once so neat and regular, seemed to have altered and lost their definition, and as far as Aurian could tell many of those homes had been destroyed. Lower down there was similar ruin. Though the great domed edifice of the circular Guildhall seemed unscathed, part of the roof of the Grand Arcade had fallen in, exposing the labyrinth of stalls, aisles and walkways to the elements. A broad fissure ran right across the garrison parade ground, making Aurian wonder uneasily if the edge of the plateau would eventually break away and crash down on the lower part of the city.

As the light continued to grow, the Mage lifted her eyes from what had once been a deep, wide river, and looked upon the ravaged landscape and altered city. She shook her head in dismay. 'What in the name of the gods can have happened here?' Taken with the landslip that had dammed the river, the destruction seemed to point to some kind of earth tremor. But why? The land around Nexis had always been stable before. She remembered – how could she forget? – that Eliseth had possessed the Cauldron of Rebirth when she had arrived in the Vale. That implied that she had found some way of defeating Miathan. Had the two Mages fought? Was that the cause of this extensive damage to the city? Yet if the Archmage had been killed, surely she and Anvar would have felt his death. So where was Miathan now? Aurian shuddered, remembering her nightmare.

'How much time do you think we've missed?' Maya asked softly.

Aurian shrugged. 'Who knows? That kind of destruction could have taken place over years – or in a single day.'

'I don't think so,' D'arvan demurred. 'Not in one day – at least, it's more than a day since the earthslip happened. Look there –' the Earth-Mage gestured at the sprawling hillock of earth that slanted across the river. 'It's hard to tell for sure, but there's at least one year's growth on that newly exposed soil – probably more, I should say.'

'You could be right.' Aurian squinted across the intervening distance, wishing that the light were better – and wishing still more for Chiamh, with his cheerful good humour and his ability to take her riding the winds so that she could look more closely at the ruined city.

'Of course I'm right,' D'arvan replied firmly. 'Your mother was a good teacher.'

Maya was looking troubled. 'But if you're right, love – and I'm not saying that you aren't – then why in the name of all creation haven't they *done* something about it? If the folk in the city had organized themselves properly, it would have taken far less than a year to shift that mudslide and let the river flow again.' She frowned. 'Which begs the question . . .'

'Who is leading the Nexians now?' Aurian finished for her. 'Who could possibly benefit from leaving the city in this ruinous condition?' She swung round to face her companions, her face drawn in lines of bitterness. 'We may have no notion of what's going on down there, but we *do* know that neither Vannor, nor Parric, nor any of our other friends are in charge. None of them would ever abandon the city to such desolation. And if our friends don't rule Nexis . . .'

'We must assume that the city is in the hands of our enemies,' Maya finished grimly.

When the Mage and her companions returned to the horses they discovered that Khanu and Shia had been hunting, and had saved two fat rabbits for their human friends. The companions decided to rest and eat before going down into Nexis to search the Academy for clues to the whereabouts of Miathan and Eliseth. Even Aurian, who was consumed with impatience, had sense enough to realize that it would be plain stupidity to face unknown danger with her strength and judgement impaired by hunger and fatigue. Besides, nightfall would be a safer time to enter the city unseen. As soon as Maya and D'arvan were busy preparing the rabbits, the Mage slipped away by herself among the trees. She was sure that, after their long separation, her companions would appreciate a little time together – and as for herself, she wanted to be alone to think.

As the sharp odour of scorching flesh stung her nostrils, Maya extricated herself reluctantly from D'arvan's embrace. With a curse she fumbled for the rabbits that had been spitted over the fire and turned the sizzling carcasses, moving them a little further from the flame.

'Careful.' D'arvan met her eyes with a half-guilty grin. 'Aurian won't thank us for ruining her breakfast.'

Maya, busy straightening her clothing, returned his smile. 'I'm sure she'd forgive us, in the circumstances, but it wouldn't be fair to starve her for our sake.' Try as she might, however, the warrior couldn't make herself sound repentant. Though it had seemed rash and self-indulgent to be thinking of such things now, she and D'arvan had been so long apart that the urge to make love had been irresistible. Besides, she knew that Aurian had tactfully departed to allow them a few moments' privacy – though if she and D'arvan had been embracing long enough to let the rabbits burn, then the Mage should have been back long before now.

Stifling a stab of guilt, Maya berated herself for being so inconsiderate. It's all very well for us, she thought, but poor Aurian has lost her lover. For the second time. It still hurt to remember Forral – he had been Maya's commander and close friend, but Aurian was her friend too, and she did not begrudge the Mage another chance of happiness with Anvar – if only Anvar could be found. And we should be helping her find him, Maya thought. She turned to D'arvan with a frown. 'Don't you think one of us ought to go after Aurian? She shouldn't be brooding alone right now.'

'I don't suppose that Aurian is really brooding – but Shia went, in any case.' D'arvan gestured to the now vacant spot on the opposite side of the fire. The warrior raised an eyebrow, then shook her head ruefully. 'I just can't get used to it. Not only the fact that those creatures are so fearsome, but the idea that you and Aurian can go around talking with them exactly as though they were ordinary folk.' Much to Maya's surprise, it had been Shia who had filled in a great deal of the background of Aurian's quest for them, while the Mage had been asleep.

D'arvan grinned. 'From their point of view, they *are* ordinary folk, love. Shia is as close in friendship to Aurian as we are – probably closer, in fact.'

Maya grimaced. 'Maybe I'm only jealous. I wish I could talk to her as you can.'

'I wish you could, too.' D'arvan smiled. 'I think the two of you would get along very well. You have a good deal in common – and when you come to consider, it's no stranger than the fact that those two horses over there used to be men.'

The warrior's eyes flew open wide. 'Don't tell me you can talk to them, too!'

D'arvan's expression sobered. 'I wish I could. But not even Aurian can reach into their minds to find the humans they once were. Unless my father is persuaded to change them back, Chiamh and Schiannath – along with the rest of the Xandim – are as good as dead.'

Maya shuddered at the bleakness in his voice. 'And you resent Hellorin for what he did,' she added with instinctive certainty.

'Of course I do!' D'arvan slammed his fist impotently against the ground. 'How *could* he act in such a callous fashion! I – I loved him, Maya, despite the difficult things he asked of us, and the loneliness and danger he put us through. When he betrayed the Xandim, I feel as if he betrayed me, too.'

'All the legends warn us that the Phaerie are tricky folk,' the warrior murmured.

D'arvan's jaw tightened. 'Then I'm going to have to live up to my inheritance and be just as tricky as my father. Because I promise you, Maya – one way or another, I'm going to make my father the Forest Lord restore the Xandim to what they were.'

Maya smiled at him, burying the shiver of dread that ran through her in the glow of her pride. 'I rather thought you might,' she told him softly. 'But first we'd better tell Aurian. I think it might ease her mind a little if the Xandim can be saved.' Her eyes twinkled. 'Which do you want to do? Tend the rabbits or go and find her?'

'Ugh!' D'arvan shuddered. 'You know what the Magefolk are like at cooking. If you want any breakfast at all, I had better go and look for Aurian.'

As Aurian wandered through the misty woodland, there was a chill around her heart that had nothing to do with the bright summer day. How much time had passed? Months? Years? Centuries? What had happened to Yazour and Parric; Vannor and Zanna? Were all the people she had known and loved dead now, and gone to dust? And what of Wolf? She had left him safe with the smugglers, but what had happened to the Nightrunners since she'd departed the world? What had become of her son? Had she failed him, too? Should she have kept him safe in the south until he was old enough to take care of himself, before going after the Sword?

The Mage walked on blindly. As the questions circled in her mind without respite or answer, the desperate loneliness and isolation she had known in her dream returned to swamp her.

Then suddenly Shia was beside her, pressing against her reassuringly. 'You are not alone,' she said. 'Khanu and I are here, and your friends the warrior and the Mage. Chiamh and Schiannath . . .' She bit off her words quickly, but it was too late.

'Schiannath and Chiamh are no more than dumb beasts,' Aurian retorted bitterly. 'Thanks to my stupidity –'

'Your stupidity lies in carrying on in this fashion!' the cat retorted sharply. She looked into the Mage's face, her golden eyes blazing. 'So events have gone awry? When has that ever stopped you before? Will you give in now, and flounder in guilt and self-pity? Can you afford such a luxury? Can your friends the Xandim? Can Anvar?'

Aurian's head came up sharply. 'How dare you say such things? I thought you were my friend!'

'I *am* your friend,' the cat retorted. 'You have no time to indulge in such destructive thinking. We must discover what has befallen us, and make our plans. Besides,' she added softly, 'I understand what truly lies behind your despair. It is Anvar, is it not?'

Aurian knelt and put her arms around the great cat's neck, hiding her face in the cat's silken fur. 'Partly it's Wolf – but partly, yes, it's Anvar. Shia, I miss him,' she confessed. 'And I'm terribly afraid for him. If Eliseth has harmed him . . .'

'She will not,' another voice put in firmly. D'arvan had stolen up on her unnoticed. Aurian looked round at him in surprise, and not a little indignation. She had forgotten that there was another Mage present who could understand her mental dialogue with the great cat, and was embarrassed that he must have heard Shia rebuking her.

'Has everybody in the bloody camp been following me around the woods?' she demanded in acid tones.

D'arvan coloured, but did not flinch from her angry gaze. 'Maya thought you shouldn't be alone,' he replied calmly, 'and from what I overheard – I'm sorry but I *did* overhear you and Shia – she was right.' The young Mage smiled sympathetically and held out a hand to her. 'Remember how I came to you when I was in trouble at the Academy? You were the one who saved me from Eliseth, and from my brother. You helped me then – and now, at last, I can return the favour. Eliseth was never one to discard what might be useful,' D'arvan went on. 'My guess is she'll use Anvar as a pawn, or as bait, or a hostage – or more likely, given her vindictive nature, she will try to turn him against you, Aurian. Think how she would revel in such a victory!'

Aurian clenched her fists tightly. 'Then she'll be disappointed,' she snarled. 'D'arvan, you're absolutely right. As soon as it's dark, we'll creep down to the Academy and find out what –'

Suddenly the forest's silence was split asunder by the harsh shrilling of many horns. Through the trees, Aurian heard Chiamh and Schiannath screaming in terror. Shadows swept across the clearing, obscuring the pale sunlight, and a capricious wind swirled leaves and dust into the Mages' eyes as the Xandim steeds churned the air with flashing hooves.

As the Phaerie came hurtling down like meteors towards the treetops Aurian thought, for one horrific instant, that she had somehow slipped back into the past to the battle in the Vale. The truth was worse. Even as she drew her sword and groped for the Staff of Earth at her belt, two Phaerie had swooped down upon D'arvan and borne him, screaming, aloft. The Mage, aghast, ran back towards the place where she had left Maya and the horses – but she stood no chance in the race against the airborne Phaerie steeds. Before she could come anywhere near, she saw Maya in mid-air, screaming curses as she struggled in the iron grasp of a Phaerie warrior who had thrown her across the withers of his horse. Chiamh and Schiannath followed, each of them cruelly bridled in burning light and ridden by one of Hellorin's bright-eyed folk.

Then the leaves and dust settled as the wild wind sank

away, and the sky was empty once more.

Aurian stood for a moment, hurling curses at the unfeeling sky. Then, as though the last of her strength had left her, she slumped to the ground and put her face in her hands. Shia, exchanging a worried glance with Khanu, tentatively touched her friend's mind, but could sense nothing but a numb blankness.

After a time Aurian looked up, her eyes gleaming like frosted iron, her jaw clenched. 'They won't beat me,' she muttered fiercely. 'Supposing they take everything I've ever loved away from me, I *still* won't let them beat me.' She put her arms round Shia. 'We'll get our lost friends back, every one of them – I swear it. Somehow, I'll get them all back, if it's the last thing I do.'

'You still have Khanu and me,' Shia told her, 'and anyone who tries to part *us* from you will discover that they've made a grave mistake! But where to next, my friend? What do we do now?'

'Well, we can't go chasing after the Phaerie yet – I wouldn't know where to start,' Aurian sighed. 'We'll take things one step at a time, as Forral always used to say. First I'm going to eat, and then I'm going to force myself to keep it down. I think we should rest until nightfall – then we'll go across the valley to the Academy. Maybe we'll find some answers there.'

'If you wish to sleep,' Shia said, 'Khanu and I will guard you.'

'Right now,' the Mage said bleakly, 'I feel as if I'll never sleep again.'

8

Thief in the Night

Since the Phaerie attack had, by some miracle, missed the city entirely, Lord Pendral had seen no reason to postpone his entertainment – which came as a considerable relief to Grince. Now he could go ahead as planned with the greatest theft of his career. Silent as a shadow, the thief sneaked along a deserted corridor in the upper storey of Lord Pendral's mansion. He had eluded the guards that patrolled both staircases by entering through one of the great chimneys – a route that was normally only used by the skinny brats who were sent up to negotiate the baffling maze of flues and sweep the soot away. The thief grinned to himself. Throughout his life, he had found considerable advantage in being small and under-nourished.

It was early in the evening yet – far from the usual hour that Grince began this kind of work. Dusk was just closing in, but the gardens surrounding the great house were ablaze with torch and lantern light. The sound of laughter and mingled voices floated up to the thief through a window on the second storey, along with a rich aroma of roasting meats that set his stomach growling. A slowly moving line of carriages stretched down the long gravelled drive, paused one by one on the circular sweep in front of the mansion to drop their richly clad passengers, and continued round to the stableyard at the rear of the house, for tonight Lord Pendral was holding a great banquet for his fellow members of the Merchants' Guild.

For Grince, the feast was a god-sent opportunity. At any other time, the grounds of the High Lord of Nexis would be guarded tighter than a maiden's honour. After the latest Phaerie attacks, Pendral was taking no more chances. Even today, the place was bristling with soldiers, but it was also swarming with Pendral's servants and a great many other

111

people: the High Lord's well-born guests along with their servitors, coachmen and guards – and the resulting chaos suited Grince's plans exactly. His escape – always the most important part of his plans – should be fairly easy, for this evening, with so many strangers in the gardens, the huge killer dogs that Pendral had purchased recently would be safely locked away, instead of being loosed to run free in the grounds all night. The guards would be looking for someone who was breaking *in*, not out, and so he ought to be able to sneak away among the departing guests without much trouble.

Grince's unauthorized entry into Lord Pendral's premises had gone perfectly. The previous day, the thief had stolen a suit of livery from one of Pendral's fellow-merchants' washing lines. Thus disguised, he had gained access to the High Lord's grounds. Knowing full well that the stairs leading to the upper floors and Pendral's private chambers would be guarded, he had found an empty fireplace in the drawing-room that was big enough to admit him, and had scrambled into the interconnecting maze of flues, emerging in a cloud of soot in one of the bedrooms. There he had rubbed his stinging eyes, removed the kerchief he'd tied over his face to save breathing too much soot, stripped off the blackened uniform of the servant and rubbed his hands, face and the soles of his soft, flexible shoes on the curtains before slipping out into the corridor in search of Pendral's strongroom.

Checking the doors that opened on either side along the carpeted hall, Grince moved as fast as he could, all the while keeping his ears open for the sound of any approaching footsteps. Though Lord Pendral and his guests would be downstairs stuffing their fat faces for ages yet, it would still pay to hurry, lest a servant should chance to come this way with a lamp, and discover the telltale trail of soot that led from the guest chamber to the lord's apartments.

Grince had done his preparation well in advance, by bribing one of Pendral's guards with enough drink to loosen his tongue. Now, the thief knew exactly where to find Pendral's chambers. Finding the door he wanted, the thief entered quickly, closing it behind him. Thick drapes were closed at the windows, shrouding the chamber in gloom, but Grince could make out the angular shapes of storage chests, a night table, and a large curtained bed.

The thief took a candle stub from the handful he always kept in his pocket, and lit it quickly. He stood without moving, looking around the chamber. Across the room from where he stood was what he assumed to be an alcove, curtained with dark hangings that matched the window drapes. The guard was unsure, but had assumed that Lord Pendral hid his riches there. Grince paused, scanning the floor with great concentration; moving the candle slowly back and forth until eventually a fine glimmer of silver, close to floor level, caught his eye. Ah, there it was! The slender filament of the tripwire was almost invisible in the gloom, stretching across the chamber about a hand's span above the richly patterned carpet.

A broad grin spread itself across the thief's face. This was going to be child's play. If that fat fool Pendral hadn't even the sense to put a trip wire by the door, he deserved to be robbed. Grince stepped carefully over the wire, reflecting that the precious coins he'd expended getting the young guard drunk in one of the town's more expensive taverns had not been squandered. He would almost certainly have missed the wires otherwise, and triggered the alarm.

Grince tiptoed to the far side of the vast chamber and blew out the candle, putting the stub back in his pocket to leave his hands free. Carefully he pulled the drapes aside, holding his breath in case the brass rings should rattle and give him away. Inch by inch, the heavy velvet curtains slid aside, to reveal, not the alcove he had hoped for, but a small, arched door, its dark wood strengthened with bars of iron. Grince felt his heart quicken with excitement. Surely there must be treasures concealed within . . .

The door presented little challenge to a thief of his calibre. Within minutes, the lock had yielded. With a shiver of excitement, he set his hand against the panels and pushed the door open to reveal a narrow, windowless room, scarcely more than a closet. Within lay a massive wooden chest, securely banded with wide strips of iron that gleamed darkly in the feeble lantern light.

113

Grince let his breath out in a long sigh. He knelt on the cold, polished boards before the heavy chest and slid another small, fine tool out of his belt. The stiff padlock cost him a tense, sweating struggle to open, but finally sprang free with a loud click. Muscles straining, Grince lifted the heavy lid. And there they were! The little thief could not suppress a gasp at the sight. The piles of jewels lay shimmering within their sturdy casket, striking myriad incandescent sparks even from the dim light of his lantern. Unset gems of all sizes and hues lay heaped in glorious profusion among long, twining ropes of pearls and necklaces of fine stones set in delicate filigrees of silver and gold. The back of the chest was divided into small wooden drawers and compartments that held rings, earrings, brooches and bracelets.

The thief let a glittering stream of diamonds slip through his fingers like cold, sparkling spring water, trying to keep a hold on his elation. With a grim smile he began to stuff great handfuls of the glistening treasure into the sack that he had hooked to his belt to leave his hands free for climbing the chimneys. This was long-overdue revenge. The value of the treasure wouldn't begin to compensate for the loss that Grince had suffered at Pendral's hands – but now the thief had deprived the cruel lord of what *he* loved most in the world.

Grince wasted no time in making his escape. Once more he tied the blackened kerchief round his face and headed for the fireplace in Pendral's chamber, repeating his careful negotiation of the tripwire. As he scrambled up the chimney he could feel the heavy sack, filled now with the lord's precious jewels, dragging at his belt.

When he had gained the safety of the rooftop, the thief leaned back against the chimney, closed his eyes, and wiped a sooty hand across his brow. He was overtaken by a surge of raw elation mixed with inexpressible relief to be safely out in the cool, fragrant air of a summer's evening. Taking deep, gasping breaths, he tried to calm himself sufficiently to complete his escape. His luck could hardly hold out much longer. He had lost his way in the labyrinth of chimneys, and at one point had begun to despair of ever finding his way out. But

114

everything would be all right now, Grince reassured himself. Soon he would be well away from this place.

Wiping his smarting eyes, the thief inched his way carefully down the sloping roof and turned to climb down the rough and crumbling brickwork of the mansion's wall. He could see the first handholds clearly, but the lower walls were already well in shadow. Grince sighed, and doggedly began to search in the dusky half-light for the best footholds to descend the wall. He would go home, clean himself up and dispose of the gems – then he would go in search of a very large drink.

He was halfway down the wall when the guard spotted him. 'Hey! You there!' As the shout rang out the horrified Grince froze in position, clinging to the rough stonework until his arms and fingers ached. Maybe if he didn't move the fragging sentry would take him for a shadow . . .

No such luck. Grince cursed as the blare of a horn sounded the alarm. Now that a thief had been discovered, it would take Lord Pendral no time at all to discover that his precious jewels were missing. Shouts came from the garden below, and he heard a clatter of running feet that was rapidly growing louder. An arrow whizzed past his ear, making him flinch. It bounced harmlessly from the stonework to his left, and another hit the wall above his head. So far, their aim was being confused by the shadowy grey stonework and deepening dusk, but if he stayed where he was it wouldn't be too long before the bastards found the range. Rapidly, Grince reviewed his options. Down? No good. Sideways? Not much better – he would still be within bowshot, and even if he found an open window they would see which one he entered and trap him in the house. The thief wasted a breath on another curse, then began rapidly to scramble up the way he had come. At least it was further away from the sodding arrows.

Grince took a firm grip on the guttering and swung himself up, leaving dark smears behind him from his bleeding fingers. The slanting peaks of the roof were slick with dew now, and the going was far more difficult – and dangerous – than it had been earlier. Breathing hard and balancing carefully he inched his way up the gradient on hands and knees, praying, though he was not normally a praying man, every inch of the way. If he should fall . . . Well, it would be better to break his neck than allow himself to be captured by that brute Lord Pendral. At least the arrows had stopped now. Grince reached a cluster of chimneys and slipped between them to rest for a moment and catch his breath, though he knew he hadn't long before some clever bastard thought to bring ladders. The idea of being hunted – or shot at – on these slippery slates so high above the ground didn't appeal to him at all. The cool night breeze ruffled his hair and chilled the sweat on his back and brow. He craned outward and looked down over the edge of the roof as a clamour of voices rose from the garden. Down in the darkness, a cluster of golden lights sprang forth one by one and the drifting breeze carried an acrid smell of smoke. Someone had brought torches – he knew the ladder would be next.

As before, the thief had only one option – and he knew he'd best get on with it. The iron door where he'd exited from the flues was on the other side of the roof, and he had no wish to risk another journey across the dew-slick rooftop. Sighing bitterly, he tied the cloth back around his face, and lowered himself feet first into the widest chimney pot.

It wasn't Grince's lucky night. Somehow, he lost his sense of direction in the complex system of flues, and came out in the worst possible place. Fortunately, the chief part of the feast had been cooked already, and the great kitchen fires had been allowed to sink to embers for simmering and keeping some of the dishes warm. The thief burst out of the broad fireplace in a cloud of soot and ashes, beating frantically at his smouldering clothing. Pots and kettles went crashing from their trivets, spilling their contents in a glutinous, scalding cascade as they fell. Coughing and choking, his eyes streaming, Grince scrambled across the spreading lake, slipping and sliding on sauces and vegetables that squelched under his feet at every step.

Luckily, the kitchen staff had been lured away from the fire by the commotion in the garden. Unluckily for the thief, they were all clustered in and around the doorway. A screech went up from the cook as she saw her entire day's handiwork destroyed by the smoking, blackened apparition that had

116

erupted from her fireplace. Then they were after him.

It was as well for Grince that Pendral's kitchen staff had not been selected for their wits. If one of them had run for the guards while the rest stayed where they were and blocked the doorway, he wouldn't have stood a chance. Instead, they all gave chase, pursuing him round the spacious kitchen. He vaulted across the top of the table, scattering crockery in every direction with a resounding smash. He dodged and dived, the precious sack of jewels still swinging from his belt, catching on chairs and tables and hampering his every step – but having gone through all this trouble for his ill-gotten loot, Grince was buggered if he was going to let it go now. He threw a stool behind him to trip his pursuers and rolled underneath the table, coming out on the other side – and suddenly there was a clear aisle between himself and the door. He gritted his teeth and ran for it.

He hadn't gone a dozen yards before he was spotted, though the cook and her helpers were raising such a ruckus behind him that it was bound to draw attention to him in any case. Grince sped round the corner of the house, wincing each time the scorched soles of his feet hit the ground, and thanking the gods that the soles of his shoes had protected him from worse injury. He took the back way into the stable yard – and ran straight into a group of four guards carrying a long ladder. They went down like ninepins, but they had companions nearby who were drawn by the commotion. Increasingly desperate, the thief disentangled himself, bleeding now from a shallow sword cut in the leg. Guards – more and more of them – burst through the arched gateway to the stable block and fanned out in his direction. Grince turned tail, doubled back towards the house – and the kitchen workers who were charging at him from that direction. *Shit!* he thought, diving to his right, into the narrow space between the two pursuing groups, and heading for a row of long, low buildings. With nowhere else left to go, he chose a door at random, went through it like an arrow, and slammed and barred it behind him.

The air in the stable was warm, and thick with the robust scents of hay and horseflesh. The only illumination was a slip of pale yellow lamplight from the half-open door at the far end of the building. Grince ran along the central aisle, ignoring the sleek inhabitants of the stalls on either side. Though he had originally run in this direction with the idea of stealing a horse, it was no good trying now, when the yard was full of armed guards. Concealment seemed his only hope, but the stable seemed singularly free of places to hide. The thief moved faster – he was running out of time. Already he could hear the barred door creaking alarmingly under repeated blows. The wood was already beginning to splinter and crack beneath the onslaught.

When the thief reached the far end of the aisle, it seemed that luck had deserted him. Beyond the further door was a large, square room filled with bins of grain, and rows of saddles and bridles hung on pegs, lit by a lantern hanging from a rafter. There was no way out. He had come to a dead end. Fear kicked like a jolt of fire up his spine, but there was nothing he could do. He would be caught red-handed.

Grince raised his eyes heavenwards and muttered: 'Thanks for nothing, gods, you bast –' and that was when he noticed the trapdoor in the ceiling.

'I take it back, I take it back.' There was no ladder to be seen, but it was the work of an instant to scramble up the pegs, kicking and knocking the saddles to the ground as he went. The tricky part was reaching over to undo the catch, without unbalancing . . . Holding on to the topmost peg with one hand, Grince stretched until he felt his arms were coming out of their sockets, and at last the finicky bolt yielded and the trap swung open, fetching him a solid clout that almost knocked him from his perch. Making a wild grab for the edge of the opening, he hung by his fingertips for a desperate moment, before panic lent him the strength to scrabble his way to safety. Heaving his body up over the edge of the trapdoor, he rolled over on to his back and found he was lying, gasping for breath, on a bed of prickly hay, looking up at the web-festooned rafters of the stable roof. He felt as though he would never move again, but there was no time to rest now. He leapt to his feet at the sound of splintering wood and angry voices. His pursuers were in the building!

There was no way to close the trapdoor from the inside.

Desperately he looked around, seeking another way out. Bales of hay were piled up against the long wall at the back of the loft, while on the other side the floor was clear, and Grince could see a row of small openings in the floor, where hay was lowered directly down from the loft into the mangers of the horses who waited below. Briefly, he considered them, but they were no use to him save as a last resort. They would put him right back into the hands of Pendral's guards – if the horse didn't trample him to death in the confined space of the stall.

The door to the tackroom slammed open. They had almost found him. *Come on, Grince. Think!* Then he had it. There had to be a way to get the hay up here. They had seen the trapdoor – he heard them shouting. Thinking fast, he dropped to his knees and reached down through the opening to knock the lantern from its hook. The guards scattered as it plummeted to the floor and smashed in a fireball, hurling flaming oil in all directions. A blast of heat came up through the trapdoor – the room below had turned into an inferno. He heard screams of agony below him, and voices cursing and yelling. 'Quick!' someone shouted. 'Get the horses out!'

He was just congratulating himself on his cleverness when it occurred to him that if there wasn't another way out, or he couldn't find it, he had killed himself.

'You bloody fool!' Grince knew he would have to be quick. The loft was filling with smoke, and he could feel the wooden floor growing hotter through the thin soles of his shoes and stinging his feet, already scorched by the kitchen fire. Choking and half blinded, he began to grope his way along the nearest wall – the narrow side wall of the building. Nothing. Bugger it. The floor around the trapdoor opening was beginning to blacken and char, so he fled to the other end of the loft. At least it was safer there, and if nothing else, he could get through one of the little openings into the stalls below.

The loading door was at the far end of the loft, partly concealed behind a pile of bales. Coughing fit to turn himself inside out, the thief flung open the double doors and took blessed gulps of clear night air. As he leaned out, still rubbing his streaming eyes, he hit his head hard on something that

119

swung back again an instant later and gave him another clout for good measure. Blinking away the last of the tears, Grince discovered an iron hook connected to a block and tackle near the ceiling. He followed the rope down into the gloom at the side of the door and loosened it, letting it slide through his fingers until the hook had reached the ground. Making it fast again, he slid down too quickly, cursing as the rough rope burned his hands raw. His feet were running before they hit the bottom.

Grince had come out behind the stable block into an unfamiliar part of the grounds, but that didn't bother him, so long as it stayed empty. He pounded downhill on painful feet, knowing he must eventually reach the dry bed of the river. At least there might be a chance to lose his pursuers there. Behind him, he heard the stable roof fall in with a crash, and his shadow sprang out darkly before him as flames leapt high into the night sky. A vivid image of the past – the soldiers raiding Jarvas's sanctuary, the roof of the warehouse collapsing in flames, his mother gutted by a sword . . . Grince stumbled, rolled, and picked himself up with a curse. He used the horrific childhood memory to help him, letting the terror lend impetus to his flying feet. With luck they would think he'd perished in the stable.

A shout went up. Some bastard had found the blasted rope. Just to plague him further, the path began to meander, turning away from the river. Swearing bitterly, Grince pushed his way into a shrubbery at the side of the path. He expected to hear the sounds of pursuit behind him, and was surprised when nothing happened. Then, after a moment, the air was ripped by the sound of a deep, discordant baying. They had loosed the dogs!

Up to that moment, Grince had thought he could go no faster. His muscles burned, his heart was pounding fit to burst, and his wheezing lungs were starved of air. Hearing the deadly ululation behind him, however, he discovered a new and unexpected turn of speed. The baying grew shrill behind him. Pendral's killer hounds had discovered his trail.

His mind blank with panic, Grince ploughed through the shrubbery, hampered at every step by treacherous roots and tough, springy branches with thorns that tore at his clothing and unprotected face. Oblivious of bruises and scratches he struggled onward, forcing his way through the thicket, the baying of the dogs growing ever louder. Soon they were closing on him: he could hear the crack of splintering branches as they crashed through the undergrowth, and the hoarse exhalations of their panting breath.

Before he knew it, Grince had erupted from the shrubbery and was back in the open once more. Thanks be to the gods! He could move faster now. Somewhere behind him, he could hear the cries of guards and the shrill whistles of the dog handlers, spurring on their charges, but he paid them no heed. About a hundred yards below him, down a sloping stretch of lawn, he could see the torches on the edge of Pendral's jetty, guarding the drop from careless feet in the darkness – but if the thief could run fast in the open, the dogs could run much faster. One by one they burst out of the bushes behind him. In seconds they were snapping at his heels.

He felt a tug on the back of his tunic, and heard the material tear. Somehow, Grince forced himself to one last, desperate burst of speed. If this failed, he would have nothing left, and death would follow swiftly. Time seemed to spin out to an eternity. He was conscious of each laboured breath, each aching stretch of muscles that propelled him forward. The river was nearer, now – but even as he heard the hollow drumming of his feet on the wooden jetty an immense weight hit his back and he felt tearing agony in his upper arm and shoulder, where the hound's great teeth ripped through muscle and skin. The momentum of thief and dog carried them forward, rolling over and over. Abruptly, Grince felt himself falling.

He would have hit much harder, had the hound not broken his fall. None the less, it was a sheer drop of about fifteen feet from jetty to dry river bed, and enough to deter the remainder of the pack, who clustered on the bank above, barking and whining. The impact knocked the breath from him, but he knew the soldiers would be there at any second. Wheezing and gasping, he started to crawl away on his hands and knees, to hide beneath the shadow of the overhanging bank before the soldiers arrived above him. There was no time to lose – the minute they found a way to bring the dogs down, they would be after him again.

Already, Grince could hear voices on the bank above him. He started to creep away, keeping well beneath the jutting side of the gully, out of their line of vision. A blood-chilling noise stopped him dead in his tracks. Fearfully, he glanced behind him, and discovered that the worst had happened. The hound, stunned by the fall, was beginning to awaken. He could see it looking at him, its yellow eyes blazing in the lamp-light reflected from above. Its lips were skinned back from fearsome white fangs in a menacing snarl. Grince swallowed, his mouth gone suddenly very dry. Moving with extreme slowness, and praying to every god he could think of, he began to inch cautiously away from the killer. Slowly, stiffly, the dog rose to its feet, its baleful eyes fixed unblinkingly on the thief.

'Look – the dog has seen something,' came a shout from above. 'Go on, boy – get him! Kill!'

Grince's plan to sneak away down the shadowy watercourse evaporated into thin air. As the dog came at him and leapt for his throat, he unhooked the heavy sack from his belt and swung it with all his might at the beast's broad skull. It impacted with a resounding crack, and the hound dropped back, yelping and shaking its head. He fumbled for his knife to cut its throat, and found nothing. At some stage in his flight, he must have dropped the weapon. *Bugger!*

Once again, fear forced Grince's aching body to run – down the gully, until he could see the great cliffs of the Magefolk Academy rearing their shadowy bulk above him. He came to the first bend, and here, as he had hoped, the stony bank sloped more gently, and could be climbed. Even as he scrambled upward, he heard the dog snarling in the river bottom as it resumed its chase, and the shouts of approaching soldiers on the bank.

Despair swept over the thief. They had him cornered now. He could have wept – it was so unfair. He had outwitted his pursuers so many bloody times, yet he just couldn't shake them completely.

'There he is!'

'Get the little bastard!'

'Grab him when he comes up!'

The soldiers were clustering round at the top of the slope, unwilling to risk a descent of the slippery gradient. Their voices drowned out the scrabbling of the dog's claws on the stones behind him. Grince was trapped, with nowhere left to turn. Dazzled as he was by the lanterns of the many guards above, he didn't see the hole until he fell in it, and found himself in a peculiar tunnel whose walls and floors were smooth, curved, and sloping slightly upward. Grince's forward momentum took his feet right out from underneath him on the slippery floor, and he fell full length, covering himself from head to foot with slimy muck. Rubbing the stuff from his eyes, he turned his head to see the hound's massive silhouette, blocking the entrance behind him. He was finished. Grince tensed himself and closed his eyes, whimpering with terror, waiting to feel the hound's sharp teeth tear his flesh . . .

Nothing happened. With a weird, dreamlike sense of utter disbelief, he realized that the men were calling off the dog. Grince opened one eye in time to see the great brute back out of the tunnel, and slink reluctantly away. What in the name of all the gods is going on, the thief wondered. The bastards almost had me – why stop now? Then he heard a shred of conversation as two men walked to the edge of the bank above him: '. . . and send some men down into the gully to watch the hole in case he comes out again.'

'Lord Pendral won't be too pleased that we've lost him – not to mention the jewels.'

'I'm not here to do his fetching and carrying – I'm a soldier, not a bloody servant. If Lord Pendral wants his damned jewels he can send a menial in for them – or go in there and fetch them himself. Maybe the ghosts wouldn't bother him. The thief is finished, so I've done my job.'

'How can you be sure?'

Grince heard the first man sigh. 'Look, you idiot. He can either starve in there, or come out and face the consequences – I'll leave some men stationed round the outlet. Or he can follow that drain as far as it goes, which is straight to the Academy and its ghosts. They're welcome to the little sod, after all the trouble he's caused us . . .'

The voices drifted away, out of earshot. The thief couldn't believe his luck. He didn't care about the ghosts – he didn't believe in them, and was far more afraid of Pendral's wrath than he was of the so-called shades of the Magefolk. If the Lord of Nexis sent someone to collect his stolen property, he would find Grince and the jewels long gone. He had escaped after all! Relief made him light-headed. Had it not been for the slippery floor, he would have danced. As it was, he couldn't keep a huge grin from spreading across his face. I can go home via the sewers, and they'll never get me, he thought. This may turn out to be the best night's work I've ever done.

Chuckling, Grince shouldered his sack, and set off into the tunnel. Above him on the hilltop, the Academy waited.

Shia, Khanu and the Mage struggled up the switchback road that led to the Academy's upper gates. Though Aurian chafed at their slow and careful pace, she knew she could go no faster. The climb, which in former times had been made so easy by the gentle gradient of the zigzag roadway, was awkward going now, especially in the dark. The road's surface was badly worn and pitted. The cracked, loose paving stones left projecting shards and unexpected holes, and tilted sharply at the pressure of an unwary tread, with an ever-increasing risk, for the Mage at least, of breaking an ankle or trapping a foot.

Aurian didn't know what she really expected to find in the Academy, which was clearly a desolate ruin now. Surely, though, Eliseth and Miathan must have left *some* clue as to their whereabouts? I hope so, the Mage thought. Right now I'm truly lost – I don't know what to do next or where to turn. Desperate for reassurance she touched the Staff of Earth at her belt, feeling comforted, a little, by the warm glow of power that pulsed beneath her hand. The Harp of Winds was slung on her back as Anvar had always carried it, and it thrummed unhappily, protesting its new ownership. Aurian could feel its magic reaching out longingly to Anvar, its true wielder. The Artefact, lacking a conscious intelligence, had no way of knowing that Anvar was gone.

At last they reached the top of the hill and stepped beneath the crumbling arch of the gate into the ruined courtyard.

Aurian paused and looked around her with a shudder of unease. Save that there was no moonlight yet, the place looked eerily similar to the way it had appeared in her dream – right down to the silhouette of the shattered weather-dome, and the same spine-chilling feeling that the place was thronging with the ghosts of the past. The wind seemed to sigh and whisper to itself in corners, and every black and vacant window about the shadowy courtyard seemed to be filled with watching eyes.

Keeping together, Aurian and the cats searched the lesser buildings in turn: the guardhouse and stables, the chambers devoted to Fire and Earth-magic, Meiriel's infirmary and the kitchens with their adjoining hall. All of the buildings were deserted, and appeared to have been for some considerable time. Webs stretched undisturbed across doors and windows, and the dusty floors were void of footprints. A sickly, waning moon was just rising as they stood at last in the cold shadow of the Mages' Tower and looked across the courtyard at the library, with its endless maze of archives beneath. To Aurian, either option was equally disagreeable, but she decided on the tower as the better of the two. With a shudder, the Mage looked into the open doorway of the building that once, in happier times, had been her home. It gaped like the dark, ravenous maw of a monster that waited to devour her. 'Well – I suppose we'd better get it over with,' she muttered. Leaving Khanu at the bottom to guard her back she stepped into the darkness with Shia at her side.

The wan moonlight had not yet reached the doorway of the tower, and it was pitch black inside. Even her night vision needed some amount of light, however small, to work upon, and Aurian strained her eyes to peer into the thick darkness at the bottom of the stairwell. She wanted to avoid using Magelight if she could, so as not to give herself away to anyone who might be watching. The tower reached high above the walls of the Academy compound, and any lighted windows would be visible from the city below.

'We'll start at the bottom,' the Mage told Shia, glad that their mental speech removed the need to speak aloud. 'If there's anything in one of these rooms, we don't want it getting between us and the way out.'

125

The first room was the tiny cell that had been Aurian's first home at the Academy. It was as bare as ever it had been while she was in residence, and she closed the door quickly, with a shudder. It brought back too many memories of the unhappy little girl who had been a victim of Eliseth's cruelty. The next rooms were one floor higher on the spiral of stairs – the chambers that had belonged to D'arvan and Davorshan. These also proved to be empty, their dust undisturbed for long ages, and Aurian was dismayed by the extent of the damp and decay that she found within. Bragar's chambers were the same.

So far, the Mage had only given the rooms a perfunctory glance, not even bothering to make a light, as she suspected that there would be little there to interest her. She hoped that Eliseth's suite would yield more clues as to the whereabouts of the Weather-Mage. It was only when she reached the next floor, and Eliseth's chambers, that Aurian noticed the footprints. At her startled exclamation, Shia came leaping to join her. The Mage was kneeling on the landing in the doorway of Eliseth's rooms, tracing outlines in the dust on the floor. 'Look. Someone's been here.'

This high in the tower, fingers of moonlight could reach through narrow windows placed at intervals in the outer walls. Where the beams touched the floor, the thick dust glimmered with a soft silvery light save for a series of darker patches – the smudged and dusty prints of feet leading up and down the stairs, and into the Magewoman's chambers and out again.

Muttering an oath, Aurian loosened her sword in its sheath. 'These look like a woman's booted foot – it's far too delicate to be a man. Eliseth must have been here! But what about the other? The boots are of similar make . . .' A prickle of fear coursed through her. 'Gods! Can Miathan and Eliseth still be in the Academy?'

'I doubt it. Whoever it is, they haven't been here for a long time.' Shia was peering hard at the tracks and following them back down the stairway with her nose. 'See? In the darkness, you must have missed the prints in the lower chambers. But see how blurred the prints are – and I can pick up no scent. There was no one in the courtyard, and we've looked every-

126

where else. I would say that no one has been in this place for many months – probably longer.'

'It should be safe enough for me to go on alone, then,' Aurian said. This place was so full of memories for her that somehow she wanted no one – not even a friend as close as Shia – to be with her when she revisited her old rooms. 'If you go back to watch the entrance with Khanu,' she told the cat, 'I'll take a quick look upstairs – and then we can get out of here.' She shuddered. 'The Academy has changed so much – I hate to see it like this. I can't believe now that it was ever my home.'

Eliseth's rooms had been ransacked – by the intruder, or by Eliseth herself, Aurian did not know. Nothing of value was left, nor was there any clue to the whereabouts of the Weather-Mage, so Aurian went up to the next floor, and her own chambers. Fighting a deep feeling of reluctance, she opened the door. As she looked around the room, grimacing at the dust and disorder, her eye fell upon the fireplace with its high, carved mantel, and the hearth where, long ago, Anvar had dropped his bucket and covered her in a choking cloud of ash. The door into the bedchamber was ajar, and through it she could see the bed that she had shared in happier times with Forral.

She should never have come in here. Aurian felt the tightness of unshed tears in her throat as she was swamped by memories of the two men she had loved. She blinked, and swallowed hard. 'Damn it, this won't help,' she muttered to herself. Quickly, she checked both rooms. The intruder had been here – she could see the telltale footprints plainly in the dust – and cupboards and drawers had been pulled open and their contents strewn about the room. 'Whoever did this, they'd better not let me catch them,' Aurian growled. It was easier to be angry. It was the best way to take her mind off the sorrowful memories. There was no point in looking in through the chaos for old possessions. Everything would be ruined by now, and besides, the Mage wanted no reminders of the past.

As she climbed the last flight of stairs and approached the Archmage's door, Aurian drew her sword, and took the Staff of Earth in her other hand. As she grasped it, the thrill of power that coursed up her arm helped to stiffen her courage. Just as in her dream, there seemed to be no wards on Miathan's door. In her dream, the Mage remembered, she had taken the heel of the Staff and pushed it open. This time, to deliberately break the sequence, she gave it a good hard push with her booted foot and sprang back quickly as it creaked ajar.

She was met by darkness – a solid blackness so profound that it defied even her Mage's sight. It was as though the moonlight reached the threshold of the room and then stopped. Aurian stepped forward, her heart hammering wildly, and summoned a sphere of actinic Magelight. Miathan's chamber leapt into glaring light, and proved to be as empty as the others. Feeling slightly foolish, Aurian pressed on into the bedchamber – and stopped dead. There, upon the bed, lay a long, shrouded outline, all details obscured at this distance by the crawling blue web of a time spell. Biting her lip, the Mage crept forward, both sword and Staff at the ready. Then, as she approached the figure, the features resolved and became clear to her.

'Anvar!' Aurian cried, and ran forward, almost weeping with relief. She wasted no time in wondering why Eliseth had chosen to leave him here – she was just so glad to see him again, and anxious to make sure he was all right. It was the work of a moment to remove the spell. She hovered over him anxiously as his blue eyes opened. In an instant, his face became alight with joy at the sight of her – and then creased with puzzlement as he lifted up one hand and looked at it as though he could not believe his eyes.

Aurian halted in the act of reaching out to him, for there was something in his expression that stopped her – something unplaceable, but dreadfully wrong. The Mage realized, belatedly, that this could be a trap, and stepped back, her knuckles whitening as she tightened her grasp on the Staff of Earth. 'Anvar?' she asked tentatively.

The figure on the bed sat up, and ran a hand distractedly through his hair in a gesture that Aurian recognized. 'No, love,' he said softly. 'It's me – Forral.'

128

9

The Calling

It never occurred to Aurian to doubt. The face and body of the man on the bed belonged to Anvar, but his gestures, the way he held his body, the animation of his features – everything brought memories of Forral flooding back to the Mage. Though the figure had spoken with Anvar's voice, the inflexions of speech, the intonation, the choice of words – they could only have come from the long-dead swordsman.

Aurian's breath stuck in her throat. She couldn't speak – the words refused to come. Forral. Impossible. *And where was Anvar?* What had happened to the mind, the spirit, the soul who once had occupied his form?

Only when she felt the firm pressure of the door against her shoulder blades did the Mage realize that she had been backing away. The touch of solid wood – something ordinary and real – pulled her back to herself, out of the numb miasma of shock.

'Aurian, don't you know me? I . . .' Forral sat up; made as if to rise from the bed.

It was more than Aurian could face; too much for her to assimilate all at once. Was she joyous? Aghast? She hardly knew. She thrust her sword back into its scabbard and her hand, groping behind her, found the latch of the door. A whirl, a slam – and she was gone, bolting recklessly down the tower steps as though a horde of demons pursued her, her fists clenched into knots of bone around the Staff of Earth and her eyes blinded by tears.

Forral swore, and leapt up to follow Aurian, but the balance of his body was all wrong, the legs longer than he was accustomed to and the weight and muscle differently distributed. His feet tangled under him and he fell heavily, bruising knees and elbows, and only just preventing his face from smashing into the floor. Half dazed, the swordsman pulled himself up to his knees, a vivid image of Aurian's horrified face seared on his mind's eye. What had happened to him? he thought. How had he managed to return to the realms of the living? Overriding the joy that had exploded within him at the sight of his lost love was a sinking sensation in his heart that something had gone terribly, horribly wrong.

Though Forral wanted badly to go after the Mage, he stayed where he was for the moment, trying to put everything that had happened into perspective. When Aurian had gone she had taken her Magelight with her, plunging the room into darkness that was barely alleviated by the gleam of sickly moonlight through the casement. There was just enough light to let him see the candle in a tarnished holder on the night table beside the bed, but it took him some time to find flint and striker as he rummaged through unfamiliar leather clothing that seemed oddly put together. He lit the candle. Once more, he held his hand out in front of him in the flickering amber light, really looking at it this time.

Forral frowned. What was this? Lightly tanned skin and long, tapering fingers. A dusting of pale golden hair on the back. Callused fingertips, but none of the heavy scarring from sword nicks that had striped his own hands and forearms. Forral's skin crawled. The hand was not his own. Frantically he groped at his face. No beard. He clenched his jaw and shook his head as if to clear away a veil of cobwebs. 'Well, what the bloody blazes did you expect?' he asked himself gruffly. Anger was better than fear. 'You've been dead and buried for years, you poor fool – *your* body was worm fodder long ago!' A sick shudder went through him at the thought. His mind was working sluggishly, as though it had not quite accommodated itself, as yet, to its new vessel.

Then it struck him like a thunderbolt. *So whose body have I stolen?*

Aurian had fallen twice during her headlong descent of the tower, but the curve of the spiral staircase had slowed her momentum, and she had not fallen far. The second time she went sprawling, Shia came charging up the stairs just as the Mage was picking herself up. Pushing the cat aside, she rushed down the remainder of the staircase, aware that Shia was following but unable, as yet, to respond to the frantic queries of her friend. Not now. Not yet. First, she must get out. Bruised and shaken, Aurian staggered out of the tower and doubled over, vomiting, in the courtyard. She stood there gasping, taking deep breaths of cold night air and trying to steady herself with the mundane. Now she had put some distance between herself and that *creature* upstairs, who had worn Anvar's body and spoken with Forral's voice, she could start to think sensibly again.

'What *happened*?' Suddenly Shia was there, beside her. 'Is Anvar up there? I saw from your mind that he was – then he was not. Is he there? Can we help him?'

Taking deep, gasping breaths, the Mage leaned against the cold, white stone of the curving tower wall, and took a firm grip on the whirling confusion in her mind. 'No,' she said flatly, not knowing what else to say. She wouldn't cry. She *must* not, or the gods only knew when she would ever stop.

Now that Aurian was calmer, she could feel her friend beginning to pick out the memories of the ordeal from her mind. 'Are you certain it was Forral?' Shia asked her. 'Remember the desert. Eliseth has used such deceits as these before. What you thought you saw – surely this must be impossible? How can a living spirit be ousted by one of the dead?'

For an instant Aurian's heart leapt at the possibility, but her mind knew better. She was no longer the inexperienced young girl, confused and grieving, who had been duped so easily in the desert. She knew exactly what she had heard and seen. Also, she could feel the intense distress behind Shia's thoughts, and realized that the cat was closing off her own mind to the possibility of Anvar's death.

'No, I'm not deceived,' she told her friend. 'Anvar is really gone, and it seems that Forral has taken his place within his body.'

Aurian smashed her fist into the wall, unable to give vent to her inner turmoil in any other way. I can't believe this, she thought. It's just too cruel. All that time spent mourning Forral – I wanted him so much. I still wish he could come back, even though it would tear my heart in two – but as himself, not like *this*. I had just found peace and happiness with Anvar – must I now start mourning *him*? Go through it all again?

And what of Forral, who had come back to her in a deadly exchange that had taken one love for the other? He had been her first love – she *still* loved him. He was the father of her child, but . . . I fled from him, Aurian thought, as though he were a monster. And if there should be some way to get Anvar back, then I'll lose Forral all over again. Even as she put the dreadful truth into words, she felt a savage anger stirring deep inside. How could this have happened? How had the swordsman managed to steal Anvar's body? And why not displace someone – *anyone* – else? The more Aurian thought about it, the more she became convinced that it could be no accident. It must be the swordsman's revenge, because she had turned to another man after his death. How *could* he? she thought. I loved Forral. Throughout all my childhood, he was the one man I could trust. How could he do this to me?

'Can this be possible?' Shia asked her softly, breaking in on the Mage's thoughts. 'And if it is, what do you intend to do about it?'

Aurian scowled. 'About Forral? I know what I have to do. I must confront him and find out the truth. It's just a matter of finding the courage to do it.'

Forral's heart gave a wrenching kick within his chest as he recalled Aurian saying Anvar's name. He turned cold all over. It wasn't possible . . . it couldn't be. But he remembered Anvar's arrival Between the Worlds and recalled Death's warning. Then the portal had opened again . . . 'No,' he muttered desperately. 'It was an accident – I didn't mean to . . .'

Did you not, jeered a small voice at the back of his mind. *Are you sure?*

'No, no! It isn't true – it *can't* be.'

A stray gleam of light kept catching at the edge of his vision, like a child tugging at his sleeve for attention. Forral half turned, and saw the slip of candle flame reflected in a looking-glass that hung on the wall at the foot of the bed. He hadn't noticed it before – nor, until that moment, had he realized that he was once again in the Archmage's chambers – ironically, the very place where he had died.

Where is that bastard Miathan anyway? Forral thought. Has he somehow contrived to bring me here? Has he placed the mirror there, to hurt and confound me?

'Don't be a damned fool, Forral,' he snarled at himself. 'The bloody thing was there all the time. You wouldn't have noticed it until you'd lit the candle.'

The mirror waited, hanging there, dark and enigmatic. The swordsman knew he couldn't put it off for ever. He had no choice but to look, and discover the truth. And Aurian – Aurian had fled from him with horror in her face. He should-n't be wasting time here – he ought to go after her, to find her, and reassure her that everything was all right.

Is it really? Will it ever be all right again? Forral ignored the insidious thought. Taking a deep breath, he scrambled to his feet and stumbled to the mirror.

The candle, held high to illuminate his features, began to tremble in Forral's hand. He recognized the man in the mir-ror, though the tawny hair was longer now, and bleached by the sun. The face, too, was tanned; its features older, more firmly defined, more mature and confident than those of the terrified boy Aurian had rescued, and Forral had befriended. Aurian's lover had become a man now – but Forral had dis-placed him.

'Oh gods,' the swordsman groaned. His legs folded beneath him. He dropped slowly to his knees, moving like an old, old man, and put the candle down on the floor. He buried his face in his hands, as if to hide Anvar's stolen features – as if to deny the truth. 'What have I done?' he whispered. 'What have I done?'

'What *have* you done?' The voice was unwontedly sharp. Aurian stood in the doorway, square-shouldered and resolute. Her jaw was clenched with determination, though her eyes glittered darkly with pain. He leapt to his feet, wanting des-perately to run to her, to enfold her in his arms and comfort

133

her as he had done when she was a child, but something in her face forbade him.

Anvar was not the only one who had matured, the swordsman thought. This was not the naive, trusting young girl he remembered. Even when they had become lovers, Aurian had still retained a quality of uncorrupted innocence at odds with the arrogant, invidious nature of the Mageborn. Why, up to the very last, she had still been trying her hardest to think well of that black-souled monster Miathan. In those days, Aurian had never made an issue of her magic, preferring indeed to play down the legacy of her Mage blood in the company of Mortals. Now, he could see the power blazing from her. Her gaunt, grim face was that of a warrior, with the pain-chiselled features and guarded eyes that had looked too often on suffering, betrayal and death. A shiver passed through him as he remembered the little girl he had warded and guided long ago. What in the name of all the gods had been happening to her, while he had not been there to protect her?

Forral couldn't hide his bitter disappointment. 'Is that all you have to say to me after all this time? Aurian, don't you recognize me?'

Grince's last stub of candle guttered and went out, and the blackness pounced on him like a lurking wild beast. *Supposing the ghosts of the Magefolk really* did *exist?* Grince wished, now, that he had left the Academy and its hidden secrets alone. Using the candle stubs from his pocket, he had made his way through the sewers and managed to find a crevice that led into the tunnels beneath the Academy that Hargorn had told him about. It had seemed a good idea at the time – clearly Pendral's guards didn't dare follow him into the haunted lair of the Magefolk – but he had never imagined that the tangle of passages beneath the promontory would be so complex. Even before the light had failed, he'd been wandering around for what seemed like hours, and he was well and truly lost.

The thief was exhausted, and desperately thirsty. He hurt from his head, where the swinging iron hook had hit him, to his feet, which still stung from the scorching they had received when he came down the kitchen flue. He was

134

scratched in a hundred places from his headlong flight through Pendral's shrubbery (wouldn't you know that the crafty bastard would have filled his garden full of thorns?) and bruised and aching from his fall. The shallow sword-cut in his leg was stinging, and his shoulder and side were stiff with dried blood where the dog's great teeth had torn him. That was the worst of his injuries by far. Every step jarred it into an explosion of blinding pain.

The darkness of the underground tunnels pressed close around him and the air was dusty and stale, making it difficult to breathe. Grince crept slowly along the passage, feeling his way along the rough-hewn wall with both hands and shuffling like an old man so as not to trip or stumble on the uneven stone floor. So much for the ghosts of the bloody Magefolk, he thought bitterly. *My chief enemy in this place is my own accursed stupidity. Why didn't I just stay in the sewers until the coast was clear?*

It was greed that had brought him into the Academy archives. Greed and curiosity. Once he had shaken off his pursuers he should have given up the insane scheme and gone home, but he knew he would never have the nerve to come here again, and had been unable to resist the challenge to explore. Surely there must be *something* of value down here! 'Something of value, my arse,' the thief muttered sourly. Why had he been so stupid? Even now he could be sitting by the fire, warm and well fed, with his injuries treated and a mug of ale in his hand. A small, cold knot of panic began to form in Grince's chest. His heart began to race and clammy sweat sprang out on his skin. *I've got to get out of here!* He never did remember starting to run. The next thing he knew, he was falling.

The impact knocked the breath from him before his scream had become more than a squeak. Grince lay there, gasping, until his heart stopped trying to hammer its way out through his ribs. For one appalling second, he had not known how far he would fall – it could have been one foot, or one thousand. Not since he was a child, and the soldiers had attacked Jarvas's refuge, had he known such abject terror. He supposed he must have started running when he had panicked, and had simply run into thin air as the level of the passage dropped. A shudder ran through him as he realized how lucky he had been. Right now, he might only just be hitting the bottom of a chasm.

'Grince, you damned idiot! That's where the panic gets you,' he told himself, merely for the comfort of hearing a voice in the black and silent void. Cautiously, he eased himself up into a sitting position and began to feel his limbs for damage. Apart from some bruising, however, and the feeling that every bone in his body had been jolted loose, he seemed to have taken little harm – though when he got out of here, he assured himself grimly, he would probably find that his hair had turned white. Feeling around himself in the darkness, he discovered that he had fallen down three steps into a shallow alcove in the passage wall. Grince stiffened, as his groping fingers encountered a different texture: smoother, warmer than the rugged stone of the tunnel. Of course – there was a door in the alcove, and the steps led down to it. Even as the thought crossed his mind, the smooth wood slipped slowly away from the pressure of his fingers, and left him reaching out into empty space. The creak of the hinges sounded loud in the shattered silence, and Grince felt a sudden cold draught on his face as the unlatched door swung open.

What should he do now? Frankly, Grince wanted little to do with mysterious doors that opened, seemingly, of their own accord, and even less to do with the chambers beyond them. He should be trying to find a way out through the corridors, he told himself – not poking around in bloody Magefolk rooms. He had learned his lesson. If there were any secrets – or even valuables – down here, they could remain hidden for all he cared. Then it occurred to him that he would never find his way out groping blindly around in the darkness. He had found no lamps or torches in the passageways, but surely they must keep some kind of illumination in the chambers themselves? If he worked his way round by the walls, he was bound to find a sconce, or a shelf with a candlestick, or *something*. Grince hauled himself to his feet. Oh, please let there be a lamp or a torch, he prayed. Just let me out of here, and I swear I'll never meddle with the Magefolk again . . .

Keeping one careful hand on the door frame to guide himself, he stepped carefully over the threshold and into the room beyond.

The last time Forral had looked, as a living man, upon Aurian, they had been here in this very chamber. At the sight of her, the memories came flooding back to him: the thick, clinging darkness that reeked of rot and decay, the maniacal cackle of Miathan's laughter, the high-pitched buzzing snarl of the Wraith as it swept down upon him, and Aurian's desperate, doomed attempt to save his life. He remembered the blackness sweeping over him – then the grey door had slammed shut behind him, and he had heard Aurian's voice, frantic and tearful, calling, calling, from the other side. *Then*, the swordsman thought bitterly, she would have stolen the very sun from the heavens to save him. Now she sat facing him as though she couldn't bear to be too close, her eyes cold, her face a picture of misery as she tried to explain what had changed. And every word she said was breaking his heart.

'But you *aren't* Forral – don't you see? Forral is dead – I was there when he died. If you'd come back in your own body, as the Forral I knew and loved, I would have been overjoyed to see you.' Aurian sighed and looked away. 'I'm sorry if this hurts you. I know you might have expected – and deserved – a different welcome, having been away so long and having returned so miraculously. But you've got to understand. I never thought you were coming back – there was no way that you *could*. I went through a lot of anguish before I would even admit to myself that I loved Anvar, but finally I did. And remember, you said yourself I should find someone . . .'

'I know, damn it!' Forral roared. 'Don't tell me what I said! If I'd known how eager you'd be to take me up on it, I would have kept my stupid mouth shut!'

'That's not fair!' Aurian was on her feet now, her eyes blazing with the cold, inhuman light of Magefolk anger. 'I mourned you. I grieved for you. I certainly didn't expect you to come back in a stolen body and throw it all in my face!'

'I did *not* steal Anvar's body!' Now Forral was on his feet, too.

'What would you call it, then, if not stealing? Where is he now? Why did you do this to him?'

Forral felt as though she had struck him – indeed he would have preferred it if she had taken her sword and thrust it through his heart. It would have hurt less. During the long, aching wait of his exile Between the Worlds, the swordsman had held fast to the conviction that if only he could find a way back to the world of the living he could put everything right. Now, with his treasured goal achieved at last, he was aghast to discover how wrong he had been. He had taken the stolen glimpses of Aurian that he'd snatched from the Well of Souls and woven them into a flimsy fantasy held together by hopes and wishes. But since his murder the world had moved on without him, and he, Forral, no longer had any place in it. One look at Aurian's face was enough to tell him that. Death had been right all along – there was no going back.

Sudden tears spilled from Aurian's eyes, and she dashed them away with angry haste. 'I never stopped loving you, don't you realize that? Anvar understood that. He made his own place in my affections – he didn't try to take yours. What hurts me most is that you would be capable of this dreadful act. I would rather have gone on grieving for you to the end of my days than discover that you were never the man I thought you were – that I had been living a lie for all those years . . .'

'No! Stop! Stop right there!' Forral's own bellow could have carried right across a battlefield. He was astonished to find that Anvar's voice could also produce such volume. Aurian shut her mouth with a snap, but continued to glare at him. A mixture of relief and dismay flooded over the swordsman. So that was why she was so angry at his return. She thought that *he* was responsible for Anvar's loss! He held out his hand to her, and concealed his disappointment when she would not take it. 'Aurian, listen, please. Just sit down and hear me out while I explain what happened. If you want to go on hating me after that – well, it's up to you. But at least you'll know the truth.' Seeing her hesitate, he added, 'Please. After all our years together, you owe me the chance to defend myself.'

Aurian hesitated for only a moment. 'All right,' she replied quietly. 'That's fair.' Folding her legs gracefully beneath her, she sank down to the dusty floor, at the side of the empty hearth. Holding the serpent-carved Staff with its eerily glowing green gem across her lap, she stroked the smooth, twisting wood with restless fingers, and Forral knew that she was attempting to control her anger and anxiety so that she could give him a fair hearing. He concealed a sigh of relief and sat down opposite the Mage. Never taking his eyes from hers, he began to speak.

Lord Pendral's florid face turned purple with rage. 'What do you mean, he just vanished? You imbecile! He didn't vanish – *you* let him get away, you sorry excuse for a human being!'

In contrast to his master's puce complexion, the Guard-Commander's face was deathly white. Coadjutant Rasvald, watching from his safer position to one side of the High Lord's chair, watched his commander shift from foot to foot, transfixed by Lord Pendral's ire like a rabbit impaled upon a spearpoint. 'But – but my Lord,' the unfortunate man stammered. 'The thief fled into the sewers beneath the Academy. I never thought he'd have the nerve to *stay* there. I thought the ghosts would drive him out, and I had men stationed ready.'

Pendral's expression grew darker. 'Oh, what a splendid plan. So you decided to waste my troops, waiting for a man who never came out!' His words started in a menacing snarl and ended in a bellow.

'My Lord, please . . . I was only trying to *avoid* wasting your troops, by not sending them into that evil, haunted place . . .'

The cringing performance of his superior officer was embarrassing to witness. Coadjutant Rasvald directed his gaze discreetly elsewhere – he had discovered long ago that for a man in Lord Pendral's employ there were many things it was safer not to see. Rasvald looked at the walls of the mansion's library, where a coating of paint obscured the scars where the old bookcases had all been torn out. Pendral had changed the purpose of the chamber to an audience room, where he heard petitioners and – more often – dispensed justice to those who had defied or crossed him or broken one of an increasing number of laws – not to mention those who had failed in his service, such as the luckless commander.

'Cease whining, you brainless, spineless worm!' Pendral shouted. 'Spare my men, would you! Why, pray? I have hundreds more! No . . .' He pointed a pudgy finger like a bejewelled sausage at the cowering man. 'Admit it – thoughts of your men couldn't have been farther from your mind. It was your own skin you were considering. *You* were afraid to go near the Magefolk haunts, so you stood by and let that accursed whoreson of a thief take my jewels and lose them in the bowels of the earth!' By now Pendral was positively screaming with rage. Veins stood out on his neck and forehead. His eyes bulged and a shower of spittle sprayed from his lips into the face of the quaking commander.

Abruptly, the High Lord fell ominously silent. Rasvald felt his guts loosen as Pendral turned his bloodshot gaze on him. 'You,' he said with deadly softness. 'You were with this pile of ordure, were you not, when he lost the thief?'

The coadjutant's tongue fused to the roof of his mouth. He prayed the floor would open up and swallow him – any fate was better than encountering Lord Pendral in his wrath.

'Well?' the High Lord barked. 'Have you lost your wits, or just your tongue? If you don't wish to use it, I will have it cut out for you.'

Rasvald gulped. 'Lord, I – yes, I was with the commander when he called off the dogs. But it wasn't my idea, my Lord. I spoke out against it. I told him it was stupid . . .'

The Guard-Commander drew in his breath in a sharp gasp at such barefaced treachery. 'Why, you back-stabbing, lying bastard!' he shouted. 'It's not true, he never . . .'

'It makes no difference.' Pendral spoke loudly enough to drown the man's protests. 'You,' he pointed at Rasvald. 'As of now, you're promoted to Guard-Commander. Be silent,' he cut off the former coadjutant's babbled attempts at thanks. 'I'll tell you when you can speak. These are your orders.' He began to tick off points on his fingers. 'First, you will nominate a new second-in-command to take charge of a house to house search of the entire city. Second, take this piece of trash outside and kill him. Yourself.'

140

The ex-Guard-Commander threw himself to the polished floor. 'Mercy, Lord – mercy!' he wailed.

'Guards!' The High Lord snapped his fingers and two burly figures left their post by the door. One of them seized the former commander from behind, while the other hit him several times in the face and the belly. Without a word, they dragged him away, choking and dripping blood from his nose and mouth.

Pendral sighed. 'I keep telling them and *telling* them not to get blood on my floor,' he muttered peevishly, 'but do they ever listen? Now, where was I?' His eyes, like two saw-edged daggers, impaled Rasvald once more. 'Oh yes. Once you've finished with the prisoner, take as many men as you think you'll need, and get down into this sewers.'

'What, now, Lord? At night?' Rasvald quavered.

'Of course now!' Pendral's malevolent gaze narrowed. 'And don't come back without my jewels and that misbegotten turd who stole them, or you'll be buried in the same grave as your commanding officer.'

It was as well that Grince had learned caution. Just within the entrance of the chamber was another step leading down into the room itself, but this time his groping feet felt the edge, and he negotiated it safely. Taking a moment to steady himself in the darkness, he set off to his right, feeling his way along the wall like a blind man.

To the thief's dismay, the room seemed to be covered from floor to ceiling with nothing but books, all stacked on shelves that stretched as far and as high as he could reach. But surely there must be a candle or maybe a lamp somewhere nearby, or what was the point of all this? No one could read in the dark. Grimly, he continued his search. He had no choice if he wanted to get out of this dreadful place. Once, his fumbling hands dislodged a pile of volumes that cascaded down upon his head, adding to his bruises. Grince cursed aloud, and the sound of his voice echoed, unnervingly loud and harsh, shattering the silence of the chamber.

A sliver of ice ran down Grince's spine. There couldn't possibly be anyone – or thing – in the room to hear him, yet suddenly he was sure that he was not alone. Though he told himself not to be ridiculous, the feeling would not subside. He remained huddled on the floor in the midst of the pile of fallen volumes, not daring to get up and move, even towards the door, for fear of what he might run into in the darkness. Long minutes passed while he waited, trying to breathe silently and straining his ears for the slightest sound of movement in the chamber. Eventually, it occurred to him that he was being foolish. There was nothing there – of course there wasn't. And even if someone *was* in the room with him, he didn't need a candle to see them – he had been sitting in the midst of the solution all the time. Grince rummaged in his pocket for flint and striker, then, picking up the nearest book, he began to tear out the pages one by one.

A spark caught on the fourth or fifth attempt, and a thread of acrid smoke drifted up, making the thief's eyes water. He blew on the smouldering spot of red until at last a tiny flame snaked its way up into the pile of crumpled pages, where it blossomed like an opening flower. Grince's heavy sigh of relief made the flames move out then in, as though the fire itself were breathing. He began to feel warmth on his hands and face. As the hungry fire took hold, amber light began to consume the darkness, spreading out towards the edges of the room. Quickly, Grince crumpled fresh pages to throw on the flames. Until he could work out a way to make it portable, he needed to keep his light source going. Paper alone would burn too fast for his needs, but if he could find some wood in the chamber – a chair, perhaps, that he might break up, or even a shelf – he might be able to fashion some rough torches that would suffice to light his way home.

This must be one of the larger chambers. The light of his little fire was not enough to illuminate the corners or the shadowy alcoves set here and there along the nearest wall. The smoke didn't help the visibility, either. It was rolling upwards now in choking clouds that stung his eyes and closed his throat against the suffocating fumes. Flinging another hand-ful of pages on to the flames, Grince got up hastily and moved away from the fire, heading away from the door towards the far right-hand corner of the chamber. When he reached the first alcove, he stepped into its shadows, narrowing his eyes in an attempt to make out details in the gloom. As another page of his makeshift bonfire caught and flared, the shadows fell back to reveal a towering figure with coldly glittering eyes. *There was someone in the alcove!*

Grince screamed. He wanted to run, but all power of movement had left him. He crumpled to his knees. Behind him, the shadows encroached once more as his fire began to die, but even in the gloom Grince kept his face tilted to look upwards. He was utterly transfixed by the hypnotic gaze of those glittering blue eyes.

As they waited at the foot of the tower, Shia saw Khanu's eyes glow bright with reflected moonlight as he turned to her. 'I wish Aurian would hurry,' he said. 'She's taking so long, I'm getting worried. And what's the mystery? What can have happened to poor Anvar?'

'I wish I knew – I don't understand half of what Aurian told me,' Shia admitted. 'I don't trust this place – and I don't trust this human she's found, who can take over another's body,' she added darkly.

'You don't trust *any* humans apart from our own,' Khanu pointed out, 'and neither do I. I don't like this city place, either – it's unnatural. Dangerous. I wish we were back in the mountains.'

Shia gave him a forbidding look. 'Where Aurian goes, I go,' she said severely. 'I don't wish to be anywhere else.'

'Well, you might try asking *her* to go where *you* want to go, for a change,' Khanu retorted, unabashed. Delicately, he ran his tongue over his nose and whiskers. 'Already I can scent the changes that will soon be happening within you, Shia. It will not be long before –' His words were cut off in a strangled yowl as a heavy paw cuffed him across the nose.

'*Be silent!*' Shia told him furiously. 'Stay out of matters that are not your concern!'

'Not my concern?' Khanu's moonlit eyes glinted wickedly. 'As the only male within hundreds of miles, it can't help but be my concern – and I'm far from sorry.'

Shia's tail lashed back and forth. 'If you say any more, I'll

143

make you worse than sorry,' she warned him with a rumbling growl.

'You're foolish to ignore what will soon happen. Sooner or later, Aurian or no Aurian, you'll have to face it,' Khanu muttered sulkily. When Shia snarled again, he took himself quickly out of reach of her swift paw with its flashing claws. 'I'm going to explore this big place across the courtyard,' he said, with a pathetic attempt at nonchalance.

'Don't hurry back,' Shia snapped at him, and went on trying to eavesdrop on the conversation Aurian was having upstairs. Just as she was thinking about giving it up as a bad job and actually going to find the Mage, she heard Khanu's mental call: 'Shia, listen . . .' In the distance, from the other side of the courtyard, Shia's acute feline hearing could just pick up a distant sound, very muffled and faint.

'Did you hear *that*?' Khanu demanded. 'I think it's coming from underground. You had better talk to Aurian. That sounded to me like a human, screaming.'

As she listened with horrified fascination to the swordsman's tale, Aurian found her anger beginning to ebb away. Despite everything that had happened this was still Forral, her first love, and as he told her of his ordeal in the endless grey monotony Between the Worlds her heart ached for him. She heard how he had used the Well of Souls, until Death had stopped him to watch over her – no wonder she had often felt that he was close – and how he had learned that by dipping a hand into the waters he could send his shade into the world to help her, as he had done in Dhiammara.

Then Forral related the mysterious arrival and departure of Vannor. Aurian's heart gave a lurch as he mentioned Death's admission that the merchant had been poisoned by none other than Eliseth. A dreadful suspicion had entered her mind. Her fingers tightened on the Staff as her thoughts began to race. 'Damn that bitch to endless torment,' she snarled, but collected herself quickly. 'Go on, Forral,' she urged the startled swordsman. 'I'm beginning to guess what must have happened – but tell me the rest.'

But when Forral's tale came to Anvar and his plight, Aurian

144

could scarcely bear to listen to his account of Anvar's arrival in the realm of Death. 'I tried to talk to him,' the swordsman told her. 'I was desperate for news. If Anvar was dead, what had happened to you? Death tried to persuade him – both of us in fact – to come away. He said we couldn't stay there – it wasn't safe. Someone was misusing the Caldron of Rebirth . . .'

Dear Gods, Aurian thought wildly. I knew it! Then she noticed that Forral had stopped speaking. He bit his lip and looked away from her. 'You were probably right to blame me,' he muttered. 'It could have been my fault. Maybe Anvar would have come back to his body if I hadn't delayed him – but you see, Death had tried so many times to get me to enter the Well of Souls and be reborn – I thought he was trying to trick me again.' He frowned. 'I don't exactly know what happened then – everything was confused – but I think that whatever the Cauldron does to bring people back, it caught hold of me instead of Anvar.' He held out his hands beseechingly. 'Aurian, you've got to believe me. I didn't do it deliberately – I was just *taken*. Even if I had worked out what was happening – well, I simply wouldn't have known how to put myself into Anvar's place.' Forral looked unflinchingly into the Mage's eyes. 'We've been apart too long if you could even suspect that I'd do such a thing – but do you want to know the truth, love? I thank the gods I was never called on to make that choice – because I missed you so much there's no telling what my heart might have misled me into doing.'

When she heard the plea for understanding that lay behind Forral's words, and saw his distress so plainly written on Anvar's face, the anger seemed to go out of Aurian. There was no doubt that he had told her the truth. If nothing else, his final admission proved it. Besides, if Forral had been able to return unaided, surely he would have done so long before now. At least now the Mage knew who was truly responsible for this disaster. Only Eliseth was sufficiently inventive to inflict such an agonizing dilemma on her enemy – and she was now in possession of the Cauldron of Rebirth.

What a bloody awful mess! And there seemed to be no way out of it. Even if she could get hold of the grail, would she be able to bring Anvar back? And if she did, it would mean sacrificing Forral all over again. The Mage's shoulders slumped, and for a moment she was left vulnerable and uncertain. Then she became conscious of Forral's eyes on her. The swordsman was still holding out his hands, waiting for some kind of answer.

'I believe you,' Aurian said softly. 'You aren't to blame for this. I should have known better – and I'm sorry I doubted you.' Then, steeling herself to put the heart-wrenching thoughts of Anvar and his plight out of her mind for the present, she reached out and took Forral's hands. 'We'll get through this somehow – and at least it gives us a chance to be together again.'

'For a while, anyway,' Forral said – and then, to the Mage's relief, he changed the subject abruptly, as though aware that they were straying once more on to dangerous ground. 'Aurian, it's a long time since Death allowed me to look into this world. What about our son? Where is he now? Is he all right?'

Oh gods – Forral didn't know! Aurian's heart sank. How can I answer him? she thought. How can I tell him that Miathan cursed his son to take the form of a wolf – and then I abandoned the poor child so that I could fight Miathan and Eliseth? Why, I don't even know where Wolf is now – or if he's alive at all. How can I confess that to Forral?

The Mage was spared from having to break the dreadful news by an urgent message from Shia. 'Aurian, come quickly. Someone *is* here. Khanu went into the big place across the courtyard. He says he heard screams coming from somewhere underground.'

146

10

The Messenger

The feeble moonlight stood little chance of penetrating the thick stained glass of the library's windows, and it was pitch black within. Aurian created a slip of ghostly Magelight and sent it floating ahead to light the way. This was the first time she had set foot in the library since Finbarr had met his fate, and she looked around in dismay at the mouldering, rat-gnawed volumes, many of which had been dislodged from their shelves and lay open on the floor like birds with broken wings, barely recognizable beneath layer upon layer of mildew and dust. The Mage was glad to reach the filigreed metal gates at the opposite end of the vast chamber. Though she had been dreading the thought of entering the maze of freezing black catacombs beneath the library, it came as a welcome relief to escape the heartbreaking sight of such needless ruin and destruction.

Aurian had not heard the screaming. By the time she had reached the door of the library it had stopped, and now the passages beneath were silent, cold and dark. Aurian was glad that Anvar – no, Forral – had stayed close to her, always keeping to her right, so that his sword hand stayed free. He was keeping a wary distance from the great cats, even though Aurian had explained that to friends they were not as fierce as they looked. Clearly the swordsman was far from inclined to take her at her word, and Shia wasn't helping the situation. Having looked into his mind and found someone other than her beloved friend Anvar, she had flattened her ears and kept glancing sidelong at him with a baleful glare.

With the cats pacing beside them they looked in one room after another on the upper level but found nothing to furnish them with a clue to the identity of the screamer, or the where-abouts of Miathan and Eliseth.

147

'This is ridiculous,' Forral said at last. 'We're just wasting our time – freezing to death for nothing. It can't be much further down, or these big beasties wouldn't have heard it. I don't know what you expected to find down here, but –'

'Whoever screamed, of course,' Aurian retorted sharply. '*And* what made them do it.'

'Are you absolutely sure the cats heard something?' Forral insisted. 'I'm sure they must have been mistaken – it would have taken a pretty loud scream to penetrate through all this stone. We may as well go back, if you ask me.'

It was plain that the swordsman didn't like the place. Ever since they had come down here, he had been fingering the hilt of Anvar's sword, which they had found discarded in Miathan's chambers before they had left the tower. Aurian, however, had grown used to trusting her instincts, and something still prompted her to remain. 'Let's go on just a little further,' she insisted. 'If Shia says she heard screaming she did – and it didn't come out of nowhere. There's something close by that we need to find – don't ask me why, but I'm sure of it.'

Forral looked thoroughly unimpressed by this reasoning – or lack of it. 'Aurian – will you come on *back* . . .' He grabbed her hand, tugging her with him, but dropped it when Shia gave a warning growl.

'It's nearby, I'm sure. Somehow I have the feeling . . .' With Forral trailing reluctantly behind her, the Mage opened the next door.

It was the last thing he had expected to see. Aurian cried out in shock and her Magelight went out, plunging the chamber into merciful darkness. With a stifled oath, Forral yanked her back into the corridor and slammed the door behind him. 'Get away from there, you idiot! *Move!*' Groping in the darkness, he grabbed her tunic and began to pull.

Aurian resisted his tugging and leant back against the cold stone wall, gasping for breath. Unable to stop herself, she began to laugh weakly.

'Curse you, Aurian, there's no time for this!' Forral yelled at her. 'That room is full of bloody Nihilim!'

'Forral, it's all right.' At last Aurian managed to get hold of

148

herself. 'The Wraiths can't hurt us. When my Magelight went out I saw the glimmer of a time spell. They must be the Nihilim that Finbarr took out of time to save me.' She laid a hand on his arm. 'I'm sorry, Forral. It must have been a horrible shock for you, seeing them like that.'

In the dark there was a small silence from Forral, then: 'Bugger it,' he muttered. 'I feel stupid now.'

'You're not the only one,' Aurian admitted. 'They had me fooled at first.' She pulled herself together and kindled a new light to hover above them. 'For a minute there, when I first opened the door and saw them, I thought my heart was going to stop.' She was about to put her arms around him, but when she looked up into Anvar's face, something seemed to shrivel inside her, and she turned away hastily. 'Come on,' she said softly. 'Let's get away from here. The Wraiths may be immobilized and if they've been here all this time they must be harmless, but they make my flesh creep, all the same.'

Forral nodded. 'That's the first sensible thing you've said since we came down here.'

Shia had nosed the door ajar once more, and was peering curiously at the Wraiths through the narrow gap. 'So *those* are the creatures that haunt your nightmares,' she said to Aurian. Her tones held a slight edge of puzzlement.

'Take my word for it – they're considerably more terrifying when they can move – and feed,' the Mage assured her.

They were just turning away to retrace their steps when the voice came.

Aurian stopped dead. 'Can you hear that?' she demanded. 'What *is* it . . .?'

The swordsman looked puzzled. 'Hear what?'

They turned to one another in consternation. 'Something that only communicates with Magefolk, apparently,' Aurian whispered.

Forral's hand went to the hilt of his sword. The Mage gave him a chance to draw it and then, as the echoes of the steely slither had died away, she held up her hand for silence.

'Can you hear that, Shia, Khanu?' Aurian asked hopefully after a moment.

'I'm sorry,' Shia told her. 'I can't hear anything but us.'

'Nor I,' Khanu added.

The voice, however, had not ceased. The Mage could still hear it in her head – a thin, cold, high-pitched call. It had no discernible words, but none the less it was clearly a beseeching, a beckoning, a summoning. Aurian felt a shiver go through her. 'It wants us,' she murmured. 'It wants us to follow.'

'What? You have *got* to be joking!'

'No, truly,' Aurian insisted. 'The gods only know what it is, but it can't be a Wraith, or it would certainly have found a way to free its comrades by now. Besides, if it was something that meant to harm us, why didn't it attack when we were helpless in the dark? That would have been the obvious time.'

'You'd better be right,' Forral retorted, 'because you'll be staking our lives on that quaint notion.'

Aurian scarcely heard him. Already she was setting off in pursuit of the phantom call. She was barely aware that the others followed reluctantly, Forral muttering darkly under his breath.

The Mage crept on down the passage, following the irresistible murmur of the summons, which did not waver or vary in tone unless she attempted to stop or turn aside into one of the chambers that lined the corridor. If she went the wrong way, the incomprehensible whisper turned into a screeching whine that made Aurian's head throb as though it were about to burst. The same thing happened when she tried to turn back. Soon, she had no choice but to continue.

Aurian could tell that Forral was worried. Anvar's face, starkly illuminated by the pale Magelight, looked sickly and wan, his dark eyes shaded to fathomless voids. 'Aurian, will you *stop* this?' he hissed.

The Mage shook her head. 'I'm sorry, Forral – I can't. It's too late now – if I don't follow, the voice will drive me mad.'

It was easy enough to find the right chamber – Aurian only had to follow the luring call that whispered, with increasing urgency now, in the recesses of her mind. Forgetting all caution she hurried along, drawn by the summoner's spell, ignoring Forral's increasingly frantic attempts to slow her down. Her Magelight streamed behind her, trailing a comet-tail of sparks. The voice was still whispering, louder and more urgently than ever. Though Aurian could not have said how she could tell, the summons seemed to emanate from a doorway further along on the right. Dragging Forral along behind her, she rushed towards the open door, and as soon as she laid a hand on it the voice abruptly ceased.

'I can't hear it any more,' she said softly. 'But it's here – I know it is. Whatever was calling me is in this room.'

As the door swung open it broke Grince's terrified trance. He whirled around, and felt his guts shrivel. There in the doorway stood a pair of what could only be Mages – tall, intimidating, and with eyes that seemed to pierce the thief's very soul.

After the first moment of startled confrontation with the tall, red-haired Magewoman, her grim companion, and the fearsome, clawed, fanged black monsters – plainly magical demons or something of the like – Grince had no other recourse save to throw himself to the floor and plead for his life. The Academy was *not* deserted after all – and he had been caught trespassing in it! As he lay there, not daring to raise his head and waiting for some terrible fate to strike him down, a whole lifetime seemed to pass.

'Oh, don't be ridiculous!' snapped a female voice. 'Get on your feet, man, and stop this pitiful grovelling. Come on – we don't have time to stand here *all* bloody night.'

Her companion chuckled dryly. 'That's a good way to persuade him not to be scared.'

The female ignored him, continuing to concentrate all her attention on Grince. 'Come on, you – answer me! What are you doing down here? Was it *you* who called me?' Her words were punctuated by bloodcurdling snarls from the demons.

'Lady – spare me!' Grince's voice was little more than a terrified squeak. 'I couldn't help it! I didn't take nothing, honest I didn't! I didn't touch a thing! I didn't call you – I would never presume to bother your Ladyship. The guards chased me here and I got lost, that's all. If you'll only show me the way out, I'll never, ever, ever come back!'

The Mage made a small sound of impatience, halfway between a curse and a sigh. 'Gods help us,' she muttered.

'Look, you stupid Mortal. No one's going to hurt you, all right? Now just pull yourself together and get up off the floor. As soon as you've answered my questions, I'll show you the way out of here.'

The thief risked a sneaky glance at her through his fingers, and began to relax a little. It was difficult to be afraid of even a dreaded Mage when she was standing over the fire rubbing her cold hands in such an ordinary, homely way, with the two black demons sitting at her feet and gazing blissfully into the blaze like a pair of fireside cats.

Watching his unnerving visitors closely to be sure that they had no objections, Grince rose slowly from the floor. As he did so, the leg with the sword-cut gave way beneath him and he fell heavily, jarring his torn shoulder and crying out in pain.

The Mage was at his side in an instant. 'You're hurt?' She brought her light down to hover just above the thief. 'Melisanda save us – what *have* you been doing with yourself?' She looked down at him sternly. 'I suppose you did all this damage when you were being chased by those guards you mentioned. Maybe you had better tell me just why they were after you in the first place.'

Transfixed by her frank stare, Grince suddenly found that he couldn't lie to her, as he had intended. 'Lady, I – I –'

'By Chathak's iron britches! Where did he get these?'

Grince jumped guiltily at the other Mage's voice. He had found the thief's sack, and was upending it near the fire. The Magewoman gave a low whistle as a cascade of gems came rattling out to heap themselves in a sparkling pile on the dark floor. Once more, she turned her stern gaze on the thief. 'You stole these. Who do they belong to?'

Grince's mouth went very dry. 'P-Pendral,' he choked. 'The High Lord Pendral.'

The Mage burst into peals of laughter. 'Pendral? Is that filthy little pervert still alive?'

Dumbly, Grince nodded, utterly astounded by her reaction.

'And you stole his beloved jewels? Well done, you. It serves him right, the tight-fisted bastard.' She chuckled to herself

152

and almost slapped him on the back. She stopped herself just in time, and ran a light but expert hand over his injuries instead.

Grince, aghast to see a liquid shimmer of violet-blue radiance coming from the Mage's fingers, shrank instinctively away from her touch before he realized, to his surprise, that she wasn't hurting him in the least. In fact the opposite seemed to be happening. Where the tingling violet light fell on his wounds, the pain and stiffness suddenly vanished, to leave a wonderful feeling of ease and well-being. Before his disbelieving eyes, the gaping sides of the sword-cut on his leg began to close up and knit together.

The Mage chuckled again. 'You'll have to sew up the rip in your breeches yourself,' she told him kindly. 'I'm useless at that kind of thing.'

Grince looked at her wonderingly. He had lost his mother at the age of ten, and she had never bothered much about him in any case. Since then he had always shifted for himself, even though Jarvas kept a place for him at the sanctuary. No one had ever taken care of him like this. 'Thank you, Lady,' he whispered. She smiled back at him, and in that moment he knew his life would never be the same again.

The other Mage had perched on the edge of a table and was smiling encouragingly, though the thief noticed that his hand was never far from his swordhilt. 'Now listen,' he said firmly. 'We came down here because we heard somebody screaming. Was it *you* who screamed?'

The female Mage turned from Grince with a startled exclamation. 'The screaming! What with that other call, I had forgotten.'

'Wait, love.' The other Mage held up his hand for quiet, and turned his gaze back to Grince. 'Now,' he said gently. 'Why did you scream, lad? You look in a bit of a mess – who hurt you? Did that same person frighten you? Is someone else down here with you?'

Numbly, Grince shook his head. 'It – it was horrible. It's in there . . .' Unable to say more, he pointed into the unseen depths of the gloomy alcove.

Aurian glanced sharply at Forral, then stepped away from

the fire with a shrug. 'We'd better find out what he's talking about.' Concentrating on the slip of Magelight that hovered above her, she made it flare into brilliant life once more. As the light leapt into the corners of the room, her eyes were drawn across the room to an alcove whose depths were lost in shadow.

'There,' the little Mortal repeated, pointing. 'That's where it is.'

'Be careful,' Shia warned. 'It may be a trap.'

'There's only one way to find out,' Aurian replied. 'Keep an eye on this Mortal for me, will you? I think we can trust him, but I don't want to risk him stabbing me in the back while I'm preoccupied.'

Forral slid off the table to join her and together, they stole cautiously across the room towards the dark void, with Aurian's Magelight high above them. As the light reached into the recesses of the alcove, the swordsman cried out and the Mage recoiled in astonishment. 'Gods preserve us,' she gasped. 'It's Finbarr!'

How many more shocks did the Academy have in store for her? Aurian was aghast at the sight of her dear old friend, changeless and stark within the blue network of a time spell, frozen in time like a lifeless statue. She took a deep breath and bit her lip hard. 'I don't believe this,' she said angrily. 'Finbarr was killed in the attack of the Wraiths – I felt him die. Why would the Archmage want to take him out of time like this? It's insane!'

'When was Miathan ever sane?' Forral replied grimly. 'But Aurian, are you absolutely *sure* you felt Finbarr die?'

The Mage was frowning, trying to think herself back into the past. 'It was the first time I had ever experienced the death of another Mage. It's not a thing you'd mistake, believe me. So why is Finbarr's body preserved this way? I just don't understand.'

'Miathan had the grail, remember.'

Aurian glanced back at the figure of Forral, wearing Anvar's body. 'We've already had an example today of the Cauldron's powers,' she told him thoughtfully. 'After what happened to you and Anvar, do you think this could be something of the same kind?'

'Who can say?' Forral shrugged.

'Well, I think we should release him,' the Mage said decisively.

'No!' Forral said urgently.

'No!' Shia's voice resounded sharply in Aurian's mind. 'What good can this do? You said yourself that the human was dead – and there is bad magic here. Leave him be, my friend, and let us get out of this dreadful place. Only harm can come of meddling.'

'That's the best advice I've had all night.' Aurian smiled wryly at the swordsman, then down at the cat. 'Sadly, I can't take it. Finbarr was my friend – I can't leave him here like this, without knowing. I would wonder ever afterwards if I had been wrong about his death after all.'

'Aurian, you're making a big mistake,' Forral warned her. 'Whatever is happening here, you shouldn't be meddling with it.'

'You're saying this to a *Mage*?' Aurian replied. 'You might as well tell that fire not to burn as tell one of my blood not to meddle.' She turned towards the tall, immobile figure of the archivist. 'All of you had better stand well clear,' she told her friends.

No one took any notice of her, which was about what she had expected. Stepping back, Aurian breathed deeply and calmed her mind, concentrating and gathering her powers. Carefully, she began to unravel the time spell. The crawling blue haze surrounding Finbarr writhed sluggishly and grew still. Then with a loud cracking sound it disintegrated into a cloud of tiny blue sparks that fell away as though a sheath of ice had shattered and fallen from the archivist's body. Finbarr's eyes cleared. He blinked and staggered but pulled himself upright before they could help him, backing away from their outstretched hands.

'Do not touch me. I am not what I seem.' The voice was light and dry, and completely devoid of inflexion or emotion. It was not the voice of a human.

Deep in Shia's throat a snarl began. Under her hand, Aurian felt the hair on the great cat's back beginning to rise.

155

She felt much the same way herself. 'Then what are you?' she demanded. 'What have you done with Finbarr?'

The voice gave a deep, eerie chuckle that echoed hollowly throughout the chamber. The sound stirred uneasy memories that lurked just out of the Mage's reach. 'Surely you remember what I am, O Mage. The Nihilim remember *you*.'

Aurian gasped in horror and took an involuntary step backwards. It felt as though ice were sheeting across her skin. Behind her, Forral gave a cry of horror, and she heard the rasp of steel as his sword left his sheath.

'Don't let it see you're afraid!' The sharp warning from Shia halted the Mage's retreat.

'You're right,' Aurian replied grimly. 'These foul monsters killed Forral.' She raised the Staff of Earth and the air was torn by a deafening thunderclap. Suddenly the chamber was limned in an explosion of sizzling emerald light. 'I recognize you, creature,' she snarled. 'And I can send you back to the oblivion you deserve.'

'Wait. Please. Do not.' Though the words contained no trace of emotion, they were spoken rapidly enough to convey great urgency. 'The Nihilim can help you, Mage – if you will allow it.'

'What?' Aurian felt as though a thunderbolt had struck her. Of all the uncanny events that had befallen her since her return to the Academy, surely this must be the most bizarre. '*You* want to help *me*?' She didn't know whether to laugh or cry.

'Aurian, no. Don't trust this – this *thing*.' Forral was at her side, his voice low and urgent. She saw that his hands – Anvar's hands – were shaking, and despite the dank chill of the chamber his skin was slick with the sweat of profound fear. Her heart went out to him. Poor Forral. The Nihilim were the only things the swordsman truly feared – the hideous creatures had killed him. Aurian understood – she had been there when he died, and the Death-Wraiths filled her with a similar terror and revulsion. None the less, if these monstrosities could give her some kind of advantage over Eliseth, then she could not afford to give in to her fear and dismiss them out of hand.

156

With an apologetic glance at Forral, the Mage turned back to the hideous creature that wore the guise of her old friend. 'Very well. I'll hear you out – but be aware that this time you are alone. If you make a move against me or my companions, it will be the last move you make.'

'I understand.'

'Good.' Aurian took a deep breath. 'Well, Wraith? What is it you want of me? I know better than to believe that you're offering me your assistance for nothing.'

The inhuman blue eyes glittered with a fiery light. 'My people need you, Mage. I want you to set them free.'

Aurian felt her jaw drop. At her side, she heard Forral gasp. 'What?' he shouted. 'You must be mad! Let the Nihilim loose upon the world? What sort of bloody idiot do you think she is?'

'Shut up, Forral,' Aurian muttered. She turned back to the Wraith. 'What sort of bloody idiot do you think I am?'

'Patience, Mage. Permit me to explain. I do not wish you to release us into *this* world – we do not belong here. I want you to help us return to our own home.'

'Your *home*?' Aurian's eyes widened. She forgot to fear the creature as, once again, the Magefolk curiosity stirred and awakened within her. 'And where is your home?' she asked softly.

Finbarr's glittering blue eyes took on an avid gleam, and for the first time the Mage heard a swell of emotion in the Death-Wraith's voice. 'We were not always as you see us now,' it told her. 'Once, we lived Between the Worlds in beauty and in grace. We were Death's dark angels – his servants who flew forth into the world to end the pain and suffering of living creatures. We would come to the old, the sick, the wretched and the weary, and bear them gently home so that they could enter the Well of Souls once again, and begin a bright new life.'

The Wraith sighed, and its voice darkened once more. 'All this we were and more – Keepers of the Balance, Guardians of the Door – until the accursed Magefolk intervened, creating the Artefacts of Power and meddling where they had no right. In the Wars of the Cataclysm, Chiannala enslaved us to the

Cauldron to turn us from givers of mercy into a deadly weapon. And so we have remained down the long, weary ages: hideous and twisted, our powers maimed and unbalanced. Without us, death has become a fearful thing for Mortal creatures.'

Once again the inhuman eyes fixed on Aurian. 'Help us, Mage – I beg you. This chance may never come again. Undo the evil committed by your ancestors and release us. Break the slavery of the Cauldron, and set us free.'

'And you will help me recover the grail that was once the Cauldron?' Aurian asked softly.

'We will. For our own sakes, we must.'

'And what about Finbarr? If I help you, can you return him to me?'

The Wraith sighed. 'That I do not know. We had no means of communicating with you humans without using a human form ourselves. I entered this body at the moment of the owner's death – but your enemy took me out of time before I could act. Finbarr's spirit did not have time to pass Beyond, but I fear that when I quit this shell it will be forced to do so. If you wish to prevent his death from becoming complete, your only hope is to capture the Cauldron and put it to the use for which it was intended.'

'And what about *my* death?' Forral broke in angrily. 'You had no compunction about finishing *me*.'

The creature's cold gaze fell upon the swordsman. 'I told you – the Nihilim were not responsible. It was not your time to die, but we are enslaved by the Cauldron. We are compelled to do as its wielder commands.'

Forral scowled, brushing aside Aurian's attempts to hush him. 'Well, that makes you very unsafe allies, doesn't it? Eliseth has only to command you to turn on Aurian, and we're finished. Do you really expect the lass to take that kind of risk?'

Aurian glared at him. 'Do you *mind*? He's right, though,' she told the creature. 'For a moment, I thought you'd be our secret weapon to defeat Eliseth, for what can withstand the Nihilim? But while she holds the grail, you're a weapon that can turn in our hands.' She held out empty palms to convey

158

her helplessness. 'What can I do? I daren't take the risk. If I gain control of what remains of the Cauldron, I give you my word I'll use it to release you, but sadly it seems I must manage without your help.'

'Wait,' the creature said. 'Think. The risk is small, for the wielder of the Cauldron must return here to undo the time spell. Until then, he –'

'She,' Aurian interrupted. 'Ownership of the grail has changed since you were first released – and the current wielder is even more to be feared than the last.'

'She, then,' the Wraith replied. 'What does it matter? The identity of our slavemaster makes little difference to the Nihilim. She cannot make use of us until she returns to remove the time spell – and until she returns, how can she know we are at large once more?'

'If you help me attack her, she'll know all right – and I daren't take a chance on her finding out.' The Mage thought hard for a moment. 'Look – you said that Finbarr's spirit hasn't departed yet – is there any way I can talk to him?'

'You are aware that my power is all that binds him to this world? You understand that even if I permit him to speak to you I cannot cede control of this form to him, or we are both lost?'

'I understand,' the Mage replied. 'Still, I think we may need his wisdom. It seems to me that you must depend on one another – for the time being at least.'

'Very well. I believe that we can share this form, at least.'

Even as Aurian watched, the monster's features altered – that arcane, unearthly glitter disappeared from Finbarr's eyes. His face took on animation and life, and he looked like himself again. He jerked into motion as though suddenly awakening from a dream and looked around wildly, his hands crackling with the blue energy of the time spell and the shadow of horror still in his eyes.

'Finbarr,' Aurian cried urgently. 'It's all right. They've gone!'

Without warning, the tall, gawky figure tottered from the alcove. He flung his arms around the Mage. 'Aurian! My dear! You're all right! And Anvar! Thanks be to the gods.' Finbarr peered around him, rubbing his eyes, his brows drawing together in a puzzled frown. 'But where are we? These aren't Miathan's chambers. These are my archives, surely. How did we come to be here? And where are the Nihilim? Did we get them all? Where is poor Forral . . .' His voice hardened. 'And that thrice-cursed renegade Miathan?'

Aurian realized, to her horror, that the archivist could have no idea that Meiriel was dead. And how could she tell him of his soulmate's insanity, and her murderous attempt on Aurian's life, and that of Wolf? Yet Finbarr would have to know.

The Mage sighed. 'Finbarr, you were taken out of time by your own spell. A very great deal has happened since that battle with the Wraiths – and a good deal of it is bad news, I'm afraid. If I help you, will you be able to take the information directly from my mind? It'll take hours, otherwise.'

Even using such a direct method, it took some time to bring the archivist up to the present. By the time Aurian had finished, she was wringing with sweat and thoroughly exhausted. It had been hard for her to relive the past – both the good and the bad. For Finbarr, it had been even harder. The archivist was weeping openly. 'Why?' he demanded. 'Why didn't you leave me in peace? Why bring me back to break my heart like this?'

Aurian took his hand. 'Because we need you, Finbarr. You know more about the Nihilim than any of us – at the moment, you have a chance to know one of them intimately. Can we trust them? Dare we remove your old time spell and release them, or is the risk too great?'

The archivist closed his eyes, his concentration so intense that Aurian could almost feel it. 'You can trust them,' he said at last. 'What one knows, all know – and they are all desperate to be free of the Cauldron's chains. You are the only one who can aid them, and in return they will do anything in their power to help you. But unfortunately, until they *are* free of Eliseth's control, they will always remain a risk and a threat to you.'

Finbarr opened his eyes. 'This doesn't please the one who shares my body, but I would advise against releasing them from the spell. The risk is far too great. You must fight your own battles, Aurian – but you're used to that.' He smiled wryly. 'One thing I would advise, however, is that you leave the Wraith that occupies my body free to act. Let it come with you – if the worst came to the worst, you could deal with a single Wraith.' His eyes twinkled. 'You must decide for yourself whether I'm advising you through selfish motives here, for if the Wraith goes with you, then so do I.'

'If it means having you with us, I'll do whatever it takes,' Aurian assured him. She looked round at her companions. 'Finbarr's advice sounds good to me.'

'As long as I am here to protect you,' Shia said. 'I like your human friend, but I don't trust that other thing – the Wraith.'

Then Forral intervened. 'No. This is lunacy, Aurian. I won't have it – you're taking too great a risk.'

He wouldn't *have* it? And who did he think he was, to be giving orders? Aurian glared at him stonily. Just because *he* was afraid . . . 'No,' she replied shortly, 'I can't agree. I understand your doubts, but –'

'Doubts? Those things are cold-blooded killers,' Forral roared. 'They're *evil* – no one should know that better than me.' With a visible effort, he got hold of his temper. 'Listen, love – I appreciate the advantage that this might give us, but in my opinion . . .'

'In *my* opinion, the risk is justified.' Aurian took a firm hold on her temper. Be patient, she told herself. Remember that Forral was killed by these creatures. He has more reason than any of us to fear the Nihilim.

'I see,' Forral said coldly. 'In my absence you've learned all there is to know about the art of war, is that it? Well, come back in another thirty years, Aurian, and tell me that – and even then it won't be true. Let me tell you, you're making a big mistake. I know your stubbornness of old, my girl – but this time you're putting all our lives in danger.'

At Aurian's side, Shia snarled softly. 'Will you let this human speak to you like that?'

The Mage rested her hand lightly on the great cat's head. 'Forral is still living in the past. Things have changed a good deal since he was alive, and he must learn about me as I am

161

now. I'm afraid it won't be easy for him.'

'Nor for you,' Shia added softly.

Mage confronted swordsman, until the tension in the air had reached breaking point.

'I value your experience, Forral,' Aurian said firmly, 'but this is a matter of magic, not Mortal war. I know more about our enemy – and about the Artefacts – than anyone else. I'll take advice, but ultimately the decisions are mine to make, and that's the end of it.'

'It is *not* the end of it!' Forral raged. 'By all the gods, Aurian, I brought you up! I don't have to stand here and take this from you!'

Aurian lifted her chin and looked at him levelly. 'That's true,' she said quietly, 'you don't. You're free to leave at any time.'

Forral gaped at her. 'What? And where the bloody blazes am I supposed to go? Do you really think I'm going to just go off and let you get yourself into all kinds of trouble?'

'That's up to you,' Aurian told him implacably, 'but if you stay, I don't want to hear any more argument about this. You taught me yourself, long ago, that only one person at a time can be in command.'

Forral was looking at her as though he had never seen her before. 'So I did,' he said softly. 'So I did. So what do we do now, *commander*? Lurk here underground until we starve and freeze?'

Aurian gritted her teeth. She was damned if she'd let him needle her. 'We need information,' she said. 'We don't know how long we've been away from Nexis, let alone who rules the city now that the Magefolk have gone.'

Grince, forgotten in his corner, had watched in awe as the Mage had freed the creature in the alcove. So this was the legendary Lady Aurian, who had been lost for so long! Old Hargorn had spoken of her often, with great fondness and regret. She had been kind to him, had healed him – and the thief admired the calm way in which she'd stood up to the other Mage when he had tried to bully her. Though common sense told him that it would be a grave mistake to get mixed

162

up in the affairs of the Magefolk, he wanted to repay her for helping him – and besides, a little magic had come into his hard and brutal life along with her. He didn't want to lose it so soon.

'Lady, I can help you,' he said, before he could stop himself. 'I can tell you whatever you want to know.'

11
City of the Flying Horse

From the air, it looked to be no more than a hill. D'arvan, hanging face down across the horse's withers, his hands bound tightly behind him with what felt like thin strands of flexible metal, tried to turn his head and blot his watering eyes against his shoulder in order to see better. It wasn't easy. The Phaerie steeds were moving so fast through the thin, cold air that the Mage's long, flaxen hair kept blowing in his face, and he'd been plagued by streaming eyes and a running nose for the entire journey, which had lasted through the night and into morning. D'arvan blinked again and squinted down towards the craggy, tree-covered eminence. Surely this pinnacle of rock in the middle of nowhere couldn't be their destination?

Apparently, it could. One by one, the steeds of the Phaerie peeled off from their phalanx and began to spiral down towards the steep, forested slopes of the summit. As D'arvan's captor began to descend, the Mage's eyes and mind seemed to blur for a nauseating instant. With a dizzying lurch, the scene below him snapped into its true perspective in the clear, cold northern light. The hill was far, far bigger than he had thought – and every one of those trees, though given the outward appearance of a woodland giant by Phaerie magic, was a soaring tower.

The Forest Lord and his subjects had clearly done their best to make this city a true reproduction of their magical citadel Between the Worlds. Using their powers to transform nature, they had created a beautiful, functional – and living – home which extended high into the air via the groves of tower-trees, and, D'arvan guessed, continued deep into the ground beneath the hill itself, for he could see many balconies and windows embellishing the ledges and sheer rock faces. Woodland glades were blooming gardens with bowers, streams and fountains, and waterfalls cascaded down the hillside like drifts of pure white lace.

Behind the hill a range of towering mountains marched along the skyline. When the Mage saw streaks of snow on their peaks and the blue-shadowed walls of icy canyons he was horrified to discover how far north he had been brought. Closer to his destination, the scattered peaks dwindled into a less rugged range with lower crests. The nearest stretched long arms out towards the Phaerie city, enfolding its eminence within a sweeping broad green glen whose sides were cloaked in the darker green of forest. As the Phaerie steed continued its curving descent around the side of the hill, D'arvan could look into the valley, where a long and shimmering stretch of water lay, with cultivated farmland round its shores, and plentiful herds of cattle and sheep to graze the sheltered fields.

It was impossible not to be awed by the sight of this magnificent new kingdom that Hellorin had carved out of the lonely northern wilderness. While the Phaerie were exiled from the world, it had been easy to forget just how powerful, capricious and dangerous the Forest Lord had really been. Now, seeing the scope of his father's vast accomplishments spread out below him, D'arvan's heart beat a little faster with apprehension. They had not exactly parted friends, yet to have found him so quickly after his return through time, Hellorin must have maintained a constant vigil throughout all the years of D'arvan's absence. And now that he had captured him, what fate had the Forest Lord in store for his wayward son?

The Phaerie steeds landed on a plateau far up on the eastern side of the hill. D'arvan was hauled down from the horse's back and surrounded by a group of Hellorin's warriors. He just had time to hear Maya cursing at the top of her voice before he was dragged away. He caught confused glimpses of trees, smooth lawns dotted with flowers, and paved and gravelled paths that wound uphill amid the glades. Curious Phaerie faces, with their large, deep eyes and sharp-boned features, watched curiously as he was hurried along in the relentless grip of his guards, until at last he was pushed through a pair of large double doors that pierced the hillside, and into the gloomy corridor beyond.

'Take your bloody hands *off* me, you outlandish bastards!' Maya snarled. Neither her protests nor her struggles were any use – her abductors simply manhandled her more cruelly. Realizing that this was the time for circumspection, not fighting, Maya let herself go limp as she was borne away. 'But when I finally get my hands free to hold a sword again, Hellorin will be finding himself a few subjects short,' she vowed to herself grimly.

Her captors took her in a different direction from D'arvan, away round the side of the hill, always leading downwards. Maya, though she was being jarred and jounced along, noticed that the trees grew thinner as they came to the northern face. The slopes became rougher and more desolate here, with stiff bracken and spiky gorse obscuring the winding trails. Great boulders patched with yellow lichen and shaggy green moss thrust through the thin soil like bones through the skin of a crow-picked corpse.

At the bottom of the hill on the northern side, the rock face was honeycombed with tunnels, each one closed off at its entrance by a barred iron gate and guarded by Phaerie bearing tall spears tipped with long blades that glittered with the same sharp cold, merciless light that sparked from their eyes. Brief words in the incomprehensible Phaerie language passed between Maya's abductors and the guards, then she was passed like some inanimate package from one group to the other. Her new captors plunged into one of the dark openings, and Maya lost sight of the daylight as she was carried inside.

The tunnel was damp, its earthen sides and roof shored up with rough planks. Straggling roots protruded like reaching fingers through the cracks between them. The damp wooden boards were crawling with a skin of slimy mould whose greenish phosphorescence was the only light. The air was heavily tainted with the odours of wet soil and decaying leaf-matter, and cold with the bone-deep chill of the grave. The voices of the Phaerie, who had been talking softly amongst themselves

166

in their own, strange, sibilant tongue, sounded flat and dead, hushed by the all-absorbing clay that surrounded them like a suffocating shroud. Maya, her body still numb with cold from the interminable journey through the thin, icy heights, her limbs held fast in the vicelike grip of her Phaerie guards, felt as though the walls and roof were closing in on her. It was as though her captors were trying to bury her alive. She fought hard against the panic that was threatening to rise within her. It seemed that the best way to overcome her overwhelming sense of dismay and dread was to close her eyes and blot out her surroundings by trying to think of some way out of this impossible situation.

After a time the almost soundless whisper of soft-shod Phaerie feet on the moist earthen floor of the tunnel changed to the scuff of leather against stone, and the alien voices were sharpened by a ringing echo. At the same time the grip of her abductors shifted, her head was suddenly lower than her feet, and the jouncing became far more pronounced than before.

Maya's eyes snapped open. The walls of the tunnel had turned from earth to rough-hewn rock, and she was being carried head first down an uneven stone staircase that was lit at intervals by crystal globes that glowed with a warm, dancing, green-gold light like sunlight seen through trees. At the bottom of the staircase was a pair of tall gates with bars of twisted iron that blocked the passage from floor to roof. These were watched by another pair of Phaerie guards, one of them a woman. Again, uncomprehended words passed between the new captors and the old, and Maya was lowered to the ground and held upright as the female Phaerie ran expert hands over her body and limbs – just as though she had been a horse at market.

The warrior, humiliated and incensed, drew back her head to spit in the woman's face, and was brought up short by the cold, pitiless iron of the alien creature's stare, which turned her blood to pure ice. The Phaerie lifted a warning hand, and Maya swallowed the mouthful of saliva hastily. The woman hit her anyway – left, right, once on either side of her face – and Maya's head exploded in pain as the touch of the Phaerie left behind a trail of freezing fire that seemed to eat like acid into the tortured bone of her skull. She was still screaming when they tore the clothes from her body and fastened a slender chain of some ice-cold metal around her neck. Then they opened the tall iron gates and thrust her through them, to fall down a short flight of half a dozen steps and roll to a standstill, naked, breathless and bruised, on the dusty cavern floor below.

'My dear – are you all right?'

Maya, her vision blurred with tears of pain, couldn't see who was speaking, but at least the voice sounded female, briskly kind – and human. 'Of course I'm bloody not,' she muttered thickly, for she had bitten right through her lip. None the less, she groped for the hand that reached out to help her, and used it to lever herself to her knees, where she spat out a mouthful of dust and blood. Knuckling the salty moisture from her eyes, she looked up to see a tall, bony woman of middle years stooping over her, wearing nothing but a thin gold chain around her neck and a frown of concern.

Rubbing gingerly at the side of her face, which still throbbed with the ebbing remnants of that deadly, aching chill, Maya blinked up at the woman. 'Who in Chathak's name are you?'

The frown went through an infinitesimal shift from concern to disapproval. 'I'm Licia,' the woman replied. She withdrew her proffered hand and with a brusque, embarrassed gesture smoothed her silver-shot brown hair, which was scraped severely back from her face into the sternest of knots. 'The lacemaker from Nexis,' she added, as though that explained everything.

Maya rubbed harder at her aching head, sure she was missing the significance of all this. She looked beyond the woman to see that she was in a gigantic cavern, lit by further clusters of the golden globes that starred the roof and walls. The ground sloped downhill from the level area at the bottom of the stairs where she knelt, and below her the warrior could see a cluster of small stone shelters built around the edges of a shimmering dark mere. What in the name of all the gods *was* this weird place?

Still confused, she turned back to Licia. 'If you're from

Nexis, what in perdition are you doing here?' she demanded.

'Good gracious, where have *you* been for the past few years?' The woman sounded shocked. 'How can you possibly not know what has been happening?'

The air of the cavern was dry and comfortably warm, yet Maya shivered, wishing desperately that she had something to cover her nakedness. She felt oddly and unpleasantly vulnerable like this, and somehow that made it hard to give her whole attention to what the woman was saying. The Phaerie's blow seemed to have scattered her wits far more than an equivalent clout from a human being would have done. And deep in her heart, a small, cold core of fear was beginning to expand like a germinating seed.

She glared at the woman. 'What sort of a stupid thing is that to say? Quite obviously I don't have a bloody clue what's been going on . . .' All at once, she realized that she would gain absolutely nothing from antagonizing this woman, who, from her stony expression, didn't look as though *she* suffered fools gladly, either.

Maya bit off her angry words. 'I apologize,' she sighed. 'I might be sore, confused, and downright scared, but there's no need to take it out on you.' She held out her hand. 'My name is Maya, and I'm a warrior. And you're right – I've been away from Nexis for several years.'

Licia's stern expression softened. 'You unfortunate girl – of course you're afraid, and you're bound to be confused. These abductions didn't come easy to any of us – it's always a dreadful shock at first. You come back with me to my shelter, and I'll get you something warm to drink.' She reached out with a surprisingly strong grip and helped the warrior to her feet.

'And please – could you spare me something to wear?' Maya asked hopefully. 'Any old rag . . .'

'I'm afraid not.' Licia shook her head regretfully. 'When the work gangs go outside the Phaerie allow them clothing, but it's taken away from them again when they return. In the caverns they keep us naked. Like animals.' She spat out the words as though the taste of them disgusted her. 'It all helps to wear down our hope and spirit – to tame us, as the Phaerie put it.'

Shock coursed through Maya, and she stopped dead in her tracks. Suddenly she understood. 'You mean the Phaerie are using humans as *slaves?*' She remembered Hellorin, D'arvan's father, and his wry, half-amused kindness towards her. Did he know she was here? Had he ordered it? Surely he wouldn't do this to his own son's lover? Then she remembered the long months he had condemned her to spend as that double-damned unicorn, unable even to communicate with the one she loved, and suddenly she wasn't so certain. When it came down to it, she was only a mere, despised human, and Hellorin was capable of anything – anything at all. And if he would do this to her, what would he do to D'arvan, his delin-quent son? A shiver of dread coursed through her.

Licia tugged at her elbow, urging her forward between the rows of rough shelters. There was not another soul in sight. 'Of course they use us as slaves – those bastards.' The epithet, spoken with such venom, was startling, coming as it did from a woman who looked so old-maidish and prim. 'What did you expect – they brought us here because they like our com-pany?' An ugly scowl settled across the lacemaker's heavy brows. 'Although they like the company of *some* well enough,' she added bitterly. 'There's many a young lass has bought herself out of here by joining the enemy and mothering Phaerie offspring – for some reason the immortal blood always seems to run true.' She sighed. 'There are some days down here in the dark, when I would sell my soul for fresh air and a glimpse of sunlight, I can hardly blame them. Other times, I would stick a knife through their treacherous hearts as soon as blink – but there, I was too old and barren to be asked, so maybe I'm only jealous.'

'What do the others do – the folk down here?' Maya asked, in some trepidation.

Licia shrugged. 'Some wait on the Phaerie as servants, cooking and cleaning, fetching and carrying and the like. Some folk labour at building and carving new living quarters under the hill, and some work in the fields and barns, tending the crops and herds. After all,' she added nastily, 'it would be far too much to expect the great and powerful Phaerie to plough or hoe or shovel cowshit. They wouldn't sully their

170

skinny white hands. We others – the skilled artisans,' she added proudly, 'we make whatever our masters need, and our only reward is the food in our bellies and the continuing absence of pain.'

The woman, her head lifted high and proud, strode along with great dignity despite her nakedness, and Maya had to stretch her legs to keep up with her. As she walked, some soldier's instinct told her she was being watched, and gradually she became aware of stealthy movement within the gloom of some of the stone shelters – the pale shadow of a face or hand round the edge of a doorway, the flash of an eye in a window embrasure as a head ducked quickly beneath the sill. All too soon, this furtive spying on her began to turn from irritating to unnerving. 'Licia . . .?' she asked uneasily, not wanting to betray her disquiet.

'Don't worry,' the lacemaker shrugged. 'They're nervous of strangers, that's all. We have a rule that only one of us comes out to greet a newcomer – usually, incomers are either terrified or dangerous. We've found from experience that it's wisest to give new captives a little while to settle in. You'll meet the others later, when the work gangs return from the fields, and we can introduce you to everyone, all together.'

Soon they reached a low, windowless stone dwelling, indistinguishable from the rest, near the shore of the lake. Licia ushered the warrior inside, into a single room with nothing but a thick layer of some thick, soft, fibrous stuff on the floor. Nevertheless, the hovel was spotlessly clean and brightly lit with more of the glowing golden globes that burned, this time, with a clear and steady light instead of the usual irritating flicker.

Maya reached up a curious hand to the Phaerie lamps that hung from the ceiling like clusters of some alien fruit. Her fingers were bathed in a deep and steady warmth, like summer sunlight. 'Why are these different?' she asked Licia.

The lacemaker snorted. 'Those wicked buggers keep the big cavern lights flickering like that all the time, so none of us can think straight – you'd be surprised how it gets to you after a while. But they can't do that in here because of the lace. I need a clear, bright, steady light for that kind of fine work, or

I'd go blind – and what worries the Phaerie more, the lace turns into a mess of tangles.' Her face twisted in a humourless smile. 'I'm the best lacemaker in Nexis – or I was.'

With a wave of her hand she indicated a plain wooden table at one end of the room, on which lay a thick pad of cloth, a cluster of delicate, spindle-shaped lace bobbins, each topped with a coloured bead, and spools of shimmering, rainbow-hued thread that looked finer than spider-silk. 'My work is in tremendous demand among the Phaerie,' she told Maya with no modesty at all; 'even the males, including Lord Hellorin, are very conscious of their finery. So that gets me the occasional favour. And at least I get a table and a stool for working. Most folk have to make do with squatting on the floor like dumb beasts in a byre.'

She reached out and hooked a long-legged stool from beneath the table. 'Here, girl – sit down. You look a bit shaky, which is no surprise. Put it in the corner, so you can rest your back against the wall.' She reached deep into a shadowy niche hollowed into the thick stone of the wall, and produced a roughly made pottery cup. 'Here –' she handed Maya an apple and a hard heel of dark bread. 'We won't be fed again until evening, when the workers come back from outside, but I usually keep a little something back for emergencies. You'll feel better for some food inside you, and I'll go and fetch you some water. You take your ease a while – I won't insult you by saying don't fret, but you can put it off till later. Worry's like yeast – if you go on feeding it, it'll keep indefinitely. I'll be back before you know it.'

Left alone, Maya sat down gratefully as instructed, feeling too weary, beaten and betrayed to wonder or care where the lacemaker had gone, although the warrior had a strong suspicion that Licia had used the fetching of water as an excuse to go and report to her fellow-slaves. Though her stomach was aching with hunger, Maya left the food untasted on the table. She knew she should be thinking of ways to find D'arvan, she ought to be planning some sort of escape, but she was tired, so very tired . . .

'There – I told you I wouldn't be long.'

'What?' Maya's eyes flew open. She jerked upright, just

172

saving herself from falling off the stool.

Licia held out the crude cup and Maya, who would have sold her soul just then for a mug of taillin laced with strong spirits, sipped, and made a face. It was water, plain and simple, but harsh with minerals and warm, not hot – about the temperature of a comfortable bath. The lacemaker, watching her, raised a sardonic brow. 'You'll have to excuse us, but the wine consignment doesn't seem to have arrived yet.'

'Is *this* all they give you to drink?' Maya asked in dismay.

'Not at all – you can have it cold, if you'd prefer.'

'Seven bloody demons! Licia – do the Phaerie treat you cruelly?' Judging from the cold-blooded severity of the blow she had received from the Phaerie woman, Maya suspected she already knew the answer.

'What do *you* think?' Licia's pale blue eyes were smouldering with bitter rage. 'We're less than insects to them. We artisans are lucky – they appreciate our skills and take better care of us – but the lives of the common labourers have absolutely no value to them at all. If they injure or kill a few Mortals, why should they worry? There'll always be plenty more.'

Maya was appalled. Somehow, she had never suspected her lover's people to be like this. Suddenly the Magefolk insistence on banishing the Phaerie made a great deal of sense. 'Has no one tried to escape?' she asked.

The lacemaker shrugged. 'You think they haven't dealt with *that* little problem? What do you think these are for? Decoration?' She fingered the slender chain around her neck. 'They do say this metal is a mixture of true gold and Phaerie blood, and it contains part of their magic. It may not look like much, but believe me, it's absolutely unbreakable. There's no way to get it off – folk have died trying. And these chains don't just mark us as slaves, as property. They also keep us here. The Phaerie have set fields of magic all around the boundaries of their realm, and if anyone should try to pass through them wearing one of these, the chain will turn white-hot and literally burn their head off their shoulders.'

Maya was too aghast to speak. Involuntarily, her hand went to her throat, as if to persuade herself that her captors had not placed the hideous device around her neck. The chill of the metal seemed to eat into her fingers, and her heart brimmed over with dread. 'These – they don't come off?' she whispered. 'Not *ever*?'

Licia shook her head. 'I'm sorry, my dear. In all the years the Phaerie have been keeping Mortal slaves, not one of those chains has ever been removed. We don't think they can.' She scowled. 'Even the accursed Magefolk were better than this lot,' she burst out angrily. 'At least under their rule we were free to go our ways – until they all got themselves killed, that is, and let the Phaerie run amok.'

For a moment, a faint, flickering spark of hope flared up in Maya's heart. Ah, she thought, but the Magefolk were *not* all killed. She could only pray that D'arvan possessed enough strength and power to force his arrogant father to see that Mortals should not be enslaved. 'We're more than brute animals,' she whispered to herself. 'We're *not* put here just to serve them.' She was enough of a realist, however, to know perfectly well that right and wrong had little influence on the world. Again, she touched the chain around her neck. *Slave*, it said. *Base and lowly animal.* In the end, it all came down to a question of might. The Phaerie have the power to enslave the Mortals, Maya thought, and there's nothing we can do to stop them. The fate of our race is entirely dependent on their mercy, and our only hope is that somehow they can be persuaded to spare us.

The tall tower was the crowning point of Hellorin's palace, and as such it was also the only place in the Phaerie city from which both sides of the Forest Lord's domain could be seen. D'arvan looked down from the southern window across the city, the symbol of Phaerie wealth and luxury, the tangible evidence of their supremacy and power. The northern window, looking up the deep green glen towards the mountains, showed a very different scene: Hellorin's quarries and mines half concealed among the heavily wooded slopes, and his farmlands, all tilled and planted, burgeoning along the valley bottom. Symbols, all of them, of human slavery.

Peering through the northern window with the longsight that was his father's legacy, D'arvan watched the captive

174

Mortals, labouring like so many swarming ants, while the Phaerie took their ease, or hunted in the surrounding woodland, or sailed in little boats upon the tarn. A faint sense of guilt writhed within him like a tiny serpent as he realized that before the Cataclysm, the Magefolk, his own people, had enslaved the Mortals in exactly the same way – and that even in his own time, most of the Mages had felt that this should still be the natural order of things.

Neither his mother's race nor his father's was blameless, and D'arvan's heart was scalded with rage and shame that such iniquity could exist. Damn the Phaerie! Hellorin had already snuffed out the humanity of the Xandim like a candle, without a single qualm. Now he had subjugated yet another race in an equally callous fashion. And what had he done with Maya?

D'arvan shook and rattled the locked door, hammering on it with his fists for what seemed like the hundredth time. 'Answer me, damn you – is anybody there? How dare you lock me up like this – don't you know who I am? Let me out of here, you slug-witted bastards! You fetch my father here – right now!'

A plague on all the bloody Phaerie! For all his protests, it was patently clear to D'arvan that he had been locked up here on Hellorin's orders, and left in this luxurious chamber at the top of the highest tower in his father's palace to cool his heels until the Forest Lord was good and ready to deal with him. It was a power ploy on Hellorin's part, to establish his dominance from the start. Well, if the idea was to humiliate D'arvan and make him feel helpless, it was beginning to work.

'I won't *let* it,' D'arvan muttered savagely. 'I won't let him get to me like this.' He knew what Maya would have done, as clearly as if her voice had whispered it in his ear. The best way to keep up his courage was to fight back with anger. Scoring the mossy carpet with his bootheels, he paced the many-windowed room, stoking his fury like a great red blaze, kicking at chairs and tables in passing for want of a better target for his rage, and heaping muttered maledictions on his father's head.

'Have a care for the furnishings – some day they may be yours.'

D'arvan swung round to see Hellorin standing in the door-way, an obvious smirk on his face. 'You!' he snarled, snatching up the first thing that came to hand.

The Forest Lord stepped easily to one side and the flung chair smashed to splinters on the edge of the door frame.

The Forest Lord's smile of welcome froze as he saw the expression of scowling fury on the face of his long-lost son.

'You vile, unspeakable monster! Have you no conscience?' D'arvan spat. 'Those are *people* out there – your labourers, your beasts of burden. People who had lives and families, dreams and plans. And what about the Xandim? Poor bastards – you've stripped them of their humanity for ever! How can you live with that?'

There was a cold, bleak, implacable look in D'arvan's eye that somehow reminded the Phaerie Lord of that dratted Magewoman, the last time he had crossed swords with her. *Don't you dare get in my way*, it said.

Hellorin swallowed the cordial greeting that had leapt to his lips, and thought rapidly. His estrangement from Eilin had taught him to deal more carefully and considerately with the Magefolk than had been his wont – and D'arvan was half-Mage, after all. He had no wish to lose his son as he had lost Eilin – but Mage blood or no, he was the heir to the Forest Lord's realm, and must be made to recognize and understand his responsibilities to the Phaerie. None the less, Hellorin was determined to begin in a conciliatory manner. Only if D'arvan should prove obdurate would there be any need to deal with him harshly. 'Will you at least have the courtesy to listen to what I have to say *before* you start throwing the furniture?' he asked in a mild and pleasant voice.

The young Mage's expression darkened further. 'Give me Maya back – *then* I might consider listening to you,' he retorted.

The Forest Lord shook his head. 'Not yet, my son. First we will talk, and then, if the outcome is favourable, I will release your little Mortal to you.'

'And if it isn't favourable?' D'arvan asked softly. His lips thinned into an obdurate line. 'No, that's not good enough. I

176

want her here, with me. I want to be sure she's safe, away from your damned tricks. Until you bring me Maya, I will not exchange another word with you.' He deliberately turned his back on his father and stared out of the northern window at the Mortal slaves who laboured in the valley far below.

A plague on this impudent whelp and his pig-headed Magefolk pride! Hellorin's anger was nearing boiling point. He clenched his fists at his sides and breathed deeply, fighting back the rage. 'So you will not talk – but you have no choice but to listen. D'arvan, there is no need for this animosity between us. You are my son, and for the love I bore your mother you are also my heir. Your true home is here, with us, your people. You could have great power here, and wield considerable authority among the Phaerie. All would defer to you. Would you let a handful of mere Mortals come between you and your own father? Your own true and splendid destiny? Mortals! Dull-witted, short-lived creatures with no magic – they are little more than animals. They were put here to serve us. It is their fate, their reason for existence.'

All the while that Hellorin had been speaking, D'arvan had not moved a muscle. Now he turned, very slowly, and there was iron and granite in his face, and a look in his eyes that made the Forest Lord's blood run cold. 'And supposing I say that you are a foul, depraved despot, and that I am no son of yours,' he hissed in a thin, tight voice that was wound up with rage to breaking point. 'What if I tell you that I abhor and despise you, and I would hang myself, or drink poison, or put a dagger through my heart, rather than take any part in your revolting schemes?' D'arvan met his father with an unblinking stare, and their gazes locked and clashed like two deadly swords. 'I wish it could have been otherwise. But I cannot and will not condone this slavery.'

The Forest Lord was struck to the heart by D'arvan's words. He felt his bitter disappointment crystallize into a twisted, misshapen core within him, cold as ice and hard as iron. So this craven-hearted, whining puppy had the temerity to repudiate his own father?

Hellorin scowled. You've just made a grave mistake, my son, he thought grimly. I gave you some latitude, I tried to appeal to you, to persuade you – but now it's time you were brought to heel. Shrugging off his human guise like an unwanted cloak, he stood revealed before his son in the full might and majesty of the Phaerie Lord, resplendent and terrifying with the raw, wild elemental power of the Old Magic pulsing from him like the fierce energy of an exploding star. He had the hollow satisfaction of seeing D'arvan blanch, and take a furtive backward step.

Hellorin flung back his head and roared with laughter. 'Spineless, witless young fool! How could I ever have fathered you? So you'd hang yourself, or drink poison, or put a dagger through your heart, would you?' His voice lifted in cruel mockery of D'arvan's empty threats. 'I wonder, my fine son, do you think that Maya would feel the same?'

'*What?*' the young Mage shouted. 'Damn you, you can't . . .'

'Can I not?' Hellorin's voice was like a knife blade dragged along bone. All his original good intentions had vanished. 'If D'arvan wanted to join him, that was well and good – but if not, he must be broken, and taught his place. 'Maya is my possession now, my plaything,' he told his son in a soft, insinuating voice. 'I can dispose of her as I please – not to mention those two strayed Xandim that you so kindly brought me.' He shrugged, feigning indifference. 'As for you, you are free to leave at any time. Of course, since you abhor the use of the Xandim you will have to walk, but I dare say your lofty ideals will sustain you over the endless miles of empty wilderness.'

'No,' D'arvan shouted. 'I am not leaving here without Maya!'

Hellorin fixed him with a flinty stare. 'Be assured, you will not be leaving *with* her. You gave up all your rights to her when you repudiated your father and your heritage.' He licked his lips. 'Perhaps, since I have no heirs now, I will take your little swordsmaid for myself. What sons she will breed me, eh?'

Before he had time to register what was happening, a fireball was hurtling towards his face. Gasping with shock, he threw up his will to form a shield, only just in time. Close enough to singe his skin, the balefire spattered against the barrier and dissipated in an incandescent starburst. Droplets of

178

liquid flame burned a pattern of small, dark holes in the moss-green carpet.

Hellorin, recovering quickly, threw back his head and laughed. 'Well done indeed, my son! I am glad to see that my cub has teeth after all.'

D'arvan leaned back weakly against the wall, gasping for breath, his face chalk-white.

Hellorin's lips curled in a feral smile. 'I would wager, however,' he added in conversational tones, 'that you couldn't do it again – not for some time, at any rate. You are an Earth-Mage, D'arvan – to hurl fire in such a profligate fashion demands too much of you.'

He approached the reeling D'arvan, and looked deep into his eyes. 'Enough of this nonsense. I have given you every chance to co-operate as a dutiful son should, yet you have met me with nought but insolence and defiance. Now, let me tell you what *will* happen. The days of the Magefolk are over – the Phaerie will rule their lands in their stead. Now that my city has been built, I fully intend to subjugate Nexis once and for all, and bring the Nexians under my sovereignty. I was merely awaiting your return, for it seemed fitting that I should present your native city to you as a gift.'

'What?' D'arvan choked. 'But that's preposterous!'

'Why so?' Hellorin shrugged. 'Someone must rule those hapless Mortals, and even I cannot be in two places at once. So, my son, it comes down to a plain choice for you. You can accept my offer and take up the rule of Nexis for me – for only in that way will you see the Mortals treated as *you* would have them treated. Also, you will have your she-wolf Maya for your queen – and breed me some grandchildren, eh?'

'And what if I refuse?' D'arvan said slowly. 'What will you do to me then?'

'To you? Absolutely nothing. As I said before, you will be free to leave this place, to go your own way. But you will no longer be my son, and someone else will rule over Nexis and oversee my Mortal slaves. Also, I will keep Maya for myself.' He paused. 'Decide, my son. Already you overstrain my patience. I will not ask you twice.'

D'arvan dropped his face into his hands, and let his

shoulders slump in defeat. 'Very well, my father,' he whispered. 'I'll do what you ask of me.' Then he straightened his back and looked unflinchingly into the Forest Lord's eyes. 'There will, however, be certain conditions.'

12

A Price to Pay

'Now it begins.' As Death stepped away from the Well of Souls, the vision cupped within it vanished, and the figures of Aurian and Forral were replaced by boundless depths and the whirl of infinite stars. Within the shadows of his deep cowl, the Spectre smiled a wry, secretive little smile. That incorrigible, unstoppable Mage had returned to the world and discovered the substitution of one love for another. This should make matters interesting! Death made his way back through the sacred grove, wondering which Magewoman he would soon be welcoming to his realm: Eliseth or Aurian.

As he left the trees, the Spectre stopped, cursing softly. There, waiting for him, was that pig-headed fool Anvar.

The Mage confronted the implacable figure. 'What did you see in there?' he demanded. 'She's back, isn't she? After all this time, Aurian has returned to the world – I can feel it. We're Magefolk, soulmates and custodians of the Artefacts – it would take more than mere death to sever our bond. You've got to send me back now. I can't stay here – I'm not really dead, in any real sense of the word. *You've got to let me go!*'

'By all means.' Death's voice was light with mockery, but his cold gaze never faltered. 'I grow weary of your incessant whining and complaints. That swordsman was bad enough, but you . . .' Red sparks of anger kindled in the black depths of the Spectre's eyes. Anvar said no more, but stood his ground. After a moment, the twin sparks flared brighter.

'Go, then,' Death snarled. 'I will not hinder you. Leave – if you think you can find a way out. You have been here long enough to explore every corner of my realm – you should know by now that the only way out of this place is through the Well of Souls.'

'There must be another way out,' Anvar insisted stub-

181

bornly. 'Aurian and I were here once before, and we got away. I'm willing to wager that you'll tell me eventually, when you've grown tired of playing games with me. Let me warn you – Death or no Death, you'll tire of me long before I run out of ways to plague you!'

'You tire me already, believe me.' The Spectre sighed. 'Very well – I cannot help you escape from this place, but I will tell you the one way in which you can leave. Do you remember our encounter when you and that wretched Mage were in the desert? Her spirit passed beyond the Door, and you came in search of her?'

'It's not a thing I'm likely to forget,' Anvar replied. 'I followed her to this place and you sent us back together. So why can't you send me back now?'

'Because at that time one of you was still anchored in life. This served to draw you both back to the mundane world.'

'But I am still anchored in life,' Anvar protested. 'My body is still there. It was stolen by that treacherous son of a bitch, and –'

'And therefore it no longer belongs to you,' Death said flatly. 'Dispute the matter as you will, you are dead. In order for you to return to the mundane world, one of the living must come in search of you – so you had better hope that Aurian does not decide that her swordsman is a fair exchange for her former soulmate. Even if she should seek you and guide you back, until the Cauldron is found you will exist as nothing but a bodiless spirit – a ghost, if you will. And, should that Mage of yours regain the Cauldron, you must still persuade Forral to give up your body. He may well be determined to stay where he is – and if that is the case, you must return to me or be doomed to roam the earth as a ghost for ever, until you are entirely forgotten. Then your spirit will be snuffed out, and will cease to exist. Heed me, Anvar, for that is the risk you run, if you persist in wishing to return. If the swordsman refuses to quit your body, your only hope is to fight him for possession.'

Forral tried to fold Anvar's long legs beneath his threadbare cloak as he huddled, shivering, in a draughty corner of the

182

underground chamber. He didn't mind the cold and darkness
– he was savouring Aurian's sweet presence as she sat beside
him, talking softly with the shabby little thief. Though he had
found it difficult to accept her new air of command and the
core of steel that seemed to have grown within her in his
absence, they seemed to have reached a fragile understanding
at least – though so far, he admitted ruefully, it seemed to be
entirely on the Mage's terms. It was something to build upon,
however, and Forral was privately glad that he'd been able to
return in time to help her with the culmination of her quest.
Had he not always taken care of her? Aurian had spared no
pains, however, to point out to him that she was a Mage and a
warrior, and she neither wanted nor needed his protective
presence hovering over her as though she were still a child.
Well, time would tell. He had always protected her, and he
wasn't stopping now.

The swordsman knew he should be concentrating on
what Grince was saying, but his attention kept wandering.
Although he felt weary, he was too caught up in the wonder
of rebirth to lose a minute of this first, miraculous day in
sleep. After the endless deprivation and numbing monotony of Death's kingdom, the dank, dusty air of the underground room seemed as fresh and fragrant as a draught of
sparkling wine. The sullen fire and even the gloomy
shadows it cast seemed ablaze with colour and light. The
interplay of the two murmuring voices sounded loud and
harmonious in his ears, and he thrilled to feel the textures
of clothing against his skin, and the warmth of Aurian's
body beside his own.

Experimentally, Forral flexed his right arm. Though it
lacked the heavy musculature of his old body the joints were
limber and the grip was strong. With some regular training,
he thought drowsily, I could soon get this body into shape . . .
Abruptly the swordsman snapped wide awake, horrified by
the direction of his thoughts. This was *not* his body – it
belonged to Anvar. He must learn to think of it as merely a
garment – a borrowed cloak that must be returned some day
to its rightful owner.

Why? There was no quelling the insidious little thought

that lurked at the back of his mind. *Why give up all this wonder and joy when you've only just won it back again?*

Forral looked for a long time at Aurian as she sat beside him, her head cocked attentively towards the thief. If he were to keep this body, she could be his forever. 'But it's not mine,' he told himself weakly.

Maybe not – but it's half the age your body was when you died – and we already know, don't we, that Aurian seems to like your new shape well enough?

A thin tendril of jealousy for Anvar curled itself like bindweed through Forral's thoughts. Why should *he* have her? the swordsman thought. She loved me first. Anvar is no longer here, and I have taken his place. In time, I could win her back . . .

Of course you could, the insidious voice began once more. *And why shouldn't you? It wasn't your fault that you were killed. You weren't ready. You weren't finished. Aurian will come to accept it – she loved you for most of her life. You have a son together . . .*

Stop this! Forral told himself angrily. You know it isn't right. You should be ashamed of yourself. But then he thought of everything that could be his once more: the dew-drenched stillness of summer dawns on campaign, the smell of leather and woodsmoke, hot baths, cold beer, riotous nights of warm companionship in crowded taverns, the unknown joys of fatherhood . . . He looked at Aurian again.

All this can be yours once more – and so can she, whispered the voice. Forral forced it back into the depths of his mind as though he were strangling a snake. After a struggle it subsided – but he knew it would be back.

As his attention returned to his surroundings once more, the swordsman suddenly had the uneasy feeling that he was being watched. He looked around to see one of the great cats staring at him intently with blazing eyes. Forral shivered. The creature looked so fierce and *knowing* – almost as though it had been looking into his innermost secret thoughts. Firmly, he pulled himself together. 'Don't be a bloody fool,' he muttered to himself. For all of Aurian's fond imaginings that she understood every word the cat was say-

184

ing, it was only an animal, when all was said and done.

Shia stifled a growl and flexed her claws, digging them into the crumbling stone of the chamber floor. Stupid human! He was lodged in the body of a Mage, but he had no idea of the powers that were available to him – nor was she about to enlighten him, for it was plain that he could not be trusted.

Anvar's old channels of mental communication were still open to the cat and she had overheard every word of Forral's inner battle. Shia loved Anvar with the same fierce protectiveness that she felt towards Aurian, and to hear this interloper planning to steal the Mage's body left her smouldering with rage.

Shia knew she must be patient, however. This human also meant a great deal to Aurian, and in any case, until the grail was regained, nothing could be done to change the situation. They must all work together to defeat their common foe, therefore it would do more harm than good to precipitate a conflict now.

Reluctantly, Shia decided not to tell Aurian what she had overheard. This was not the right time – but none the less the cat resolved that in future she would watch this human very closely indeed.

Rasvald thanked the gods for Lord Pendral's hounds. Without them, he would never have found the thief in ten thousand years, and besides, it seemed from all the twists, turns and backtrackings he and his men were making that the wretch had managed to get himself utterly lost in this tangle of passages. The two dogs, however, followed the fugitive's scent unerringly. Rasvald, who had less confidence in the animals' ability to find their way back, was careful, at each intersection, to mark the return route with chalk.

There were so many tunnels beneath the promontory that it was a wonder the entire hill didn't collapse, and the Academy with it, Rasvald thought sourly. Though he had brought a dozen men with him – a ridiculously large number to track down a solitary thief – he still didn't feel at ease. It wasn't just the cold and darkness, he was sure, that caused his crawling skin and the itch between his shoulder blades – there was a *feeling* down here, as though some hostile presence left over from the Mages' reign still walked these passageways.

'There's no such thing as ghosts,' Rasvald whispered to himself, over and over. '*There's no such thing as ghosts!*' Somewhere, at the back of his mind, he heard an echo of hollow, mocking laughter.

Whether the phantoms of the Magefolk were present or not it was impossible to tell. The leaping torchlight made a confusion of shadows and, though he had long ago silenced their grumbling and whispering, the heavy footfalls of the men still obscured all other sound. The whines and harsh panting of the leashed hounds sent a rippling cloak of echoes across the other noises. None the less, Rasvald knew that they must be closing in on their quarry, for the dogs were becoming increasingly excited now. The big animals strained ahead, pulling so hard on their leashes that their two handlers were forced to quicken their pace, simply to stay on their feet.

'Keep those bloody animals quiet!' Rasvald hissed. 'They'll warn him.'

One of Pendral's kennelmen gave him a withering look. 'Sithee, mister – how would *you* like to try? Maybe you'd put your hand in his mouth to silence the hound? Or better still, your head?'

'Mind your tongue,' Rasvald snapped – but he had more sense than to push the issue. Instead, he sent a man to run ahead to the next junction of the passage and listen there – then, when the dogs caught up and pointed the new way, he sent the runner on again. Once more the man went out, and then came racing back up the tunnel. 'Sir, I can hear voices up ahead.'

Grince scowled. 'New laws here, new rules there, and bloody garrison troopers everywhere! Truly, Lady, when Lord Vannor was ruling Nexis it got so an honest thief couldn't make a living any more.' He sighed. 'I have to admit, though, that most folk were a lot better off – until the stupid sod decided to go and make war on the bloody Phaerie.'

'He decided to do *what*?' Aurian gasped. 'But that's insane!'

186

'Vannor would never do that – he's got too much sense,' Forral protested.

'Oh, but he did – believe me.' Grince waited until the ensuing uproar had died down and then, in a grim voice, described how, some ten months ago, a large force made up partly from the garrison and partly from Nexian conscripts had gone north to attack the new city the Phaerie had built. Parric had denounced the affair as pure insanity and refused, at first, to waste the lives of his troops. Eventually, however, in the face of Vannor's determination, he had been persuaded to lead the Nexian forces – not a single one of whom had returned. It was assumed that he, too, had died there. The Phaerie, however, came back to Nexis with a vengeance, indulging in a frenzy of destruction and causing almost as much devastation as the earthquake that had happened some months before.

'It was a bad time,' Grince told the horrified Mage. 'A lot of folk were killed, a great many more were stolen away. The Phaerie took Lord Vannor, too – snatched him right out of his house. I would have said good riddance, but then that evil bastard Lord Pendral took over in his stead.' His voice turned low and hard, and his face contorted with hatred. 'Pendral keeps a tight grip on the city now. He has to – folk would see him not only deposed but dead besides, given half a chance.'

The Mage was utterly devastated by his words. This is my fault, she thought. It was my failure to master the Sword that unleashed the bloody Phaerie in the first place.

'Nonsense!' Shia snorted. 'Did you compel that stupid human to make war on the Phaerie? Did you force them to attack the city?'

'You have a point,' Aurian told her. 'None the less, I'm not entirely blameless.' She clenched her fists. Maybe Parric was captured, she thought. He's a tough old bugger – I refuse to believe he's dead. Not without some proof. 'Listen, Grince,' she added aloud, directing her query towards the thief. 'Where exactly is this Phaerie city?'

The thief shrugged. 'How in perdition should I know? I've never been out of Nexis in my life.'

Forral, who had been very quiet until Grince had mentioned Vannor's attack on the Phaerie, nudged the Mage.

'Isn't there anyone left in this benighted city that we know and trust? Preferably someone with a small amount of intelligence, at least.'

Aurian closed her eyes and thought hard, trying to remember the faces of former friends and companions. So many were dead now, or vanished. Some must even be growing quite old . . . 'I've got it!' she shouted. 'Grince, have you ever heard of an old soldier called Hargorn? I'd guess he must have retired from active service now.'

Grince's face split in a grin. 'Has he ever!' he said. 'You'll never guess what –'

'Danger!' Shia and Khanu roared the warning almost simultaneously. 'Enemies attack!'

Then the air was filled with a fierce, deep-throated baying, and two massive hounds burst into the chamber, followed by a horde of men with swords.

At the first hint of a threat, Forral's old instincts took over. As his sword left its scabbard, he was faintly surprised to hear the sound of Aurian clearing steel, so quickly that the ring of the two blades being drawn might have come from a single sword. Beyond them, there was a flare of light as Finbarr ignited a searing fireball and held it at the ready. Grince scrambled away behind the Mages and cowered in the farthest corner of the alcove, a knife, pathetically inadequate, in one clenched fist, and his face contorted with terror. 'Don't let them get me,' he whimpered. 'Lady, I beg of you – Pendral will cut off my hands . . .'

Forral felt faintly stung that the thief had turned to Aurian for succour, rather than himself. Who was supposed to be the warrior here, anyway?

'They won't get you, Grince,' Aurian reassured him. 'We won't let them.'

The guards, expecting to find only one small, fairly defence-less thief, took one look at what appeared to be three armed and angry Mages and stopped dead – unlike the hounds, who, with their quarry in sight, kept right on charging.

Shia launched herself at the foremost, knocking it off its feet with the force of her spring. The two massive creatures rolled right across the chamber, toppling bookcases and scat-

tering volumes in a snarl of claws and fangs and flying fur –
then Shia had the dog cornered, darting from side to side to
contain the clamouring creature as it tried repeatedly to
charge its way past her and make its escape. The other hound,
finding itself face to face with the snarling Khanu, turned tail
and fled, bowling two guards over in the process, and dragging its handler behind it for several yards before the man
could manage to get his hand unwrapped from the leash.

The leader of the guards stepped forward, pale and appre-
hensive. Incredulously, Forral recognized him as Rasvald,
who had come to the garrison as a raw green recruit – and had
later been thrown out again because, as Parric had so suc-
cinctly put it, 'that one will never make a soldier as long as he's
got a hole in his arse'. Clearly, Rasvald had finally found a way
to prove the cavalry master wrong.

'S-sirs and Lady,' stammered the quaking commander, 'I
apologize for trespassing, but our orders come from Pendral
himself, High Lord of the City of Nexis.'

Forral was impressed by the way in which the fellow managed to apologize while putting the blame on someone else at
the same time – and then he remembered that Parric had also
referred to Rasvald as 'that two-faced weaselly little bastard'.

The two-faced weaselly little bastard was still speaking.
'Your honours probably weren't aware that you'd caught a
criminal nosing around in your – er – home, but you don't need
to trouble yourselves, we'll take care of him. Believe me, once
Lord Pendral has finished with the little vermin, he won't be
in any condition to steal again . . .' Catching Aurian's expression, which had turned at his last words from frosty to positively glacial, Rasvald faltered for a moment, then rallied again.
'I beg you, Lady, don't be angry with us. We're only following
orders – doing our job, as you might say. We'll leave here and
never come back, I swear it. All we want is the thief . . .'

'Well, you're not having him,' said Aurian, very clearly and
distinctly, 'so I suggest you take your men out of here before
somebody gets hurt.'

'Lady, please – I don't think you understand,' the commander protested. 'If I go back without the thief, Lord
Pendral will kill me.'

189

Aurian didn't even blink. 'Him or me,' she said evenly. 'Take your pick.'

Rasvald, not the tallest of men, looked up into the face of the Magewoman. Her stony expression was bleak and forbidding, and there was death in the unyielding flint of her cold grey stare. All at once, the prospect of Lord Pendral's wrath seemed far less terrifying than it had been a short time ago. Besides, *someone* must survive to bring back the news that the Magefolk had returned to Nexis. He only hoped the High Lord would be sufficiently grateful for the warning to spare his commander's life.

'Lady, please forgive me,' he found himself saying, almost before he was aware of his own decision. 'I must have made a mistake. I see now that your friend couldn't possibly be the man we're looking for. By your leave, I'll take my troops back up above now, so we can get on with searching the city.' From behind him, he was positive he heard a collective sigh of relief from his men.

'Why, of course, commander, by all means. We won't detain you.'

Rasvald shivered. Somehow, the Magewoman's haughty graciousness was even more unnerving than her outright hostility. Afraid to say more lest he dig himself deeper into trouble, he sketched a bow and ushered his men from the chamber – not, however, without one last, venomous glance for the thief, who paused in the act of putting his knife away to make an obscene gesture at Pendral's soldiers behind the Mages' back.

I'll get you, you cocky little bastard, one way or another, Rasvald thought. You can't hide behind your Magefolk friends for ever. It's not over yet.

Shia stepped back to permit the kennelman to leash his savage hound. As the invaders crowded their way out of the chamber with indecorous haste, Aurian struggled with her conscience. Full well she knew that not a single one of them must be permitted to return to Pendral with word that there were Mages in the city. Possible solutions cascaded with lightning speed through her mind.

190

A dozen soldiers, two great hounds and their handlers would be too large a number to guarantee the success of an all-out attack. With Forral beside her and the great cats in support, Aurian had little doubt about the outcome, but she knew it could not be accomplished without risk. The possibility of serious injury or even death for herself or some of her companions was high – and in the end, there was no guarantee that some of the enemy might not escape into the catacombs after all.

The Mage knew she could unleash the Death-Wraith that occupied Finbarr on the soldiers, but she shrank from that dreadful option. It would also be impossible to take the men out of time – she could not ensorcell all of them at once, and before she had frozen more than a handful of their number the rest would be turning on her. Also, there was still the possibility of losing one or more of them – and not a single one must escape.

Only one option remained – evil, dark and dreadful. She knew there would be a price to pay, but what else could she do? *I have no choice*, Aurian thought desperately. And she would have to act fast – there was no time for discussion, or pondering the repercussions of her deed. Taking the Staff of Earth from her belt, she grasped it tightly in both hands, invoking its powers as she had done so many times before. Her mind went forth into the labyrinth, seeking the retreating soldiers among the twisting, intersecting tunnels. When she found them, the Mage set her will against the rock of the ceiling above them, and found a fault line where the planes of the rock had sheared and slipped a little. Sliding the tendrils of her power into the tiny crevice, she struck at the weak spot with all the power of the Staff.

Forral heard the distant rumble, and then felt the slight vibration as the earth trembled beneath his feet. 'What the . . .?' Then Aurian crumpled to the ground beside him, and as he caught a glimpse of her stricken expression he knew at once what she had done.

Horror claimed him – horror and utter disbelief. She could not have done that – not his Aurian. She would no more be

191

capable of using magic to murder a dozen men in cold blood than . . . But she had done it. All those men, plain soldiers like himself who had only been following orders, lay dead and buried under tons of rock. Killed, not in a fair fight, but from afar, by foul magic.

Aurian was in a huddled heap on the floor, her hands over her face as though to shield herself from her own ghastly handiwork, her breath coming in harsh, racking sobs that were more like retching than weeping. Forral looked down on her, his feelings a roiling mixture of revulsion and icy rage, unable to believe or accept the change in the young girl he had known and loved.

'Damn you,' he said softly. 'Damn you.' Then he turned on his heel and walked away from her.

13

Master of the Unicorn

After a sleepless night, Jarvas, now seriously worried, left Benziorn in charge of his sanctuary on the quayside and went out into the city to search for Grince. The thief had not returned last night, and Jarvas feared the worst. He alone had known what Grince was planning, and he blamed himself for having failed to dissuade the lad from such insanity. He should have knocked him out or locked him up – even if Grince had never forgiven him for the lost opportunity, it would have been better than letting the idiot suffer the consequences of trying to steal from Lord Pendral.

Jarvas had felt responsible for Grince ever since he had caught him – a wild, scruffy fourteen-year-old ruffian in those days – trying to rob the sanctuary one night. Under Lord Vannor's prosperous rule the Grand Arcade had reopened, and the newly-staffed garrison had been so successful in controlling the city's petty crime that the boy had lost his home and his livelihood, and fallen on hard times. He had been raiding Jarvas's refuge not for himself, but in a desperate attempt to get food for his dog.

Until he saw Warrior, and recognized the animal as one of the distinctive offspring of Emmie's dog Storm, Jarvas had not realized that his burglar was Tilda's son. He and Benziorn had been certain that the boy had perished in the initial destruction of the refuge, and he was aghast to discover that Grince had been living as a criminal in the city ever since. For the last half-dozen years or so, Jarvas had tried to fill a father's place for the young orphan, but since the lad had never had anyone to depend upon, even when Tilda was alive, he remained as wary and untrusting as a wild animal, refusing to respond to either authority or kindness. Emmie might have been able to win him over, but she had remained with the smugglers and married Yanis, the Nightrunner leader, taking over most of the domestic running of the secret underground complex from an increasingly frail Remana. She was happy, he heard, but had not been back to Nexis in years. Jarvas had never told her that the lad had turned up again – she had enough on her plate these days, and had probably forgotten all about him in any case.

As the years passed, Grince had refused to mend his ways and settle down to learn a trade, as Jarvas had suggested. Nothing had cured him of his habit of stealing – neither cajolery nor punishment. When Jarvas, out of pure desperation, had eventually tried taking a stick to him, Grince had simply started disappearing for weeks at a time, only coming back when he had some pressing need – usually for Warrior's sake rather than his own – that only Jarvas and his refuge could supply. At heart, he was not a bad lad – had he been sunk in villainy or vice, it would have been easy for Jarvas to wash his hands of the entire problem. But surprisingly, given his background, there wasn't a vicious bone in Grince's body. Thievery was simply a way of life to him – and sadly, he was proud of his skill and the independence it gave him.

Jarvas had been determined to shoulder the additional burden of responsibility for the difficult boy, but Grince's intense hatred of authority caused him deep concern. The makeshift home in the Grand Arcade had represented the only security the lad had ever known, and he blamed the High Lord for its loss. When Lord Pendral had come to power following Vannor's disappearance, he had instituted severe penalties for stealing which put Grince into constant peril. Jarvas sighed. The thief was taking risks that increased with time – and in a city the size of Nexis, it had been inevitable that he would eventually be caught.

That was not the worst of it, however. Something had happened last year to fan Grince's hatred into a deadly blaze. Pendral's troops had killed the white dog, Warrior. A patrol had recognized the thief and given chase, and Warrior, ten years old now, had not been able to run fast enough to escape. Before Grince could rush back to help, a soldier, enraged at the escape of his true prey, had put an arrow through the fleeing dog.

For a time Jarvas had despaired of Grince's life. He had been stunned by grief, unwilling to talk, refusing to eat, unable to sleep. Warrior had been everything to him – family, companion, protector and friend. For days he had remained in his little cubicle in the refuge dormitory, sitting on the bed and staring at the thin partition with unseeing eyes. Jarvas, watching him with increasing concern, never saw him weep. About eight days after Warrior's death, the boy vanished into the night. A worried Jarvas was organizing searchers when Grince returned with the dawn, a boy no longer. There was blood on his hands and a bleak, cold, adult look in his eyes that had not been there before. None the less, he had thrown himself into Jarvas's arms and sobbed like a broken-hearted child. He never talked about where he had been, but no one was surprised when the reports came in of a soldier who'd been found in a lonely alley with his throat cut.

From that day onward, Jarvas saw a change in Grince's personality. Though he was still the same amiable, rather shy lad to his cronies at the refuge, he smiled rarely, and never laughed at all. He became more furtive and secretive in his doings. His stealing, which he had once treated in the light-hearted spirit of a game, suddenly turned into a deadly serious business. Grince was playing for higher stakes now – whereas previously he had contented himself with food and clothing, and small amounts of money to buy his needs, he was now stealing gold and jewels, and raiding the cash boxes of the fat, wealthy merchants to spirit away a month's profit at a time. At first, Jarvas had decided that he must be amassing a hoard, to buy himself – what? Companionship? Security? Escape from the rootless life of poverty that was his lot? Now, though, it had become clear that Grince had extended the scope of his operations for another purpose. He had been rehearsing last night's job. Pendral had deprived the thief of what he loved best in the world, and ever since that day Grince had been planning his revenge on the High Lord of Nexis.

A shiver ran through Jarvas's bony frame. Poor Grince! He had his faults, it was true, and he had certainly been in the wrong to steal those jewels, but the danger into which he'd put himself made the big man's heart quail. Petty criminals might be flogged, or set to work for a number of days or months with the gangs of labourers who were gradually rebuilding the damaged areas of the city. For such a serious crime as stealing from Lord Pendral, however, there could be only one penalty. Tomorrow, if he had been arrested, they would cut off Grince's hands.

By the time he finally reached the garrison plateau, the muscles in Jarvas's calves were beginning to knot in cramp, and his face was running with sweat. He was badly out of breath, but there was no time to stop and recover. With every passing minute he had grown increasingly certain that Grince had been caught. Each morning, the names of the miscreants who had been arrested the previous day were posted on the gates of the garrison, and though he dreaded the tidings he was about to receive it was better to know at once – though his knowing would make little difference to the thief, who would be doomed in any case. Jarvas sighed and braced himself. Turning right, he left the steps and made his way towards the garrison as fast as his aching legs would carry him.

The postings went up at dawn, with those who'd been arrested the previous day listed in order of the severity of their crimes – and with the consequent penalties they would suffer. A small knot of people were already clustered in front of the great, arched garrison gates. Some wept silently, while others cursed and shouted abuse, from a safe distance, at the two stone-faced sentries who stood there on guard duty. Now that he was finally here, Jarvas felt an uneasy reluctance to go any further. Cursing himself for a coward, he gritted his teeth and began to shoulder his way through the crowd, towards the ominous square of white that was pinned to the heavy timbers.

There were not many names that day – a number of floggings and one execution, for tomorrow's dawn, but no Grince. Jarvas sagged with relief and felt his weary knees begin to buckle. Groping like a blind man he pushed his way back out of the crowd. Suddenly feeling as though a huge weight had been lifted from his shoulders, he stumbled down the street towards the Invisible Unicorn. Had his legs been working properly, he felt as though he might have danced.

When Jarvas arrived at the tavern, formerly run-down and dingy, he was impressed, as always, by its current look of cleanliness and prosperity, with its sparkling windows, gleaming paintwork and new shutters. The taproom, once so rough and dirty, was a haven of warmth and comfort, and a gleaming new wooden counter stretched across the far side of the room. Behind the counter, in the host's position and radiating contentment and good cheer, stood Hargorn.

The taproom was already beginning to fill with its regular early-morning customers who came for breakfast – mostly traders and labourers from the city, and the occasional garrison soldier just off the night watch. Nowadays, the Unicorn had become one of the most popular inns in the city. Despite his advancing years, Hargorn maintained a reputation as a man who could take care of both himself and his premises. After the vanishment of the Magefolk, the veteran had decided to retire from military life, and had taken on the tavern in partnership with – of all unlikely people – Vannor's old cook Hebba.

When Lord Vannor had returned to the city following the disappearance of the Mages, his cook had come with him, but not to stay. She had hatched a plan with Hargorn when the veteran had forsworn the sword, and with generous assistance from Vannor they had purchased the Unicorn, which in its finer days had been the favourite haunt of the troopers – Hargorn in particular. During the depredations and shortages of Miathan's rule the tavern near the garrison had become badly run-down, but in their hands the business had soon begun to flourish.

Hargorn and Hebba seemed an odd combination, particularly to those who knew the couple well. How would the practical, laconic, imperturbable soldier ever manage to put up with the vapours, panics and incessant chatter of the rotund little cook? How could such a fussy, houseproud woman ever stand for his rough soldier's ways, learned during a lifetime spent in barracks and camps? But though it was only a business partnership it had gone from strength to strength.

Word soon got round the citizens of Nexis that they would find the warmest of welcomes at the Unicorn. Hargorn had been a well-respected and popular soldier at the garrison. He was easy to get along with, and one way and another he had been specializing in ale for most of his life. He was qualified in every respect to be the host of an alehouse – right down to his ability to deal with any trouble that might arise.

Hebba had turned the tavern's interior into a haven of homely comfort, with sparkling brass lamps replacing the dim rushlights of former days, and the scarred old tables polished each day to a blinding sheen. Not only that, but she believed in mothering her customers, which included feeding them. The meals she served had become a legend throughout the city.

Hargorn had been a good friend to Jarvas over these last difficult years, and, in addition, his tavern was also a trading post of gossip and rumour, information and innuendo. If there had been any word of Grince at all, Jarvas knew he would find it here. Just as he was approaching the counter, however, Hebba came bolting out of the back room in even more of a flutter than usual and pale as if she'd seen a ghost. Grabbing Hargorn's arm in a vicelike grip she reached up on tiptoe and whispered something in his ear.

Jarvas saw his friend's expression alter from the usual look of long-suffering patience with which he greeted Hebba's fussing. Hargorn blanched, and went absolutely rigid, swaying alarmingly on his feet as though he had received a blow. For a dreadful moment, Jarvas thought the older man was about to have some kind of seizure, and then Hargorn seemed to collect himself all of a sudden. His face split into the biggest grin that Jarvas had ever seen and he grabbed hold of Hebba, lifting her right off her feet and dancing her round in the confined space behind the bar, oblivious of her shrill protests and squeaks of alarm. The room rang with cheers, jeers and cat-calls as customers began to whistle and applaud. Hargorn, beaming all over his face, looked up and noticed his audience at last. 'What are you lot all staring at?' he demanded belligerently, and there was a sudden clatter of knife on plate as the regulars turned back to their food with great industry and interest. The Unicorn was such a pleasant, homely place that no one wanted to get on the bad side of the landlord.

As Hargorn called a young woman who was wiping tables in a corner to come and take his place, Jarvas remembered why he had come here, and realized that he was about to lose his chance of speaking to the landlord. 'Ho, Hargorn. Wait!' he shouted, rushing up to the counter. Hargorn, already vanishing into the back room, still with his arm around Hebba, half turned with an impatient sigh. 'Not now, Jarvas. Can't you see I'm busy?'

'But . . .'

'Not *now*, I said. Whatever it is, it'll have to wait. Look, get Sallana to give you a drink, and Hebba will fetch you some breakfast. I'll be back in a little while, I promise.'

'Plague take it, will you just *listen* for a minute. Grince has stolen Lord Pendral's jewel collection and the guards are combing the city for him right now!'

Though the veteran's grin faded a little, he looked completely unsurprised. 'Well, Jarvas, the way the daft beggar was acting, it was inevitable that something like this would happen sooner or later.'

'Curse you – is that all you can say? It was bound to happen sooner or later?' Jarvas demanded angrily.

The grin returned to Hargorn's face. 'What I can say and what I can do are two different things. Stop scowling like that, man – your face is ugly enough without making it worse. Keep your mouth shut and come with me.'

Hargorn ushered Jarvas down a short corridor and into a cosy sitting room with comfortable padded chairs and a bright fire crackling in the hearth. As Jarvas entered the room a tall figure pushed him aside, almost knocking him off his feet, and hurtled past him through the doorway to envelop the landlord in an enormous hug. He was even more surprised when Hargorn, who never stood for any trouble in his tavern, did not throw his assailant off the premises; and was totally astounded to see that the tall figure was a woman in warrior's garb. Hargorn – not usually known to his customers as an emotional man – was hugging her and laughing and crying all at once.

'Gods, lass, but you're a sight for sore eyes – I never thought

I'd live to see this day! And Anvar too! You know, I had a wager of fifty silver pieces with Parric that you'd come back to us!' As he mentioned the cavalry master, the joy in Hargorn's face dimmed for a moment, and Aurian had not missed the way he had raked the room with his eyes on entering – in the hope, she suspected, of seeing Maya. But now Hargorn was pulling her towards the fire, without, as yet, giving her a chance to speak. 'You look terrible, Aurian – terrible weary, I mean. Here – come and sit down, lovey. Rest before I start on you with all my questions. Let me get you some beer.'

Aurian didn't protest as Hargorn led her to one of the deep chairs by the hearth. She stretched out her legs before the blaze, and closed her eyes. When her old friend thrust a deep, brimming tankard of ale into her hands, she felt as though she had just sailed through a hurricane and battled her way to a peaceful shore at last.

It was thanks to Grince that they had managed to get here at all. With Finbarr still confused and disorientated, and both the Mage and Forral suffering in their different ways from Aurian's attack on the soldiers, the thief had taken charge. He had brought them out of the Academy and into the city, using the sewers as far as they were passable, and then using one of his own secret routes via little-used ginnels and byways, taking occasional short cuts through back yards and derelict houses. Shia and Khanu had accompanied their human friends by a tortuous but less conspicuous route over rooftops and along the tops of walls. After the precipitous slopes of Steelclaw, they found human structures no challenge to their climbing prowess. Without drawing attention to themselves, the companions had approached the Unicorn through the alleyway at the rear, and entered at the back door, practically terrifying Hebba out of her wits.

Aurian took a deep swig of Hargorn's excellent ale. On the other side of the room she could hear Grince greeting the ugly man who had come in search of him, and Forral trying to convince his old friend that despite appearances he was truly not Anvar. The Mage was content to leave them to it and snatch a few blessed moments of peace, for she was weary indeed, and racked by guilt over her use of magic to slay Pendral's soldiers. The act of violence had contravened everything she had been brought up to believe – it was the action of a Miathan or an Eliseth, but not herself. This was not the first time she had used her magic to kill a helpless Mortal – well she remembered her voyage to the south, and her slaying of the men who had tried to slaughter the Leviathan. Yet it could not be avoided, either this time or the last, and done was done.

Aurian knew, however, that there would be a penalty to pay. Last time, on the ship, she had given her position away to Miathan and he had sent his storm with devastating effect. What would happen this time, she didn't dare imagine. She could only wait, and pray that those she loved would not be the ones to suffer for her deed.

Out of the whole sorry business, it was Forral's attitude that caused Aurian most distress. You'd think that as a soldier he, of all people, would have understood the necessity, the Mage thought bitterly. What gives him the right to judge?

'He has never seen you wield such power.' The voice that entered Aurian's thoughts belonged to Shia. 'You tended to keep your magic apart from your life with him – except once . . .' The cat sounded puzzled. 'He's remembering something about you and rain – and for some reason he was angry with you then, too. But he is angry with himself more than with you, because while he knows in his heart that you did what you must, your power makes him afraid.' The cat laid back her ears in disgust. 'Humans! If I live to be older than Hreeza I'll never understand them!'

'Just a minute.' Aurian looked at the great cat. 'Shia, how do you know all this?'

Shia would not meet her eyes. 'How do you think?' she said at last. 'That man has stolen Anvar's body – the physical form of a Mage. It still possesses Anvar's powers – including the means to communicate with me. The fool has no idea of his new abilities, though – he doesn't know how to shield his thoughts. I'm surprised you haven't heard them yourself . . .'

'What?' Aurian interrupted. 'You've been *eavesdropping*?'

'Yes I have, and I don't intend to stop, either,' said Shia unrepentantly. 'I don't trust him, Aurian – *you* might, but *I* do not.'

The Mage looked deep into the golden eyes of her friend, and knew it would be pointless to argue. Besides, who could say that Shia was not right?

'Aurian, where is Maya?' Hargorn's voice interrupted her train of thought.

'She came through the transition safe and well, but then the Phaerie took her and D'arvan, shortly after we returned to the world.' Aurian knew there was no point in hiding, or even trying to soften, the truth.

Hargorn swallowed hard. 'I'm going after her,' he said flatly. 'First Parric and Vannor, and now Maya – I'm going to find the lair of those Phaerie vermin if it's the last thing I do. Even if I fail, at least I'll still be with my friends.'

The Mage laid a hand on his arm. 'There'll be time for that,' she said softly. 'The Lord of the Phaerie won't harm D'arvan, and he'll make sure that Maya is safe. If they don't come back soon, I'll be heading up there myself.' She scowled. 'I have a thing or two to dispute with the Forest Lord.'

Hebba's sitting room was stuffed to capacity, though she was not there in person. She had taken one horrified look at Shia and Khanu, and fled with a shriek into the sanctuary of her kitchen. Aurian, who had been close friends with Shia for so long that she tended to forget that first impressions of the cat could be terrifying, found herself hoping that the woman would make herself useful while she was there by cooking some food and heating water for baths.

Forral was discovering that his hopes for understanding from Hargorn were in vain. While Aurian was away bathing, he had taken his old friend aside and told him what the Mage had done in the tunnels beneath the Academy. Hargorn's reaction came as a surprise.

'Well, you can say what you like, Forral, but I think you're a bloody fool,' the veteran said bluntly. 'Honest, I don't know what you're getting so upset about – you said yourself there was no way any of those soldiers could be allowed to escape. Dead is dead – what's the difference between Aurian dropping the roof on their heads and you running a sword through their guts?'

'Magic is the difference,' the swordsman insisted. 'Don't you see – those men had no chance to fight back? They never even knew what happened to them. Aurian is leading herself along a dangerous road with this business. Her actions were the very abuse of magical power that she's fighting *against*!'

'And don't you think the poor lass knows that?' Hargorn retorted. 'I could see it in her face – and knowing Aurian, it'll take her far longer to forgive herself than it'll take you to forgive her.' He sighed. 'Forral, you've been away too long. I think you've built up some notion of a perfect Aurian who never existed. You know as well as I do that in war we all do things we're not proud of, and you've forgotten that Aurian has been at war for a very long time now – a weird, inhuman war where there are no great battles, and most of the skirmishes go unseen by our Mortal eyes. I'm not excusing what she did – it's worrying, I agree. But so long as she doesn't start making a habit of it, I don't think you should fret about it too much. I think she's learned a lesson today.'

Forral opened his mouth to protest, but before he could say a word Hargorn forestalled him. 'Now you listen to me, Forral. You tell me you're disappointed in Aurian. How much more must she be disappointed in *you*? When she felt bad she knew she could always count on you, no matter what. You can't just suddenly reappear and start judging her like this. She's managed well enough without you for a long time now – or is that what's really eating at you?'

The swordsman scowled. 'Now look here . . .'

'No, you look. Instead of getting angry at me now, just think about it for a while. And for the gods' sake, and your own, make up your quarrel – if quarrel you can call it – with Aurian. She needs you, Forral, as she's never needed you before, and you can keep her out of trouble far more easily if the two of you are friends.'

Forral sighed. 'I suppose you're right, Hargorn. You old bugger – when did you become so wise and sensible?'

The veteran grinned. 'Living with Dulsina, Vannor's woman, if you must know. I got to know her when we were both with the rebels.' He shook his head sadly. 'It just about broke her when Vannor was taken by the Phaerie. Afterwards, she came here to stay with Hebba and me for a while, but then she went to the Nightrunners – that's where she is now. Zanna is taking good care of her.'

To the Mage's delight, the redoubtable Hebba had provided baths for those who wanted them, in a scullery behind the main kitchen where a blazing fire heated the water in the copper set into the side of the wide fireplace. A pile of clean clothing that looked approximately the right size was folded on a chair nearby, and several towels were warming on the drying rack above the fireplace. Aurian, soaking in a hot tub with the cold tankard balanced on the rim, felt her heart beginning to warm to Hebba. The kindly woman had thought of everything, and the Mage was reminded, with a wistful pang, of Nereni. She wondered what Eliizar's wife was doing now – and how she was enjoying the surprise gift that Aurian had left for her at their parting.

When the Mage came out of the scullery, still drying her hair, she found that Hargorn had managed to master his shock at seeing Forral in a different body. He and the swordsman were deep in talk, and Aurian smiled to herself, touched by the quiet, undemonstrative pleasure they clearly found in each other's company.

Forral looked up and saw her. Hargorn gave him a vicious dig with his elbow, and he held out his arms. 'I'm sorry, lass, for blaming you so harshly,' he said simply. 'I wasn't thinking straight.'

Aurian went to him, but instead of embracing him she stood back and took his hands in her own. Somehow she couldn't bear to have Anvar's arms around her when another soul looked out from behind his blue eyes. 'Do you recall that first day we met, and you told me off for playing with fireballs in the wood? Do you remember what I said?'

The swordsman grinned. 'Aye, you wretch – you said it was an emergency.'

'Well, it was an emergency today, too. I know it was wrong – I just couldn't think of another way.'

Forral sighed. 'I know, lass. But don't be tempted to do it again. Remember what happened to you the *next* time I caught you playing with fireballs.'

'Indeed!' Aurian snorted. 'You'd have your work cut out to do *that* again!' And, feeling lighter of heart, she suddenly embraced him after all. It had taken a while, but now she was getting used to the idea she could admit to herself that she was glad to have Forral back, though she still missed Anvar desperately. His absence was a constant, unalleviated ache inside, and she knew that the pain would never leave her until she could hold him in her arms once more. If only Forral could stay without sacrificing Anvar, Aurian thought with a sigh. There must be a way out of this dilemma – but I'm damned if I know what it could be.

'Listen, Grince.' Jarvas's ugly face creased in a frown. 'I want to talk about you in private, while everyone is distracted.'

Grince's heart sank. While Jarvas was, at heart, a gentle soul, he had an uncertain temper and an uncompromising way of looking at the world. The thief wondered if his escapade the previous night had upset the big man, and if he would be going home tonight with more bruises to add to his collection.

Jarvas took the thief by the elbow and drew him into a quiet corner. 'Grince – I've known you since you were a lad, and frankly, it's about time someone made you pull yourself together.' Jarvas was frowning, his ugly face furrowed in concern. 'Look,' he went on, 'I don't blame you. Everybody round here knows what a bastard Lord Pendral is. I know what he did to you, and I understand why you want revenge. But don't you understand what you've done? Pendral has his troop of armed bullies combing the city for the jewel thief, and even if you give the jewels back now it won't make any difference. He'll never rest until he tracks you down – and he's bound to catch up with you sooner or later. You've put yourself in deadly danger, lad. I'm afraid you'll have to disappear for a while – and fast.'

Grince stared at Jarvas in dismay. Bent on revenge as he was, he had never truly considered the repercussions of his action. What a fool he had been. He had dug his own grave last night, if word got back to Pendral.

Jarvas put a big, rough hand on the thief's shoulder. 'Don't fret,' he said kindly. 'We'll get you out of this yet. Pendral's men won't come in here, so you're safe enough for now . . .'

'I can make arrangements to smuggle him out of Nexis,' Hargorn put in. He turned to the others. 'And sorry though I'll be to lose you so soon, I think you'd better go with Grince. Neither Eliseth nor Miathan is here, Aurian – you must seek them elsewhere. And with Pendral running the city, you'll be better off away from here before you draw the wrong kind of attention. Jarvas is right – Pendral's men won't be in a hurry to search this place – in fact I doubt that they'll search here at all. They value the Unicorn far too highly – it's their haven away from the barracks. They won't want to risk offending me.'

Grince felt the cold hand of fear close around him at the idea of leaving the city for the first time in his life. 'But where can I go?' he protested. 'How will I live?'

Hargorn grinned. 'Don't worry,' he said. 'The Nightrunners will take good care of you. They can probably use someone with your talents.'

Aurian was grinning. 'You sly old fox! That's where you get your spirits, isn't it?'

Hargorn looked injured. 'Of course it is! What do you take me for? Did you think I'd be daft enough to pay that bastard Pendral's levies? What's more, I have a consignment coming in this very night.'

Aurian's heart had leapt at the mention of the Nightrunners. 'Hargorn – what about Wolf? Have you seen him? Is he all right?'

The innkeeper's expression clouded. 'Parric told me about Wolf,' he said softly. 'I'm sorry, Aurian, Forral. Wolf is not with the Nightrunners, I'm afraid. On the day you left for the Vale, the wolves that were guarding him vanished with the cub. No one has seen them since.'

For an instant, Aurian's heart stopped beating. It felt as though the earth had opened up beneath her feet. 'No,' she whispered.

Unseeing, she felt Forral take her hand. 'It's all right, love.' The Mage heard a catch in his voice. 'We'll find him, never fear. He's a tough little lad by all accounts, and you got him safely through all the dangers that beset you when you were carrying him. You didn't go through all that to lose him now.'

'You don't understand,' Aurian cried. 'His foster-parents were southern wolves, lost in a strange country and far from their pack. They had no territory of their own and no other wolves to help rear a cub. It's likely that the native wolves would kill them – and Wolf along with them.'

Forral squeezed her hand so tightly that it seemed the bones would break. 'Now listen,' he said firmly. 'Likely isn't certain, and I refuse to believe my son is dead until events prove otherwise. Remember, love – I told you, many years ago, to do the first thing first and the rest would follow?'

Without looking at him, Aurian nodded.

'Well, that's what we're going to do. First we'll get to the bottom of what's been happening in Nexis, then we'll rescue Parric. *Then* we'll find Wolf – and after that, we'll deal with Eliseth and the grail. How does that sound?'

Aurian took courage from his words. She took a deep breath, and gave him a grateful smile. 'When you put it like that, it sounds like a superb plan.'

Forral did not let go of her hand. 'It *will* be all right, love,' he said in a low voice. 'You've got to keep believing that. All the time I was haunting Death's domain, I never saw anyone like Wolf pass through. It's my guess he's still alive – and so long as he's alive we'll find him, if we have to look behind every blade of grass from here to the northern ice.'

The Mage could not help but be cheered by the magnificent meal Hebba had prepared, with soup, a roast goose, root vegetables and late-summer greens, all washed down with peerless ale from Hargorn's barrel. Everyone sat around the large kitchen table, save for the cats, who were in the nearby scullery making short work of a pig that had been slaughtered especially for them by the generous Hargorn.

After the first few mouthfuls, Hebba, who had begun the meal in a strained and watchful silence, with many dubious glances towards Hargorn's unnerving collection of visitors, soon found herself beaming and blushing beneath a barrage of compliments. Aurian gave her wholehearted attention to the

207

food on her plate. It seemed an endless age since she'd eaten a decent meal – and she hadn't eaten one as good as this since Queen Raven's coronation feast.

Finally, as Hebba was clearing the empty plates away, Hargorn filled their tankards with more of his excellent brew. 'Now,' he said. 'Let's see if we can find you all some gear – clothes, blankets and the like, to tide you over. We can always talk during the journey.'

'What?' Aurian exclaimed in delight. 'You're coming with us?'

'Only as far as the Nightrunners,' he told her. 'I have some folk there I want to see in any case, and I'll probably escort Dulsina back here.' He looked significantly at Hebba, who was busy bustling back and forth, and laid a finger to his lips. Aurian realized, with a sinking heart, that the old warrior was thinking about picking up his sword once more. Hargorn had no intention of returning to the Unicorn.

14

Heir and Hostage

Maya was awakened by the sound of voices and many foot-steps passing by Licia's shelter. 'What's happening?' she asked drowsily.

'It's the labourers,' the lacemaker told her. 'They're home for the night.'

'What?' Slowly, the warrior's sleep-fuddled wits returned to her. Scrambling to her feet she peered out of the shelter to see a ragged trickle of weary workers trailing past her door. As Maya scanned the passing faces, a small, familiar figure caught her eye. For a moment she could not believe it. 'Parric?' Filling her lungs, she summoned the battleground bellow that Forral had taught her. '*Parric*!'

Down the street, there was a stir among the crowd. 'Get out of the bloody way, will you?' Maya grinned as she heard that familiar testy voice. 'Gods blast you to perdition, *let me through*!' Then two burly labourers went staggering, one to either side, and the short, wiry form of the cavalry master came bursting through between them.

Parric stopped dead when he saw her, his face blank with shock. Then without a word he ran to Maya, and caught her up in an embrace that almost broke her ribs. They stood there for a long time, without speaking, too deep in the emotions of their reunion for words.

The cavalry master shared a dormitory cavern with two dozen other labourers, so for privacy they retired to Licia's shelter. The lacemaker was very good about it. 'If we can't help one another now and then it's a poor look-out. Why, we'd be no better than those steel-eyed cold-blooded bastards who call themselves our masters.'

Maya shook her head reprovingly. 'Licia, to look at you a person would never imagine that you knew such language.'

The lacemaker blushed, and gave a sheepish shrug. 'Well as a matter of fact I didn't. Back in Nexis I was just an old maid; prim, proper and plain – before I wound up here and started mixing with these reprobate warriors.'

'Anyway, being stuck here with these whoreson Phaerie would make anyone swear,' Parric added in support.

Since it was the hour of the evening when the food would be handed out, Licia offered, with kindly tact, to leave them alone for a time while she went to fetch the rations for all three of them. Parric told the warrior of Vannor's insane behaviour, and the disastrous campaign with the Phaerie that had followed, then Maya quickly sketched the details of all that had happened since she had left Nexis so very long ago, to take D'arvan to the Vale. She then brought him up to the present with the tale of her re-emergence with Aurian through the gate in Time, and the abduction of herself and D'arvan by the Forest Lord.

When she had finished, Parric gave a long, low whistle. 'You spent all that time as a *unicorn*? It beggars belief!'

'Well, that's what happened,' Maya assured him. 'And now, I'm just wondering what Hellorin will have in store for D'arvan and myself *this* time.' As she spoke, she fingered the chain around her neck. 'Anyway,' she added in a brisker tone, 'that's *my* story. What I still don't understand is, what happened to you and Vannor? What in Chathak's name possessed the fool to make war on the Phaerie?'

Parric shook his head. 'I could never fathom it. Truly, Maya, you could hardly even call it an attack. They just waited until we'd worn ourselves out tramping all the way up here, then threw some kind of magical field around us and mopped us up from the air. That was when Sangra died.' His face creased with the memory of old pain. 'You know, old Vannor always had sense. He used to be a good man – a man I liked and respected. I knew him as well as anyone when we were with the rebels, and for the life of me, I can't imagine why he'd be so stupid as to attack the Phaerie. He must have known what the cost would be in human lives, and even if he didn't there were plenty of folk to tell him – me included, not to mention Dulsina, and you know how much influence *she* always had with him. Not this time, though. The whole business eventually drove them apart, in fact. It was as though . . .' He shrugged. 'You'll probably think I'm daft, Maya, but at that time it seemed as though he wasn't himself any more – the old Vannor had disappeared completely. It was just like talking to a stranger – and a nasty piece of work at that.'

Parric sighed, and shook his head. 'Well, he won his way in the end. To tell you the truth, everyone was a bit afraid of him by then. You got the feeling he'd be capable of anything – anything at all. It was as though that poison had somehow addled his wits . . .'

'What poison?' Maya asked sharply. 'Someone tried to poison Vannor?'

'Oh, I forgot you didn't know about that. Someone did – we still don't know who it was, but they bloody nearly succeeded . . .'

Maya listened, appalled, as Parric told her of the attempt on Vannor's life, and the earthquake that had followed soon afterwards. 'So that's what caused all the damage,' she murmured. 'I thought it must have been the Phaerie.'

'Oh, the Phaerie caused enough, by all accounts,' the cavalry master retorted bitterly. 'Our attack on them – if you can call it that – seemed to stir them up good and proper.'

'It certainly did.' Licia's voice came from the open doorway. She walked across to the table and put down the food she was carrying, then turned to face the others, her expression bleak as the memories crowded round her. 'They swept down on Nexis that night like the wrath of all the gods,' she said quietly. 'No one was expecting it, and what chance did we have, with all our best warriors already away? They took men and women both – the only limit to their depredations seemed to be the number of folk they could carry off.'

Her fingers clenched tightly around the edge of the table behind her. 'The ones who were taken were lucky – for every one they seized, three more were killed, in the streets or in their beds. Ah, it was easier for me than for some folk. At least I had no family to mourn . . . I saw them trample little children beneath the hooves of their great horses, with no more thought or remorse than you or I would have in swatting a fly.

211

People were screaming, buildings were burning . . .' she shook her head. 'It was too dreadful to describe. They broke into Lord Vannor's mansion, I heard, and took him too – though we never see him. He's imprisoned somewhere else, up in the citadel.'

Licia's voice grew hard. 'Just as well for him – I think if he was sent down here, the folk would tear him limb from limb. I only hope he had a chance to see what I saw, as they bore him off. If there's any justice in this world, it should haunt him for the rest of his days –'

Her words broke off as a shadow darkened the doorway of the shelter. Some half-dozen Phaerie guards stood there, tall, grim, and forbidding. To Maya's astonishment, one of them was holding a bundle of clothing. 'You two.' One of them indicated Parric and Maya. 'You are summoned. Come with us.'

'Dear gods have mercy!' D'arvan exclaimed. 'What have you done to him?'

'I? Nothing.' Drawing his sword, Hellorin gently prodded the figure that knelt motionless on the floor. Vannor swayed at the jab of the blade, but otherwise did not move, nor did his expression change in the slightest – a pity, D'arvan thought, for beneath the wild tangle of long grey hair and long white beard there was something deeply unnerving about the way the prisoner's face was contorted in a soundless scream of agony.

'How long has he been like this?' the Mage demanded.

Hellorin shrugged. 'Ever since we brought him here – slightly more than a year now, I would say. The night we captured him he shrieked abuse at us and cursed us with the direst of dooms – we locked him up when we returned, and in the morning, when the guard came to fetch him, he was exactly as you see him now. It takes two slaves to feed him, wash him and see to his other needs, and there he stays: uncommunicative, unchanging, lost in some private torment.'

'Why did you bother keeping him alive?' D'arvan asked.

Hellorin shrugged. 'I was curious. Something about that attack on us did not sit right with me. Unless Mortals have changed in some fundamental way in our absence, which I doubt, there seemed no sense to this man's actions. Only someone with powers close to our own would even consider making war upon the Phaerie – only someone with the sheer arrogance and ambition of a Mage, in fact.' Suddenly the Forest Lord swung round, piercing D'arvan with a sharp, shrewd gaze. 'Are you sure this Mortal is all that he seems?'

D'arvan struggled to conceal his shock. 'Aurian told me that Miathan could control another's mind from a great distance,' he admitted, 'but that was with the victim's full consent, apparently. From what I know of Vannor, he would never submit to such an intrusion.'

'Who knows what these Mortals will or will not do?' Hellorin replied with distaste. 'Maya, in all justice, seems sharp-witted enough – from mixing so much with the Magefolk, I've no doubt – but I fear that due to your attachment to her you give the rest of the flock too much credit for intelligence. Do you really believe that a strong-minded Mage might not control a mere Mortal at will?'

'Well, I couldn't,' D'arvan said firmly. 'But then I never wanted to. Besides, if Vannor had been under the control of a Mage, why wouldn't they try to force him to escape from here, or even use him to spy on you?'

'That's what I was hoping you would find out.'

'Me?' gasped the Mage. 'What can I do?'

'Oh, come,' Hellorin said impatiently. 'Mortals are a completely alien species to us Phaerie. You, with your Magefolk ancestry, are that much closer. You could probe his mind, D'arvan, and discover what I could not. As a condition of your co-operation, you asked me to release Vannor. Well, before I do, I want to be certain his mind is unaffected by any trace of Magefolk meddling – if indeed he has any mind left at all. But I will not set him free to plot against me further . . .'

The Forest Lord was interrupted by a respectful tapping on the door. 'Ah – I expect your other Mortals have arrived. Enter,' he added in a louder voice.

'Get your bloody hands off me!' D'arvan heard Maya's voice before he saw her. Then the door burst open and she came hurtling into the room, wearing nothing but an ill-fitting

213

man's shirt that hung down below her knees. Parric followed her, similarly attired and glowering blackly.

Maya rounded on Hellorin like a tigress. 'You treacherous snake,' she spat. 'You slimy son of a pox-ridden harlot! To think I once called you father.'

Hellorin smiled at her. 'Maya, you are a pure delight. You never change.'

'And neither do you,' Maya growled. 'You were a heartless, murdering butcher then and you're still one now.' Seeing his lover's hands clench into fists, D'arvan stepped up quickly and put an arm around her shoulders before she could do something stupid in her rage.

'It's always nice to be appreciated.' Hellorin made her a mocking bow, and headed for the door. 'D'arvan – I leave it to you to explain the bargain you made. My presence seems to be upsetting your Mortals.' With that he was gone.

'*Your* Mortals?' Maya turned to D'arvan, a dangerous glint in her eye, then, just as abruptly, she hugged him. 'Thank the gods you're all right,' she muttered into his shoulder. 'When they brought us up here I didn't know what to expect.'

'We still don't know what to expect.' Parric, ashen-faced, was looking down at Vannor. 'What in the name of perdition have they done to him?'

D'arvan sighed. This wasn't going to be easy. 'According to Hellorin, the Phaerie haven't done anything to him. They found him like that the morning after they captured him.'

'Rubbish!' Parric snapped. 'No one gets a face like that for no reason.'

Maya walked to Vannor's side, and laid a tentative hand on his shoulder, beneath the bird's nest mane of shaggy grey hair. 'Vannor?' Frowning, she touched his face, but he showed not the slightest flicker of reaction.

'Listen to me, both of you.' D'arvan took command. 'Never mind Vannor for a minute, we'll worry about him presently. Sit down and have some wine. We have to talk, the three of us.' He took a deep breath, wondering how he could break the news to his beloved. 'There's no gentle way to tell you this,' he said at last. 'Hellorin demands that I stay here, and take up my duties as his son.'

'*What?*' Maya shouted. 'But you can't! What about Aurian?'

'I have no choice, my love,' the Mage told her flatly. 'Already, the other slaves must have told you the significance of that chain you wear. My father is using you as a hostage for my co-operation. If I don't obey him, he'll kill you.'

For a long moment, a variety of emotions chased across Maya's face: shock, indignation, and rage being paramount. Then, as the horrified silence stretched out between the three of them, D'arvan saw her brows knot together in thought. She looked up at him. 'If Hellorin kills me,' she said slowly, 'then he'll no longer have any hold on you. You can go back and help Aurian.'

The Mage could read the other thought in her mind, the one she had not spoken aloud, as clearly as if it were written on her face. *And if I kill myself, D'arvan will be free.* Striving not to panic, knowing that his next words would decide the matter and desperate to convince her, he reached out and took her hands in his own. 'Maya,' he said gently, 'try not to be hasty. Just listen with an open mind to what I have to say. I've spent a long and wearisome day wrangling with my father over this matter. He's more stubborn than the most mule-headed Mage, but I finally managed to wring some concessions from him – so long as the two of us consent to stay.'

'This had better be good,' Maya growled.

'It's better than nothing – which was what he originally offered me.' D'arvan squeezed her hands tightly. 'I wanted him to liberate the Nexians, but he refused outright. He will, however, release Parric and Vannor to go back and help Aurian . . . if I can manage to free Vannor from his evil trance, that is.'

'Is that *all*?' Maya bristled. 'I can't say I'm very impressed so far with your father's magnanimity.'

D'arvan, however, looked across at Parric and saw his eyes burning with a fierce, joyous, desperate light. Too proud to plead, too level-headed to influence the discussion with an emotional appeal, the cavalry master was rigid with the effort to keep silent, but his heart was in his eyes.

'There's more,' D'arvan told Maya hastily. 'Again, I

215

wanted Hellorin to let the Xandim return to human form, but there was no chance of that. Frankly, he'd rather lose the Nexians. He said, however, that he would agree to disenchant Chiamh and Schiannath, and let them return with Parric.'

'My, how generous,' Maya said bitterly. 'And dare I ask what your father wants in return for these great favours? Am I to remain a slave for the rest of my life? There's something you're not telling me, I know it.'

'Well, he says he'll remove your chain eventually –' D'arvan prudently stepped back out of striking range – 'as soon as we produce a son together.'

'He *what*?' Unexpectedly, Maya burst out laughing, but from the shrill, wild peals D'arvan could sense that her control was very close to the edge. 'Why?' she demanded. 'What in the name of perdition does an immortal, all-powerful magical being want with a bloody *heir*?'

'He wants to extend his realm.'

Maya's laughter ceased abruptly.

'Hellorin wants the Phaerie to rule the entire northern continent,' D'arvan went on into the ensuing silence. 'He wants scions of his own blood to wield power in his name in various regions – that way he feels he'll have better control over the fractious Mortals.'

Narrow-eyed, Parric looked at the Mage with suspicion and undisguised hostility. 'And just where do *you* fit into this grand scheme?' he asked coldly.

D'arvan sighed. He had been dreading this moment. 'He wants me to rule Nexis,' he answered quietly.

Parric kicked the wall of the shelter as hard as he dared with his bare toes. 'That traitor! That thrice-damned backstabbing chicken-hearted turncoat! I might have known we couldn't trust a bloody Mage!'

'For the last time, Parric, will you shut up!' Maya snarled. 'If you hadn't created such an uproar and brought the guards down on us, you stupid fool, we'd have had a chance to discuss it with him.'

'What's to discuss? At heart he's nothing but another power-hungry tyrant, just like the rest of his ilk.'

'Like Aurian, you mean?' For a moment Maya actually thought he would strike her. She had never seen such rage on Parric's face. But though she had felt equally betrayed by D'arvan when he had broken the news to her, she now felt a perverse need to defend her lover in the face of Parric's virulent attack.

Controlling himself with difficulty, the cavalry master turned away in disgust. 'How can you stand there and say that?' he asked in tones of biting contempt. 'Unlike your precious Phaerie stud, I never saw Aurian try to enslave an entire race.'

'It wasn't his idea!' Maya shouted. 'You heard what he said – Hellorin will enslave us anyway! D'arvan was trying to give us a chance . . .' Her voice trailed away into silence as she was struck by the inadvertent truth of her own words.

Licia, an unwilling spectator to the quarrel, seized the moment. 'Parric, I want you to leave, please. Now. You can continue your discussion later, when tempers have cooled.'

'Gladly. I've had enough of listening to this Phaerie-loving garbage in any case.' With one last venomous glare at Maya, Parric stamped out of the shelter, muttering imprecations and pushing his way roughly through the knot of curious bystanders who had gathered near the door.

Maya stood like a statue in the centre of the room, one hand lifted to her lips, her eyes turned inward, blind to her surroundings. 'D'arvan is our only chance,' she murmured softly. 'Our one slim chance to beat Hellorin at his own game . . .' So deep in thought was she that she barely noticed when the lacemaker tiptoed out.

'Please . . . I must see Lord D'arvan.' Maya tried to conceal her annoyance as the guards at the gate looked down their noses at her. Try to *look* respectful, at least, for your own sake, she told herself. She had by no means forgotten the blow they had given her earlier.

'Ah, Lord D'arvan's little lapdog,' the female guard sneered. 'Mortal, you seem to have forgotten your place. You may be assured that when Lord D'arvan wants to see you, he will send for you.'

'But –' Maya got no further.

'You dare dispute with me, Mortal?' The guard's eyes glinted with anger, she made a complex gesture – and the warrior suddenly found herself lapped around from head to foot in the clinging briars of a thorny rose. Instantly, the supple green vines tightened around her body, cutting painfully into her limbs and constricting her breath. As the tendrils tightened further, the long, sharp thorns drove deep into her flesh.

Maya fell writhing to the cavern floor, driving the manifold claws of the rose still deeper beneath her skin. Choking for breath as she was, she could not even scream. Already there was a high-pitched buzzing in her ears and her vision was fading to glittering black . . .

'Curse you, let her go!'

The roar was so loud, so angry, that it penetrated even as far as the deep, dark pit into which Maya was falling. She heard a fierce sizzling sound then a loud crack, like the sound of a spitting spark, followed by a cry of pain. Abruptly, the strangling briars and their piercing thorns were gone, and Maya took a deep draught of sweet, sweet air. With a clang, the gate swung open, and as her vision began to clear she saw D'arvan kneeling over her, his eyes diamond-bright with rage and glittering with unshed tears.

As the Mage scooped her into his arms and bore her from the slave cavern, Maya saw that the female guard lay crumpled against the wall, her face disfigured by a blistered brand as though she had been lashed by a fiery whip.

'Never again,' D'arvan snarled. He raised his voice. 'Hear me, you Phaerie,' he grated. 'If any one of you ever hurts this woman again – if you so much as look at her harshly – I will slowly burn the flesh from every inch of your vile bones. I am the son of the Forest Lord – you know that I can do this. And for your own sakes, you had best believe that I will.'

Maya wanted to tell him how very glad she was to see him, but as yet, she lacked the breath.

When he laid her on the couch in the tower room, Maya gasped in pain as her abraded flesh touched the silken fabric. Her pale skin was mottled with bruises, and each laboured breath scraped harshly in her throat. Though D'arvan as no expert at healing, the Lady Eilin had taught him the techniques to suppress pain and to stop the bleeding and seal the flesh of simple wounds. It was not enough, however, to overcome his guilt. As the tension of pain began to smooth itself from Maya's face, he leapt to his feet and started to pace back and forth across the tower room, unable to face the condemnation that would soon appear in her eyes. 'I wouldn't blame you for hating me,' he told her wretchedly. 'It's all my fault. I should never have let them take you back.'

'Don't talk so daft, love – we don't have time for that.'

D'arvan spun, an astonished exclamation on his lips, to see Maya holding out a hand to him, an expression of fond exasperation on her face. 'Come here and sit down,' she told him in a hoarse, scratchy voice. 'On second thoughts, bring me a drink, *then* sit down.'

'Now,' she said, when he had obeyed her, 'let's get this out of the way once and for all. It's not your fault your father treats his slaves this way, and it wasn't your fault that we were taken back to the cavern – it was because that hothead Parric went and lost his temper.'

'I should have come for you sooner . . .'

'D'arvan, shut up. It's done now – and at least that guard will think twice in future about mistreating Mortals.' Her eyes glinted with malicious glee. 'I liked what you did to her face, by the way – I hope it teaches her a lesson.' She squeezed his hand tightly. 'Anyway, listen. I've been thinking . . .'

D'arvan felt a frisson of unease at her words, like a finger of ice trailed down his spine. He knew Maya well, and he could tell from her brisk, businesslike tone that he wasn't going to like this in the least. He looked down into her beloved face, wishing he could stem the flow of what she was about to say, and knowing already that it would be impossible, and unwise.

Already, Maya was speaking. 'Am I right in believing that it takes Phaerie magic to make the Xandim horses fly?'

Surprised by the direction her thoughts were taking, D'arvan nodded. 'The magic is in the horses and the Phaerie both. Only together can they fly.'

Maya bit her lip and looked away from him, staring out of

219

the window as though fascinated by the reflections of the lamplit room against a black background of midnight sky. 'Then you can do it,' she said at last.

'Do what?'

Maya gripped his fingers tightly, her face aglow with urgency. 'D'arvan, go back to Hellorin and renegotiate. *You* must return to Aurian, and take Chiamh and Schiannath with you. Flying steeds may give Aurian the edge she lacks.'

'Woman, have you lost your mind?' D'arvan exploded. 'Were you not listening when I explained? Hellorin wants me to stay and rule Nexis. I'm his heir, as he calls it – his only son. He'll never let me escape him again!'

'He will if I stay behind as hostage for your return,' Maya argued stubbornly.

D'arvan scowled at her, both angry and alarmed. 'Maya, if you think for one minute that I would be so careless of you as to risk a repetition of what happened tonight . . .'

Maya's eyes sparkled with mischief. 'But I've thought of a way for Hellorin to keep his heir and ensure my own safety. No one would dare hurt me, D'arvan – not if I carried your child.'

15

Wyvernesse

Now that the river no longer ran as far as Nexis, the Nightrunners had been forced to resort to other means to smuggle their goods in and out of the city. Aurian and her companions left that night concealed, along with various artefacts made by Nexian craftsmen, in a row of gaily painted wagons which, to all intents and purposes, appeared to be a travelling carnival. The Mage had to smile at such a fanciful method of moving illicit goods. Zanna's idea, I'll be bound, she thought.

Such a thing would never have happened during the rule of the Magefolk – in fact this was the first travelling carnival that Aurian had ever seen, though Forral told her he could remember them from his childhood. Miathan, objecting to the wayfarers' light-fingered ways and their light-hearted manner that, by their very presence, spread a general air of restlessness and disaffection among the townsfolk, had forbidden them access to Nexis many decades before. They were a good disguise, though – for one thing, there was something very satisfactory in being able to hide in plain sight like this, and for another, respectable folk tended to give the travellers a wide berth. When not parting them from their coin, wayfarers were generally very private folk, defensive and hostile to strangers and outsiders – often with good reason. Also, they had a reputation for being notorious thieves, so people, quite wisely, approached them with wariness, if at all.

'Stop right there!'

Clearly, the caravan had reached the city boundaries. The Mage, huddled in the hay-scented darkness, crossed her fingers as her wagon came to a juddering halt. Now, if we can only get past these accursed guards, she thought. With her ear pressed to the thick planking, she could hear every word of the

221

conversation that was taking place outside.

There was a squeak of leather as the guard walked over to the wagons. 'Who's in charge of this rabble? Identify yourself.'

The second voice was rich and mellifluous – and very, very loud. 'I, sir, am the Great Mandzurano,' it declaimed. 'I am the master of this exceptional troupe.'

Aurian grinned. She had only met the Great Mandzurano briefly, but she had already discovered that he was a former sailmaker's son from Easthaven, and his name was actually Thalbutt. She had been surprised to discover that many of the jugglers, acrobats, conjurers and trick-riders came from similar backgrounds, lured by the romance of the wandering life.

Outside the wagon, the guard seemed less than impressed with the carnival folk. 'Really?' he said in acid tones. 'Well, Master Mandzurano, kindly tell your exceptional troupe to get their arses out of those wagons right now. We're looking for the thief that robbed Lord Pendral. Get a move on, there! I've a search to conduct, and I don't have all bloody night.'

'My good man, are you insinuating –'

'No – I'm telling you. No respectable folk would feel a pressing need to be leaving the city in the middle of the night. You wayfarers are always up to no good, and tonight is no exception, I'll be bound. Get your rabble out here now, or I'll arrest the lot of you.'

In the darkness of the wagon, Aurian smiled to herself. Apparently Mandzurano had a particularly aggravating effect on persons in authority. It was good to have something to smile about, she thought ruefully. It was suffocatingly hot and desperately cramped in her hiding place, crammed as she was in the darkness together with Hargorn and all of her companions, including the little thief she had rescued the previous night. If they managed to get out of the city, however, all the discomfort would be well worthwhile. They would soon find out.

'Come on, you lot. Everybody out!' The guards were walking along the wagons, clouting the wooden sides with their sword hilts. Aurian could hear a ragged chorus of complaints and oaths as the carnival folk hauled themselves reluctantly outside. Angry accusations and outraged protests marked the progress of the search. As the guards drew gradually nearer to her hiding place, Aurian clenched her fists tightly around the hilt of her sword, unable to bear the agonizing tension of this wait.

The guard had reached her wagon. The Mage could hear his voice directly outside. 'And what's in here, that you've got it locked up so tight? Come on, let's have it open!'

'Please, sir – do not open that door if you value your life,' Mandzurano was protesting. 'There are dangerous wild beasts within!'

'Dangerous wild beasts, indeed! Pull the other one, master. As if some ragged-arsed bunch of travelling vagabonds would have real wild beasts . . .'

Within the wagon, Shia and Khanu waited until the man's hand was actually on the latch. As he began to pull back the bolt, they broke into a deafening cacophony of bloodcurdling roars and snarls.

'Thara's titties!' shrieked the guard. Even above the row, Aurian heard the bolt go crashing back into its socket. As the wagons moved on again, she buried her face in her sleeve and shook with laughter.

Aurian was awakened by the noon sun in her eyes, shining through the open doorway of a small and gaily striped tent. She felt wonderfully snug and relaxed in her cocoon of blankets, warmed by the two guardian cats who slept on either side of her. In the background she could hear the soothing burble of a stream mingled with a murmur of low voices and the sharp crackle of burning twigs. The glorious piercing song of a skylark rained down like a shower of silver from far above her head. The Mage felt her spirits rise with the sound. How good it was, to be back in the living world!

A whiff of frying bacon drove her from her blankets, and as she emerged into the open she was struck by the chill of the moorland air. Although it was summer, there was no warmth at all in these northern uplands, not even in the midday sun. The camping place was in the bottom of a secret dell, formed and sheltered by three swelling green hills, with a stream for water and thickets of bramble, gorse and whin to provide fuel, swift-burning though it be – enough for a small cookfire, at least. The colourful wagons had been drawn together in a sheltering semicircle near the banks of the stream. The horses, almost as colourful as the wagons, being mainly piebald, skewbald or spotted, were picketed nearby.

Most of the carnival folk were up and about, moving drowsily from tent to wagon in what was clearly a regular routine, as the striped canvas shelters were struck with the swift ease of long practice. The Mage hid her cold hands in her sleeves and looked around for her companions. Grince was nowhere in sight but Finbarr – or rather, the Wraith that was occupying Finbarr's body – she spotted immediately, sitting huddled in the lee of a wagon, his cloak wrapped tightly around him. Though its borrowed corporeal shell could be nourished in the normal way, Aurian wondered, with a pang of disquiet, how soon the creature would need to feed, now that she had removed the spell that had taken it out of time.

Beyond the wagons, Forral was exercising Anvar's body, sparring with a wiry young carnival lad using wooden staves. Aurian turned away and went to the fire, where Hargorn and the Great Mandzurano were engaged in the homely task of frying bacon.

'Aurian, lovey.' As Hargorn rose to greet her, Aurian noticed how happy he looked to be out of the city, out of retirement, and back to a soldier's outdoor life again. 'Sleep well?' he asked her. 'There's some taillin in the pot there, by the fire's edge.'

'Thanks, Hargorn.' The Mage poured taillin into a tin mug and cupped her hands around it, appreciating the warmth that leaked into her frozen fingers. 'I slept wonderfully well – surprisingly well, in fact. I think it was pure relief at getting out of Nexis – the city has turned into an evil place since I was last there.' She shook her head. 'I could feel it in the air the whole time: the sense that dreadful things have already happened – and far worse is yet to come.'

Hargorn, his grey hair bound back in the neat tail he had always worn as a warrior, handed her a tin plate laden with bacon fried crisp and a large, soft hunk of bread. 'I couldn't agree more. I didn't even realize how bad it had become until I left last night. It felt as though a huge weight had been lifted off me.' He shook his head. 'I'd as soon sell the Unicorn and get right out of the place, but I worry about Hebba. I know she would never leave Nexis again.'

Forral joined them, his face gleaming with a sheen of sweat and his chest heaving. 'Out of condition,' he panted.

Aurian put down her plate. 'Anvar was a Mage, not a warrior,' she said shortly. 'Have a care you don't do yourself some permanent damage . . .' She swallowed what she had been about to say, but her unspoken words hung in the air between them as though illuminated in letters of fire: *because it's Anvar's body, and some day he may want it back.*

Hargorn broke into the strained silence. 'Now then, what do you say to us getting on our way? Now we're safely out of Nexis, Thalbutt – sorry, Mandzurano – can give us horses and we can travel to Wyvernesse far quicker than the caravan.'

'Sounds good to me.' Aurian scrambled to her feet. 'Has anyone seen Grince this morning?'

Hargorn and Aurian finally ran the thief to ground in one of the wagons. His skilled fingers had located the catch for one of the secret compartments that the smugglers used, and he was now prying into a variety of boxes and bales that had been sneaked out of Nexis under the very eyes of the guards.

'Grince!' thundered the Mage. 'What do you think you're doing?'

Grince started violently, then turned round with a broad smile and a carefully studied air of nonchalance. 'Just looking.' He shrugged. 'My compliments, Master Mandzurano. You wayfarers are very clever folk. Who would have thought that all this could be hidden in an innocent-looking wagon?'

Mandzurano preened himself. 'The guards are looking for items pilfered from townsfolk, you see, not contraband . . .'

Aurian, however, went on looking severely at Grince, until he began to fidget uncomfortably beneath her relentless gaze. 'We don't steal from our friends,' she said.

Grince leapt to his feet. Digging deep in his pockets, he hurled a handful of small items to the wagon's wooden floor.

225

'I don't have any friends.' He pushed past her, jumped to the ground and ran.

Stooping, Aurian sifted through the scattered objects – a pathetic collection of painted trinkets, cheap copper bracelets and carved wooden combs. 'There wasn't even anything of value here.' Looking in the direction Grince had fled, she shook her head sadly.

Hidden from curious eyes among the rolling swells of the northern moorland, the small group of travellers made their way swiftly eastwards. For Grince, who had never ridden a horse before, the journey was an experience he could well have done without. There was no time for him to learn horsemanship – all he could do was cling to the saddle and bump painfully along, while one of the others took his reins and led him as though he were a small child. It was utterly humiliating – but had only his pride been hurt, Grince could have put up with it. The aches and bruises, however, were a far more serious matter. During the first day he must have fallen off a dozen times at least, and on one unforgettable occasion the horse tossed him right into a bramble thicket.

'Serves him right,' Hargorn had muttered as the Mage struggled to disentangle the cursing, yelping thief from the mesh of thorny briars. The veteran had still not forgiven Grince for attempting to steal from the smugglers. 'Maybe that'll make up for the thrashing you wouldn't let me give him, Aurian.'

Nursing his hurts and scratches, Grince glowered at the veteran who was riding up ahead and hauling him along as though towing a cart. The horse didn't like such treatment either, Grince could tell from its laid-back ears and the direful expression in its rolling eyes. The minute Hargorn lets go of those reins, he thought ruefully, with a sinking sense of the inevitable, this accursed creature will fling me off its back again, and I'll have even more bruises to add to those it's given me already.

Much to Grince's dismay, they rode on well into the night, navigating by the stars and seeing their way by the merest sliver of moonlight. Aurian, with her Mage's vision, rode ahead to pick out the easiest path. The two cats, who tended to scare the horses if they came too close, flanked the procession well out on either side. The thief was so exhausted that despite his hurts he fell into a half-doze, half-reverie as the miles passed by. His mind went back to earlier that day, when he had run from the smugglers' camp.

Having more sense than to lose himself in the bleak, trackless wilderness, Grince had followed the course of the stream up between the hills, until all sight and sound of the encampment had vanished. Damn them! He hurled a stone into the stream with all the force he could muster. Why had he left the city with these cold-eyed, hard-faced strangers? He could have dodged that ass Pendral's guards with both eyes shut and one hand tied behind him! In the end the High Lord would have forgotten . . .

Grince's thoughts wound down into a small, cold silence, in which he realized all too clearly that Pendral would *not* forget – not while he had a breath left in his body. All at once, the thief was seized with panic. Gods help me, I can't go back to Nexis, he thought. I can never go back there – I've lost everything! He threw himself to the ground and huddled there, oppressed and terrified by these vast, empty open spaces that stretched out around him, without a building or a fireside or a person within dozens of miles. And Grince needed people. Stealing was the only thing he knew. Out here he couldn't feed himself, shelter himself, or even make a fire.

'Grince? Are you hurt?' A hand touched his shaking shoulder. Looking up, Grince discovered that Aurian had used her friends the great cats to track him down. She squatted down beside him, frowning. 'What happened? Did you fall?'

It took a moment for the thief to realize that the look on her face was not condemnation but concern. 'What do you care?' he snapped.

'Well, somebody has to,' the Mage retorted, equally brusque. 'Clearly you don't.' She held out her hand. 'Are you coming back to the camp? We're getting ready to leave.'

Grince looked away from her. 'They don't want me.'

'I wouldn't be at all surprised, after the way you behaved – but whether they want you or not has nothing to do with it,'

227

Aurian told him briskly. 'They certainly wouldn't leave you alone out here to starve. Anyway,' she went on, 'no one is really angry with you, Grince – just disappointed, that's all.'

'What's the difference?' the thief muttered sullenly.

'A whole lot of bruises, for a start.' A cold grey spark of anger was beginning to kindle in the Mage's green eyes, and Grince felt an obscure satisfaction at having put it there. He had been snatched away from everything he had known, he felt lonely and scared, uncertain and helpless in this strange new world, but at least he had managed to influence something in his immediate surroundings.

Then it all went wrong as Aurian got to her feet and began to walk away. 'We're leaving soon,' she flung curtly over her shoulder. 'You'd better be ready, because we're not waiting for you, we're not coming back for you, and Mandzurano certainly won't let you ride with his folk now that you've been pilfering his cargo. To perish of cold and starvation on these moors would be a very unpleasant way to die, but it's entirely up to you.'

She was almost out of sight before Grince realized, to his horror, that she really meant what she'd said. With a thrill of fear he thought of wandering these desolate uplands all alone. What about when night came? He'd be stuck out here in the cold and darkness . . . Clearly the wayfarers steered clear of well-travelled trails – no one might pass by this place in months, if ever. And were there wolves on these moors?

Grince took to his heels and pelted after the vanishing figure of the Mage. 'Wait!' he shrieked. 'Lady – wait for me!'

His reception had been cool when he had returned to the camp, but Aurian, without really saying anything much, always seemed to be between himself and the wrath of the others – Hargorn in particular. It had been she who had selected the quietest of the ponies – the spotted mare – for him to ride, and she had taken pains to see that he was as comfortable as could be expected, for a raw novice. It had also been the Mage who had picked him up and dusted him off every time he took a tumble. And everything she'd done had made Grince feel increasingly guilty.

The feeble moon was dipping down behind the hills, and

Grince was feeling the shivery, light-headed weariness that came of still being up and about in the deepest hours of the night. He snatched at the horse's mane with a curse as Hargorn, in front of him, stopped suddenly and the spotted mare barged into him from behind. Hargorn's animal let fly with a vicious kick, the mare plunged to one side, and the thief found himself on the ground once more. As Aurian had taught him he rolled to one side, out of range of the pounding hooves, and simply lay there, too miserable and weary to rise.

The Mage materialized out of the darkness and snatched at the mare's bridle before the beast had time to bolt. 'Don't bother remounting,' she said – rather unnecessarily, Grince thought – 'we're stopping here.'

The thief awakened to a cold, grey world. He was wrapped in a blanket and the cloak that Hargorn had found for him back at the Unicorn, and he was curled up in the midst of a nest of springy bracken. Dimly, he remembered his bitter resentment the previous night, when Aurian had made him gather the stuff. He could see the sense of it now, however – it was bed and windbreak both, and far preferable to lying on the short, unyielding turf of a windswept hillside.

The thief rubbed bleary eyes and got to his feet – or rather he tried to. To his horror, he found he was so stiff that he could barely move, and he ached as though someone had sneaked up in the night and beaten him with a stout stick while he slept. Too wretched and dispirited even to curse, Grince flopped back into the bracken with a despairing whimper.

'What's wrong with you? Come on – you can't laze around all day. We've got to get moving soon.'

The thief looked up to see Hargorn standing over him. Glaring up at the elderly warrior, Grince told him in acid tones exactly where he could go, and what he could do when he got there.

Hargorn burst into mocking laughter. 'Why don't you make me?' he taunted. 'You gutless, ball-less little turd.'

With a yell of rage, Grince leapt to his feet, fists clenched, to find that Hargorn was already standing several feet away. The veteran held up his hands placatingly. 'Steady, Grince –

I didn't mean it. See, though – I knew you could get up if you tried. Instead of killing me, why don't you go and get yourself some breakfast, lad.' He walked away chuckling.

'Poor old Grince, you look terrible.'

In his rage at Hargorn, he hadn't noticed the Mage approach. 'Here,' she said, 'sit down for a minute and I'll help you.'

'I daren't sit down – if I do I might never get back up again,' Grince told her sourly. None the less, he did as she asked. Aurian knelt down behind him and laid her hands on his shoulders, and immediately the thief felt a tingling wave of warmth and well-being flood through his battered body. Within minutes, it seemed, the aches and stiffness had melted away as though they had never existed.

'There.' The Mage was smiling. 'That should get you through the day. No doubt you'll have collected another set of aches and pains by tonight, but I can always help you again – and it will get better, I promise you. In a few days you'll be thinking you were born in the saddle.'

'Why – why thank you, Lady.' For the first time in his life, the words came easily to Grince's lips.

Aurian laid a hand on his arm. 'You told me yesterday that you have no friends. Well, you were wrong about that. You have friends here, and I'm sure you'll find others when we get to Wyvernesse. But friendship works both ways, you know. You must trust people, and they must be able to feel they can trust you. You won't need to steal from the Nightrunners. They're generous folk, and they'll provide what you need.'

She rose to her feet, dusting bits of grass from her knees. 'You think about it. Anyway, there's taillin in the pot and some bread by the fire. Eat quickly – Forral is getting the horses ready now, and we must be on our way again.' She walked away towards the horses, leaving a very thoughtful thief behind her.

The Mage and her companions rode eastwards for another three days, across the bleak and windswept moors. At last the land began to dip, and sunrise on the fourth day found them in a wild, primitive stretch of salt-marsh and dune where a river had carved a shallow vale on its way down to an estuary. The land was grey and drear, the only vegetation sharp-edged marram grass and thorny sea-holly. The shrill, lonely cries of gulls and wading birds sounded on the bitter wind, as the red sun struggled vainly to free itself from the blood-tinged clouds smothering the hills to the east.

The Mage turned her horse northwards along the coast and the others followed her in a straggling, weary string. Aurian chafed at their slow pace, anxious to get back on the trail of her foe. She was almost certain that Eliseth must have gone south, across the ocean, for scrying had failed to find a trace of her. At Wyvernesse, where the vast Earth-magic of the mysterious standing stone might be harnessed, she hoped to find out more. The Mage remembered the stone from her previous sojourn with the Nightrunners, but at that point she'd had neither the time nor the need to examine it more closely. She had never forgotten it, but had stored its existence in her memory for the future.

As the companions rode northward, the coastline gradually grew more rocky, until at last they were riding along the top of a craggy cliff, looking down upon narrow beaches of shingle guarded by fanged and jagged rocks. Then, breasting one last rise, Aurian suddenly found herself in sight of her destination. There was the crescent bay, embraced by the reddish cliffs that rose behind it. And there, above the cliffs, was the smooth green knoll, crowned by its dark and sinister stone.

Even from this distance, Aurian could feel the stone's power beating around her like dark, gigantic wings. She inhaled deeply and threw back her hood, letting the fierce exhilaration course through her body and taking it for her own. At her side, she felt the Staff of Earth begin to pulse in time with this other source of power, and at her back the Harp began to thrum in harmony with them both. *Soon*, she promised them. *We'll come back soon.* Then she turned away from the glory and took her tired horse along the clifftop, towards the smugglers' haven.

After a short distance the Mage came to a v-shaped niche in the cliff. Looking down, she could see the beginnings of a path in the crevice – a narrow ledge that followed a fault line where the slabs of rock had slipped. It doubled sharply back the way they had come. Forral, who had never been here before, looked at it dubiously. 'We have to take the horses down there?'

Aurian shook her head. 'No, thank goodness. There's a tunnel somewhere around here that they use to take their horses down when the weather's bad. The only trouble is, it's very well hidden, and I'm not sure I could find it again . . .'

Hargorn rode up, dragging Grince's horses behind him. 'If I remember rightly,' he said, 'it's in one of those gorse thickets, over there.'

The horses, who had been here before, delivering contraband goods to the Nightrunners, also seemed familiar with the way. They pressed forward eagerly, knowing there was food and a well-earned rest nearby. But when the companions reached the thicket of tall, leggy gorse, there seemed to be no way in. 'Are you sure this is the right place?' Aurian was asking doubtfully, when a voice that seemingly came from nowhere cried: 'Hargorn! By all the gods – what are you doing here?'

One of the bushes was pushed outwards, supported at the back by a wooden frame, and revealed a narrow, thorn-fringed passage that sloped down into the ground. From its entrance a lithely built young man with tow-coloured hair stepped into the open. He gasped in astonishment as his eyes fell on the Mage. 'Lady Aurian! It *is* you! At last you've come back to us!' His face lit up with the broadest of smiles. 'And Anvar too,' he went on joyously. 'How lucky that I was keeping watch today, dull task though it usually is. Come, come,' he gestured them inside. 'Zanna will be so glad to see you! I can't wait to surprise her.'

The Mage leapt down from her horse and embraced Tarnal with delight, then followed him down into the steeply sloping tunnel, the others close upon her heels. They left their weary mounts in the stable cavern, where a young Nightrunner lad came up to care for them. Aurian glanced back as they left the cavern to see the youth staring with wide-eyed curiosity after them; wondering, no doubt, who these strange visitors might be.

The huge torchlit cavern with its shingle beach was astir with people, all going about their daily business, mending fishing nets and sails, performing essential repairs on the anchored smuggler vessels, and transporting bales and crates ashore from one of the ships and taking them into the storage caverns whose tunnel mouths spotted the rear of the massive cave. Tarnal stopped a little girl, who was running along with the serious mien of someone on an important errand. 'Can you fetch Zanna –' he began, but the child interrupted him. 'She's just over there.'

Zanna was dressed identically to the Nightrunners, in supple, waterproofed boots and sturdy seaman's clothing. She was bending over one of the bales that had burst open, seemingly during transit, and shaking her head. 'No, there's water damage here, sure enough. This fabric will be stained for good. By all that's holy, Gevan – can't you be more careful? The whole bale's lost. We can't trade this – we'll have to use it ourselves for –' At that moment she looked up and saw the Mage. '*Aurian!*'

For the first time, Aurian became truly aware of how many years had passed during her absence. Zanna was a woman now: capable, confident, and very much in command. She had cropped her hair short and her skin was brown and weathered by sea and wind. Yet many of the fine lines had been pencilled on her face by laughter, and there was wit and wisdom in her eyes. Joyfully, the two women embraced, then, as if conscious of the palpable curiosity emanating from the folk around them, Zanna swung round to face the interested throng. 'Now, you lot – no need to stand there gawking. You'll meet our visitors in good time. If anyone has no work to do, I can soon find them some,' she added ominously. The crowd melted away as if by magic.

Aurian chuckled. 'I recognize Dulsina in those words,' she teased.

A fleeting shadow dimmed Zanna's smile for an instant, and was gone almost before the Mage could be sure it was there. The Nightrunner woman shrugged. 'If a ploy works, why not steal it?' She turned to the others. 'It's wonderful to see you, Anvar, Hargorn . . .' Her words tailed off as she looked doubtfully at Grince, and the silent, shrouded form of Finbarr.

'Let's go somewhere private,' Aurian suggested in a low voice. 'We have a tremendous lot to tell you and Tarnal.'

Zanna nodded. 'I can well imagine. Besides, you must see Dulsina – I'd better let her know we have visitors, or we'll hear about it. Yanis is away at sea at present, but we're expecting him back in a day or two . . .' As she spoke, she was leading Aurian and the others up the beach and into one of the tunnels, which Aurian recognized as leading to the cosy cavern with the wide fireplace that the Nightrunners used as a general common room and meeting hall. Zanna paused with her hand on the door frame. 'By the way, I have a surprise for you. Another visitor arrived here a few weeks ago.' She opened the door and stood back to let the Mage pass first.

Aurian stopped short on the threshold, utterly thunderstruck. There, sitting alone by the fire, was one of the Winged Folk.

16

Snowsilver and Frost

Aurian stared in amazement at the slender, brown-winged young woman. Something about her seemed vaguely familiar . . . The young girl had no such doubts. She leapt to her feet and made a deep obeisance, her pointed little face wreathed in smiles of pure relief. 'Lady! By the grace of Yinze you are here. This is good fortune beyond my wildest hopes!' As she straightened, the veneer of formality began to crack. 'I never thought I'd get here,' she confided. 'I would have perished in the ocean for sure, had I not found Master Yanis's ship.'

For the first time, Aurian noticed that the girl's limbs bore a colourful collection of fading bruises, and that her wings were tattered and bedraggled, with pinions frayed and flight feathers missing. One wing was held at a skewed, unnatural angle, with its tip trailing along the floor. The Mage came out of her daze of astonishment to peer closely into the young girl's face -but it was the thick mop of lustrous brown curls that finally jogged her memory. 'I know who you are!' she said suddenly. 'You're *that* child – the one who found Hreeza in the temple.'

'That's right, Lady, I . . .'

'Come along, Linnet,' Zanna interrupted firmly. 'Where are your manners? Let the Lady Aurian and her friends get to the fire – they've had a long and wearying ride, and there'll be time enough for your news when they've rested a little. Run along to the kitchen, why don't you, and tell them we have five hungry visitors, then bring Dulsina back here.'

Linnet looked crestfallen. 'All right, Zanna.' Lifting the dragging wingtip the girl scurried away, with one last, reluctant glance over her shoulder at the Mage.

Aurian shook her head, still dumbfounded. 'My dear Zanna – where in the world did *she* come from?'

'You'd be amazed at the things we smugglers manage to find,' the Nightrunner woman chuckled dryly, 'though that one surprised us all. There was a dreadful storm, near on a month ago, and Yanis was out in the midst of it. It's as well he's such a good seaman – he was lucky not to lose his ship and all hands. Linnet was lucky too, that he happened to be there. She landed on his deck during the tempest, otherwise she would have drowned for sure. The poor creature was exhausted from battling the wind – she would never have reached land.'

'But what in the world possessed her to make such a long and dangerous journey?' Aurian said wonderingly.

Zanna shrugged. 'She was looking for you, apparently. It broke her heart when I told her you had vanished – but I'll let her tell her own story.' Her expression clouded. 'It's been nothing but grief and heartache for all of us, this last year or so.'

Aurian took her hands. 'Yes, I know about Vannor. Zanna, I'm so sorry . . .'

'Vannor brought his troubles on himself,' said a harsh voice from the doorway. 'Unfortunately, he brought them on the rest of us, too.'

The Mage turned, and struggled to keep her dismay from showing on her face. But Dulsina wasn't old, she thought. Alas, that was no longer true. Dulsina was almost unrecognizable from the straight and sprightly woman she remembered. Time and grief had fallen heavy on her shoulders, bowing her back as though she carried some incalculable burden. Her glossy dark hair, always so impeccably neat, had turned snow-white and straggled in wisps about her face, and her once flawless skin, of which she'd always been so proud, was now furrowed with bitterness and anger.

When she saw the Mage her eyes flashed, and she drew herself stiffly back as though she were about to spit in Aurian's face. 'You came back too late, Mage,' she hissed. 'It was you who loosed the Phaerie on us, and then went away to escape the consequences of your deed. Well, it's too late now.' She jabbed an accusing finger into Aurian's face. 'The damage has been done, and for all your magic you can't bring back the lives that have been sacrificed.'

236

The stricken Mage backed away from her, utterly lost for words. What can I say, she thought, in the face of such hostility? What could I do to make amends? How can I even be angry with such a pitiful, ruined creature?

'Dulsina, you forget yourself,' Zanna said sharply 'Aurian is not accountable for the evil of the Phaerie, nor is she responsible for Vannor's folly. One was brought upon us by the other, when that poison robbed my father of his wits. You'd do better to put the blame where it truly lies, at the feet of his would-be assassin. You do neither yourself nor the rest of us any credit by carrying on in this fashion.'

His eyes dark with sorrow, Hargorn stepped between the three women and took Dulsina's arm with care. 'Don't distress yourself, old friend,' he prompted. 'Come and talk with me a while instead. Hebba gave me all the gossip from Nexis to pass on to you.' With gentle solicitude, he led her from the room.

The Mage stood without speaking, her face pale but rigidly expressionless. Only Forral, who had known her for so many years, saw the depths of her dismay and the distress that she so carefully concealed. He went to her and took her arm, unconsciously echoing Hargorn's gesture. 'Come on, lass,' he said into the awkward, uneasy silence that had settled on the room. 'The poor old creature is deranged – she didn't mean it.' Feeling the infinitesimal tremor that ran through her body, he led her to a chair near the fire. 'Come now – rest a while, love. We're all tired.'

'Aurian, I'm so sorry.' Zanna was crimson with embarrassment, and she was all but wringing her hands in distress. 'Dulsina hasn't been well since – but I had no idea she would act that way. I – I'll go and see what has happened to that food.' She scurried from the room.

What in the name of perdition had that been all about? the swordsman wondered. Once more he cursed Death for blocking his access to the Well of Souls and preventing him from observing the world he had left. There were so many hidden undercurrents in this place – so much was going on that he didn't understand. When he had been commander of the Garrison, for instance, he had never known that Wyvernesse

237

existed – and he would have paid good gold for the information. These blasted Nightrunners had been a thorn in his side for years, and it had never occurred to him what kindly people they might be.

That winged girl, too, had been a shock. She had left him reeling. Though he had once glimpsed Raven, Aurian's former winged companion, in the Well of Souls, that was a far more detached experience than actually meeting one of the legendary Skyfolk face to face. And how can I help Aurian if I don't know the half of what's going on? he thought despairingly.

Well, he would do what he had always done – his best. Looking around, Forral realized with a twinge of unease that both Grince and the eldritch creature who had once been Finbarr had disappeared. Then he put them out of his mind. Save for the two great cats, he and Aurian were left alone for the first time since their initial meeting in the Mages' Tower.

The Mage was gazing bleakly into the fire, and Forral, desperate to comfort her but unsure of her reaction, knelt down beside her and reached out a tentative hand to ruffle her hair, as he had done when she was a child. Aurian turned sharply, but there was gratitude in her eyes, not hostility. With a sigh, she took his hand and rested her head against his shoulder. 'I know I find it difficult to show you, Forral,' she said softly, 'but truly, I'm glad to have you back.'

Grince had taken advantage of everyone's preoccupation with the mad old woman to slip away and do a little exploring on his own account. It's all very well for the Mage to tell me to trust these folk, he thought, but I'd prefer to know a little more about them first. Where would I possibly fit into a place like this?

Retracing his steps, he made his way back to the huge cavern that berthed the Nightrunner fleet. He had been intrigued and entranced by the ships – even before Nexis had lost its river, he had never seen vessels such as these, with their intricate figureheads and sleek, rakish lines. Also, it wouldn't do any harm to see what was in those bales they had been unloading . . .

On the busy, crowded shore, no one noticed one small, extra figure. Grince loitered for a time near the men who were unloading cargo, but to his disappointment they did not open any of the boxes but carried them away just as they were. After a while he lost interest and wandered off along the curving beach, giving a wide berth to an old man who was seated on a low stool at the water's edge, gutting a pile of slimy, smelly fish. For a time he watched the men and women who mended the nets and sails, but it was a dull activity that soon palled.

The thief was just about to leave them to it and go in search of something to eat when his attention was drawn to a whole spate of swearing coming from one of the ships that was anchored nearby.

'Bugger it! The bloody main gaff's jammed solid!'

'Well climb up and free the cussed thing then.'

'Me? Not on your life, mate. My mast-climbing days were over long since. That's a young man's game.'

'Well there's a young man, across the shore. You! Hey *you*! Hop in a dinghy and get your lazy backside over here!'

To his horror, Grince realized that they were shouting at him. 'Me?' Hastily he backed away from the water's edge. 'But I don't know how . . .'

The two old shipwrights exchanged a look of disgust. 'I'm not having this. You go and get him.'

'No, you go.'

The greybeard who was gutting fish looked up from his work and spat into the water. 'Don't strain yourselves, will you?' he said derisively. 'I'll bring the lad.' He grabbed hold of Grince, covering his tunic with smelly fish scales, and bundled him into a small boat. Before the thief knew what was happening, or could explain that he didn't even know how to swim, he was afloat and heading out into the deeper water of the bay.

Ignoring his protests, they hauled him aboard the smuggler ship. One of the old men looked at him, a slight frown creasing his forehead. 'Whose lad are you?' he demanded in puzzled tones. 'You know, I can't quite place you . . .'

'Oh, come on, Jeskin,' the other cut in, 'or we'll be here all bloody night. What difference does it make whose lad he is, so long as he can climb?' He turned to Grince. 'Lad, can you climb?'

239

'Can I climb?' The thief couldn't conceal his grin. Perhaps these Nightrunners would have some use for his unorthodox talents after all. 'Can a fish swim?'

The two old men looked thoroughly unimpressed. 'Well climb up that mast and cut the gaff free.'

Immediately, Grince regretted showing off. What in the name of all the gods was a gaff supposed to be? Why and how was it stuck up the mast? And the mast itself seemed awfully high and spindly, and the ship was rocking on the water in the most unnerving way . . .

But a new feeling had come over the thief. Here he was, in a different place, his previous background unknown, the slate wiped clean. Suddenly he was fired by a newfound determination to prove himself among these folk, to fit in at last with those around him. Grince pulled out his knife and stuck it between his teeth. He spat on his hands, swallowed back his fears, and began to climb the mast.

In fact it was quite easy. The rough, damp wood gave him a good sure hold and there were plenty of ropes and things to help him on his way. He shot up the first part at speed, showing off again, and was more than halfway up the wretched thing when everything changed. Gradually the mast began to narrow, making it more difficult to get a firm grip with his legs. Also, the further he got, the more violently the ship began to rock, and the more he could feel the swaying motion as the top of the mast tipped back and forth through the air. Grince's stomach lurched and heaved. His palms began to sweat, causing him further difficulties with the climbing. Rashly, he looked down, and froze with a whimper, his teeth clenched tight around the haft of the knife as he clung like a leech with his arms and legs wrapped tightly round the swinging pole.

Only professional pride made the thief continue. Cautiously he inched his way higher, carefully not looking down at the narrow deck and all that water far below. After what seemed like a year or two, his groping hand fell upon a tangle of ropes and a long wooden spar caught up in them so that it drooped at an acute angle that looked wrong even to Grince's inexperienced landsman's eye. 'This must be that gaff thing, I suppose,' he muttered to himself. Hanging on tightly with one hand he sliced through the entangling ropes – and nearly went crashing to the deck with the gaff as it struck him hard on the shoulder in falling, narrowly missing his head.

Afterwards, he had no memory whatever of climbing down. Grince came back to himself to find that he was standing on the blessed, solid deck with the two men clapping him on the shoulders hard enough to rattle his teeth.

'Well done, lad!'

'You did a good job up there – it wasn't easy.'

'Come on, Jeskin – let's see if we can't find him a drink somewhere.'

Filled with a warm glow of belonging, Grince managed to conceal his utter relief to be back on shore again. The old men beached their rowing boat and led him off down a different passage, which twisted and turned until it reached what was clearly a vast kitchen that fairly hummed with the purposeful bustle of a meal in preparation.

Dodging their way between the busy workers with utter unconcern, Grince's new friends towed him across the cavern. 'Emmie – hey, Emmie? Have you a drop of rum in the pantry for a handy lad?'

'Have a heart, boys – can't you see I'm busy?' The slender figure that had been stooping over the fire turned to reveal a fair-haired woman whose delicate elfin features no longer held the smooth glow of youth.

Grince looked at her and the world seemed to whirl around him. For a moment he was a ten-year-old boy again, who had just been given the first real possessions of his life by the first person to be truly kind to him. 'You!' he gasped. 'Emmie! I never thought I'd see you again!'

The woman's silvery brows drew together in puzzlement. 'Do I know you?'

The thief was just opening his mouth to explain when it happened. There came a low whine from under the table, and a huge white dog emerged, yawning and stretching its great limbs. Memory struck Grince down like a sword. His throat clogged, and his vision swam as his eyes flooded helplessly

241

with tears. The dog could have been the ghost of his own lost, beloved Warrior.

The crowded kitchen with all its heat and noise vanished from the thief's perception. He and the white dog were the only creatures in the world. Grince couldn't speak. His heart was foundering in a vast and swirling wave of mingled memory, sorrow and joy. The dog, noticing a stranger who had plainly been accepted into Emmie's pack, came ambling over to investigate, and thrust a cold nose into the thief's hand, its tail sweeping back and forth. Grince ruffled the sharp-pricked, silken white ears and dropped to his knees, throwing his arms around the broad, shaggy neck as tears ran down his face.

Emmie looked down at the lad, trying to remember where she had seen him before. He wasn't part of the Nightrunner community, and yet, and yet . . . The memory lurked teasingly at the edge of her mind, but she couldn't bring it to light. She was sure the youth must be older than he looked – his short stature and ragged appearance were deceptive – but he couldn't be more than twenty, if that. And what was the mystery with Snowsilver? Clearly, the white dog held some tremendous significance for him. It was difficult to interrupt such an emotional scene, but after a moment's hesitation Emmie reached out gently and touched the stranger's shoulder. 'Are you all right?'

The lad started and looked up at her, and gradually his expression cleared and composed itself, as though he was coming back from a far, far place. He sniffed hard and rubbed his face on his ragged sleeve. Then, to her astonishment and faint alarm, he scrambled to his feet and grabbed hold of her hand. 'Emmie, don't you remember me? It's Grince – from Nexis. You gave me the puppies . . .'

'Grince . . .?' As the memories came flooding back, his smudged, unshaven face resolved into the pinched, unhealthy features of the neglected, starveling child she had rescued from the squalid back streets of Nexis.

Grince's expression changed to a sullen scowl and he turned away from her abruptly. 'Never mind,' he muttered. 'Forget it. Why should you remember me?'

242

'No! Wait! Grince, I do remember.' Though he resisted, Emmie grabbed his shoulder and pulled him firmly back to face her. Gently, she touched his face. 'Truly, I remember,' she told him softly. 'You pulled a knife on me and told me to bog off, and . . .'

'And you took me to see the white dog and her puppies,' the young man finished for her. 'You were the first person who was ever kind to me.' His voice was thick with emotion.

'All these years, I thought you were dead.' As she reached out to hug him, Emmie was suddenly aware that the burden of the past had been lightened, and one, at least, of the wounds of grief she had carried with her from those dreadful, tragic days had been healed at last. She tugged Grince's hand. 'Come back to my rooms with me. We have so much catching up to do – I want to hear everything. I can't believe you managed to survive that terrible night. Come on –' She scooped up some pasties that were cooling on the table and folded them into a cloth. 'This lot can make their own bloody supper for once.'

Zanna strode purposefully down the corridor, trailed by a pair of chattering young Nightrunner lasses bearing fresh linens, dustrags and brooms. She was on her way to prepare the chambers for her guests, having volunteered to undertake the task herself in the hope that brisk activity might dull the scalding sense of shame she felt at Dulsina's hostile welcome of the Mage. It's my fault, she thought for the hundredth time. I knew perfectly well the uncertain state of Dulsina's mind since dad was taken. I should have known better than to let her near Aurian . . . The rest of the thought was lost in the surge of dull and empty pain that accompanied any memory of Vannor – not only a loss, but a betrayal. I lost him before the Phaerie took him, she thought. After he was poisoned, he was never the same.

Zanna shook her head and pushed such sad thoughts to the back of her mind. After all, she had so much to be thankful for – Tarnal and their two boys most of all. Valand and Martek, aged eight and six, were growing up to be fine, sturdy boys, and she was proud of them. Indeed, since Emmie and Yanis had no children and looking unlikely to have any now, the Nightrunner leader had named Valand his successor, and the lad, taking after his father no doubt, was already proving himself to be a natural seaman – in fact he had already been brought back twice from attempts to stow away on board the smuggler ships.

Feeling cheered by the thought of her family, Zanna hastened on her way. She had decided to put Aurian in the guest quarters near her own rooms, but as she passed the chambers that she shared with Tarnal she was halted by the sound of raised and angry voices coming from within.

Zanna frowned. 'You two girls start without me – go on, get busy, if you want to be finished by suppertime. I'll follow you in a few minutes.' When they were safely gone, she stood for a moment outside the door, trying to get some idea of what was going on before she went bursting into the middle of it.

'And I say we don't want 'em and we don't need 'em. They have no business here.'

'Gevan, Aurian and Anvar are our friends. They have every right to be here.' Though Tarnal was trying hard to be patient, Zanna recognized from his clipped tones that his temper was fraying. She sighed. For her mild-tempered husband to be that exasperated, the two men must have been wrangling for some considerable time.

'Damn all Mages – they're nothing but bad luck and trouble! Why couldn't they stay gone, and leave the world to decent folk? *She's* bad enough – last time she came it was bloody wolves and I don't know what else – but have you seen that Anvar? He don't look right – there's something badly amiss with him, you mark my words. And what about that other one, that spook, all muffled up like that and never showing his face nor saying a word. Not to mention that other lowlife little blackguard they dragged along. There's trouble there for somebody, you mark my words. You'd best make bloody sure the storerooms are locked up tight!'

'Gevan, that's *enough*!' Finally, Tarnal had been goaded to anger. 'Let me remind you that in Yanis's absence *I* am in command here. Now you either accept that, or you go.'

Zanna caught her breath sharply. Yanis had used this ploy

often enough to put Gevan in his place – but it worked for him because he was Leynard's son, and Gevan had first and foremost been Leynard's man. Whether he would accept it from Tarnal . . .

'All right then, if that's the way you want it. But mark my words, you'll be sorry!' Wrenching the door open, Gevan strode out of the room, white-lipped with anger. Pushing Zanna roughly aside, he rushed away down the passage, and was gone. As Zanna entered the room, her husband was rubbing his forehead wearily. Rushing to his side, she put her arms around him. 'Never mind,' she said. 'Gevan's just a loud-mouthed, bad-tempered fool. He'll never change.'

Tarnal grimaced. 'You heard, then?'

'The last part, anyway,' Zanna admitted.

'You probably missed all the best bits then – he's been at me ever since Aurian arrived.' Tarnal groaned, and went to pour himself a cup of wine. 'Gods, but my poor head is ringing . . .'

A prickle of unease crawled across Zanna's skin. 'Tarnal, do you think he'll really leave?'

'The gods only know, love. If he does or if he doesn't – I don't know which will cause us more trouble.'

The white dog accompanied Grince and Emmie. When they entered the woman's chambers it vanished purposefully behind a curtain at the far side of the room, which clearly concealed an additional area beyond. Having not yet seen a Nightrunner living chamber, the thief looked around him curiously as Emmie went to stoke the fire.

Emmie's rooms were pleasant and homely – not like living in a cave at all, Grince thought, though like all the accommodation in this place the suite of chambers had been hollowed out of solid rock. But thick, gay, woven rugs covered the floor, and the walls were warmed by colourful hangings. Small lamps burned brightly in wall niches or were suspended from chains bolted into the uneven stone ceilings, and though there was no fireplace a sturdy iron stove burned driftwood, a pile of which was stored in a basket nearby. The furnishings were simply and rustically constructed from a mixture of smooth planed wood and driftwood whose fluid, curving shapes added interest and character. There were wooden shelves, cupboards and chests for storage, and the chairs were padded with cushions stuffed fat with dried grass and fragrant herbs.

'This calls for a celebration.' Emmie took a bottle of wine and two cups from the cupboard, and laid out the pasties on the table.

It was the best meal of Grince's life. As they ate, Emmie told him of her escape from Nexis, the night that Pendral's men had attacked with such tragic and destructive results. 'There was so much to do when I got here that I ended up just staying on, when the rest of the Nexians went home,' she told the thief. 'There was a place for me here – the Nightrunners lacked a healer. And Remana needed my help more and more, then when she died last year, I took over completely. Then there was Yanis.' To his surprise, Grince saw her blushing. 'Well, he's a good man – his heart's in the right place and the gods only know, he needed a wife to look after him.' Emmie shrugged. 'What could I do? He pestered and pestered me so much that I finally said yes. But what about you, Grince? I was so sure you were dead. What happened to you that night? How did you manage to escape?'

Reluctantly at first, Grince began to tell her. He had never spoken to anyone of that dreadful night, but to his surprise, once he had started, the words seemed to flow from him with increasing ease. He wept when he told her of his mother's death, and the horrors he had seen in the burning stockade. His tears began afresh when he told her of Warrior, and how the beloved white dog had perished – ironically, at the hands of Lord Pendral's soldiers once more. Emmie held him like the child he had been when they first met and shared his grief, and when his tears were over, Grince felt transformed. It was as though he had been carrying a festering wound within him for half his life, and tonight the poison had been drained.

The thief pulled away at last, and blew his nose on the handkerchief that Emmie had thoughtfully provided. He gave her an unsteady smile. 'I'm sorry. I –'

'No, you needed that.' Emmie smiled warmly. 'You've been saving up all that grief for too long a time, Grince – not only for your mother but for poor Warrior too.' She sighed. 'I know how that feels. When I lost Storm, his mother, two years ago, I thought I'd never get over it . . . Some folks would say it was ridiculous, really – I had already lost a husband and two children, yet here I was, grieving so deeply over just a dog.'

'Ah, but she wasn't just a dog,' Grince put in softly. 'She was your friend.'

Emmie nodded. 'That's right – she was. And a better friend no one ever had. At least I was luckier than you, Grince. Storm died peacefully of a ripe old age, right here in this room – and I had Snowsilver, her daughter, to comfort me. You know, it was strange – she was the only one of Storm's off-spring that ever bred true to her mother, and she was one of Storm's last litter. It was almost as though Storm had left me a gift, for when she had gone . . .' A sudden smile lit Emmie's face. She thrust her chair back with a jarring scrape and leapt to her feet. 'Grince, come with me. I have something to show you.'

Burning with curiosity, the thief followed Emmie as she pulled back the curtain at the far end of the room. Beyond was a short corridor with three doors leading off at intervals. The single door on the right was slightly ajar, and Emmie pushed it open then stood back and gestured for him to precede her. 'I think there's someone in there who may want to meet you,' she said. Grince saw the twinkle in her eye, and wondered. His stomach felt hollow with a sudden, inexplicable surge of excitement as he went through the door.

The small, cosy chamber was some kind of study or work-room. A cluster of quills stood in a small pot on the desk, and the shelves were stacked with volumes and scrolls. A cabinet, two big chests, two hard chairs and a low wooden couch com-pleted the furnishings. Another stove, unlit, squatted in one corner, and the ceiling lamp was turned down low.

Every one of these details was blotted from Grince's mind by the occupants of the couch. There, curled up on the cush-ions, was Emmie's dog Snowsilver – and beside her sat a young dog who was the living image of Warrior.

Grince stood as if stricken, lost in memories of a young boy and a puppy who had been forced to make their way alone in a hard and dangerous world. The young dog looked at him and barked once on a high, clear note. It scrambled down from the couch and ran towards him, wagging an unruly tail, and as Grince squatted down it leapt up and put its paws on his shoulders, licking an ear until he laughed.

'Amazing. He likes you, and he doesn't take to many folk.' Emmie's voice came softly from behind the thief. 'He's five months old – the only one left of the last litter. I decided to keep him myself, because he looked so like Storm. His name is Frost – and if you want him, Grince, he's yours.'

Years had passed since Aurian had healed a wing. She had been forced to examine the healthy one first, taking its structure as her example and trying to make its injured fellow match it as best she could. At last she straightened from her cramped position, stretched her spine and rubbed her eyes. 'There – how does that feel?' she asked Linnet.

'Better, I think.' Carefully, the girl opened her wing, stretching the great feathered span out as far as the confines of her bedchamber would allow. 'Why, yes.' Her face brightened in a smile. 'I can move it again. It feels as good as new!'

'Well, not quite,' the Mage told her. 'You'll need those flight feathers back before you can get airborne again, and I can't fix them, I'm afraid. You'll have to wait till new ones grow.' Looking down at the winged girl, she shook her head. 'You took an awful chance, you know. You're extremely lucky not to have been killed. What was so desperately important that you had to risk your life to come here?'

Linnet shrugged – always a rash exercise for one of the Skyfolk in a cramped space. A cup went spinning from the table, caught by a sweeping wingtip, and Aurian caught it just before it hit the floor. The winged girl took no notice. 'I had to come – it was our only chance,' she explained.

Aurian frowned. 'But surely Queen Raven would have more sense than to send you . . .'

'There is no Queen Raven.'

'*What?*'

Linnet flinched. 'No, it's all right. I mean, she's all right – or she was when I left. It's just that she isn't Queen of Aerillia any more.'

248

'And why is that?' The Mage's voice was dangerously quiet.

'I'll try to explain, but I'm not sure I understand it myself,' Linnet said. 'In fact I'm not sure that anyone does, really, except the priests.'

Aurian bit her lip, counted to ten, and reminded herself that Linnet was very young. 'Linnet, just tell me what happened, *please*!'

'I told you, I don't really know. Suddenly Skua the High Priest developed powers of magic. He said that Yinze had brought back the powers of Incondor and the Skyfolk Mages. He said it was a sign from the gods, that Aerillia should be ruled from Yinze's Temple. He was backed by Sunfeather and the Syntagma, and there was a terrible battle against Queen Raven's Royal Guard – until Skua brought down lightning bolts from the sky and incinerated half of Raven's warriors.'

Linnet shuddered. 'It was dreadful. The queen was far advanced in pregnancy at the time. She and Lord Aguila were forced to flee for their lives. In a matter of days the city had become a place of fear and suspicion. Lord Skua claimed that he could read people's minds, and that the wrath of the gods would descend upon those who still supported the queen. Certainly folk began to disappear, and were never seen again. I was one of Queen Raven's ladies-in-waiting – that was her reward for my saving her when I was a little girl. I offered to stay behind and collect information, but after a while I got too scared. Skua's mind-reading claims were starting to ring true. I was going to flee and join the queen in the new southern Skyfolk settlement, but then I thought of you. I was sure you were the only one who could help us, and so I headed north instead.'

'And I'll wager you had some adventures, too,' said Aurian with a kindly smile, 'but they can wait for another day. You'll be tired after the healing, so I suggest you get a good night's sleep now, and we'll talk again soon.'

'All right. And thank you, Lady – thank you so much for repairing my wing.' Linnet looked up at the Mage, her eyes frank and pleading. 'Lady Aurian – you will come back with me to Aerillia and help my people?'

Cold seemed to strike through Aurian's heart. Suddenly she felt old, and very weary. *I wish people would stop asking me that,* she thought. But Linnet's tale had stirred her suspicions . . . 'It looks very much as though I will,' she told the girl.

Lost in thought, Aurian walked back towards her chamber – and went straight past the door. Forral was there, and just now she didn't want him asking any awkward questions, such as where was she going, and why. Linnet's tale had simply served to confirm her suspicions that Eliseth must have gone south. It would be just like the Weather-Mage, to usurp power in an alien city by manipulating people's lust and greed from behind the scenes. Also, something about the situation that Linnet had described struck a chord with the Mage when she considered the events in Nexis of about a year ago. *I can't quite put my finger on the connection,* she thought, *but a connection there is, or I'm a Mortal.*

Well, there was one way to find out. Normal scrying wouldn't work, not across the ocean, but using the nearby standing stone she would be able to take herself Between the Worlds. From there, she would be able to discover what was going on . . .

And you might also find out what happened to Anvar, said a little voice at the back of her mind, *which is why you really want to go risking your life on such a rash, insane venture.*

'Oh, shut up,' Aurian told it, and went to find Shia.

17

The Way Through the Stone

The eerie darkness pressed close around Aurian, dimming even her Mage's sight. She could hear nothing save the boom and hiss of surf on rocks, somewhere below her and off to her left. Carefully, she altered her path away from the sound, away from where she guessed the cliff edge must be. Shia accompanied her on that side, but that was no guarantee that the Mage might not miss her in the dark and go hurtling to her doom.

When she could feel that she had started to climb, Aurian knelt for a moment and touched the ground around her feet. When her fingers encountered short, soft turf instead of the tough and wiry dune-grass she knew she had reached the Hallow.

The Mage was uneasy. She had never known her night vision to fail like this before, yet in this place she was utterly blind. From the thunder of the surf there must be a stiff wind blowing in from the sea – indeed, she had felt its cold pressure on her left cheek all the way here – yet in this place not a breath of air stirred against her face. Well, what did you expect? she told herself irritably. You always suspected that this was one of the Gateways, where the barrier between the worlds grows thin and fragile – and that's exactly what you want and need. This strangeness only proves that you were right.

'Aurian, I can't come any further.' Shia's mental tones were taut with distress. 'The magic – I have never felt anything like this. It forms a barrier I cannot pass.'

'Don't worry,' Aurian told her friend. 'Where I'm going you couldn't follow in any case. Just stay there, if you will, and watch for my return.'

'If you do return,' the great cat muttered direfully. 'You don't need me to tell you that this is an act of utter folly.'

'You're right,' Aurian told her briskly, 'I don't. I already know that, but this is something I must do, Shia. One way or another, I have to speak to him again. Take care, my friend – I'll see you soon.' With these parting words, Aurian put all thoughts of her companions firmly from her mind. Now she must concentrate all her energies on the journey before her.

As she began to climb the steep slope of the knoll, the feeling of unease grew into fear, and finally to stark terror that became worse with every step she took. Soon she found herself beginning to tremble. Her heart raced, and her mouth became dry. 'It's nothing but a cheap trick, to guard the Gateway,' the Mage told herself firmly. She put forth all her power to shield herself and clamped down firmly on the fear. Gradually, she brought the incipient panic under control, then banished it altogether.

Aurian reached the broad level plateau where the monolith stood, and located the great stone by touch alone. As her fingers met the icy surface, the terror lashed out at her again, multiplied a hundredfold, but this time she was ready. Snatching the Staff of Earth from her belt, she raised it as if to block a physical blow. The Artefact blossomed with an emerald flare, sending the shadow of the stone flashing across the plateau. Its power shielded her and reflected the fear back to its source. Aurian's night vision suddenly returned and the stars appeared, sparkling in the deep blue canopy above.

'First blood to me, I think,' the Mage muttered grimly. With a sigh of relief she allowed the flames to die from the Staff, leaving the smooth, dark wood with its twining serpents unsullied. Quickly, she found a place near the stone where the turf was sufficiently smooth and level to make a comfortable resting place. She lay down on her back with the Staff resting on her breast, her hands clasped tightly around its smooth-worn wood. She closed her eyes and breathed deeply, willing herself to relax.

After a time, the Mage felt her inner form become discrete from her corporeal shell. She sat up and opened her eyes. There was no trace of the starry night above her. Instead the entire knoll was bathed in an eerie amber glow that seemed to emanate from the pillar itself. Aurian stood up, still clasping the Staff whose earthly form had also been discarded. Without glancing back at the body she had left behind, she made her way to the tall standing stone. It was cold to the touch, though not unpleasantly so, and the power that emanated from it sent a thrilling tingle through her hand and arm. As the Mage exerted her will the stone beneath her hand vanished, leaving a dark, narrow doorway in the face of the monolith. Holding tightly to the Staff of Earth she stepped inside, and as she did so the doorway vanished behind her, cutting off all trace of the amber light outside.

Aurian found herself in a narrow tunnel with a low roof that came dangerously close to brushing the top of her head. The walls were featureless black rock, but a faint silver light came from the floor, which was coated with glimmering dust the texture of fine ash. It stirred in clouds about her feet as she moved, sheathing her boots in a skin of starlight.

Sword at her belt, Staff in hand, Aurian moved forward cautiously. After a while, the tunnel grew progressively narrower, until pale light shining through a slim crack finally marked its end. Turning sideways, the Mage slipped through, stepping out into an alien and colourless world. The light was dim and opalescent. Soft grey moss carpeted the ground, and vision was limited by a pale mist that swirled and swelled in an unnerving fashion, though there was not a breath of wind. The depth of silence was sinister and profound.

Aurian grasped the Staff of Earth more tightly and stepped forward. The mist swirled aside, revealing a patch of dark grey turf. She took one step forward, then another, and suddenly her way was blocked by a tall, darkly shrouded figure.

'You know this is forbidden, Mage.'

'I don't think so,' Aurian told Death flatly. 'I have a right. I have passed through one of the Gates of Power, and you cannot turn me back. Besides, you are holding someone who should not be here.'

'No one who comes to this place believes they should be here.'

Aurian curbed her impatience and bit back her anger. 'I'm not speaking of belief. I'm speaking of injustice. How can you possibly justify keeping Anvar here?'

The Spectre's voice rang out, chilling and harsh. 'I am Death. I justify nothing, and none can gainsay me.'

Fear clawed at the Mage's heart like a living, feral creature trapped within her. To bolster her courage, she thought of Anvar, alone and lost in this dread place. Death was silent now, awaiting her reply – or her retreat. 'True,' Aurian told him. 'No one may gainsay you – even a Mage would be a fool to try. But surely, a Mage may ask?'

'Foolhardy Mage!' The Spectre laughed out loud. 'Now it comes. I must encourage her effrontery or live for ever with my curiosity. Very well, so be it. And what, exactly, would you ask of me?'

Aurian bowed to him. 'Two things, in truth. Anvar you already know about; the other matter is also of vital importance – perhaps as much to you as it is to me and the world from which I came. I want to know what's happening – how the exchange took place between Forral and Anvar, and also what happened to Vannor, who so nearly came here and was snatched away again. Was it Eliseth? Did she use the Cauldron of Rebirth? And is she using it still? If you would permit me, I would like to look into the Well of Souls, and find out what she is doing now.'

Death was silent a moment. 'I admit that the Magewoman Eliseth is involved, but as for the rest . . . You ask much, O Mage,' he said at last.

'Surely this situation cannot be to your liking,' the Mage suggested tentatively. 'People coming here to be reborn, then being snatched away again before they have the chance to reach the Well. People getting into the wrong bodies . . . If Eliseth is not stopped, where will it end?'

'This I cannot deny.' The Spectre seemed to be unbending a little, and for the first time, Aurian dared to hope. 'Would that the Cauldron were lost again, or even unmade . . .'

'Or brought to you?' Aurian put in quietly.

The Spectre's head came up sharply. 'Brought to me?'

Aurian nodded. 'It's the only way you'd gain true peace of mind,' she argued. 'Otherwise, it'll just keep turning up across the centuries, and you'll be constantly wondering where, and when, and in whose hands it will appear next.'

'You would swear to this?' Death demanded. 'If I help you to regain the Cauldron, you will give it to me?' Though she had heard both his anger and his mocking laughter, it was the first time that Aurian had heard genuine eagerness in his cold, unemotional voice.

'Release Anvar, too, and I'll swear.' She was unable to keep her voice steady.

Death sighed. 'Aurian, you do realize that even if I let Anvar go back with you, he must go as a disembodied spirit? Even one with your powers could not see him, or speak to him, in the mundane world. Without the grail he cannot return to his own body – and even then he may be forced to dispute ownership with the present occupant.'

'But he'd be willing to take the risk, I'll wager,' Aurian insisted.

'To be with you, my love? I would risk anything.' Anvar, who had been wandering aimlessly and disconsolately over the rolling hills, had come to this place with no idea what had drawn him there, but as soon as he heard Aurian's voice everything fell into place. Instinctively, he had sensed his love's closeness – her very presence had summoned him to her side.

Aurian looked at him, her heart brimming over in her eyes. 'What kept you?' she said dryly. With a hoarse, inarticulate cry that held all his past fears and present loneliness, all his love and joy, Anvar threw his arms around her. It was difficult to embrace within the realms of Death. Even though he knew he held Aurian, though she was right there in his arms, Anvar could feel nothing. Just to have her with him felt wonderful, none the less. 'I didn't know how I'd ever find you again,' he whispered into her hair.

'You might have spared yourself the worry.' Death's sardonic tones cut into the moment. 'It seems that not even I can keep the pair of you apart for any length of time. Remember, this is not the first occasion one of you has ventured into my realm in search of the other.'

Aurian faced Death squarely, though Anvar kept an unrepentant arm around her shoulders. 'True enough,' she said. 'You must be sick of the sight of us by now.'

'Very cunning, Mage – but it will not work,' the Spectre replied sternly, and with rising anger. 'On the contrary, I do not see enough of you. You come, you go. You have no regard whatever for the sanctity of my office and my realm. I would see you – *both* of you – come here, remain here, and pass through the Well of Souls to be reborn like any natural beings. Then I might, perhaps, recover some peace and order within my kingdom.'

With an effort Death mastered himself, and when next he spoke his voice was calm again. 'But this one last time, my children, I will let you pass.' Bowing low, he gestured towards the path they were to take. 'The Well of Souls is there, Mage. See what you will, then take your lover and depart.' With that, he disappeared.

'That was a sudden change of heart.' Anvar glowered suspiciously at the spot the Spectre had just vacated.

'Too damn sudden for me.' Aurian, too, was frowning. 'All this sweetness and co-operation strikes me as not only out of character, but just a bit too easy . . .'

Anvar felt a frisson of unease. 'We'd better not waste time,' he said hastily. 'Let's see whatever you want to see, then maybe we can get out of here before he changes his mind.'

'And springs his trap,' Aurian finished the thought for him. As Anvar looked at her his heart was kindled with a blaze of courage, confidence and joy.

'Gods, but I've missed you,' he said softly.

'And I you.' The Mage took his hand and clasped it tightly. 'Come on, let's go – and as we walk you can tell me how you managed to get into this mess,' she added soberly.

Hand in hand with Anvar, Aurian entered the sacred grove and bowed to the trees, who stood aside to let the Mages pass. Within moments they came to the clearing where the Well of Souls lay cradled in its bed of soft, deep moss.

'Will you watch over me?' the Mage asked Anvar softly. 'I don't want to go falling in – who knows where I might end up.'

'Or as what,' said Anvar soberly. 'Don't worry, I won't let you go.'

'Keep a sharp look-out for Death, too. He's up to something, I'm sure of it . . .' She knelt reverently on the pool's cushioned brink and laid the Staff down on the moss beside her. Lowering her head, she peered down into the infinite starry depths. Great spears of light lanced up from the surface, dazzling the Mage's eyes. When her vision cleared, the galaxies within the pool were whirling, spinning, in a maelstrom of streaked light. Biting her lip with concentration, Aurian dipped a finger into the Well of Souls and bent her thoughts upon her enemy . . .

The winged priest lay twisted on the floor of the temple precincts, a long spear transfixed through his heart. Eliseth knelt over him, the grail clutched in her hands. 'He's dead all right.' She smiled up in satisfaction at the winged warrior who stood over her, wiping the blood from his hands. 'Nice work, my Lord Sunfeather. He won't have known what hit him. Now, for the second part of our plan – if you would just pull out the spear first.' She gave a short and mirthless laugh. 'I doubt if even the Cauldron of Rebirth could keep him alive very long with a spear stuck through his heart . . .'

The winged man planted a booted foot on the High Priest's chest and wrenched the bloody spear loose with a vicious twist. 'And get rid of the accursed thing,' Eliseth hissed at him. 'When Skua returns he won't have any memory of what happened, but we might find *that* a little difficult to explain.'

Quickly, the Magewoman poured water from the chalice into the gaping hole in Skua's chest, and watched with satisfaction as the mangled flesh and splintered ribs began to piece themselves together again. She was accustomed now to the fact that the grail's magic took a few minutes to work, and sat back on her heels to await the outcome with calm confidence. 'There,' she said with great satisfaction. 'Now Skua is ours. Now that I've brought him back with the Cauldron's power, I can control his every move if I so will it – and he'll never know a thing about it.'

'He was ours in any case,' Sunfeather grumbled. 'I don't see why it was necessary to go through all this. I don't think –'

'I told you before – leave the thinking to me!' Eliseth

snapped with a flash of irritation. A plague on this innocent who lacked the subtlety for intrigue. The thick-headed warrior might know military strategy but he had absolutely no feel for the finer nuances of plot and counterplot.

Seeing Sunfeather frown, the Magewoman reined in her temper. 'I already explained,' she said with laboured patience. 'Skua was getting too many ideas of his own about what the gods wanted and didn't want. He was beginning to actually believe that the powers he's been using are his own – a gift from Yinze. The Father of Skies, indeed,' she snorted. 'In whose name he would eventually have betrayed us both. Well, we'll have no more of that!'

The Skyman looked doubtful. 'You think he would have betrayed me?' he asked.

'I know he would have betrayed you, you idiot. He was already trying to persuade me that he could handle things, and we didn't need you to command the Syntagma.' Eliseth glanced up shrewdly at the warrior. 'And if he was conspiring with me against you, it's almost a certainty that he was plotting with you against me.'

'Nay, Lady – there was never any suggestion . . .' But Sunfeather could not quite meet her eyes, and Eliseth knew, with malicious glee, that her words had hit their target, and she'd been right about Skua all along.

Sunfeather was scowling and shuffling his feet – just like a young lad caught out in mischief, the Magewoman thought. 'And what about me?' he demanded sulkily. 'What if you decide that *I* am a danger to your plans? Do you intend the same dire fate for me?'

'You?' said Eliseth dismissively. She turned away from him and back to Skua, who was beginning to stir and groan. 'You won't betray me, Lord Sunfeather. You have more sense – and you've just had a demonstration of exactly what will happen to you if you try.'

Aurian, looking at the scene through the Well's clear, glassy surface, saw the High Priest open his eyes. She remembered Skua – a malign, ambitious, treacherous piece of work if ever there was one. Though these developments boded ill, and she viewed them with grave concern, she was spitefully glad that a nemesis such as Eliseth had been wished upon the base, perfidious, self-serving . . .

'Aaaah . . .' Skua opened his eyes. 'In the name of Yinze, what happened to me?'

'Hush, High Priest,' Eliseth soothed him. 'You were taken ill – I have warned you often of the dangers of overextending yourself in your zeal.' She laid a hand on his arm. 'We must take better care of you – you are far too valuable to be allowed to jeopardize your health in this fashion.'

'I'm fine, I'm fine – just help me up. That is, if you please, Lady.'

'I'll do it.' Sunfeather extended a brawny arm and hoisted Skua to his feet.

'Now, High Priest, you must rest,' the Weather-Mage insisted, swirling the remains of the water in the grail. 'There will be time enough later for you to tell me how went the meeting between your courier and the Queen-Regent of the Khazalim . . .'

'What?' Aurian gasped in shock. 'Where in the name of all the gods does Sara fit in with this particular vipers' nest?'

'Sara?' Anvar leaned over the Mage's shoulders to look into the pool. 'She's viper enough to fit right in with the worst of them. What are they say –'

'*Now, I have you both at last! And this time you* will *be reborn!*'

Aurian caught a glimpse of the Spectre's dark, looming figure, and then she felt Anvar stagger against her, pushing her off balance, down towards the surface of the Well.

The Mage got one flailing hand deep into the moss beside the brink. Clenching her fingers, she hung on with all her strength and braced herself, giving Anvar a split second to get his legs beneath him and hurl himself to one side.

Then Aurian saw movement from the corner of her eye. The Staff of Earth, dislodged by their struggles, was rolling into the pool.

She made a desperate grab with her free hand. Her fingers brushed the Staff even as it splashed into the Well and she clamped them tight around the very end of the serpent-carved shaft. But the Well clung to the Staff of Earth, holding it tightly and sucking it deeper beneath the surface. Leaning perilously out over the water, Aurian held on until she thought her arm would tear loose from its socket. She was damned if she'd let go of the Artefact. Once it vanished into the Well of Souls it could end up on one of a million worlds and would be lost for ever.

Anvar, she was half aware, was on his feet now, confronting the dark and eldritch figure of the Spectre, putting himself between the Mage and Death. Aurian had no attention to spare for them, however – her entire being was focused on maintaining her hold on the Staff of Earth. And as she looked back into the pool she saw two things happen, so close together that she could never, afterwards, decide which had come first.

Beneath the rippling surface of the pool, the outline of the Staff began to alter. The two carved serpents, their jaws still conjoined about the great green stone that held the powers of the Artefact, began to take on vivid colour, one patterned in brilliant red and silver, the other green and gold. One of them stirred – a flick of the tail, no more – then the other began to writhe, and untwine itself from around the wooden shaft. Aurian's jaw dropped open. The Well of Souls had brought the Serpents of the High Magic to life!

One by one, the snakes wriggled loose and dropped away from the Staff, the red serpent still bearing the green crystal in its jaws. The Mage was left holding a plain stick of lifeless wood, that slid from the water so easily that she almost over-balanced. The stone that held the Staff's powers was lost to her, held by the serpent that had swum, with its mate, far out to the centre of the pool, where she could not reach it. Side by side, the snakes reared up their heads and defied her, their cold gaze sharp with a mocking glitter. Clearly, this was another test – if the Mage could not take back the stone, she would have lost the Staff for good.

So aghast was Aurian that she almost missed the other threat. But some instinctive sense of warning drew her eyes away from the living serpents, and down into the pool towards the vision of her nemesis. Eliseth, ignoring the puzzled stares

260

of the two Skyfolk, was staring into the grail, her silver eyes ablaze with rage and hatred. 'Aurian,' she said, her voice hard and intense with loathing. 'So, you have returned at last. But you've returned too late!'

Aurian gasped. The Staff! It had reached out through the medium of the Well to touch its fellow Artefact. And seemingly the water in the chalice was showing Eliseth as clear a picture of her foe as the Mage was seeing in the pool Between the Worlds. Inwardly, Aurian groaned. Right now, when she must focus her wits and her will on the recovery and restoration of the Staff, this was one distraction she could have done without. She looked at Eliseth, her gaze like ice and whetted steel. 'Too late, perhaps to prevent your mischief,' she said in biting tones, 'but not too late to put an end to it.'

Eliseth threw back her head and laughed. 'It will take more than your empty bragging to do that, but feel welcome to try! The first day we met I punished you for defying me, and I look forward to doing it again – I have been waiting to crush you for a long age now.' Her eyes flashed. 'Your day is done, Aurian – you are too soft of heart to prevail. Your pitiful, pathetic attachments to the Mortals will weaken and betray you for the last time, if you dare encounter *me*!' Quick as a whiplash, Eliseth made a stabbing gesture at the grail she held – and suddenly the Mage's vision of her enemy vanished as a film of ice spread across the surface of the Well of Souls, solidifying rapidly from the centre towards the brink.

As ice began to form around them the serpents streaked towards the pool's edge, a hair's breadth ahead of the lethal crust that was congealing around them, threatening to trap their bodies in a cold, crystalline tomb. Thinking quickly, Aurian stretched out her arms to the threatened creatures, as far as she could reach. The intense chill rising from the surface of the Well burned her hands with a cruel, bone-deep ache, yet she held firm until the threatened creatures could reach her.

Rearing from the pool, the serpents leaned towards her, but the Mage drew back slightly. 'First, give me the stone,' she ordered sternly. With a savage hiss, the red snake dropped the precious crystal into the palm of her outstretched hand. As

261

Aurian extended her arms again, each serpent fastened its coils around one of her wrists and she leapt to her feet, lifting them out of danger. The power of the Staff enveloped her, running into her from the crystal in her hand. A surge of even greater power came from the Serpents of the High Magic, in a surge of ecstatic elation that nearly knocked her off her feet as she raised her snake-twined arms above her head, crying aloud in joy and triumph.

The serpents hissed in warning. Aurian spun. Behind her the towering figure of Death stood over Anvar, who was doubled over on the ground in agony, his mouth distorted in a silent scream. 'A soul in torment,' the Spectre hissed. 'An unpleasant sight, is it not?'

A cold, sick feeling of dread washed over Aurian. Slowly, she lowered her arms. 'Let him go,' she said evenly. 'Your quarrel is not with Anvar.'

'You are wrong. My quarrel is with the two of you. I am done with humouring you and your recalcitrant paramours, Mage. You will go into the Well. Both of you. Now.'

Aurian stooped to pick up the inanimate shaft of the Staff of Earth. Though it would be no defence whatsoever against Death, it made her feel better to have some kind of weapon in her hand. 'If you do this, you will lose the Serpents of the High Magic,' Aurian threatened, desperate enough to clutch at any straw. 'I have claimed them, they have come to me, and there's nothing you can do to stop me taking them back with me to my own world.'

'You will do as you must – it changes nothing. You will return to your own body. Anvar will be reborn.' Death shrugged. 'Say your farewells to one another. It may be long indeed ere you meet again on any world.' So saying, the Spectre seized hold of Anvar and lifted him to his feet with one hand. A single shove sent him staggering to the brink of the Well of Souls. 'Aurian . . .' he shouted despairingly, and flung out an arm towards her as he fell.

'No!' Aurian cried. Even as Anvar plunged into the water she dived forward and caught hold of his outstretched hand. Then the waters closed over Aurian's head as the two Mages fell together, whirling down and down into starry infinity.

18

The Sunrise Hawk

Finally, Forral abandoned the idea of ever getting to sleep that night. With a bitter sigh he got out of his lonely bed, lit the lamp, and poured himself a cup of wine. It had been a long, long night. Though these underground caverns tended to baffle his instinctive sense of time, he was sure it must be nearing dawn by now. Pulling a blanket around his shoulders, the swordsman drew his chair close to the stove in the corner and stuffed a log from the basket into its maw, huddling over the embers until the fresh wood had time to catch. Cradling the cup in his hands, he sipped abstractedly at the drink as he struggled with his disappointment. He told himself that he'd been a colossal fool to count on Aurian's joining him tonight, but when something meant so much to a man how could he help but hope?

With a sigh, Forral poured another cup of wine. Though Aurian had told him why she was reluctant to let him come any closer to her, it was difficult for the swordsman to understand. She'd said that it was hard for her to adjust to the mind and personality of one love within the outward form of the other, but considering what they had been to one another surely she ought to have welcomed him with open arms? Forral, who was finding it easier and easier to forget that he was not occupying his own true form, was hurt and frustrated by her attitude.

'You've only been back a few days,' he told himself. 'Give the poor lass time – she'll come round . . .' But would she? Well did he remember Aurian's stubbornness of old! No, even if it was the middle of the night, it would probably be better for them to have the whole business out right here and now where they were safe and private. With sudden decision, he drained the cup, and went off in search of the Mage.

Her room was empty, save for one of the great cats who was curled up asleep, occupying the whole of the neatly made bed. It lifted its head as he opened the door, and opened one lazy eye, yawning to show a truly fearsome collection of sharp and gleaming fangs. Though Forral was fairly sure it wouldn't hurt him, he backed out hastily none the less. Aurian was a fool to trust these dangerous wild animals as she did, and the swordsman had too much sense to follow her example and take risks with beasts of such vast size and power.

A quick search of the kitchen and community caverns told Forral all he needed to know. He raced to the door of Zanna's headquarters and began to hammer on it loudly. After a few moments Tarnal answered, barefoot and clad only in breeches, his brown eyes glinting with ire. 'What the bloody blazes is going on, man? Have you been drinking? You've wakened the children!'

'Where's Aurian?' the swordsman demanded. 'Where has she gone?'

'How should I know?' the smuggler demanded irritably. 'In bed if she's got any sense – where we all should be . . .'

But over Tarnal's shoulder, Forral caught a glimpse of Zanna, in her nightgown and with a shawl around her shoulders, peering tentatively from behind the curtain that led to the sleeping quarters. With an oath, he shouldered his way past the young smuggler and wrenched the curtain aside to confront the Nightrunner woman. 'Where is she, Zanna? Curse you, woman, tell me!'

Even in his new body Forral was very much the bigger and stronger of the pair, but Zanna stood her ground. 'Aurian asked me to see her past the sentries. She told me not to tell anyone where she went – and I promised,' she said firmly.

'Now look here, Anvar, or Forral, or whoever you are.' Tarnal put himself between the pair, his voice low with anger. 'How dare you come barging in here in the middle of the night, threatening my wife? Get out of here right now, or I'll put you out.'

The old brawny Forral would have laughed at such a threat, but Tarnal, though wiry, was strong and fit from hauling on rope and oar, and the swordsman wasn't entirely confident of

264

his ability to handle his new body if it came to a fight. Besides, looking at it through the eyes of the two smugglers, his anxiety about the Mage had made him act like an ill-mannered lout. Backing up a step, Forral held out a hand in apology. 'I'm sorry, Zanna, Tarnal. But Aurian's bed hasn't been slept in, and if she's been away all night she may have got herself into some kind of trouble. I only want to assure myself that she's in no danger.'

He managed to summon a smile. 'Come on, Zanna,' he coaxed. 'Think how you'd feel if Tarnal had vanished who knows where. Wouldn't you be worried? And if she's been gone all night, then surely I'm far too late to interfere with whatever she had planned? It wouldn't do any harm to tell me now, would it?'

'I have to admit, Zanna, that Forral has a point,' Tarnal put in. 'Aurian has been away for hours now. If she has managed to get herself into danger, I wouldn't like to think we just stood by and did nothing.'

Zanna frowned thoughtfully. 'Very well,' she said at last. 'You're right – I don't see what harm it could do now. Aurian went to the Hallow.'

'What?' Tarnal shouted. 'And you let her?'

'The standing stone?' Forral asked in puzzlement. 'What's the significance of that?'

'Aurian said it was a matter of great urgency. She knows what she's doing,' Zanna insisted, answering her husband. 'She can take care of herself – and besides, Shia went along to guard her.'

'What *is* this about the stone?' Forral bellowed. 'Someone tell me what's going on!'

'It's magic. It's dangerous. We don't go near it,' Tarnal said tersely, struggling into a tunic and belting on his sword. 'Zanna, you must have lost your mind letting her go up there. Come on, Forral – we'd better go and find her.'

'I'm coming too.'

Forral and Tarnal spun to see Grince standing in the doorway. 'How long have you been there?' the swordsman demanded.

'You woke me with all that yelling.' The thief looked at

Forral gravely. 'The Lady Aurian was kind to me. If she's in some kind of danger, then I want to help.'

Forral shrugged. 'Suit yourself.' He strode off down the passage, leaving the others to follow as they might.

Although Forral did not count himself a cowardly man, he was unable to suppress a shudder of awe as he set foot on the sloping turf of the Hallow. Last night's wind had dropped and the sky was pale with cold pre-dawn light. The flat sea below him was the colour of iron and lost dreams. On the hill above, he could see the top of the tall stone, towering black and sinister against the dreary sky. There was no sign of Aurian.

'She must be at the top,' Tarnal muttered, as though he had read the swordsman's mind. 'We wouldn't see her from here.'

'No, but she would see us,' Forral replied doubtfully. 'Which must mean either that she's hiding something from us, or she's hurt in some way, and can't call out.' Without another word, he set off quickly up the slope.

A finger of blood-red light touched the top of the standing stone as the rim of the sun reared itself above the horizon. A hawk swooped low over the swordsman's head and hovered over the top of the stone, hunting the small creatures of the dunes. Forral had no eyes for such details. As he reached the brow of the hill and came in sight of the summit, he encountered a sight to chill his blood. Aurian's body lay on the ground beside the stone, composed as if for burial with her hands clasping the Staff of Earth at her breast. The great cat was standing over her, guarding her seemingly lifeless form.

The swordsman acted without thinking. With no sight for anything but the Mage, and no thought of her guardian, he ran towards Aurian, calling her name. Shia's head came round. She left the Mage and stalked, stiff-legged, towards him, snarling menacingly. Swearing, Forral slowed his pace and drew his sword. The cat circled warily, her blazing, baleful eyes never leaving his face. Tarnal tried to creep past her while her attention was fixed on the swordsman, but the cat sprang towards him with a growl, forcing him into a swift retreat. The thief had vanished – the little rat probably ran away, Forral thought. While Shia was distracted, Forral had managed to get a few steps closer to the Mage. She darted back towards him, trying to watch the two men at once.

'Stay away from her!'

'What?' Forral shook his head. Where had that voice come from? It sounded nothing like Tarnal. Had he imagined it?

'Stay *back*, human! If you disturb her body while she walks Between the Worlds, Aurian may die!'

Glancing past the threatening cat, Forral saw the thief creeping out from behind the great stone. While the others were preoccupied, he had worked his way around the back of the hill and crept up behind Shia. He reached Aurian, knelt over her still form, and took her hand. His voice came clearly to the swordsman in the stillness of the dawn.

'Come back, Lady! Don't leave us now – come back, please.'

Then everything seemed to happen at once. With a savage snarl, Shia sprang at the thief, knocking him away from the Mage and bowling him over on the grass. Dark clouds came boiling across the sky on an icy wind from the north, and gathered in a dark, coiling mass, the colour of a bruise, right above the stone. The air turned icy cold, and stinging flurries of hail and sleet blew across the exposed hilltop. With an ominous rumble, the monolith stirred and shifted, rocking back and forth on its base. The Mage's body gave a convulsive heave, and a great breath sucked into her lungs with a ghastly wheezing sound. Her eyes, huge with panic, shot open, and her staff rolled away as she tried to rise, grasping frantically at the air with empty hands. The hawk that had hovered above the hill came plummeting down from the sky as though shot, and thudded to the turf close to Aurian's outstretched hand.

The Mage scrambled to her hands and knees, and snatched up the Staff. '*Run!*' she screamed at the top of her voice. Grince scrambled up, took one look at her face, and obeyed. Reacting to her urgency, Forral, no longer hindered by the cat, grabbed her arm to haul her to her feet and together they fled down the hill, Shia flanking them and Tarnal and Grince running ahead down the slope, their feet slipping on the wet and frozen turf.

Suddenly Aurian turned her head, as though reacting to some call that only she could hear. With a stifled cry she

267

dragged her arm free of Forral's grasp and ran back up the hill.

'What the . . . Come back, you idiot!' The swordsman spun on his heel and hared back up the slope in pursuit. Aurian ran to the stunned bird and scooped it up, then came racing back the way she had come.

Lightning sheared down from the crown of tenebrous cloud and struck the monolith with deadly accuracy. With a tearing crack like a thunderclap, the great stone split asunder and a massive explosion ripped the top off the hill.

The distant deathsong of the Phaerie was like the whine of steel as a sword blade splits the air. The fierce, wild cries of their silver horns were like the raw breath of winter on the wind. Vannor, in his sleep, turned restlessly and dreamed of the Valley, and the Lady Eilin with a glowing sword clasped in her hand. Then he awakened, bolting up from his blankets with a hoarse cry of dismay. The horns and cries were louder now. This was no dream – the attack on Hellorin's city must have failed, and the Phaerie had come to Nexis to extract their vengeance.

Pulling on whatever garments came to hand, Vannor ran to the window. Already the wild hunt could be seen as streaks of glittering light arcing down through the sky like shooting stars. In the city, the brassy calls of horns arose to combat the sounds from the sky, while the great forewarning bell of the garrison had begun to ring, alerting the Nexians to their peril as it had done in times of danger throughout all the centuries since the Cataclysm itself.

Much nearer than these sounds came a tumult of voices from downstairs, where Vannor's household staff were beginning to panic. Through the window he could see manservants and housemaids running out into the garden to witness the spectacle, mingling in terrified knots with the gardeners and grooms. Vannor threw the window open with a bang. 'Get inside,' he bellowed. 'Get into the house, you fools, and stay there.' Snatching up his sword he ran downstairs. For the first time since her angry departure he was glad that Dulsina had left him. At least in the secret caverns of the Nightrunners she would be safe.

268

As Vannor watched from the vantage of his hilltop mansion, the Phaerie came down on the city like a firestorm, their shimmering robes shedding drifts of sparks that swirled in the air behind them. The exultant horns had taken on a deeper, more menacing note. Spars of light leapt from the top of the Mages' Tower as the Immortals rode past on their great horses, the luminescence spreading rapidly down the curving sides of the building and throughout the Academy complex, outlining in scintillating starlight the splintered shell of the weather-dome and the rococo ornamentation of the great library. Similar patches of glimmer were springing up and spreading rapidly throughout the city, wherever the Phaerie touched down.

For the space of a few heartbeats it was a vision of breathtaking beauty. Then harsh angry light dispelled the dreamlike radiance as hungry flames leapt up in a dozen places, and the shrilling of the horns was drowned by screams.

Then Vannor was running, running through the burning streets, seeing a man cut in half by a Phaerie sword, his guts spilling out across the cobbles . . . A little girl clutching a rag doll and weeping over the body of her mother . . . A young lad running from a burning house, engulfed in a ball of flame . . . A woman shrieking as her children were snatched away from her and borne aloft, screaming, by a Phaerie woman with burning sapphire eyes . . .

The victims all had their eyes fixed on the High Lord of Nexis; accusing, condemning. Scenes of torture, torment and slaughter were repeated over and over again before Vannor's eyes, while Phaerie stalked everywhere, cold-eyed and terrible, veiled in the coruscating glamourie of their magic . . .

'Vannor is trapped within his own mind,' D'arvan muttered. 'He's a prisoner of his guilt, unable to face the slaughter he caused.' His eyes flashed with anger as he looked at his father. 'Judging from some of the outrages I've found in his memory, he'd be better off placing the blame where it truly lies. How *could* you revel in such atrocities?'

'They're only Mortals,' Hellorin said mildly. 'After the

269

endless misery of their long imprisonment, would you begrudge my folk a little sport?'

D'arvan sighed and kept his thoughts to himself. His father's goodwill was all-important. It would serve no purpose to start a quarrel. Hellorin, he knew, would never change – he was too accustomed to seeing the Mortals as nothing more than low, brute creatures, fit only to be slaves – or quarry.

'It won't be easy to release Vannor,' he said instead. 'His mind is locked into a cycle that relives the horrors of that night over and over again. I'm sorry, but I can't find any clue as to why he mounted his attack on you – he seems as genuinely baffled by his own actions as the rest of us.' D'arvan turned away from Hellorin so that his father would not see the depth of his dismay. In Vannor's memory there had been horror unending, and it had shaken him badly. The last thing he wanted was to go back into the mind of the tormented man and experience it all again. 'I wish Aurian were here. She would know what to do – she's been properly trained in the skills of healing.'

'There's no reason why *you* should not succeed.' There was an edge of impatience in Hellorin's voice. 'And if you do not – well, the world will keep on turning. One Mortal more or less will make no difference.'

'Except to Vannor,' D'arvan said firmly. 'My Lord, surely there's no need to pursue this further? I've searched all that I can access of Vannor's mind and memory – no matter how much you wish it, I can't find any reason for his attack on the city. Let him go, I beg you. He is no further use to you here. Let me take him to Aurian – it may well be that she can help him where I have failed.'

'No. Try again, D'arvan,' the Forest Lord insisted.

Vannor lay in the tower chamber that had been given to D'arvan, on the same low couch from which, three days earlier, Maya had produced her audacious plan. The Mage sighed. Unfortunately, Hellorin had liked her idea all too well – he was anxious both to extend his bloodline and obtain his son's help in ruling the Mortal race, and for this he was willing to forfeit a slave or two – or even make the greater sacrifice of releasing the two Xandim.

Putting off the evil moment when he must enter Vannor's mind once more, D'arvan turned away from the stricken Mortal and went to look out of his window at the spectacular city – a dazzling blend of Phaerie magic and Mortal labour – on the lower slopes of the hill. Over the past few days, events had moved with dizzying speed. Over the years of their long exile, the Phaerie healers had become expert in the manipulation of Mortal fertility, for the Forest Folk themselves had been unable to reproduce their own kind, thanks to a cruel twist of the Magefolk spell that bound them. Already, Maya was carrying the tiny mote of life that would one day become their child. At his insistence she had been moved into the comfort of D'arvan's chambers, away from the slave quarters and their ruthless guards. Parric, still bristling with hostility towards the Mage, had been perforce left down in the caverns until it was time to leave, and now there was only one task remaining – the reconstruction of Vannor's mind – before Hellorin gave them his permission to depart.

D'arvan, in the meantime, was being torn in two by the cruel turn events had taken. On the one hand he was anxious to obtain the release of Parric, Vannor and the two Xandim, and go to the assistance of Aurian, who had a right to expect his aid. On the other, he was desperate to remain with Maya, especially now that she was expecting his child. She was the one with all the courage – this whole mad scheme was her idea. She insisted that Aurian needed him, that she herself would be fine during his absence, yet he dreaded leaving her behind, unable to escape with Hellorin's sorcerous chain around her neck, and at the mercy of his father's capricious whims. What would become of her if he perished at the hands of Eliseth? And if he should return – what then? He had given his word to his father that he would conquer and rule the city of Nexis, as Hellorin wanted.

'Are you just going to stand there all night?' Hellorin barked, dissolving D'arvan's troubled reverie. 'I thought you were in desperate haste to abandon us and return to your friend the Mage.'

D'arvan frowned at the rancour in his father's tone. 'I am also a Mage – or do you choose to forget that? And am I not proof that you don't detest all Magefolk? I fail to understand why you, of all people, persist in continuing this ancient enmity. None of the Mages living now had anything to do with the imprisonment of the Phaerie.' He met his father's eyes, glad of a chance to revenge himself a little on the Forest Lord. 'Or can it be, my Lord, that your grievance is not with all of the Magefolk, but only with Lady Eilin, Aurian's mother?'

'Do not mention that woman's name to me!'

'I understand from Parric that she seems less than impressed with you, also,' D'arvan retorted dryly. 'Now, my father,' he went on with a malicious smile. 'Shall we resume our work with the Mortal?'

'Do as you please. You may report to me when – and if – you succeed.' Glowering thunderously, Hellorin stalked out, slamming the door behind him.

D'arvan stood a moment longer, relishing his small victory. He triumphed over his powerful father so seldom that these rare moments were worth savouring. Maya emerged from the bedchamber, stretching and rubbing sleepy eyes. The changes the Phaerie healers had made in her body would balance themselves out as her pregnancy progressed, but for now their magical intervention had left her tired, and a little more fragile than her normal, robust self.

'What was wrong with Hellorin?' she asked. 'Did I hear the sounds of a royal tantrum?'

The Mage shrugged. 'I committed the heinous offence of mentioning the Lady Eilin. On that particular subject his temper is so short it's almost nonexistent.'

'He only has himself to blame, as far as I can see.' Maya perched herself on the edge of the table, swinging her legs. She was dressed now in rich, silken Phaerie robes that had been altered by Mortal seamstresses to suit her smaller stature. The glowing, jewelled colours suited her dark, delicate beauty, but could not hide the glint of the abominable slave chain around her neck. In that moment, D'arvan was overcome by the depths of his love for her. He put his arms around her, resting his cheek against her silken, scented hair. 'I'll make this up to you,' he promised. 'When I get you out of here and we return to Nexis, that accursed chain will come off, and you'll be a queen.'

'When we return to Nexis,' Maya answered soberly, 'I'll be a traitor.'

19

Flying Sorcery

The thin air held no sound save the whine of the wind and the
reverberant thunder of Sunfeather's immense red-gold
wings. From this height, it seemed possible to see the entire
world . . . And one day, I shall rule it all, Eliseth thought. She
revelled in the excitement of soaring so perilously high, with
an abyss of empty air beneath her and the jagged rocks below,
and luxuriated in the strength of Sunfeather's strong arms
around her, bearing her securely aloft. As a Weather-Mage, it
gave her an overwhelming feeling of power to touch the
winds, to flirt with the sunshine and penetrate the clouds from
which she drew the essence of her magic. How the
Magewoman wished her own race had been fortunate enough
to possess the gift of flight. I could have achieved so much
more, she thought. Still, at least she could borrow
Sunfeather's wings, and he was so besotted with her that he
was always happy to oblige.

Today she needed the escape of flight more than ever, to
clear her thoughts and help her gain perspective on the new
challenges that awaited. The unheralded vision of Aurian had
come as a shock indeed, for lately Eliseth had been too
involved in her own schemes to give much thought to her
rival. Indeed, Aurian had taken so long to return to the world
that the Weather-Mage had almost ceased to count her as a
threat – until now.

I was lucky to be warned in time, Eliseth thought. I'm sure
Aurian had no intention of announcing her return to me that
way. It must have been an accident or carelessness on her part.
The Magewoman frowned. But where in the name of perdition
was she? What was that colourless, misty place? There was
something weird and unnatural about her surroundings
. . . I didn't recognize them. And it wasn't a clear scrying, either

– the vision seemed to be rippling, almost as though I looked up at the scene through the water, but how could that be?

'Why so preoccupied today?' Sunfeather murmured in the Magewoman's ear.

Eliseth was about to make him a short reply, but changed her mind. 'It's nothing to worry you. Will you take me back now, Sunfeather?'

'Surely there's no hurry?' the Skyman breathed. His hands began to move across her body. 'I had thought we might stay out here a while . . .'

Eliseth was tempted. It had not taken her long to discover the thrill of mid-air coupling with the winged man. Having tried it, she hadn't been at all surprised to find that this was the way the Skyfolk usually mated. Today, unfortunately, there were other matters that must occupy her time. 'No!' she told Sunfeather firmly. 'That is – not today, my dear one. Take me back to Aerillia, please. I have work to do.'

Having been flown back to the Temple of Yinze by an aggrieved and peevish Sunfeather, the Weather-Mage returned to her secret chambers in the cloisters beneath the building. She locked the door behind her and shed her furred cloak. The rooms were spacious and equipped with every possibly luxury – and it was just as well, the Magewoman thought, for she spent a considerable amount of her time in them, lurking like a spider on the periphery of her web. For though, in truth, Eliseth ruled Aerillia now, few of the Winged Folk were actually aware of her existence. Had they known, they would never have countenanced a Mage as their ruler.

Eliseth poured mulled wine from the pot that stood in a metal rack affixed to the top of the brazier, and sat down, pulling a furred blanket over her lap against the inevitable draughts. The damnable Winged Folk, she thought, never seemed to feel the cold at all, but she was not so impervious. Her chambers, with their curving walls, were in a hanging turret, one of several that thrust out from the mountainside below the level of the temple. The furnishings were a peculiar but comfortable blend of Aerillian and Nexian styles, for she had complained to Skua and Sunfeather until they had a proper couch made for her, in place of the spindly Skyfolk seats that she found so uncomfortable, and a proper bed in which she could stretch out. The bathing facilities, too, had been altered from the ice-cold cascade that flowed directly from peaktop cisterns. A bathtub had been fashioned and installed, though heating water on the brazier was such a long, slow process that baths were a rare treat, and were shallow and tepid even at best.

The quarters were spartan by Eliseth's standards, but she supposed she could put up with them for a little while longer. Only a few months ago, this place had seemed a refuge of comfort and luxury after a gruelling journey through the mountains. When the Magewoman had first arrived in the southlands she'd had nothing but Bern, the useless Sword of Flame that the Mortal carried slung on his back in an old cloak, and Anvar's stolen memories to guide her through these strange new lands.

Eliseth had felt horribly exposed on the coastal plains, like a fly crawling along the top of a vast table. She had travelled mostly at night, scrying frequently in the grail to foresee any approaching Xandim patrols. On foot, it was a long and wearisome journey – hungry too, for Bern was worse than useless as a hunter, and Eliseth was forced to obtain most of their food herself, using her magic to kill rabbits and the small deer that grazed the plain.

Eventually, as she neared the foothills of the great mountain range, Eliseth had found what she was seeking – two young Xandim herders, a man and a woman, guarding a small cluster of cattle. She had followed them for a few days as they tracked the slow-moving bovines, noting the pattern of their activities. Each day they would take turns, one remaining in human shape as the rider, and the other changing to equine form. At night they also took turns, one guarding the camp while the other slept.

At last Eliseth was ready to make her move. When the Horsefolk had made their camp for the night and fallen asleep, she had used her air-twisting spell to camouflage Bern as he crept up on the drowsy woman and cut her throat. She died without a sound, and her partner drew his last breath without even waking. Eliseth filled the grail from the herders' own waterbag and restored them, one at a time, to life. The Xandim knew nothing of what had happened to them, but now they were gripped by a strange compulsion to devote themselves to this outland woman, and to serve her in every way they could.

Once she had questioned the herders, called Saldras and Teixeira, about the habits, numbers and whereabouts of the local Xandim, they were of no further use to the Magewoman in their human form. Taking control of their minds, Eliseth forced them to change to equine shape and stay that way. Now she could continue her journey quickly, and she headed for the mountains without further delay. She had decided that the Horsefolk as a race would be of little use in her plans of conquest – she could come back and deal with them later, at her leisure. No, control of the skies was the secret of power in the south – and, among the scraps of knowledge she had gleaned from Anvar's mind, she had found the names of Winged Folk who would be only too glad to help her oust the rightful queen.

The mountains came close to putting an end not only to her plans but to her life. Eliseth had never been taught how to survive in the wild. She had been unprepared for the bitter cold, the hard, bleak surroundings, and the exhaustion that increased during day upon day of hard climbing and the strain and concentration of picking out a safe path. Had it not been for the knowledge she lifted from the minds of her Xandim captives and her ability to control the weather, she would have perished for sure.

When the Magewoman finally reached the vicinity of Aerillia, she had killed the two Xandim for good and all and enjoyed the first hot meal – of horseflesh – that she'd eaten in many a long day. Then, wrapping a concealing mist around herself, she had watched the city and its surrounds in the grail, awaiting her chance. Repeating the successful ploy she'd used to gain control of the Xandim, Eliseth had struck again, finding another solitary victim in a lonely place. This time, it was a young winged girl, out gathering berries alone on the mountainside. It had been pathetically easy to kill her – she'd

277

scarcely put up any struggle at all. Eliseth had used her victim to take a message to Skua and Sunfeather, then wiped the incident from the girl's memory. She was living her normal life now in the city: uninvolved, undisturbed – and waiting there as a pawn that could be brought into play at any time, should the Magewoman need her.

At first, Eliseth had toyed with the notion of using the grail to control the queen herself. On reflection, however, that scheme had involved too many problems. First, all members of the royal household would be guarded far too tightly for the Magewoman to gain access and use the grail. Second, Raven and Aguila ruled so closely and harmoniously together that if one should begin to act in an unusual manner the suspicions of the other would be roused at once. She would be forced, therefore, to deal with both at the same time – which brought her back to the first problem. No, it would be far easier for Eliseth to do her work through enemies of the throne – and it would also mean far less risk to herself.

It had been child's play to recruit the two disgruntled winged men. Skua bore a long-standing grievance against the queen. According to the High Priest, Raven had usurped his power and undermined her authority right from the start. Though he was aware that much of her hostility towards the temple stemmed from the heinous acts of Blacktalon, his predecessor, Skua also knew that, if it came to a question of who held the greatest power over the common folk, the contention between crown and temple must one day come to a head. Sunfeather's grudge against Queen Raven had far less to do with the subtleties of politics. He had never forgiven her for that day, so long ago now, when she had humiliated him in front of the High Council. Also, he was consumed by jealousy and bitterly resentful of the low-born Aguila, who had been raised to the exalted position of consort to the queen.

It had not taken the three conspirators long to hatch their plot. An ordinary, everyday harp was obtained and disguised by Eliseth with a small spell of glamourie. Then Skua announced to the congregation in the temple that the great god Yinze had, in his wisdom, seen fit to return the Harp of Winds into the hands of his children, the Winged Folk.

Eliseth, watching from hiding, had used her own powers to produce the carefully staged 'miracles' that the harp had wrought.

The Skyfolk were beside themselves: delirious with joy and hope. If one of their race could recover his magical powers, why not all of them? Only the queen and her consort were unimpressed by Skua's claims and voiced their doubts aloud, for Raven knew very well what the true Harp looked like, and was also aware that it had been claimed by Anvar in a joining that no Mortal could sunder, be he High Priest or no. Such reasoning, however, was the last thing her subjects wanted to hear.

Almost overnight, the ruler of the Skyfolk discovered that she had lost the support of her subjects. Folk started recirculating the old tale of her association with the groundlings, and Blacktalon's cohort Harihn. Once again, Raven's judgement was brought into question. Skua spoke out against her openly, with the public backing of the Syntagma and the temple guard. Wisely, the queen and her family had fled Aerillia – just in time to save their own lives.

Well, Eliseth reflected, sipping at her cooling wine, she was not above taking a leaf out of Raven's book. Timely action, she knew, was the secret to most success – and thanks to the warning of the grail, she knew it was high time she was embarking on the next step of her own plans. 'At the very least it'll get me out of this dungeon of a room, and this mausoleum of a city,' the Magewoman mused aloud. 'I look forward to living in a place where I can actually be warm again.'

Now that Eliseth held power here, her work was done, for she had never actually meant to make herself queen of this wretched, freezing pile of rock at the tail end of nowhere – nor would the Skyfolk accept as ruler one who was not of their own kind. And who wanted to rule a city where they were not even able to go out in public? No, Aerillia had only been a means to an end, and it would serve her purpose quite well if Skua ruled – under her instruction. Eliseth was ready to leave now, and make her way towards the place she'd planned to be the true heart and centre of her empire. Dhiammara.

The Magewoman rose and walked to the window, spilling

the blanket from her lap to the floor. There was one thing remaining to be done before she left Aerillia. She had no doubt that Aurian would soon discover that she was no longer in the north, if the Mage did not know already. Soon the eyes and thoughts of her enemy would be fixing themselves across the ocean – and before Aurian made a move, it was vital that Eliseth set her spies in place.

Eliseth took up the grail and half filled it with water, setting the cup down on the table. Then, seating herself comfortably, she gazed into the blackened depths and bent all her thoughts upon Anvar.

For a considerable time, nothing happened. The Magewoman sat there without moving, her head aching with the effort of concentration – and still no vision formed within the cup. What in perdition was wrong? This should not be happening! Eliseth began to feel the stirrings of impatience – and a shadow of doubt. Still she persisted, until the noon sun came blazing through her windows. Its glare almost burned her eyes from her head as the rays struck the surface of the water, and Eliseth sprang back with a livid curse, her carefully constructed shell of concentration in splinters.

The Magewoman couldn't understand what was happening – she had no way of knowing that the spirit she had hoped to master had not returned to his body after all, and that another had taken Anvar's place, one over whom she had no control. She only knew that one of her most precious schemes had failed. Snarling another curse, she hurled the grail as hard as she could in temper. It flew across the room, spilling water in a glittering arc. There was a searing flash as it hit the wall and a starburst of cracks snaked out around the impact point. Eliseth gasped in horror as a picture – all too clear – flashed across her mind, of the turret breaking loose from its moorings and crashing in ruin down the mountainside. 'Pox rot it – be more careful!' she warned herself. 'It's not a bloody plaything!'

She rushed over to the grail and picked it up carefully, checking it for damage and dusting it on the hem of her robe. It pulsed sulkily once or twice, and then became quiet in her hands. Cradling the precious Artefact, Eliseth began to pace the room. What could she do? She must have a means of discovering her enemy's movements. After a time, the answer came to her. She didn't really hold out much hope, but she could always try Vannor again.

The Magewoman sighed as she refilled the grail. She had abandoned Vannor long ago. After the blundering imbecile had made such a botch of the attack on the Phaerie, then let himself get captured by Hellorin's accursed folk, he had no longer been of use to her – not to mention himself or anyone else. But it had been a long time since she had even bothered to contact him – maybe something had changed . . . It had better, she thought bitterly. A slender chance indeed, it was her last and only hope. Narrowing her eyes, Eliseth bent over the grail once more and focused her will upon the former High Lord of Nexis.

Maya stood on the lush green lawn in front of Hellorin's palace and watched the early sun touch the soft grass with emerald fire. How she wished she had a sword in her hand! It might help her assume a bravery she did not feel – now, when she needed her courage as never before. This morning, her whole world seemed composed of things she did not want – she didn't want D'arvan to go, she didn't want to be left behind. And for sure, she didn't want to be carrying a child at this time – and not one conceived with the help of the arcane Phaerie magic, instead of naturally and spontaneously, as it should have been. Gods – how can I possibly cope with a child? she thought desperately. I'm a bloody warrior – I'm not the motherly sort at all. The idea terrifies me – I don't even know where to start.

She had no choice in the matter, however. The child was already within her. After she and D'arvan had lain together, the Phaerie women had come, and cocooned her in a spell of sleep. By the time she had awakened, they had quickened D'arvan's seed within her. There was no backing out of the bargain now. It was my own idea, she reminded herself. The entire plan was mine. I have only myself to blame – me and my big mouth. Around her throat Maya could feel Hellorin's chain to remind her of her new status – a glittering circle of cold that never seemed to warm to the temperature of her skin. Was this all that the future held for her? Chains?

D'arvan's arm went round her shoulders, and she knew, with a sinking heart, that the very tension of her body had betrayed her fear and doubt. 'It's all right,' he murmured. 'Don't worry – I'll be back before you know it.'

Maya glanced up at him, storing details in her memory for when he had gone: the way his fine pale hair was blowing in the breeze, the way the early light cast dark shadowed hollows beneath the sharp bones of his face. She tried to avoid the eye of Parric, who was standing nearby with a pair of Phaerie guards and the unresponsive Vannor, who had been given leave to depart at the last minute, as Hellorin finally conceded that D'arvan could not help him. Though the dreadful chain had been removed from his neck, the cavalry master was still scowling. He had been against this whole scheme from the start – he had already made it more than clear that he thought she was insane. As she was drawing breath to reply to D'arvan, there was a silvery fanfare of trumpets, and the Forest Lord emerged from the palace, nodding grandly to the crowd of brightly garbed Phaerie, courtiers all, who fringed the stretch of grass. 'Bring forth the steeds!'

Maya gritted her teeth. Why the bloody blazes didn't Hellorin just get on with it? He could have had the Xandim waiting here, as everyone else had been, but no . . . Did all kings have this ridiculous need for spectacle?

In the brief pause before the Xandim arrived, Hellorin turned to herself and D'arvan, extending his arms as if to embrace them both. If he tries it, Maya thought grimly, Phaerie or no Phaerie, I swear he'll be wearing his balls up around his ears.

Luckily, the Forest Lord restrained himself. 'Is it well with you, my children?' he cried.

D'arvan, in the same grand manner, flashed him a dazzling smile. 'It is well, my Lord.'

Maya gritted her teeth. If my child ever tries to behave like this, she thought, he won't be sitting down for a week.

Before the warrior could think of a reply of her own, the two Xandim arrived: a magnificent huge warhorse, darkly dappled in cloudy black and grey, and a somewhat smaller beast with a shining bay coat and a shaggy, crow-black mane and tail. Though Maya looked at them closely, it was hard to imagine them as men. What did they look like in human form? What must it be like, living their whole lives as two different beings? She wished she could have a chance to know them, to speak to them. She only had a fleeting, clouded memory of the one time she had seen them as humans. Then, she herself had been the one to wear the form of a beast, for Hellorin had put her into the shape of a unicorn. The warrior smiled sourly to herself at the thought. Maybe we're not so different after all, she thought. I, too, have lived as two different creatures at the Forest Lord's whim.

Maya could feel D'arvan straining forward, anxious to be away, lest his capricious father should change his mind. This was no place for farewells – it was too public, everything was too hurried – and besides, he and Maya had said goodbye already. D'arvan exchanged a few soft words with his father, too low for Maya to hear, then he was embracing her for the last time in a long time – maybe for ever . . . The warrior tightened her arms around him. 'You'd better be careful,' she hissed at him, 'or you'll have two of us to reckon with.'

D'arvan smiled. 'Trust me,' he said. 'Everything will be all right. Take care of our child, my love – no one could do it better.'

Then he was gone. With a wrenching effort, Maya stopped herself from holding her empty arms out towards him. Keeping them firmly down at her sides, she clenched her fists. Then the Phaerie guards were helping the cavalry master hoist Vannor up in front of him on the big grey horse that she knew must be Schiannath, and D'arvan was mounting Chiamh, the bay, who was clearly far from happy with the situation. He plunged and wheeled, throwing up clods of turf from under his churning hooves, until the Mage bent forward and whispered something in his ear.

Whatever D'arvan had said, it seemed to work like magic. As one, the Xandim leapt into the air, heading back to freedom. A piece of Maya's heart went with them – in one flashing instant, she knew joy, and sorrow, and bitter, bitter envy. Then the sky was empty.

Hellorin put an arm around her shoulders. 'Come, my little she-wolf. All you can do now is care for your child, and wait for D'arvan to return.'

One of the beech trees in the grove had grown too tall, and had fallen to a bolt of lightning during the last of the summer storms. Yazour was chopping the earthbound giant into logs for the winter woodpile, hurrying to get as much of the task completed as possible, for the summer was sliding gently in to autumn now, and it would not be too long before the sun went down. Already there was a lamp burning in the ground floor of the tower across the lake, and he could see a faint glimmer of Magelight moving like a firefly in the garden, where Eliseth wandered between the rows of vegetables, picking out the ingredients for supper. The evening was still and tranquil; the only sounds were sleepy birdsong mixed with the gentle rippling murmur of wavelets by the lakeside, and the rasping sound of Iscalda tearing up the grass as she grazed companionably nearby.

He never knew what made him look up just them. Some instinct, perhaps left over from his far-off days as a warrior, drew his eyes towards the north . . . 'Reaper of Souls!' Yazour dropped the axe. The next minute, he was astride Iscalda's back and galloping across the bridge, yelling frantically for Eilin. The day they had long been dreading had come at last. The Phaerie were returning to the Vale.

'Get inside, Iscalda – you'll be safe there.' Without ceremony, Yazour opened the tower door and pulled the horse into the kitchen. He met Eilin in the doorway, on her way out. The Mage, carrying his sword and her own staff, looked at the white mare and smiled. 'That's everyone safe under cover, then,' she said. 'Don't worry, Iscalda,' she added, with a glint of anger in her eye. 'We'll soon send that damned Hellorin on his way.'

Yazour and Eilin, side by side, took up station at the island end of the bridge. The Phaerie steeds were very close now. 'But there are only two of them,' Eilin said in puzzled tones. 'This doesn't look like an invasion. What in the name of perdition does Hellorin think he's playing at?'

Yazour was a little ashamed of his earlier panic. When he saw the first outriders, he hadn't waited to count heads – he had simply assumed that an attack was under way. 'Could it be some kind of trick?' he suggested.

And then, on the wind, came the sound of voices calling their names.

D'arvan dismounted a little stiffly, almost sorry that this amazing ride through the skies was over. For a brief time, he had come to fully understand why his father was so desperate to keep his Xandim steeds. Then all such thoughts were lost as Eilin ran across the bridge to embrace him. 'D'arvan,' she cried. 'Thank all the gods – you're safe.' She clutched at his tunic, her fingers knotting in the fabric. 'Did Aurian come back with you?' she asked him eagerly. 'Why isn't she with you? Is she all right?'

'As far as I know,' D'arvan told her. 'She did come back with me, but I had to leave her in Nexis.' Feeling Eilin's shoulders droop with disappointment, he added quickly: 'She had the two cats with her, though. Shia is a formidable creature, and she would never let Aurian come to any harm.'

Beyond the two Magefolk, Yazour was greeting Parric with delight. Suddenly there was a wild neighing, and the door of Eilin's tower burst open. There was a thunder of hooves across the wooden bridge as Iscalda came hurtling across to rub necks with Schiannath, her brother.

'Well, there's a happy reunion,' said D'arvan. He couldn't suppress a grin of secret delight. 'I think I can improve matters, however . . .' He fingered the talisman that hung on a silver chain around his neck. The gleaming, polished stone at its centre felt warm to his touch, and shone with a misty grey light, like the sun glinting through a fall of silvery rain. His father had given it to him just before his departure, and it was imbued with Old Magic, the essence and core of Hellorin's power. Clutching at the Forest Lord's gift, D'arvan felt the magic running through him, so strange yet so familiar, as though it had awakened a force in his blood that had long lain dormant and untapped. Taking a deep breath, the Mage unbound the spell that trapped the Xandim in their equine shape.

285

The change was unexpected. Chiamh, so accustomed now to four legs, suddenly found himself on two. He swayed, staggered, and fell flat on his face. For a long moment he stayed there, his eyes closed, his senses whirling; stunned by a joy too great to be contained. He ran his fingers through the rough grass, feeling the individual texture of each narrow blade with extraordinarily sensitive fingers. He had never expected to be human again. Cautiously, he opened his eyes, and the world sprang at him, rich in colour and depth of perception. The balance was simply different, Chiamh thought – better hearing and sense of smell were exchanged for a great improvement in eyesight and touch.

'Chiamh – are you all right?' Yazour and Parric were bending over him, and the Windeye had no idea which one of them had spoken. They both looked equally concerned.

'I couldn't be better,' he assured them with a grin, as they helped him to his feet. Parric, whose life Chiamh had saved more than once, wrung his hand and clapped him on the shoulder, so hard that Chiamh almost lost his balance again. 'By Chathak, but it's good to have you back, old friend,' he told the Windeye. 'Life's been dull without you.'

'Ah, you just miss being Herdlord,' Chiamh teased him. Nearby, Schiannath and Iscalda were laughing and weeping in each other's arms. The Windeye turned to D'arvan. 'I've never met you in my human shape,' he said gravely, 'and I know little about you, save that you are a friend of Aurian. But I owe you such a debt of gratitude for what you've done for myself and these other Xandim . . .'

Just then, the Windeye was interrupted by the light, quick sound of further footsteps on the bridge. He turned and, to his utter astonishment, saw a little, dark-haired boy about five years old, and a large grey wolf. Even though he had changed a great deal, Chiamh still recognized Aurian's son. 'Why, it's Wolf,' he shouted in delight. He looked at Yazour in puzzlement. 'But who is the child?'

The child came up and tugged at Yazour's sleeve. 'Dad?' he said.

'*What?*' Chiamh blurted in utter amazement. 'He's *yours*?'

Yazour had turned very red. 'I . . .'

He looked at the Lady Eilin. 'Don't look at *me*,' she said. 'He's your friend, you explain. I'm going to have enough difficulty breaking the news to Aurian that she has a brother.'

20

Reunions

The morning was grey, with drifts of fine rain that swept across the Vale on a fitful wind that turned the surface of the lake to roughened pewter. Eilin slipped quietly out of the tower, careful not to make a sound – though the gods only knew why, she thought wryly. There had been so many tales to tell and plans to be made the previous night, and everyone had gone to bed so late, that it had scarcely been worth the trouble. Eilin was the only one who had not slept at all, and now it seemed as though she was the only one stirring in all the world.

As she crossed the exposed span of the bridge, the wind increased in strength. Eilin tugged at the hood of her brown cloak to stop it blowing back from her face. It was not a morning for walking, but she needed the comfort of her beloved Vale. She had come out to think, but really there was little to be considered. Yazour would leave this morning with the others – even Wolf and Iscalda. He would head back to his southlands with Aurian, and she would never see him again. Eilin would be alone once more, as she had been for most of her life. And, just as had happened with Aurian, she would have another child to bring up on her own.

Why? the Magewoman thought despairingly. Why does this keep happening to me? After Geraint died, she had refused to even consider the notion of another soulmate in her life. She had never wanted to experience such a loss again – and oh, how right she had been. Yet she had taken to Yazour from the very start – from that very first day, when he had brought back Iscalda and little Wolf, there had been a spark between them – but she should never have let him charm her as he had. It had taken the young warrior a long time – almost two years – to win her over, but by Iriana he had been persistent! In some ways he'd seemed older than his years – he was strong, capable and dependable, and always calm in the midst of her storms and doubts – yet in other ways he'd been so young, so full of enthusiasm and joy . . . He made me young again, Eilin thought. He gave me back so many of the years I had lost. And she had walked into it with her eyes wide open, had even let herself be lured by the notion of another child . . . *Oh, Eilin, you fool. You poor, pathetic old fool!*

It was too wet and windy for walking. Eilin's cloak was of little use for keeping out the damp and chill of the morning. She took shelter in the birch grove on the landward side of the bridge, leaning against the solid, comforting bulk of a dripping tree. For the first time she noticed that the leaves were beginning to turn yellow and bronze. Yes, summer was truly at an end.

Well, she had the courage to face her loss. The gods only knew, she'd had enough practice. She would do nothing to hinder or hold Yazour – he must follow his own path, and go where his heart led him. She had seen his face last night as they had talked with D'arvan, Parric and the others – seen the struggle that he was trying to hide. He wanted to help Aurian, wanted to be back among the press of events: wanted to go back out into the world, with its excitement and its lures. And who could blame him? Though they had been together for nearly ten years now, he was still young enough to want these things.

At least Eilin had his son – and she would not make the same mistake with Currain as she had made with Aurian. This child would not have a bitter and neglectful mother. And it was not as though Yazour was dead and unreachable, like Geraint. Who knows, the Magewoman thought, maybe he'll come back one day . . . Angrily she berated herself for clutching at such dreams. Of course he wouldn't. He would be going home, to his own lands, his own people . . . With a sigh, the Magewoman turned and went back to the tower, composing herself to bid Yazour farewell.

It was still raining when everyone left the tower and crossed the bridge, ready to depart. Yazour lingered behind the others, wanting to be the last to leave. He wanted to store in his memory every detail of the home that he and Eilin had built together, using his strength and her magic. This is ridiculous, he told himself. It's only for a little while – when all this is over you'll come back to Eilin and Currain, and everything will be as it was before. *If you don't get killed*, said a little voice in his mind. *If you don't fall in love with the south again, and abandon these harsh, damp northern climes. If a hundred and one things don't conspire to keep you away.*

The worst part of it was that Eilin had done nothing to keep him with her. If she had wept, or pleaded, he might have had an excuse to resent her. Had she given him a sign that she even cared . . . No, that wasn't fair. The two of them had been together long enough now for him to be aware that she was deeply unhappy at the thought of his leaving – and absolutely determined that he should never know it. He admired her courage – no wonder she had spawned such a warrior of a daughter.

'Yazour, are you coming?' Parric hailed him impatiently from the far side of the bridge, and the warrior went with a sigh. Currain was watching him – he knew, with the instinct of a child, that something was amiss. Wolf sat staring, the hackles on his neck raised and bristling. Though Yazour could not talk with the wolf in mind-speech as Eilin could, he was left in no doubt that Aurian's son disapproved of his decision.

The three Xandim stood to one side. After spending so long as horses, they were waiting until the very last moment to undergo the transition once more. Eilin was filling the ears of D'arvan and Iscalda with messages and advice to be passed on to Aurian. She scarcely glanced in Yazour's direction, but Chiamh sidled up to him. 'Yazour, you're making a big mistake,' he hissed in the warrior's ear. 'There are enough of us to help Aurian – one more won't make much difference. Your place is here. Your *heart* is here.'

It was time to go. Chiamh, Schiannath and Iscalda moved aside from the others and made their transformation. Yazour noticed Currain hanging on to his mother's hand and watching open-mouthed. Feeling as though his heart was being torn into pieces, he went to embrace his family one last time. 'I'll be back,' he told Eilin. 'I'll come back as soon as I can – I swear it.'

'Of course you will.' He could hear the lie in her voice. 'Take care,' she told him. 'And give my love to Aurian.' Her mouth twisted in a crooked grin. 'Tell her about her brother – it'll get me out of the task.'

'I will,' Yazour assured her. 'And you take care too – you and Currain.' When he left her, it felt as though he was tearing part of himself away. The boy was too young to understand – he waved at his father solemnly, as he always did when Yazour went hunting, or was leaving the tower to perform some small task.

The others were waiting. D'arvan had hoisted Wolf up in front of him, holding the animal as he lay across the horse's withers. It was clear that neither Wolf nor Chiamh was entirely happy with the situation. There was no helping it, however. Though Wolf and his grandmother were reluctant to part from one another, Eilin had decided, the previous night, that he should go to his mother, especially if there was a chance that she might be able to release him from his curse. All the same, it had taken a good deal of persuasion, and finally insistence, on her part to sway her grandson, who, when he had a mind, could be every bit as stubborn as his mother.

Parric was mounted on Schiannath as before, the two former Herdlords together. He held the limp form of Vannor in front of him on the saddle. Eilin, like D'arvan, had been unable to help the merchant, though they were hoping that Aurian, more advanced in the skills of healing, might be able to free him from his self-imposed prison.

Yazour strode across the grass to where Iscalda stood, patiently waiting. He looked at Eilin one last time, then leapt astride the white mare's back – and bit his tongue as Iscalda exploded beneath him into a whirling, bucking frenzy. Good horseman though Yazour was, there was not the faintest chance that he could stay on her back. Iscalda was determined. In far less than a minute, the warrior was lying on his back on the turf, cursing profusely.

'I think she's trying to tell you something,' Parric said dryly.

'Something you know already,' D'arvan put in helpfully.

Yazour scrambled to his feet. He turned back to Iscalda, but she flattened her ears and bared her teeth at him. Gradually, a grin compounded of relief and joy spread across his face.

'If I thought for one minute that Aurian couldn't manage without you, I'd tell you,' Parric said. 'Chathak's britches, man – stay here and be happy! Do it for all of us.'

The warrior nodded. 'All the time, my heart has been telling me to stay. I didn't want to go – but I thought it was my duty.' He laughed, for sheer lightness of heart. It was as though a heavy burden had vanished from his shoulders. 'For once, I will take your advice. Go well my friends – and kiss Aurian for me.'

Yazour held out his hands to Eilin, and the Magewoman, her face glowing, stepped forward to take them. Though the Valley was still beset by the moody wind and sulky drizzle, it seemed to the warrior as though the day was growing brighter.

Aurian opened her eyes. For a moment, she was still Between the Worlds, with Death – and Anvar. Then she recognized her surroundings, and realized that she was back in the Nightrunner haven, though not in the room she had originally been given. Furthermore, she ached from head to toe, and every part of her that had not been protected by her clothes was stinging from small lacerations made by flying particles of rock. There was a solid weight upon her feet – Shia lay across the bottom of the bed, and she knew that Khanu would not be far away. As she turned her head, she saw Forral occupying the bed to the left of her, while on the other side was Grince. Some kind of infirmary, then, she thought hazily. Very well. The Mage glanced above her head, and saw the hawk she had risked her life to rescue perched on the rail at the head of the bed. All at once, a tension she had not realized she'd been feeling left the Mage. Drifting comfortably, she fell back into sleep.

Aurian woke again to find Zanna sitting by her bed. 'At last!' she said, smiling. 'I was beginning to think you were going to sleep for a century or two. Even your faithful cats have gone out to hunt for something to eat.'

Zanna settled herself more comfortably in her chair. Though she was a grown woman – older, now, in relative terms, than Aurian herself – the Mage saw a do-or-die expression on her face that reminded her of the young girl who had hero-worshipped her so long ago. 'Now,' the Nightrunner said firmly, 'I want to know what it is that you're not telling me. What with everything that happened when you arrived, I know there was never a chance for explanations, but you weren't exactly forthcoming even then. The next thing we all knew, you had dashed off to the stone. I took your word for it when you said you must go, but now you're back I want to know more. Why is Finbarr so silent? What's the matter with Anvar – he's not himself at all. And something's wrong between the two of you, that's for sure.' Her forehead creased in a frown. 'What the bloody blazes happened up there on the mound, Aurian? As far as we know, that stone has stood there since before the Cataclysm – then you come along and in a matter of hours there's not only no more stone, there's no longer any mound, even.' She fell silent and waited, an expectant look on her face.

Aurian sighed. 'Gods, Zanna, I hardly know where to start . . .'

It took a good hour to tell the Nightrunner woman the whole tale. Zanna listened, saying nothing, though Aurian could see that she was aching to interrupt from time to time. When Aurian finally finished, she let out a long whistle. 'By all the gods – that's incredible! Aurian . . .' She leaned forward and put her hand on the Mage's arm, staring at her intently. 'What you said about Forral and Anvar, and the Cauldron of Rebirth – do you think it might have happened to my father, too?'

'Why do you ask?'

'Well . . .' Zanna told Aurian about Vannor's poisoning, and the old woman who had come and healed him in some miraculous fashion. 'And after that, he changed somehow,' she said sadly. 'It's hard to explain, but he was never the same again.' She hesitated. 'Aurian – do you think that old woman might have been Eliseth? And if it was, then what did she do to my dad?'

Aurian frowned. 'Who can say, Zanna? But it looks very likely to me. As to how she changed him – well, I have no idea. From what you say, there doesn't seem to have been the kind of exchange that occurred between Forral and Anvar. Something obviously happened, though – and whatever it was, you can be sure that no good will come of it.'

'If he's still alive,' murmured Zanna, 'I'd be willing to take the risk.'

She must have been wrong about the hawk. When Aurian awakened a third time to find the bird gone, it was hard to contain her disappointment. She had been so sure . . . Well, I can't think why, the Mage chided herself. So it was the only creature around when you came back though. So you were sure that Anvar had come with you. So the creature seemed to be dead, then you saw it move . . . But a hawk! You idiot! Is it even possible for a human spirit to occupy the form of a bird? Then she thought of Chiamh and Wolf, and Maya in the shape of an invisible unicorn. If all these things were possible, why not a bird?

Grince and Forral were already up and about, and the Nightrunner healer, Emmie, pronounced Aurian fit to do the same. 'Do you know what happened to the hawk that was here?' the Mage asked her, as she clambered stiffly out of bed and began to scramble into her clothes.

The woman's face fell. 'Lady, I'm sorry,' she said. 'The poor creature looked sick, so I took it down to the kitchen quarters to see if it would eat. When I was crossing the harbour cavern, it just took off on me, and flew away out to sea.'

Aurian's heart ached with disappointment. She turned away from Emmie so that the woman could not see her face. So that was that, then. It couldn't have been Anvar – or why would he have left her? Feeling incredibly stupid, Aurian pasted a bright smile on her face and turned back to the healer. 'Never mind. He's probably better off where he is.'

When the Mage returned to her chambers, Forral was waiting for her. She took one look at his face, and Anvar's blue eyes glinting cold with wrath, and suddenly found herself wishing that she'd stayed in the infirmary.

'What I want to know is what the hell did you think you were doing?' Forral paced the floor, unable to contain his anger. 'You nearly got us all killed!'

'There's no need to point out the obvious,' Aurian retorted, eyes flashing. 'It's your own fault that you were there in the first place. *I* didn't want you to follow me. And if it's any business of yours, I was trying to find out what Eliseth was doing.'

'By going off into some trance and lying there like a dead thing? Couldn't you just scry for her, or whatever it is you Magefolk do?'

'There were good reasons why that wasn't possible,' Aurian shouted. 'You're not a Mage – you don't have the slightest idea what you're talking about! Anvar would have understood . . .'

Her words lay between them like a naked sword.

'Ah, so that's what's rankling with you – bloody Anvar again!' Forral snarled. 'Maybe you were just trying to get yourself killed so you could follow him . . .'

'Maybe you're right,' Aurian said flatly. 'That's what happened when I lost you.'

'*What?*' Forral stopped pacing and stared at her.

'It's true,' Aurian flung at him. 'I very nearly drowned myself the night you were killed, then in the days – the months, really – after I lost you, I was taking the most insane risks. It was Anvar who stopped me – he protected me and took care of me until I was thinking rationally again.'

'Well, I hope you didn't resent him as much as you seem to resent me for doing the same thing.'

Aurian stared at him, open-mouthed, for a long moment. Slowly, the anger drained out of her. 'Damn,' she said wryly. 'You've got me there. Actually, you're right – more often than not I gave him an awful time.'

'Good,' the swordsman said decisively. He turned away so that she couldn't see his face. 'That's one comfort, anyway,' he muttered.

'What?' Aurian wasn't sure she had heard him right. 'Why in the world would you say a thing like that?'

Forral swung round and glared. 'Because I'm jealous of him, that's why,' he roared. 'Insanely, murderously jealous . . .

That bastard lay with you – you *loved* him . . .' In three swift steps he closed the gap between them. Seizing the Mage by the shoulders, hard enough to wring a gasp of pain from her, he covered her mouth with his own and kissed her until she fought for breath.

For a moment Aurian struggled against him, and then she didn't care any more. She was done with fighting this insane situation. He was Forral, he was Anvar – both the men she'd loved and mourned. And she wanted him – them – whatever. Almost savagely, she returned his kisses, then they were tearing at each other's clothes. Forral picked her up and hurled her down on to the bed, and with a triumphant laugh Aurian pulled him down on top of her. That first time, they coupled with savage ferocity, blasting away the walls that had grown up between them. Then, almost before the echoes of that first, fierce passion had time to die away, they made love again, gently, this time, and with infinite tenderness.

When at last it was over, and they lay spent in one another's arms, Forral looked at her searchingly, and the Mage was moved to see tears standing in Anvar's intense blue eyes. 'So you do still care,' he whispered.

Aurian gave a languorous sigh. 'You bloody fool,' she said softly. 'Of course I do.'

Someone was pounding on the door. Aurian turned over and made a small sound of complaint, unwilling to be disturbed from her happy dreams. 'Go away,' she shouted.

'Wake up!' It was Zanna's voice. 'Hurry! You've got to come – just wait till you see who's here! D'arvan and Parric and Chiamh, and . . .' Her voice cracked. 'Oh, Aurian, they have dad with them!'

Aurian leapt out of bed and ran to the door. Forral almost beat her to it. When they opened it, Zanna's face was a picture. She looked from one to the other. 'I know I said to hurry,' she told them faintly, 'but I think there's time for you to put some clothes on first.'

As she came through the common room door, Aurian's heart leapt to see Chiamh. His face lit up at the sight of her. Their reunion was without tears or laughter; they simply embraced, with quiet delight and deep, deep joy. 'I'm so glad to see you,' Aurian said softly. 'I never thought I'd set eyes on you in human form again – and it was all my fault, for not mastering the Sword of Flame, and controlling the Phaerie.'

'No,' the Windeye told her. 'You take too much blame upon yourself. It was the Forest Lord who trapped us in our equine forms – he did not ask us to choose, or to help – he never once looked on us as human. At least Hellorin's son is far more enlightened,' he added. 'It was he who bargained for our freedom.'

Chiamh glanced over the Mage's shoulder at the inconspicuous grey shape that was hanging shyly back in a shadowy corner. 'Come with me,' he told her. 'I have someone here who very much wants to meet you.'

For an instant her heart stopped beating. 'Wolf?' she whispered. '*Wolf?*'

Then the thoughts of the great grey beast in the corner came to her, clear and strong. 'Mother?'

The Mage wanted to run to her son and throw her arms around him, but something – a trace of reticence or doubt in his mental tone – made her hesitate. She was glad that mind communication at least gave them a certain amount of privacy in the crowded room. 'Wolf, I'm so very glad to see you,' she told him softly. 'I've waited a long time for this moment. There's so much –'

'I don't remember you.' The wolf looked at her coldly. 'And I don't want to be here. My grandmother said I had to come.'

Sick dismay clenched like a fist in Aurian's belly. Everyone else in the room was oblivious of the exchange that had just taken place, and she fought hard to keep the hurt from showing on her face.

'Give him time, Aurian.' It was Chiamh's voice. 'This is all very strange to him. You two will have to get to know one another all over again.'

Thank the gods for the wisdom and kindness of Chiamh – he was a true friend. And he was right, of course.

'I'm sorry you feel that way,' the Mage told Wolf seriously.

297

'It's always a wrench to leave home – especially for the first time.'

'You seem to be good at it. You left *me*.'

The wolf fled the room, running into Forral with a snarl as he shot through the door, and knocking the swordsman right off his feet. 'What the blazes was that all about?' the swordsman demanded as he scrambled up from the floor.

'That unmannerly creature,' said Aurian, with a wry grimace, 'was your son.'

Forral gaped at her, absolutely stunned. Then he cast his eyes heavenwards. 'Great Chathak preserve us,' he muttered. 'How do you spank a wolf?'

Chiamh stared at the familiar form of Aurian's companion. There was something about the figure . . . Quickly he switched to his Othersight, and discovered that the refulgent aura of the man's lifeforce had changed completely from the one he remembered. The Windeye was too shocked for tact. 'That's not Anvar,' he gasped.

Schiannath looked at him oddly. 'What are you talking about, Chiamh? You hardly give yourself time to draw breath in human form before you're starting with that weird Windeye nonsense again. Of course it's Anvar! Anyone can see that.'

The swordsman looked Schiannath straight in the eye. 'No, he's right,' he said baldly. 'I'm not Anvar. My name is Forral.'

Oh, thank you, Forral. Thanks for breaking it to them gently – you idiot! Aurian hid her face in her hands and let the storm break over her.

Gevan was weary from sailing all night, but the tides and currents had been in his favour, and a strong, steady wind had blown him fair to Norberth in less time than he'd expected. As he sailed into the harbour, the smuggler rubbed a hand across his hot and bleary eyes, and smiled grimly to himself. It had almost seemed as though the gods themselves had been in favour of his plan. He would show them – that serpent-tongued Mage-loving little bitch who fancied herself the true Nightrunner leader, and her man, who had pushed him around once too often – with the support of that weak-minded

298

fool Yanis, who just let them get away with it. *He* was no leader – not like his da had been!

The smuggler moored his swift little craft among the fishing boats that were being unloaded of the night's catch, and climbed up on to the busy wharf. As he hurried along, he jingled the coins in his pockets. He had enough in here to buy himself a good meal and a swift horse – and once he reached Nexis and spoke to Lord Pendral, he would never want for wealth again.

21
The Old Magic

The same nightmare repeats itself, again and again. Vannor turns restlessly and awakens with a hoarse cry of dismay. The horns and cries are loud now. The Phaerie have come to Nexis to extract their vengeance. He runs to the window. In the city, the warning bell of the garrison has begun to ring, alerting him to the city's peril.

He hears a tumult of voices from downstairs, where the household staff are beginning to panic. Through the windows he sees them running outside to witness the spectacle. 'Get inside,' he bellows. 'Get into the house, you fools, and stay there.' Snatching up his sword he runs downstairs, glad that Dulsina has left him. With the Nightrunners she'll be safe.

As Vannor watches, the Phaerie sweep down on the city. The exultant horns take on a deeper, more menacing note. Light flowers from the Mages' Tower as the Immortals ride past, and spreads down through the Academy complex. Similar patches of effulgence spread rapidly through the city, wherever the Phaerie touch down – then hungry flames leap up, and the shrilling of the horns is drowned by screams.

Vannor runs through burning streets, his boots slithering on blood and entrails. He sees a man cut in two by a Phaerie sword, his guts spilling out across the cobbles. A child with a rag doll weeps over the headless body of her mother. A lad runs from a burning house, trailing streamers of flame, and falls to the ground, engulfed in a ball of fire. A woman shrieks as her children are snatched away, screaming, by a Phaerie woman with burning sapphire eyes. Scenes of torture, torment and slaughter enacted over and over again, while Phaerie stalk the streets, cold-eyed and terrible . . .

Out of nowhere, a sword swings down in a glittering arc, and the blue-eyed Phaerie woman crumples to the ground, golden blood pouring from a deep rent in her flesh. The children, released, run back to their mother, who receives them with a cry of joy. The tall wielder of the sword, whose identity is hidden in a shimmering haze, swirls a heavy cloak from its shoulders and covers the burning lad, smothering the flames. The youth springs up from beneath the cloak, restored and healed.

The mysterious warrior calls to Vannor. 'Come with me, and fight them. Fight the bastards, Vannor. Fight your way free!'

And Vannor remembers the sword in his hand, and his limp grasp tightens round the hilt. At the side of his unknown redeemer he scours the streets of his city, helping folk wherever he can, while the Phaerie fall to his sword like wheat before a scythe.

And at last he fights his way out of the city and stands on the high northern road that leads out across the clean, untainted moors. The cool, fresh wind scours the stench of blood and smoke from the air. The numinous stranger turns. The concealing cloak of mist dissolves away, and he sees the face of Aurian. She holds out a hand to him. 'You're free now, Vannor. Free to return. Come back with me, my friend, come back . . .'

Slowly, Vannor reaches out and takes the hand . . .

. . . and the high moors swirled away, and he found himself lying on a bed, in a cavern, with no memory of how he had come to be there. Everything was strange – except the face, the same, familiar face of the Mage, looking down on him kindly and holding his hand tightly in her strong, callused grasp, as if to anchor him in life.

Aurian smiled at him. 'Welcome back,' she said.

'Welcome back, Vannor,' Eliseth snarled, 'and about time, too.' In truth, however, she was not displeased, for the last three days of constant vigilance – three miserable days spent peering into the dark, dead depths of the grail until her head and eyes ached, had finally paid off. She looked at the image in the grail with narrowed eyes. Really, it was laughable. Dear, good little Aurian had kindly brought the former High Lord back to his senses – and so created her own undoing. Now, at last, Eliseth had a spy and an agent in close proximity to the Mage.

Eliseth let her consciousness mesh with the power of the grail, until, with an abrupt and dizzying switch of focus, she viewed the scene through Vannor's eyes, concealing a flash of cold hatred at the sight of Zanna. Well, now that the Weather-Mage had Vannor back under her control, there would be ample time and opportunity to deal with his daughter . . .

'I'm only too glad that it worked,' Aurian was saying to the woman. 'With luck, he should be fine now.'

'I can never thank you enough.' Zanna tucked her arm through that of the Mage, and they walked away, almost out of earshot. 'Now, do you know exactly what you'll need for your journey south . . .'

Eliseth could hear no more – but she had all the information she needed right there. Wrenching herself back into her own body, she emptied the water in the grail out of the window, and dispatched a servant to find Skua and Sunfeather. If she wanted to be secure in Dhiammara before Aurian reached the place, it was time to make a start. And the first obstacle that would have to be dealt with was Eyrie – the southern Skyfolk colony at the edge of the great forest, and the place that was currently harbouring Queen Raven herself.

Eliseth smiled coldly. The colony and its human counterpart set up by Aurian's former companions would make a superb supply base for defenders of Dhiammara – and the Skyfolk and their human friends would make useful slaves.

The hawk had flown wide and far before Anvar remembered who he was, where he had come from, and why he must return. He did not reach this awareness all at once – instead, the information filtered, very gradually, into his consciousness, like bubbles of air rising from the bottom of a pool. Only when some vague sense of identity had awakened within him could he begin to work out what was wrong. It was a difficult process, as if each thought was a tiny, glittering bead that must be taken out and examined in detail before it could be strung with the others on a thread of consciousness. The efficiency of his thinking, however, improved with practice, until finally he decided his difficulties stemmed from the fact that the vast, complex entity which was the spirit of a human and a Mage fitted ill inside the bird's small body and even smaller brain.

All the time Anvar had been deliberating, he had been flying steadily along the coast, with the ocean on his left wing and the land on his right. Suddenly he became aware of what he was doing. I'm flying! I don't know how to do this! It's impossible! The thoughts scarcely had time to flash into his mind before land, sea and sky were whirling across his vision in a disorientating jumble as he plummeted, tumbling end over end in an uncontrolled and helpless fall.

Anvar's mind froze in panic, and instinct saved him. Clearly, the automatic reflexes for flight were contained within the hawk's wings and brain. His wings flashed open, catching the wind beneath them and tilting to swoop him up at a dizzying angle, so close to the surface of the sea that one wingtip actually caught the top of a wave.

Gods – that was too close. As he careened unsteadily on his way, the Mage ordered himself not to think of the technique he was using – in fact preferably not to think about the whole business at all. It proved easy enough, for his brain seemed only capable of dealing with one subject at a time, but to be on the safe side he flew inland – almost drowning himself again with his first attempt to turn – and once he had solid ground beneath him he flew as low as he dared, to reduce the chance of his hurting himself should worst come to worst.

That was how he came to see the rabbit – several of them, in fact, in a grassy hollow a short distance back from the brink of the cliff. A red spike of hunger flashed across his brain. Instinct took over once more. He didn't have far to drop – he simply selected his prey, angled his wings and tucked them close to his sides, letting his momentum drive him, talons extended, into the fleeing rabbit. He hit the beast, knocking it off its feet, his wings extending at exactly the right instant to take him up again, a fingertip above the grass. Then he was turning at an impossibly steep angle, and gliding back to the ground to finish his stunned prey with a sharp blow of his beak. Dipping his head, he began to tear through fur into the still-warm flesh.

303

He was halfway through the grisly meal when the sense of wrongness overtook him. *No, this isn't right. This is not what I eat. Not raw!* He remembered a face – a human face, with blue eyes and blond hair. *Me?* Hands, brown, with fingertips callused, not from a sword, but from harp strings. A harp – there had been a wonderful harp . . .

Then Anvar saw another face, its sculpted features as aquiline as those of the creature he had become. There was tangled hair of a deep copper shade, and intense green eyes . . . *Aurian.* The next minute, the clifftop was empty, and a hawk was streaking along the coastline; the sea on its right wing, the land on its left, heading back the way it had come.

'If we make all speed we can get there in about three days, my Lord. Much quicker, if this wind swings round, instead of staying set against us. Your sailors wouldn't have the skill to get into our anchorage, and in any case the keels of your ships will be too deep, so we'll drop anchor in the next cove, and bring the soldiers in overland.'

From his great chair, high on its dais, Lord Pendral looked down at the unkempt, unshaven smuggler. This was a pinch-faced, unprepossessing wretch to be sure, but there were two details about him with which the High Lord of Nexis could readily identify: the all-consuming lust for vengeance, and the glint of pure, unadulterated avarice in Gevan's eyes. The man had surely been sent by the gods themselves, but if Pendral's success as a merchant had taught him one important thing it was not to appear too keen too soon. 'You seem to have thought it all out.' He laced his ring-encrusted fingers across his ample belly and narrowed his eyes at the ruffian. 'And just what do you expect from me in exchange for this information?'

Gevan's eyes shifted away for an instant, and flicked back to the High Lord. 'I want to be a merchant like yourself, my Lord – successful and respected. I want my own crimes to be pardoned, I want five hundred gold pieces to start up in trade, I want a warehouse of my own down on the wharves – and when you destroy the Nightrunners, I want my pick of their vessels.'

Pendral's eyes widened. 'Indeed? You don't want much, do you?'

Gevan shrugged, and was about to spit on the highly polished floor, until Pendral fixed him with the gaze of a snake about to strike. He swallowed the mouthful hastily. 'My Lord, think what the Nightrunners cost you and this city in trade each year. Without my help you'll never find them – no one ever has. And as I told you, they're sheltering the thief who stole your jewels. Surely it would be worth anything to you to lay your hands on him?'

Pendral nodded. Why delay on this matter, he thought. The mere mention of the thief set his guts roiling with rage, and he was anxious to strike as soon as possible lest the slippery wretch should take himself elsewhere. 'Very well – I agree. You shall have what you desire – and what you so richly deserve.'

The treacherous smuggler was effusive in his gratitude, and, as Pendral had expected, he was far too stupid to notice the implicit threat – or promise – that lurked behind the High Lord's words.

Aurian slipped out of the room, leaving Vannor to his reunion with Dulsina and Zanna. When she returned to her quarters, she was pleased to find Shia and Khanu there. 'What have you two been doing?' she asked them. 'I haven't seen much of you this last day or so.'

'Mostly, we've been hunting on the moor,' Shia told her. 'We don't like being cooped up with all these humans.' She gave the Mage a piercing look. 'Where is the other one?'

Aurian sighed. For some reason that she would not disclose, Shia had taken a marked dislike to Forral, and refused to even name him. 'Forral is talking to Parric and Hargorn,' she told the cat with a smile. 'There seems to be some kind of warriors' reunion going on, so I hope that Emmie has plenty of drink on hand.'

'Humans and their drink! We waste time here,' Shia grumbled.

'You're right, I know.' Aurian flopped down into a chair. 'We'll be going soon. I must start arranging –' She was interrupted by a knock at the door. She sighed. 'Who is it?'

'It is I – Finbarr.'

Aurian was all too aware that it was not the archivist who spoke, but the Wraith who shared his form. 'Now what?' she muttered sourly under her breath, though it struck her that she was being somewhat unjust. Ever since his arrival, the Wraith had remained solitary and apart from the Night-runners, in order to escape both suspicion and alarm. Only Zanna and Tarnal were aware of the creature's true identity, and it said a great deal for their trust in Aurian that they allowed the entity to stay.

As the tall, gangling figure walked into the room, Aurian had to remind herself sharply that some ghastly, inhuman creature controlled this body in place of her old friend. 'Is something wrong?' she asked.

'We have a difficulty.' The grating, emotionless voice sent a chill through the Mage. 'Now you have removed the spell that took me out of time, I must feed – but if I quit this body, my host will perish. Once more I need your help, Mage. When I leave this form you must take it out of time once more, and restore it only when I wish to return.'

For a moment, Aurian had difficulty finding her voice. 'Let me get this straight,' she said quietly. 'When you say feed, do you mean you need to take a human life?'

The expressionless figure nodded. 'As you say.'

'But you can't do that!' the Mage burst out. 'These folk are our friends. They have given us shelter – they trust us. I can't just let you go and kill one of them!'

'You have no choice.' The Wraith regarded her impassively, its utter lack of emotion shocking on Finbarr's face. 'My instinct for survival is as great as that of any other being – I will feed with or without your help. If you will not assist me in the preservation of this body, I will simply return to my old shape for good, and abandon this carapace to die.'

Aurian sank down into the chair. 'How much longer can you last?' she whispered. 'How soon before you need to feed?'

'I can last perhaps two or three days more – then I must feed or perish.'

*

'I must have gone mad,' Vannor said, in a voice that was heavy with shame. He looked at his daughter, and then at the woman he loved. 'There's no other explanation for the way I was acting. How could I have driven you away from me, Dulsina? I would rather cut off my other hand!'

Dulsina shook her head. 'At the time it was like a dreadful nightmare – like living with a total stranger – but it's over now, love, at any rate. I'm only too glad to have you back again, and acting like yourself. This last year has been the loneliest of my life. You know, I was so angry when I left you – I told myself I never wanted to set eyes on you again.' She shrugged. 'It didn't take too long before I discovered my mistake.'

'I'm glad to be back too – but it doesn't explain or excuse my actions. What happened to me, Dulsina? Why in creation would I want to order an attack on the Phaerie? The whole idea is insane! I must have lost my mind completely – had a fit or a seizure or something – I don't recall.' He rubbed his one hand across his face. 'Can you believe it?' he whispered, the words coming muffled from between his fingers. 'I actually ordered all those men and women to their deaths – and I can't even *remember*? What kind of monster am I?'

Zanna laid a hand on her father's shoulder. 'What's the point in torturing yourself like this? It won't do you any good, nor will it bring those people back. Besides, I agree with you – had you been in your right mind you would never have acted like that. It must have been the poison that affected you – the gods only know how you survived it at all . . .' Her words trailed off into silence as she remembered her earlier conversation with Aurian.

'Dad . . .' she began hesitantly. How in the name of the gods could she suggest that he might have been under the influence of Eliseth without alarming him so badly that he never dared make a move again? Or worse still, she thought with a shiver, actually alerting Eliseth in some way to the fact that they knew what she had done?

'Can you remember anything about the time you were poisoned?' Zanna plunged on recklessly. 'When you were actually ill, I mean? Did you have any strange dreams, or visions?

307

And what about the old woman who saved your life? What did she do to you? Have you any recollection of her at all?'

Vannor shook his head and sighed. 'I think I had some weird kind of dream about Forral, but apart from that I don't remember anything about the entire episode, love. Not a thing . . .'

'Never mind, dad – it doesn't matter,' Zanna assured him – but even as she spoke the words, a shiver went through her. Try as she might, she couldn't shake the feeling that it *would* matter – very much indeed.

Aurian sat in her darkened chamber and studied the faint and feeble glow that emanated from the crystal at the head of the Staff of Earth. This isn't right, she thought despairingly. Where has the power gone? What can have happened, Between the Worlds? The corporeal Staff that had been left in the mundane world with Aurian's body appeared to have come out of the entire episode unscathed and unchanged, but the ethereal manifestation, the core of the Artefact's power, had been virtually destroyed in the Well of Souls. Indeed, had Aurian not been able to rescue the serpents and the crystal, she had a very bad feeling that she would have had no Staff to come back to on her return. Even as matters stood, she was in serious trouble.

Wondering what she could do to restore the power, Aurian cradled the Artefact in her lap. It felt like watching over an ailing friend. Normally, when she touched the Staff a glorious surge of vibrant energy went coursing through her. Its power had a distinctive feel to it, for, like the Harp of Winds, the Staff had an intelligence and a character all its own. Now, as she held it, she could barely feel a tingle, and she could feel no more personality than was present in any other dead stick.

The Harp. Now there was an idea. Perhaps the power of its fellow-Artefact could revive the Staff of Earth. Aurian ran to fetch it. As always, the Harp thrummed discordantly when she picked it up, and the Mage found it difficult to hold, as though it was constantly trying to writhe out of her grasp. As she touched the crystalline frame, an image of Anvar leapt into her mind; so vivid that she felt she could touch him. The

Harp gave a shimmering sigh, and a cascade of notes, each one visible as a falling star, swirled away from it. 'Anvar,' it sang, over and over. 'Anvar . . .'

Aurian sighed. 'I know,' she told it. 'I miss him too. But we'll both have to do without him for the time being, and if you want him back you had better co-operate with me.'

The Mage's words cut harshly across the liquid fall of light that was the Harp's song, and abruptly the Artefact fell silent. After a moment, the frame ceased to feel slippery in her hands, and a tentative tingle of energy leaked into her fingers and ran through her arms. In her thoughts, Aurian sent out a wave of gratitude towards the Artefact, and felt it thrum in response. Carefully, she laid it down on her bed, beside the Staff of Earth. 'Can you tell me why the Staff has lost its power,' she asked the Harp of Winds, 'and what I may do to heal it?'

In the darkened room, the crystal frame of the Harp began to glow with a soft incandescence that expanded and reached out to embrace the dormant Staff, outlining the twisting shapes of the serpents in a nebulous lustre. At first, Aurian thought the misty luminescence was playing tricks with her eyes. As she watched, the serpents, still holding the dull crystal, lifted their heads from the Staff to watch her with coldly glittering eyes. In the ghostly radiance of the Harp, their colours looked flat and faded; no longer the brilliant red-and-silver and the vivid gold-and-green that she recalled.

Then, once again, the Harp began to sing in its shimmering voice. 'They say the fault is yours, O Mage. They say you abused your guardianship; that you used the Staff for ill: for death and slaughter.'

Aurian's blood turned to ice as she remembered her slaughter of Pendral's soldiers in the tunnels beneath the Academy.

'You knew, Mage, that there would come a reckoning,' the Harp sang on, its notes now as hard and sharp as diamonds. 'Firstly, there will be an equal price to pay for your deeds that day. Secondly, to win back the Staff you must prove yourself worthy once more. You must atone. And you must pay back in love and healing all the power you took from the Staff for death and destruction. Then both you and my fellow-Artefact will be renewed.' With one last shimmering note, the Harp fell silent.

It was some time later when Chiamh found the Mage, still sitting in the darkness with the dormant Artefacts laid in front of her on the bed. Gently, he wiped the tears from her face and held her in silence for a long time. 'Come on,' he said at last. 'Let's get you out of this deep darkness, and back into the open and the light.'

'You must be out of your mind! I can't do that!' Aurian looked from Chiamh to D'arvan in dismay. These last days had been difficult enough without being asked to usurp the Old Magic – the province of the Phaerie – and use it for flight. 'I'm a Mage,' she objected, 'not a bloody Phaerie – I don't know what makes the Xandim fly and I don't want to! Don't you know how I feel about heights, D'arvan? Just being out here on top of this cliff makes me uneasy, and I'm nowhere near the edge. That business with the Skyfolk and their nets was quite bad enough, but there is no way – and I mean *no* way – that you're getting me up in the air on anything I could fall off!'

D'arvan shrugged. 'Suit yourself. Of course this means you'll take months to get anywhere, with Eliseth up to all sorts of mischief in the meantime. Furthermore I'll have to come with you, and abandon Maya to the gods only know what fate . . .'

The Mage's dismay turned into stone-cold horror. 'Do we really have to fly?' she asked in a small voice. 'Surely it's not absolutely necessary . . .'

'Look,' D'arvan told her, with a patient expression that she itched to strike from his face, 'Eliseth is a long way ahead of you, Aurian. You told me yourself she's had time to conquer Aerillia. The longer you delay, the more she can consolidate her position and the more difficult it'll be for you when you eventually catch up with her.' He patted her gently on the arm. 'Come on, Aurian – think how far you've come, and all you've achieved since the night you fled Nexis. You know you can do it if you have to. You know you *will*.'

Aurian gritted her teeth. 'D'arvan' she said tightly, 'I hate you. You know me far too well for my own good.'

The Windeye held out his hands to her. 'It won't be so bad,

my friend. I won't let you fall – you should know better than that. It won't be the first time we've ridden together.'

Aurian sighed. 'That's all very well, Chiamh, but you're not exactly an expert at this business yourself. You've only done it a couple of times – and with Phaerie to assist you. What if we both mess it up?'

'We'll stay close to the ground until we're confident.' He grinned. 'Come, Mage. Think what fun we could have with this.'

Aurian held up her hands in defeat. 'All right, all right. Let's get on with it now, before I change my mind.'

D'arvan lifted Hellorin's talisman, on its glittering chain, from around his neck, and laid it in the Mage's outstretched hand. As it touched her skin the gleaming surface of the stone changed from misty grey to clear silver, and flashed once with a blazing white light. Aurian staggered as a fierce, alien power pulsed through her, as bright as suns, as dark as the vault of the universe, as strong as the very bones of the world and as ancient as time itself.

'Seven bloody demons! What *is* this?'

'The talisman has been imbued with the Old Magic by my father,' D'arvan told her. 'You hold in your hand the power of the Phaerie.'

Aurian shook her head. 'Surely it can't be *that* easy,' she argued. 'I mean, if you were to give this to Zanna, for example, she couldn't just go flitting about the sky on Chiamh's back . . .'

'She certainly could not,' the Windeye put in with a laugh, 'because I wouldn't let her.'

'Don't be daft, Aurian – obviously you'd have to be a Mage,' D'arvan told her with a touch of irritation. 'A Mortal couldn't possibly manipulate – or even recognize – power like this.'

Aurian was looking doubtfully at the talisman that lay, quiescent now, in the palm of her cupped hand. 'I'm not sure that I can, either. It's so different, this magic.'

'There's no reason why it shouldn't work,' D'arvan insisted. 'After all, the Artefacts give you access to the High Magic – this talisman gives you power of another kind. Just

311

think of it as an Artefact of the Old Magic. Go on – put it on.'

The Mage slipped the talisman around her neck – and gave a cry of astonishment. She could see the living energies of her companions, cloaking their bodies in auras of shimmering radiance that were in constant flux, renewing themselves with each thought and motion. She saw the green haze of living energy that shone from each blade of grass. The rock below her feet was like a fractured mass of translucent crystal, in shades of amber and red, and the ocean was like a silken cloak thrown over the bones of the earth, glowing softly with opal, moonstone and pearl and limned with vibrant lapis, aquamarine and amethyst to mark the movement of current and swell. The winds that swirled around the exposed clifftop streamed like glistening silver ribbons, and each gull that was wheeling and diving through the air above the ocean was a spark of silver that trailed a streaking tail of light like a shooting star.

'Aurian! Aurian – come back!'

Hands were gripping her shoulders, shaking her violently. Distantly, she felt someone lifting the talisman and pulling it over her head. With a cry of dismay she snatched at it, but was too late. Aurian's vision cleared to see D'arvan standing in front of her, with the stone at the end of its silver chain swinging from his outstretched hands. Without it the world seemed a dull, flat, colourless place, and Aurian was assailed by a deep sense of loss. 'Plague take it, D'arvan,' she said irritably, 'what do you think you're doing?'

'I had to do something,' D'arvan protested. 'You stood there for ages, not speaking or moving, just staring into oblivion. You were completely captivated.'

Aurian sighed, trying to grasp the last elusive memories of the wonder she had witnessed before they slipped away from her entirely. 'It was breathtaking, D'arvan. Why didn't you warn me?'

D'arvan looked puzzled. 'Warn you about what?'

'About . . .' With some difficulty, Aurian tried to explain what she had seen.

'Why,' the Windeye cried excitedly, 'that's exactly what I see with Othersight!'

'Well I certainly don't see anything like that,' said D'arvan.

'So how do you account for it?'

'I think I understand,' the Mage said slowly. 'Because your race was so closely connected with the Phaerie, Chiamh, the powers of the Windeye must stem from the Old Magic. But the Phaerie themselves are actually part of that magic – they're living manifestations of the Old Magic, if you like – and so they don't discern what we non-Phaerie perceive.'

'It's a pity – from what you and Chiamh say, I feel as though I'm missing something special,' D'arvan said. 'There's only one problem, Aurian – how are you going to control this Othersight? It's no good you having access to the Old Magic if it's just going to enthrall you.'

'Let her try it again,' Chiamh suggested, 'and we'll fly this time. She'll know what to expect, so it won't come as such a shock, and what's more she'll have something else to occupy her attention. I'll teach her to control the Othersight, but it will require a lot of practice – there's no time to do it now.'

'Do you think it's safe?' D'arvan began doubtfully.

'Oh, let's get on with it,' Aurian said impatiently, 'before we grow old and grey standing here on this blasted cliff. You've already explained what I ought to be doing – give me back the talisman, D'arvan.'

Reluctantly, he handed the shimmering stone to her. The Mage almost snatched it out of his grasp. When she hung the chain around her neck once more, the world sprang back into radiant splendour. Entranced, she watched Chiamh's outline change and his aura alter to darker, more stocky hues as he changed from human to equine shape. Well, standing around putting off the moment of action wouldn't make her feel any less nervous. D'arvan made a stirrup of his hands for her and, taking a deep breath, Aurian scrambled up on to the Windeye's back.

22

Departures

Knotting one hand firmly into Chiamh's mane, the Mage closed the other around the talisman. Concentrating hard to imprint her will upon the unfamiliar magic, she gathered the field of energy that constituted her own aura, and let it merge with that of the Xandim beneath her, and the swirling silvery strands that were the wind. Chiamh leapt forward with a lurch that almost unseated her, set his hooves upon a pathway of gleaming air, and stretched out his stride in what seemed like an ordinary gallop – except that with every step, he and the Mage were climbing higher and higher into the skies.

The first thing Aurian noticed was the cold, which increased as she mounted higher, and the strengthening wind that made her eyes water and her ears ache, and blew her hair back from her face. Chiamh's rhythmic stride felt similar to the way it had always felt, except that the motion was smoother and more fluid, without the jarring impact as his hooves struck the ground. Save for that one detail, Aurian could almost imagine herself riding along on the ground in an ordinary fashion – so long as she didn't look down. For a time she was very careful not to do that. She clung to Chiamh's back like a burr, crouching low over his neck with her eyes screwed tight shut, and when she did gain the courage to open them – mostly because it was more worrying not to be able to see what was going on – she kept them fixed firmly in front of her, on the Windeye's pricked, black-tipped ears.

Finally, Aurian mustered enough courage to look down at the ground. Glowing in the dazzling, crystalline configurations of the Othersight, it swung dizzily beneath her in remote but perfect detail, just as it had done when she had ridden the winds to Aerillia with Chiamh, so long ago. And here we are, riding them together once more, the Mage thought – and her fear vanished all at once, in a glow of warmth and trust for her companion, as did the many worries that had been dogging her for these last hours.

The Mage had been filled with despair ever since Anvar's spirit had failed to return with her own from the Well of Souls, for if he had gone to be reborn elsewhere he could never be restored, even with the Cauldron, to his old body. Now he seemed truly dead to her and lost for ever, so that she was forced to fight a continuing battle against her sorrow, in order to keep striving towards her goal of Eliseth's defeat. She had also been feeling hurt by Wolf's hostility, though in truth she could understand why he should feel little love for a mother who had seemingly abandoned him for so many years. Vannor, too – there was still something very much amiss with the man, though for the life of her she couldn't discover what . . . But the higher Aurian soared with the Windeye, the lighter her heart began to feel, as though she had truly left her troubles behind her, anchored to the ground below.

Chiamh circled above the cliffs and began to make his descent, losing height all the time as he angled back to where D'arvan stood waiting. He landed perfectly; so lightly that Aurian barely felt the jar at all. She slid down quickly from his back, delighted by what she had seen, but glad, none the less, to be back safe on solid ground. As she stepped back Chiamh shimmered, and changed back to his human shape. 'Well?' he asked her challengingly. 'No, on second thoughts don't tell me. You were squeezing me so tightly round the ribs that I'll probably have the bruises for a week.'

Aurian removed the talisman from her neck and dropped it carefully into the pocket of her tunic. 'I could probably get used to it,' she admitted cautiously. Then she exchanged glances with the Windeye and they both laughed. Aurian held out her hands to him. 'It was wonderful,' she said, 'as well you know . . .'

She broke off, staring over Chiamh's shoulder and up into the sky at a small dark speck in the distance. It seemed to be hurtling down towards her at a tremendous rate. The Mage held her breath. 'Don't be daft,' she told herself, 'it's probably just a chough or a gull . . .' But the sight had set a fresh spark

315

to the cooling embers of hope within her heart, and already they had flared up, renewed – to burn brighter yet when the bird came close enough for her to see that it was, indeed, a hawk.

Chiamh shook her arm. 'What is it, Aurian? What do you see?' He knew better than to try to look in the direction of her gaze – his vision was far too limited.

'I think –' the Mage began, and fell silent. Since the hawk had flown away from the Nightrunner settlement, she had derided herself as a fool for thinking that such a creature might have housed Anvar's spirit. In her embarrassment and doubt she had remained silent, therefore, and had not mentioned her suspicions to a soul. Now, however, those former suspicions were looking to be increasingly accurate as the hawk came to hover high above her head.

'Dear gods, it *is* . . .' Aurian breathed. She extended an arm to the hovering bird. 'Anvar?' she called softly.

'*Anvar?*' D'arvan exclaimed. He looked at her with deep concern. 'Aurian, you'd better come inside,' he said gently.

He reached out to take her hand, but Chiamh restrained him. 'D'arvan, look . . .' The hawk abandoned its static position in the sky and sideslipped down towards Aurian. It landed on her forearm, settling its wings across its back as though it meant to stay there, and fixed the Mage's face in its fierce amber gaze.

The warm colouration drained from Chiamh's eyes, changing them to reflective argent as he switched to his Othersight. The silver eyes widened. 'Light of the goddess,' he breathed. Though the physical form of the hawk was a drastic alteration, the spirit light that shone from it in a scintillating aureole of many hues was unaltered and familiar. Aurian, as always, had been right. The goddess only knew how it happened, but somehow Anvar was occupying the body of the hawk. 'You knew, didn't you?' he accused the Mage.

Aurian nodded, never taking her eyes from the bird. 'I suspected – I had hoped . . . I'll tell you about it later, Chiamh.'

'Me too, I hope.' D'arvan put in. 'This is one explanation I wouldn't like to miss.'

*

316

From his vantage point high in the air, Anvar had looked down on the tall figure of the woman. This was right – this was where he wanted to be. Already, he had forgotten who he was or why he had been searching, but this human had clearly been his goal. There was something in her that called to him . . . Trusting her as he would have trusted no other, the hawk folded his wings and swooped down to settle on her proffered arm.

As Anvar looked into the human's green eyes he was overwhelmed by a profound wave of joy: a feeling of *belonging*, that swept through him like some inexorable tide. Though he did not understand why, he knew that his place was here at the human woman's side.

'Has the courier been despatched to the Queen of the Khazalim?' Eliseth asked.

'Indeed, Lady. Everything is just as you have ordered,' Sunfeather told her. 'The message was worded exactly as you said, asking the Khisihn Sara if she would be willing to become your ally and supply you with troops to help defend Dhiammara, in exchange for your assistance in her own land once the Dragon City has been secured. As for our planned attack on Finch and Petrel and their colony, your warriors are assembled above, and ready to move – we simply await your word.'

The Weather-Mage turned to Skua. 'And you, High Priest? Are you ready to take on this great charge?'

Skua nodded, and though his usual saturnine expression did not alter, Eliseth could see the gleam of suppressed excitement in his eyes. 'I have been preparing all my life for this moment, Great Lady. You need have no fear – in my safe hands, the city will thrive and prosper during your absence.'

Eliseth smiled at him. 'I have every confidence in you, my Lord Skua.' If only you knew how little I have to fear from you, she thought. Your black heart may be full of treachery, but your mind is under my control.

Eliseth poured wine for her two winged cohorts, and picked up the third cup from the table. 'What do the Skyfolk think of our glorious mission to subdue the colony of Eyrie?'

317

The High Priest grimaced thinly – the nearest he ever came to a smile. 'I have preached against the evil, godless renegades in the temple,' he said. 'The populace of Aerillia are convinced that Sunfeather and his warriors will smite the Eyrians in Yinze's name, and there is a great deal of support for the notion. After a handful of dissenters had the error of their ways explained to them by the stones and cudgels of the righteous, even those who have friends and kin in the colony are rapidly learning the value of silence.'

'That's most satisfactory.' Eliseth laughed. 'By all means, let us cleanse our land of these ungodly Eyrians – not to mention the fact that the colony stands in the way of my plans for Dhiammara.' She lifted her cup. 'To our success, my friends – great deeds await us.'

By the time dusk fell the next day, Aurian had begun to feel that she was really getting somewhere with the magic that permitted the Xandim to fly. The weather had been grey but dry with a brisk wind, and she'd spent the day outside with D'arvan, Chiamh, Schiannath, and Iscalda, practising the wielding of Old Magic to include more than a single Xandim. It had not proved so difficult as she had expected, though it did require a good deal of concentration to link the energies of so many auras with the power of the winds. Linnet had joined them for part of the day, exercising her newly healed wing. Because of the missing feathers, her flight was still uneven and ungainly, but at least she was getting off the ground again.

The hawk was also present, flying around them in fluttering circles, sometimes peeling off to hunt over the cliffs, but never straying too far, and always returning to Aurian. The bird remained an enigma to the Mage. Since it had returned to her the previous day, she had become more convinced than ever that it truly held the spirit of Anvar, yet when she reached out with her mind to attempt communication with the creature it seemed to have no sense of identity, and she could make little sense of the confused jumble of simple avian images in its brain. Certainly, it was still very wild – there was no way she could persuade it to accompany her into the confinement of the Nightrunner quarters. Whenever she stepped

318

outside, however, it was there waiting for her, and clung to her with a fierce loyalty. For some reason, it also seemed to favour the Windeye, but any notion that it might have been drawn to magic was negated by the fact that the hawk treated D'arvan with utter indifference.

Shia too had been uncertain. 'I hope for all our sakes that you're right, Aurian,' she had said doubtfully, 'but are you sure your wishes aren't leading you astray? It just looks like a bird to me.'

The one person with whom Aurian had not discussed the hawk was Forral. Not only had she made no mention to him of her suspicions, but she had sworn D'arvan and Chiamh to secrecy too. D'arvan had asked her why. 'Look,' she told him, 'if I'm right about this, it will only upset and disturb Forral – with very good reason – to think that Anvar is still present in some way, watching our every move and waiting to take back his body. If I'm wrong, then Forral will be equally disturbed, but for no reason at all.' It had all sounded very plausible at the time.

All in all, it had been good to get away from the Night-runner caverns and the uneasy mix of personalities that had been thrown together these last few days. The issue of the Death-Wraith's hunger was becoming increasingly urgent, and there seemed no way to avoid a human death. The Mage could not help but think that maybe Forral had been right after all – perhaps it had been a grave mistake to bring the Wraith back into time. Wolf remained, if not overtly hostile, indifferent to his mother, and was spending a great deal of time with Zanna's sons. Iscalda said he missed Currain, who had been like a younger brother to him. Much to the swords-man's distress, he had flatly refused to believe that Forral was his father. 'You can't be my father – he's dead,' Wolf insisted.

None the less, there had also been better news. Vannor, thank the gods, seemed to be recovering his spirits thanks to the determined ministrations of Dulsina and Zanna, who were well on their way to persuading him that, rather than castigating himself over his past mistakes, he would be better off aton-ing for them with constructive deeds. That morning, Forral had come out with Parric to find out what the Mage was up to,

319

and had gone very white when he had seen her hurtling through the skies on Chiamh's back, with Schiannath and Iscalda flanking her on either side. At Aurian's urging, however, the swordsman had finally been persuaded to mount Schiannath for a trial flight, and had returned with his face glowing with delight as he enveloped the Mage in a great bear hug. 'By Chathak, lass – what an incredible experience! I never thought I'd live to see the day . . .'

'You didn't,' Parric put in dryly, and clapped the swordsman on the back to take the sting from his words. The cavalry master was in irrepressible spirits. He had flown already, of course, when the little party had left the Phaerie city, but now, racing the wind on Iscalda's back, he was convinced that he had seen the crowning moment of his life.

That night, the Mage and her companions ate in Yanis and Emmie's quarters with Zanna and her family, to celebrate the return of the Nightrunner leader whose ship had returned that afternoon (and who had been bemused, to say the least, to find a horse flying in circles around his mast when he neared the land).

Grince's eyes were on Aurian, who was seated across the table from him. Emmie had rummaged through her storerooms to find some finery for them all, and the Mage looked like a living flame in a wine-coloured velvet gown. Her hair, which was growing long again, lay loose on her shoulders in a tumbling silken cascade. The thief could barely look away from her for long enough to eat his food. Though he had been spending most of his time in the Nightrunner haven with Emmie, or learning about ships from his new friend Jeskin the shipwright, Aurian had never been far from his thoughts. She was brave and competent and compassionate, and one of the few people who had ever treated him as though he really mattered. Furthermore, she had brought some magic into a life that had been singularly short of enchantment. He had never forgotten their meeting beneath the Nexian Academy, and the rough but unreserved kindness she had shown him, both then and during their escape across the moors.

Though he'd been unaware of it at the time, Grince had

given his heart to the Mage that first day, but he had only come to realize just how much she meant to him when he had seen her lying, cold, pale and still, up by the standing stone, and had been sure that she was dead. At that moment, he had felt that something rare and precious had been taken from him; as though some vital part of himself had been ripped away. In a fit of fervour that had shocked him greatly when he came to look back on it afterwards, he had run to her, clutched at her and begged her not to leave him – and, as if by some miracle, she had not. Over the last day or two, however, he had been watching her covertly as she practised flying with the Xandim and talked to Emmie and Zanna about ships and supplies. He knew that she was planning to leave again and the thought filled him with dread and dismay. He couldn't let her go without him.

It had been a difficult decision. All too well, the thief recalled the agonies of riding on horseback, and his fear of the vast, wild, open spaces, without a house or a paved road in sight. He reminded himself of the endless misery of never feeling warm, the rough, scanty meals, the utter blackness of night, and the dreadful tension of lying awake in the dark, waiting for some vile and vicious creature to pounce. And worst of all, there was the insecurity, the constant lurking terror of being left alone in the wilderness – for if anything should befall his companions, he could measure his own life in a day or two at most.

Grince had thought about all of these difficulties constantly over the last two days, until his head was spinning, and he didn't care. He had almost lost her at the standing stone, and Aurian wasn't going to get the chance to leave him again. This time, at least, he could follow her wherever he was going, and he intended to do exactly that. The problem, however, would be convincing her to take him.

When the meal was over, Grince waylaid the Mage as she was about to follow Forral to their rooms. 'Lady, can I speak with you for a moment?' he asked her.

'Why, of course.' Though Aurian looked tired, she had a smile for him, as always. Turning aside from her planned route, she led him to the great cavern where the ships were

321

docked. They walked along the beach, crunching fragments of the white shell shingle underfoot. The Mage looked at Grince, one eyebrow raised. 'Well?' she said. 'What can I do for you?'

All of Grince's carefully prepared arguments flew right out of his head. 'I – I'm going with you,' he blurted, 'when you leave, I'm coming too.' He looked at her defiantly.

The Mage's eyebrows rose another fraction. 'I don't think so,' she said pleasantly.

The thief's heart sank. 'Lady, you've got to take me with him. That Chiamh was only saying yesterday that you'll need all the help you can get, and –'

'Look, Grince,' Aurian said firmly. 'I don't want to offend you, but when Chiamh was talking about help he meant the assistance of folk who could ride a horse and use a sword, or wield magic.'

'You're saying I'm no good,' Grince muttered sullenly, kicking sprays of sand out in front of him.

'I'm not saying anything of the kind. It's just that you're not cut out for the kind of journey we'll be making. Why, that little ride from Nexis to here nearly killed you – and don't tell me you enjoyed it, because I know very well you didn't. You had a miserable time from first to last.' She sighed. 'It's not a question of being no good – it's a question of different skills and experience. Had we been heading for a city like Nexis, you would have come into your own. Had I needed a thief . . .'

'Who's to say you won't?' Grince put in quickly.

'Then I'll just have to manage.' Aurian's tone brooked no further argument, but she softened her words with a smile for him. 'Grince, if I take you with me, I truly believe I'll get you killed. And I'm not going to do that. I've seen too many friends die – I like you far too much to let that happen to you.' With a whirl of her wine-red skirts she was gone.

Grince looked after her, not sure whether to be upset or gladdened by her words. One thing was for sure – she had achieved exactly the opposite of what she had intended. If the Mage liked him so much, there was no way he would let her leave him behind. 'It's not over yet,' he muttered. 'I'm coming with you – just you wait and see.'

When the Mage reached her chambers, Forral had stoked the fire in the stove and poured two glasses of wine. 'What was all that about?' he asked her, seeing her frown.

Aurian shook her head and sighed. 'Poor Grince seems to have taken leave of his senses. He wants to come with us when we go south. Can you imagine? It took the poor little sod all his time to get here from Nexis, he has no woodcraft whatsoever, he can't even use a sword properly, yet he's blithely talking about setting off on a journey of several hundred leagues.'

Forral shrugged. 'You've done it again, haven't you? It looks as though you've got another follower. By all the gods, Aurian – I don't know how you manage to inspire such loyalty . . .' He paused, and smiled at her. 'No – in truth, I think I do know. You care. Within minutes of meeting Grince you had healed him and helped him, you smuggled him out of the city with you, probably saving his life in the process, and then you were the only one who stood by him when he was caught trying to steal from Mandzurano. I've noticed him watching you – I reckon he's taken a real fancy to you, love.'

'To *me*? Absolute rubbish!' Aurian snorted.

'I'm serious,' Forral told her. 'For most of his life he's had no one. Just think what a lonely existence that must have been, without family or friends. He's never had anyone to love, and nobody has cared for him. Then along you come. You're kind to him as no one else has been, and for the first time someone is treating him like a human being. What do you think? It's no wonder he imagines he's in love with you.'

The Mage glared at him. 'In love, my backside. Whatever Grince imagines he's feeling, it's nothing more than hero-worship, pure and simple – and I should know the symptoms. I remember a little girl, once upon a time, who felt the same way about you.'

'Yes, and look how that ended up,' the swordsman growled.

Aurian sighed in exasperation. 'Forral, this nonsense has gone quite far enough. You're talking more like a kitchen-maid than a bloody swordsman!'

Forral shrugged. 'Well, you may be right. Maybe I can see it so clearly in Grince because *I'm* in love with you.'

'You daft bugger.' Aurian shook her head. 'Honestly – you must be going soft in your old age. If anyone should hear the world's greatest swordsman saying things like that, your reputation would be ruined for ever.' She smiled at him fondly and held out her hand. 'Stop talking nonsense and come to bed.'

Chiamh took off his clothes and threw them in the general direction of a chair, then slipped quickly between the blankets of his lonely bed. After a few moments' shivering he warmed up enough to let his body relax. Then, as always, he lay back and let his Othersight take over. Finding a slender thread of a draught, he began to follow it, sending his consciousness forth to slip through the tiny fissures and crevices in the rock, along the now familiar route to Aurian's chambers. It was the Windeye's nightly ritual. He didn't stay long – there was a feeling of wrongness and guilt in the notion of spying on the Mage while she slept. No, he simply cared about her, and felt protective of her now that Anvar had been torn away from her. After all, she was his dearest friend – what could be more natural? Chiamh would simply linger a moment and extend a tendril of his consciousness to gently touch her sleeping face. Only then could he return to his solitary bed and find sleep at last.

Tonight, he discovered the Mage asleep next to Forral, as she had been these last few nights. Though he knew that Aurian had, for the time being, managed to reconcile her feelings between the old love and the new, he had his doubts about this interloper who'd stolen Anvar's body. Seeing them together, Chiamh suddenly found himself aflame with jealousy. Appalled by the intensity of his feelings, he fled back towards his body with a soundless cry of dismay.

The Windeye's thoughts were in such a turmoil that he took a wrong turning somewhere, and his consciousness emerged, not in his chamber as he had expected, but in the main cavern. What he saw there drove all thoughts of the Mage right out of his mind. The night watchmen lay scattered; dead. Strange soldiers, all alike in black livery and with eyes like cold steel, were pouring into the cavern. Chiamh was

324

about to sound the alarm when he realized that he was out of his body, and had no voice. As fast as he could he turned, and fled back the way he had come.

Zanna was awakened from a sound sleep by a fearful commotion in the corridor. She heard shouts and screams, and one of the ship's bells was ringing wildly. Tarnal leapt out of bed. 'Get the boys,' he cried. 'We've been invaded.'

Zanna had never dressed so fast in her life. She threw on her rough seaman's clothing and boots, and dashed to the children's room. They were already awake and snuggled in a single bed with Wolf, peeping out from behind a barricade of bedclothes with huge, frightened eyes.

'Ma, what's happening?' Valand demanded. Martek, now that a source of comfort had arrived, began to wail.

Zanna didn't believe in hiding the realities of life from her offspring – they were Nightrunners, after all. 'Bad soldiers are attacking us,' she said tersely. 'Get up quickly and get dressed – we have to leave right now.'

Valand obeyed her without another word, and Zanna ran to help her younger son. Martek was still snivelling as she forced him into his clothes. Zanna knelt down beside him and cupped his damp face in her hand. 'Martek, you stop that. You don't want to frighten Wolf, do you? We have to get to the ships now, all right? Then we'll be safe.'

The child bit his lip and nodded.

'Good lad,' Zanna told him. Picking him up, she gestured for Valand to go ahead of her.

Tarnal was standing by the door, sword in hand. 'I can hear them fighting in the distance, but it seems clear outside our door. We'd better go while we can.'

Zanna nodded. 'Valand,' she said, 'you take hold of the edge of my cloak. Hold on to it tight now – and whatever happens, don't let go.'

They raced together along the corridor, their footsteps ringing on the stone floor. When they reached the main cavern the sight of the carnage stopped Zanna in her tracks. Small groups of smugglers, many in their nightclothes, were fighting desperately against well-armed professional soldiers.

With a thrill of horror, Zanna recognized the black uniforms of Pendral's troops. They seemed to be everywhere. The beach was littered with the bodies of men, women and even small children; the white sands were dyed crimson with their blood. Even as Zanna stood, transfixed with horror, more soldiers were pouring in through the narrow tunnel of the landward entrance.

'Come on!' Tarnal shook Zanna out of her trance. 'We've got to get to the boats!' Wielding his sword like a man possessed, he plunged into the seething mass of combatants.

The three Xandim had been given chambers towards the rear of the Nightrunner complex. Their rooms were the only chambers in a short, dead-end corridor that branched off the main tunnel, and by the time the sounds of fighting reached them it was too late.

Iscalda had hung up the blue gown that Zanna had given her, and was brushing her long, flaxen hair when she first heard the clamour outside. Almost at the same time, there came a hammering on her door. She opened it to find the Windeye, dishevelled and half dressed. 'Arm yourself,' he gasped. 'We're being attacked!'

Before she had time to reply, he was gone, and banging on Schiannath's door. Iscalda dragged on shirt and breeches and picked up the new sword that she had obtained through the kindness of the Nightrunners. When she left her room, she saw her brother, armed and dressed, coming out of his chamber – and a large group of soldiers, rounding the corner at the junction of the corridor. A flash of fear shot through Iscalda as she realized that the Xandim were trapped and outnumbered.

Then suddenly the soldiers were backing away, howling curses and crying out in fear. Chiamh followed them, his silver eyes narrowed with concentration, pursuing them with the vision of a hideous monstrosity that was worse than the worst of Iscalda's nightmares. 'Go,' he shouted. 'I'll hold them off.'

The moment the junction was clear, Schiannath and Iscalda fled past the Windeye, towards the main cavern. Iscalda glanced back over her shoulder to see Chiamh follow-

326

ing; scrambling backwards to keep facing the enemy and somehow maintaining his apparition without faltering. As they reached the more populous areas, they began to find bodies sprawled in the corridors – some of them soldiers, it was true, but far more of them members of the Nightrunner community. Another group of soldiers appeared from a junction ahead of them, and Iscalda and Schiannath went into action side by side, swords flashing as they carved a path through the enemy ranks for themselves and the Windeye.

Everything went well until the Xandim reached the open spaces of the big cavern, with a group of frightened smugglers, mostly elderly, that they had collected on their way. To their horror the beach was filled with a mass of struggling figures, and the fight was moving this way and that across the entrance to their passage. Iscalda and Schiannath waited for a break in the mêlée and brought the others through the entrance safely, but Chiamh, still preoccupied with maintaining his phantasm, was just a moment too late. As he emerged, the fight swept back in his direction and a duelling soldier, on the defensive, backed straight into him. The Windeye's concentration broke – only for an instant, but it was enough. The soldiers who had been following the Xandim all through the tunnels at a respectful distance saw the apparition waver.

'It's not real!'

Iscalda turned as she heard the cry, but she was too late to save him. Even as she watched in horror, the soldiers rushed forward in a solid mass, and she saw Chiamh go down, pierced by half a dozen swords. Although she knew in her heart that it was hopeless, she would have gone back for him had Schiannath not grabbed her arm and hauled her onward. 'Come on, Iscalda! You can do nothing for him now!' Then the warrior was forced to turn her full attention back to her own survival, for they still had a fight in front of them before they could reach the boats. Her last sight of the Windeye was a shapeless, crumpled form like a blood-soaked pile of rags; a discarded piece of refuse that had been kicked out of the way, against the cavern wall.

23

The Phantasm

As Zanna pushed her way forward in Tarnal's wake, she felt a tug, and then her son was no longer holding on to her cloak. 'Valand!' She whirled to see the child smashed down into the ground by a warrior's gauntleted fist and kicked repeatedly and viciously where he lay. As the man pulled back his foot for another blow, a snarling grey shape erupted out of nowhere, leaping up and tearing at the warrior's throat. Man and wolf staggered backwards and fell, vanishing into the affray.

Zanna ran back to where her son lay, white and unmoving, but could not lift him without putting Martek down. Tarnal could not help her. He stood over his family to defend them, but his sword was needed. The crowd thinned for a moment, to show Emmie and Yanis with Vannor, Parric and Dulsina. Vannor and the cavalry master were fighting valiantly, back to back; Vannor defending himself admirably with one hand. 'Dad!' Zanna shrieked. 'Help us, please!'

Yanis tugged at Vannor's sleeve and shouted something that Zanna could not hear above the screaming and the clash of swords. Then he led Emmie and Dulsina towards the boats with Snowsilver, Emmie's huge white dog, helping to protect the women from attack. In the meantime, the former High Lord carved a path towards his daughter, his old friend Parric guarding his rear. When the two men reached Zanna, Vannor blanched at the sight of his grandson, lying so limp and still. He scooped up the boy without speaking, and they headed once again towards the water's edge, Tarnal and Parric defending them. Thinking only of her children's safety, Zanna hurried towards the boats. She had completely forgotten about Wolf, left somewhere behind her in the midst of all the fighting.

*

Pendral's soldiers, who had fallen back in dismay from the red-headed fury and the tall, blond warrior who fought so fiercely by her side, now fled screaming at the sight of the two great cats, all deadly fang and claw and terrifying burning eyes, that accompanied the two human fiends. With no one to hinder them, they burst out of the passage and into the main cavern. Forral paused to take in the scene with a warrior's experienced eye, and saw that two of the smuggler ships were being manned, with a further flotilla of small boats on their way out across the harbour to join them. He knew there was not much time. The Nightrunners were badly outnumbered, and more of the enemy were appearing in a never-ending stream. 'Down there – and hurry,' he shouted, pointing with his sword, then plunged down the beach and into the thick of the fray, taking the swiftest route towards the water.

Aurian was about to follow him when she caught sight of a fallen body lying crumpled in the lee of the cavern wall. Something – some vague sense of recognition – tugged at her, and without another thought she veered back towards the inert bundle, her heart leaden with dread at what she might find.

'Chiamh,' the Mage whispered. She didn't dare touch him, not even to stroke the tangled brown hair away from his face. Blood leaked out of a multitude of wounds: the Windeye was hacked and stabbed in many places, with some deep rents and gashes too close to vital organs, and looking very bad indeed. Her healer's senses told her that if he was not dead, he must only be clinging by a thread to life, and that thread was fragile and attenuated; already stretched to breaking point. There was no time to waste. Aurian knew she must act instantly, if it was not already too late. She thrust aside her overwhelming anguish to make a cool and competent assessment of the situation. There seemed no way to save him – to move him would be to kill him, and the risk of losing her own life to the enemy swords was growing greater by the moment – yet Aurian refused to countenance defeat. 'Don't worry, Chiamh – I'm here now,' she told him. 'I'll take care of you.' Concentrating hard to block out the distraction of the battle that was going on around her, she took the Windeye out of time.

Now, an apport spell . . . The big ships were too far away –
Aurian couldn't shift the Windeye that distance without seriously depleting her own energy, to the extent that she might
not make it to safety, and without her to heal him Chiamh
stood no chance at all. There was a smaller boat that had been
overlooked, however, moored behind a low, rocky point that
jutted out from the shore at the very southern end of the
beach. The little craft had gone unnoticed in the shadows, and
she had only been able to pick it out because of her Mage's
vision. 'Fine,' Aurian muttered. She turned back to Chiamh
and –

'*Lady!* Look out!'

Aurian ducked, and as the blade went whistling over the top
of her head she brought her own sword round in an arc that
sheared right into the knees of her opponent, who toppled like
a felled tree. Turning the blade with a deft twist of her wrists,
the Mage finished her assailant before he could hit the
ground. Only then did she see Grince, who seemed to have
popped up out of nowhere, with Frost, his young white dog,
at his side. He wore a fierce expression and was brandishing a
sword that had clearly been lifted from a corpse, and was far
too big for him.

'Thanks,' Aurian told the thief. 'Watch my back a minute.'
Gathering her powers, she thought of the Windeye as *here*,
visualized him being *there*, on the boat – and, wrapping him in
her magic, gave a great mental heave. There was a crack and a
gust of wind as the air rushed in to fill the empty space where
Chiamh had been.

Aurian heard a gasp and a strangled oath from Grince.
'Come on,' she told him, 'let's get out of here.'

'There's a boat left,' Tarnal shouted. 'We're nearly there . . .'
He stopped with a cry of horror. Zanna reached him, and her
arms tightened around her younger son until he cried out in
pain. Ignoring his protests, she crushed his face into her
shoulder, where he could not see. Half in the shallows, at the
water's edge, lay Emmie and Dulsina. There was no visible
mark on Emmie, but clearly she was dead. Dulsina's skull had
been crushed by a heavy blow that had obliterated half her

330

face and left blood and brains leaking out into the sand.

Finally Zanna managed to tear her eyes away from the appalling sight. Her grief was too great to consider at present – Dulsina had been a mother to her ever since her own had died. Keeping her mind deliberately numb, refusing to think of Dulsina's death, Zanna turned to her father. She hadn't heard a single sound from him – how must he be taking this? Vannor was standing at the edge of the sea, oblivious of the water that was soaking into his boots. He was clutching the body of his grandson as though the ship of his life had foundered and the boy was the only floating spar.

Vannor looked up at Zanna, and there was a terrible emptiness in his eyes, as though his soul had been torn out from behind them. 'That's not my Dulsina,' he said hoarsely. 'That's not her.' And he turned away from the grisly corpse.

There came a hail from behind Zanna, and she turned to see Yanis at the oars of a small boat. Snowsilver, bleeding heavily from a gash in her flank, was tied to a thwart with a piece of rope. Even now the dog was straining to get back to Emmie's body. Tears streamed down the Nightrunner's face. 'I couldn't save them,' he said. 'I tried, but I couldn't . . .'

Only then did Zanna notice that his tunic was soaked in blood. 'Yanis – you're hurt!'

'I couldn't save them . . . Just couldn't . . .'

Clearly, he was in deep shock. Someone would have to cope . . . 'Dad, get in the boat,' Zanna said sharply. 'Good – now put Valand down and take Martek from me. Go on – that's it.' She scrambled into the little craft, followed by Parric, and Tarnal, with a grateful nod to his wife, sheathed his sword and took hold of the bows to push the boat off the shingle. Zanna, looking over his shoulder, suddenly shouted. 'Tarnal, wait. Wait just a minute!'

Anvar – Forral, she corrected herself – came rushing down towards the boat with the two great cats. Tarnal hailed him. 'If you're coming, get in.'

'Wait,' said Zanna sharply. 'Where's Aurian?'

'Right behind –' The swordsman uttered a ferocious oath and scanned the beach, trying to pick out the Mage among the knots of fighters.

Shia, with all her attention on the enemy, had fought her way down to the water's edge before she realized that the Mage was not behind her. She whirled with a roar. 'Aurian! Where are you?'

'I'm coming.'

'Forral has found a boat.' It was the first time Shia had named him.

'Then go.' The Mage's replies were terse and distracted – clearly she was fighting for her life up there on the beach. 'Chiamh is wounded, in another boat – I'll go with him.'

'No! Wait – I'll be with you in –'

'I said *go*! And take Forral with you. Tell him to get – oh, never mind. Make him get on the bloody boat, Shia, if you have to knock him unconscious and drag him on board. That way we'll all have a chance of surviving this. *Do it!*'

'Take care then, my friend!' Shia looked around to see Forral craning his neck for a sight of the Mage.

'Come *on*, man!' Tarnal was shouting. 'We have to go! Get in or be left behind!'

'I can't – Aurian is missing!' the swordsman shouted.

'*Get in the boat*,' Shia roared at him, using all the mental force she could muster. 'Aurian is coming.'

Forral turned towards her. 'What the – You . . .? Did you . . .?'

'Yes! Now get in the cursed boat, human, before I rip out your guts. Aurian told me to tell you.'

An obdurate expression settled on his face. 'I'm not leaving without –'

With a snarl, Shia sprang at him, knocking him backwards so that he staggered into the boat, pushing it out into the shallow water. Parric shot out a wiry arm and dragged him on board. Shia and Khanu looked at the little craft, already crowded with passengers, and an unspoken message passed between them. Plunging into the water together, they set off swimming towards the waiting ship. To cats whose great claws were designed for dealing with the cliffs and craggy escarpments of Steelclaw, it was nothing to swarm up the side of a wooden vessel. The other ship had already left. Even as

Tarnal, the last of the boat's passengers, climbed aboard the larger craft, the anchor came rattling up, and strong men, with the help of long poles, began to move the ship out of harbour.

The Mage was enraged at the foes who had inflicted such terrible wounds upon her friend. She took her anger out on the enemy, and felt a grim satisfaction as they fell beneath her blade. Then, as she neared the boat, she saw a sight that pierced the red haze in her brain and left her thoughts exposed with a raw, ice-cold clarity. Two soldiers were stalking Wolf, and had him backed in to a crevice in the cavern wall. Aurian could see blood on his mouth and on his fur, and had no idea whether or not it was his own: she only saw the danger to her son. Hearing him whimper with fear, she drowned the piteous sound with a shriek of anger so loud that every skirmish in the cavern faltered for an instant.

Wolf's assailants never knew what hit them. The Mage was pulling her sword out from between the ribs of the second man almost before the first one's head had time to hit the ground. Unwisely, though, she had drawn attention to herself with her battle-cry, and clearly the enemy had decided it was time she was stopped. Already, several of them were beginning to close in.

'Can you run?' Aurian demanded of her son.

'I – yes . . .'

'Then *run!*'

They ran, with Grince and Frost pelting at their heels. But they were never going to make it. A group of soldiers was almost treading on their cloak-hems, and another knot of foes was running around to get between them and the boat. The one gap narrowed . . . Closed . . . The Mage found herself running into a thicket of swords. One of the enemy shouted something, but it was impossible to hear through the agonizing buzzing that permeated her skull. Aurian wiped sweat from her eyes with the back of her hand. The air seemed to be growing darker; thicker. When had it turned so cold? It was becoming harder to see the outlines of the soldiers – but surely their faces were contorted with stark terror? Surely they were backing away? Breaking – running! With a jarring, high-pitched snarl, a great black shape glided over the Mage's head and swooped down upon the fleeing soldiers, settling over a group of three terrified men like a hawk on its prey.

As the Death-Wraith fed, the paralysis dropped from Aurian and her will came back to her. Turning to the mesmerized Grince, she slapped him hard. 'Get out of here – now!' she shrieked.

The Mage, the thief and Wolf arrived together at Aurian's hidden boat. A single, hunted glance over her shoulder told Aurian that the Wraith had risen from the lifeless bodies of the soldiers and was looking for more prey. She saw the smoky red eyes glance in her direction, and then the Wraith deliberately turned away from her and vanished into the tunnels, hunting the fleeing warriors.

Scooping up her son, Aurian hurled him aboard. At Grince's encouragement, Frost jumped in after him, and together the Mage and the thief pushed off, then scrambled over the side and into the boat. Aurian remembered afterwards that the water felt very cold as it flooded in over the tops of her boots, but at the time she was oblivious of such details.

Snatching up the oars she began to row as fast and hard as she could, in an attempt to speed the craft out of the cavern.

Gevan had stopped taking part in the fighting. For some time now he had lurked in the entrance to one of the passages, looking out in horror at the scenes of carnage and slaughter that were taking place in the main Nightrunner cavern. He wished he hadn't come, now. If only he had stayed safe in Nexis, or at least waited on the boats until the fighting was over and the bodies had been cleared away. It would have been one thing to walk into the empty Nightrunner complex and load his pick of the booty on to his new boat before setting off back to the city and a prosperous new life. It was quite another to see folk he had known since childhood being forced to fight or flee for their lives, and being cut down before his eyes.

There was little guilt attached to Gevan's discomfort – he simply felt that if he did not witness the massacre, he would not have to distress himself with unpleasant memories, and would soon be able to forget the part he had played in destroying the community. It wasn't his fault, anyway – Yanis was to blame. Gevan had been growing increasingly dissatisfied with the Nightrunners since Yanis's father had died. He had been Leynard's second-in-command, and as far as he was concerned Yanis owed him – favours, respect, attention and the extra share of the booty that he had once enjoyed. The new Nightrunner leader, however, had clung stubbornly to ideas of his own – which included being his own man, for better or worse, and not letting his father's old companion run things just because he had the advantage of years. Gevan had been nursing his grudges since Leynard had died, and his resentment had taken on a life of its own, growing, like any other living entity, by the day.

Notwithstanding his other reasons of wealth and respectability, Gevan had in fact betrayed the Nightrunners in order to be revenged on Yanis, and that was why, when he saw the leader escaping, he could barely contain his wrath. 'There he goes! The Nightrunner leader! Stop him – he's escaping!'

A group of soldiers had run out of opponents and were gathered near the top of the beach, picking over the Nightrunner corpses for weapons, adornments and coins. Gevan ran up to the nearest one and grabbed his shoulder. 'Yanis is escaping! You've got to stop him!'

Unhurriedly, the warrior got to his feet, drew his knife, and rammed it into Gevan's stomach, angling the blade sharply upwards. The astonishment hit him an instant before the pain. Even as he crumpled, with a thin scream of agony, scrabbling in vain at the fiery torment in his guts, he could not believe what had just happened.

The soldier spat, and he felt the gob of warm slime go trickling down his face. Then he could no longer feel anything. As Gevan went spiralling down into darkness, the young soldier's voice followed him. 'Lord Pendral said there'd be a reward for the one of us as spitted you, once you'd brought us in here,' he said. 'I reckon it might as well be me.'

D'arvan, finding himself alone and hopelessly outnumbered, had done the only sensible thing – he had barricaded himself and as many Nightrunners as he could rescue inside his chamber, and used his magic to disguise the door to look like part of the cavern wall. Much to his relief, one of the Mortals he had sheltered was Hargorn. Maya would never have forgiven him if he had left her old friend to die – not that there seemed much fear of that. D'arvan had pulled the bitterly protesting veteran from the thick of the fray, where he was taking on three soldiers even though blood was pouring down his arm from a long but shallow slice where he'd been caught by the tip of a sword.

It was a long time before they dared emerge. Hargorn, with his arm bound up, was still cursing and haranguing the Mage for his interference when they had heard screams of abject horror, and the sound of stampeding footsteps running back up the passage towards the exit. D'arvan shuddered. There was only one thing he could think of that might terrify experienced soldiers to that extent, and the gods only knew what would happen if the Death-Wraith was on the loose and uncontrolled.

When the Mage and the Nightrunners finally dared to creep out, they found the complex utterly deserted, save for the bodies. The smugglers wept and cursed as they recognized friends and loved ones, but far more numerous were the sprawled corpses of the foe. Most had died without a mark on them, save that their faces were twisted into expressions of stark terror and dread. The Wraith had fed well tonight, D'arvan thought grimly.

Feverishly, the Mage and Hargorn searched through the scattered corpses, sick to their stomachs but determined to see the dreadful business through. It was many grim and weary hours before they could comfort themselves with the knowledge that their friends must have escaped the carnage, though the veteran had wept to discover Dulsina and Emmie, lying together by the water's edge.

For D'arvan, the worst discovery was the corpse of Finbarr, lying on the bed in the chamber where the Wraith had discarded it like a worn-out garment. Without his eldritch tenant to animate his body, the archivist had finally relinquished his tenuous hold on life. D'arvan sat for a time, holding his old

336

friend's hand, appalled by the waste. We came so close, he thought. So close to restoring him. He was one of the best of the Magefolk. His tears fell on Finbarr's cold and lifeless hand.

After a time, Hargorn entered. He was clearly full of questions, but waited quietly by the door out of respect for D'arvan's grief. The Mage rose and straightened, his expression stern and unyielding. 'We'll deal with the dead now, then you can take the few surviving Nightrunners to the Vale for the present,' he said. 'It won't be the first time the Lady Eilin has harboured refugees. As for me, I intend to make that snivelling Mortal the so-called Lord Pendral rue this day's work.'

'Now wait a minute – you can't just –'

The silver flame of wrath flashed in D'arvan's eyes. 'Can I not, indeed?' he said grimly. 'Can you honestly say, Hargorn, that the mortals of Nexis would not be better off under my rule?' His lips thinned into a glacial smile. 'No, for once it will be a positive pleasure to do my father's bidding.'

The Mage was not the only one whose plans involved a return to Nexis. Already, the Death-Wraith was hurtling like a black comet through the starless night, making its way back by the straightest route towards the city. Over the last days, it had been raking through Finbarr's mind and memory for the means of negating the time spell – and now, fed to repletion with the lives of so many Mortals, it was certain it had both the power and the means to free its fellows at last. Before much longer, the Nihilim would be loosed once more upon an unsuspecting world.

Aurian emerged from an exhausted daze to find Grince shaking her shoulder. 'Here, lady – let me take over. It must be my turn by now.'

The Mage straightened her aching shoulders, unlocked her hands from around the oar. It felt good to stop rowing. She was surprised to find that her palms were stinging and beginning to blister, while the land was already a good distance away: a blacker line against the darkness of the starless night sky. We did it, she thought with dull amazement. We actually got away.

The Mage held the dripping oars steady while Grince moved on to the thwart beside her and took them from her. Then she slid down into the well of the boat, letting herself slump wearily against the wooden side.

'Mother? Are you all right?' The mental voice was tentative and scared. Aurian felt a cold nose against her arm. She opened her eyes and looked around to see Wolf. He glanced at her, then looked away, hanging his head. 'You were very brave,' he said in a small voice. 'I thought you didn't care about me, but I was wrong, wasn't I?'

An immense weight was suddenly lifted from Aurian's heart. 'Yes, you were wrong,' she told him softly, 'but I was gone for so long that I don't blame you for thinking as you did. I would have thought the same thing myself.' She put her arms around the wolf's shaggy neck. 'Poor Wolf. I haven't been much of a mother to you so far, have I? When this is all over, I hope I'll have a chance to put that right.'

'Do – do you think you'll be able to take off the curse?'

Though he was trying to hide how very much it meant to him, Aurian could detect the desperation behind his words. None the less, she wasn't going to lie to him – she owed him more than that. 'I don't know for sure,' she told him. 'But believe me, we're going to have a bloody good try.'

The wolf sighed and laid his head on her shoulder.

'Are you hurt?' Aurian asked him anxiously.

'No – well, some bruises, that's all. Most of the blood belonged to the man who hurt Valand.' Aurian heard grim satisfaction in Wolf's voice, and hugged him hard.

'That's my son,' she said proudly.

The Mage sat quietly with Wolf until he fell asleep in the bows, and husbanded her own strength against the ordeal to come. Chiamh still lay in the bottom of the boat, cocooned in the blue matrix of the time spell, and she dreaded what she would find when she removed it. In her heart, she knew there was no way that she – or anyone else, for that matter – could heal such dreadful wounds.

She could feel the hard outline of the Harp of Winds strapped to her back, and wished that it possessed healing magic. If only the Staff of Earth had its power back, she thought, her hand closing around the Artefact that hung life-less at her belt. At least it might give me the chance to do something! But perhaps this was the penalty for misusing it, she thought. If so, then her rash slaughter of the soldiers beneath the Academy had earned her a far worse punishment than she could ever have imagined.

Her anguish must have been clear on her face, for Grince reached out and gently touched her arm. 'Will he die?' he asked softly.

Aurian nodded, and swallowed hard to find her voice. 'Yes. I think he will.'

The Windeye's blood-spattered face, already corpse-pale beneath the vivid blue time spell, dissolved in the shimmer of tears. Aurian recalled their first meeting, in that sordid chamber in the Tower of Incondor that had been her prison for so long. Chiamh had been the only other person to see that Wolf as truly human – and he had taken her riding the winds that very night, all the way to Aerillia. She thought of the day, back at the Xandim fastness, when he had shown her his lonely home at the Place of Winds, and trusted her enough to change into his horse form and let her ride upon his back. She remembered saving his life with a magical shield, when the Xandim rebelled against Parric as Herdlord, and had almost stoned their Windeye to death.

Well – might as well get it over with – she could only do her best. Gods, she prayed, let me be able to help him. Don't let Chiamh suffer for my mistakes. Aurian took a deep breath, summoned her powers, and dissolved the spell.

Chiamh sprang up like an uncoiling snake and knocked the Mage back against the stern of the violently rocking boat, pin-ioning her arms to her sides. 'Don't! Don't do anything! I'm all right! I'm all right!'

Aurian stared at him. The terrible wounds had gone. The bloodstains and gaping rents had simply vanished from both his skin and his clothing, and the deathly pallor and spattered blood had disappeared from his face. After several minutes, the Mage closed her mouth. Speech, however, continued to evade her. Suddenly, she felt unstrung with relief. To her dis-may she felt a single tear spill over and go streaking down her face, and bit the inside of her lip hard to prevent any more from following.

'Oh, goddess, what have I done?' Chiamh muttered. He let go of her arms and looked away from her. 'Aurian, I'm sorry,' he said wretchedly. 'I didn't mean to give you such a dreadful shock. It was all an illusion – it was the only thing I could think of to save myself, not to mention Schiannath and Iscalda. Why would anybody bother killing me, if they thought I was already dead?'

'You complete and utter bastard,' said Aurian, enunciating very carefully. 'How did you do it?'

'Well – you remember back at the fastness when I was holding the mob off with an illusion of a demon – only they discovered it was false and nearly killed me?'

Aurian nodded. 'I was just thinking of that. Back when I thought you were dead,' she added acidly.

Chiamh flushed. 'Well,' he went on hastily, 'I almost made the same mistake tonight, but I remembered just in time, and I knew that if Schiannath and Iscalda were to get away they would need some kind of diversion. For a few seconds I was out of everyone's sight where that passage twists, and I ducked into a doorway and formed a second illusion.' He grinned at her. 'Of me this time. Then when the passage straightened, I let the demon-phantasm falter, and they all rushed forward to kill me – except it wasn't me, of course.'

He frowned. 'I was watching, around the edge of the door – it gave me an awful turn to see myself killed like that . . .'

'It didn't do much for me, either,' Aurian growled.

'The hardest part,' Chiamh went on, as though she had never spoken, 'was creating the illusory wounds as the swords went in, and managing to stiffen the air to form some resistance to the blades. I doubt that there was enough to be realistic, but they were so fired up with blood-lust by that time they didn't notice.' He shrugged. 'After they had gone, I realized I didn't stand a chance of fighting my way down to the beach. I mean I can't see much, as you know, but I could see quite enough to tell me it was hopeless. I looked down at my phantasm, and it looked so realistically dead – and that was when I thought, who would bother killing a man twice? So I dissolved it and took its place, creating the illusion of the wounds around me, instead. When you came along, I didn't get a chance to warn you before you took me out of time . . . Aurian, I *am* sorry. It must have been a dreadful sight.'

The Mage shook her head in wonderment. The glacial calm of deep shock, which had been melting with his words, finally burned away in a flash of anger. 'Damn you, do you know what you put me through?' She hauled back her hand to hit him, but somehow found herself embracing him instead. 'Chiamh, I could kill you for frightening me like that – if I wasn't so bloody glad to see you alive.'

He held her – tentatively at first, then tighter. Aurian rested her head against his shoulder and closed her eyes, buoyed by a wave of relief and a happiness that seemed totally irrational, considering the horrors she had witnessed that night, but was no less real for that. Within moments, both Mage and Windeye were fast asleep in each other's arms.

Grince, still valiantly manning the oars with more energy than skill, looked down with a scowl at his sleeping passengers. 'Why, thank you, Grince, for rowing our blasted boat for us all bloody night,' he muttered sourly. 'We really do appreciate it.'

Well, they weren't the only ones who were tired. With a shrug, he pulled the oars back on board and tried to stow them where the drips would matter least. Then he climbed over the thwart and curled up in the bows beside Frost and Wolf, who were asleep together. The weather seemed calm enough – surely the boat could take care of itself for an hour or two . . . That was Grince's last drowsy thought before he too fell asleep.

24

Zithra and Eyrie

Eliizar paced back and forth along the covered porch of the big, single-storey wooden house in the clearing, his booted feet striking a hollow rhythm on the planked floor. Though it was still fairly early in the morning, he thought it best to hurry his wife along a little. The gods only know, he thought, I'll never understand why women take so long to dress themselves for a big occasion. 'Nereni, aren't you ready yet?' he shouted through her shuttered window. 'The ceremony is due to start at noon – that doesn't leave us much time to get there.'

There was no answer. Eliizar resumed his pacing for a few minutes, then stopped with a sigh. 'What in the Reaper's name is she doing in there?' he muttered irritably.

'Swordmaster – isn't it about time you were leaving? Everyone will be waiting.' Jharav hurried through Nereni's garden and came clattering up the porch steps, mopping his face and panting from the exertion. Since his near-fatal wounding in the Battle of the Forest that had finished the tyrant Xiang, he had retired from active service and had spent the last ten years radiating contentment and good cheer – and growing a notable belly. 'It's a fair distance to the new palace and –'

'How many times do I have to tell you it's not a palace?' Eliizar snapped.

'Well, what else do you want me to call it?' the grizzled warrior retorted, equally testily. 'You are the ruler of the Forest Lands, even though you make us call you swordmaster instead of king. Your new home is the big stone building where the ruler will be living – in other words, the palace. If you ever get moved into it, that is. Aren't you ready yet?'

'*I* am.' Eliizar gestured in disgust at his new finery. 'And because of this accursed ridiculous frippery that you and

Nereni insisted I wear, I daren't even sit down in case I stain or wrinkle something. I look like a whore's trinket-box.'

'You look magnificent,' Jharav told him soothingly. 'Just like a ki –'

'If you say that word once more, I'm going to run you through with this jewelled butter-spreader that Nereni and the Skyfolk are pleased to call a sword.' Eliizar scowled at Jharav then glared with his one eye at the offending object, decorated with gems and chased with gold, that hung in the glittering scabbard at his side. 'I can promise you, it'll be a long, slow death,' he added sourly.

'It's a good thing you talked her out of the embroidered eye-patch.' The grizzled ex-soldier chuckled. 'On top of the sword, that would have been too much. You're nervous, Eliizar, that's what ails you. Here –' He unclipped a silver flask from his belt. 'This should cure you – it's Ustila's new brewing of mead. You drink some of that and the world will seem a better place. In the meantime, I had better go and fetch Nereni.'

'No, I'll go.' Taking a last deep swig from the flask, Eliizar handed it back to his friend. 'You go on up to the pa – the new house, and tell Amahli we're coming.'

Jharav went off with a cheerful wave, sipping at his flask, leaving the swordmaster alone with his reflections on the porch of the house in which he and Nereni had spent the whole of their new lives, since they had first come to the forest with nothing but their followers and a dream of living in freedom from tyrants and sorcerers alike.

Eliizar was very proud of the community he had founded, and rightfully so. From its scant beginnings of a few wooden shanties clustered together like fearful children between the gloomy trees, the settlement had grown apace in size, scope and population. Its founders, the soldiers and household servants of the ill-fated Prince Harihn, had sent a group of experienced warriors sneaking back to the Khazalim capital of Taibeth in search of friends and family to swell the numbers, and as word of the new colony had spread others, tired of living under the Khazalim yoke, had dared the lethal jewelled desert and come struggling in to join the autonomous forest community. Even a few runaway slaves had managed to make the perilous crossing, and Eliizar, with memories of Anvar, had made them welcome and declared them free and equal with the rest.

Now, the forest colony numbered three hundred and twenty-nine souls, and its growth was slow but strong. One turning point, Eliizar reflected, had been the long-ago Battle of the Forest. The threat of Xiang had been removed for good by the blade of his former swordmaster, and in the natural confusion that had followed a goodly number of folk had managed to escape from Taibeth and join the renegades, until events had settled themselves with the birth of Xiang's son Quechuan. His mother the Khisihn and Aman, Xiang's former vizier, had declared themselves joint regents, and had taken control simply by slaughtering everyone who dared oppose them. Taibeth had been placed under martial law, and the constraints upon the populace had become so tight that the trickle of escapees had dried up almost completely. On the other hand, the new rulers of Taibeth were far too preoccupied with consolidating their own position to trouble themselves about one small independent colony on their borders. Besides, they had Xiang's example to deter them – and, Eliizar strongly suspected, neither of the two rulers regretted the former Khisu's demise, and were not entirely ill disposed to those who had brought it about.

The other turning point for the settlement had also been due, indirectly, to the battle, for that was the day that Finch and Petrel, the winged couriers, had decided to throw in their lot with Eliizar and his people, and, in the truest spirit of friendship and mutual co-operation, to found an adjacent Skyfolk colony in the mountains nearby. Not only had the two groups prospered, but together they had reached heights of progress that neither one could have achieved without the other.

Eyrie, the winged community, now occupied the nearest peak to Eliizar's forested valley. Unlike the groundlings, they had started building in stone from the very outset, for, though wood was plentiful on the lower slopes, the weather at that altitude was far too savage in winter for mere timber to withstand. Eliizar had sent quarrymen and masons to assist in the construction, just as the Skyfolk had sent winged teams down into the forest to help with the felling and moving of timber for the homes of their earthbound friends.

Khazalim had helped the Skyfolk with the construction and cultivation of their terraced vineyards on the lowest mountain slopes, and winged scouts had soared over the forest, spotting game for Eliizar's hunters. As the groundling settlement – named Zithra, which meant 'freedom' in the Khazalim tongue – had grown and spread, more of the thick woodland was cleared, and fields began to be tilled. Nereni combed the forest with her band of woman foragers, discovering by trial and error which plants could be cultivated as cures for common ailments, and which were nourishing and good to eat. The Skyfolk hunted and eventually bred and herded the nimble, peak-dwelling goats and sheep, producing not only meat but soft, thick fleeces and skins of peerless quality, which they traded with the Zithrans for vegetables, fruit and sweet river trout.

Both colonies became industrious and prosperous. Folk, winged and unwinged, tilled crops, hunted or herded beasts, foraged, fished, kept bees or mined metals in the foothills that lay between the two communities. There were dyers, weavers, and tanners; carpenters, potters and smiths. And all the while, the two communities were growing in size, in comfort, and in friendship.

It was no mean achievement for a man who had started his life as a professional killer, Eliizar reflected. He knew, however, that he would never have managed it all without Nereni – and thinking of Nereni, where was she? He looked up with a guilty start to realize that the sun had crept a little closer to the zenith, and ducked quickly into the house. 'Nereni? Nereni! It's time to go – we're late. Where in perdition are you, woman?'

She was not in the bedroom, but eventually Eliizar found her, dressed in her new red gown embroidered with gold thread, and looking like a queen in such glorious finery. She was sitting at the kitchen table, crying her eyes out. He hurried to her side and took her hands. 'Why, Nereni – whatever is wrong?'

345

Nereni looked at him, and broke into a torrent of fresh sobs. 'I don't want to go,' she wailed. 'This is our home – I love it. We've been so happy here!'

Eliizar sighed. 'But Nereni, our new home is so much bigger. You've supervised the planning and the building yourself – it's just as you wanted it. The carpenters and weavers have been busy for months making beautiful new furnishings, because they love you. And someone else needs this house now.' He stood up and held out his hand to her. 'Come now, my love – it is always hard to leave the comfort of familiar things, but we've done it before, remember? When we left Taibeth with Aurian to come here. And look how well that turned out.'

Nereni managed a watery smile. 'Everything you say is true. It's just that this place contains so many happy memories . . .'

'You'll take the memories with you,' Eliizar said gently. 'Nothing can change that – and think of all the wonderful memories yet to be made in our new house.'

Nodding, Nereni got to her feet. 'I know,' she sighed. 'You're right, of course, Eliizar. Just let me wash my face, and . . .' Her words were drowned by the rumble of galloping hooves.

Eliizar laughed. 'I know who that will be.'

Instantly Nereni's tears were forgotten. 'Oh no,' she cried in dismay. 'It couldn't be!'

The swordmaster walked over to the window and looked out. A black horse was hurtling down the dusty road with a small, white-clad figure on its back. The rider jerked the huge animal to an abrupt halt in front of the cabin and slid down from the saddle. 'Mother, Father – where are you? Are you never coming?'

'In here, my jewel.' Eliizar knew that a fond smile had spread itself across his face, and he didn't care in the slightest. This child had been Aurian's surprise parting gift to himself and Nereni – not the son and heir he had always wanted, but the daughter he worshipped and adored.

'Amahli!' Nereni cried, as the slender, dark-haired girl entered the kitchen. 'Oh, you wretched, wretched girl – how could you?' She pounced on her daughter and began to beat the dust from her white embroidered dress, rather more vigorously than necessary, and scolding all the while. 'Spawn of a demon – I swear I never mothered you! Did I not tell you, most particularly, not to get dirty today?'

Whatever reply the girl had been about to make was muffled as her mother began to scrub with a damp cloth at the smears on her face. 'And there you are, riding around the countryside like a hoyden on that dangerous great beast – how you'll ever get a husband I don't know, unless you mend your ways.'

'Nereni,' Eliizar protested mildly, 'the child is barely ten years old. She's young yet to be thinking about husbands.'

'Don't be ridiculous, Eliizar,' Nereni snapped. 'The child is your heir – it's never too soon to start thinking about her future.' She had undone Amahli's braid with lightning fingers and was yanking a comb through her waist-length hair. Eliizar noticed with fond pride that though the girl scowled and wriggled, she bore her mother's brisk ministrations without complaint.

'There.' Nereni had rebraided the hair. She turned her daughter round and enfolded her in a hug. 'All beautiful again. And mind, Amahli,' she added sternly, 'you get one more speck of dust on you and I'll take a switch to your behind! Do you hear me?'

'Yes, mother,' the girl chanted dutifully, then sneaked a twinkling glance up at her father, who winked his one good eye.

'Come along now – we can't keep the people waiting any longer.' Nereni was all bustle now, disguising, in briskness, her sadness at leaving her home. 'I don't know,' she grumbled, 'between the two of you, we'll never get there at all today.'

'Stop talking then, woman, and get yourself out of that door!' Eliizar roared. Giving a hand to each of his beloved ladies, he led them from the house towards the horses that waited patiently at the bottom of the garden.

The exiled Queen Raven and her consort waited with Petrel,

347

Finch, and a crowd of other assorted dignitaries on the broad terrace of Eliizar's new palace, and looked down on the crowds of settlers, winged and unwinged, that thronged the broad lawns below. Aguila nudged his wife. 'Smile, my dear one. People are watching.'

'Let them watch,' the winged woman retorted sulkily. 'What do I care? I don't see why we had to come and watch Eliizar and Nereni show off the trappings of their power and success when we have lost a kingdom!'

Her husband gave her one of those looks that riled her so – as though he had married some ill-mannered child whose behaviour needed to be corrected. 'Nereni is your friend,' he said reprovingly. 'She has always been like a mother to you, Raven. How can you resent her good fortune?'

Raven rounded on Aguila in a flash of temper. 'Don't be such an oaf! I don't begrudge Nereni a single bit of her good fortune. What I resent, however, is losing my throne and being betrayed by my miserable, ungrateful subjects . . .'

'But your subjects here are loyal.' Aguila glanced around quickly to make sure no one had overheard his wife's outburst. 'They have made us most welcome here, and given us a home.'

'They aren't my subjects – they're an independent colony ruled by a council,' Raven said bitterly, 'and we exist on their charity.' The scene before her blurred as her eyes filled with angry tears. 'What's wrong with me, Aguila? I'm such a failure. I held my throne for less than ten years, and now I'm an exile again.'

Aguila took her hand and squeezed it hard. 'We live in treacherous times, my love – momentous days when great changes, for good or ill, are happening in the world, and in the fabric of folks' lives. For many generations before you came along, your ancestors lived out their lives in peace and plenty – and where is the skill in that? You can't say whether, as rulers, they were any better or worse than you, for they were never tested.' He looked down at her and smiled. 'Besides, our story isn't over yet, my little queen. We'll win the throne back one day – if not for ourselves, then for our children.' He glanced to one side, where their three-year-old son and their

348

daughter of a scant two moons were being cared for by their nursemaids.

Grateful, Raven returned the pressure of his hand. 'Aguila, what would I do without you? All the time I was queen, Elster gave me priceless advice, but when she told me to marry you it was the best day's work she ever did.'

'Elster was wise,' Aguila said, and Raven could hear the weight of sorrow behind his words. 'I owe her all my happiness. Would that she had lived to see her namesake.'

'She died that night to save us.' The winged woman closed her eyes, remembering the old physician's sacrifice. On the night that Skua had planned to slaughter Raven and her family, he had encircled the Queen's Tower with guards who were loyal to himself and replaced the servitors with his own people, thus effectively sealing off the royal household from all aid. Somehow – Raven never had discovered how – Elster had discovered the plot, and, once night had fallen, had managed to fly through the cordon of winged guards that surrounded the tower.

Once they had been warned, Raven and Aguila had been able to take their son Lanneret and escape on foot, with Elster, through the corridors and aerial walkways of the palace. Skua had concentrated most of his forces in the air, and the guards they met within the building could be either dodged, or dealt with by Aguila. Only when they finally took to the air at last, from a little-used exit on the lower slopes of the pinnacle, was their escape discovered. The fugitives could not fly as swiftly as they would have wished: Aguila was carrying Lanneret, at three years old a sturdy burden, and Raven was hampered by her unborn child, not yet due for another cycle of the moon. Their foes were gaining on them with every moment, until Elster had stolen Aguila's sword right out of his scabbard, and doubled back to hurl herself at her beloved Raven's pursuers. Though the queen had not seen Elster die, it had sounded from her death screams as though they had hacked her to pieces. Raven still woke in the night hearing those harrowing shrieks – she knew they would haunt her for the rest of her days – but Elster, through her courage and self-sacrifice, had bought the royal household just enough time to make their escape.

At the time, there had been no chance to mourn Elster's loss. It took the fugitives several hungry, fear-filled days to reach Eyrie, flying mostly by night and dodging the patrols that hunted for them. Once they had reached Incondor's Tower, however, the pursuit had ceased, and they were able to make faster time, despite having been weakened by hunger and cold. Before the welcome silhouette of the colony even came into view, Raven's labour pains started. Somehow, she managed to keep herself flying long enough to struggle to safety – and early the following morning, her long wished-for girl child finally made her appearance.

The queen would never forget the first time she held her daughter. The stubby little wings, that had been crushed firmly down on her back during the birth, were beginning to stretch and unfurl. Raven looked at them, and her breath caught in her throat. Though the feathers were still damp and crumpled, the black wings had the same exquisite fan pattern of white feathers that had made the healer's pinions so distinctive. In her mind, she seemed to hear that loved, familiar old voice one last time: '*How will I be remembered if you don't have a little princess to name after me?*'

Raven hugged little Elster tightly, and laughed through her tears. 'How in the name of Yinze did you manage that?' she said.

'Here they come.' Aguila's voice brought the exiled queen out of the past with a jolt. Turning to the nurse, she took her precious child into her arms, her eyes misty with love and memories. The crowd, Skyfolk and groundlings alike, erupted into cheers, and Raven tore her attention away from Elster to see Eliizar and Nereni coming up the steps of the terrace, followed by their daughter.

Amahli was so excited about the new house – she couldn't wait to live here. It had been built down near the eastern end of the great forested valley, where the major river, the Vivax – Uncle Jharav had jokingly named it after his favourite horse, and the name had stuck – poured out of the vale in a succession of rapids and cascades. In this place the northern side of the valley climbed in a gentle series of terraces, part rock and partly clad in grass and clumps of rowan, aspen and birch that turned to larch and pine towards the heights. The house sat high on the slope, with terraced gardens that stretched right down to the river. It was built of the blue-grey local stone, and, because so many people, both Khazalim and Skyfolk, had contributed to the design, it had sprouted flat roofs, sloped roofs, turrets, porches, terraces, windows that were arched, squared, pointed, or jutting out in spacious bays. Though it was new, it looked as though it had been growing out of the hillside for centuries, changing and developing all the time.

As her parents neared the top of the steps, Amahli turned her attention from the house itself to the group of dignitaries assembled on the terrace. On such a grand occasion, it would-n't do to forget her manners. She saw Queen Raven and her consort Lord Aguila, and their two small children. On the other side of the steps were Finch and Petrel, the founders of the Skyfolk colony, who, like Eliizar, had refused to accept any titles. Amahli was glad to see that they had brought their families with them: Petrel's mate Firecrest, and their son Tiercel – who, at the age of fifteen, could remember living in Aerillia – and Finch's mate Ouzel, and their daughter Oriole, who was the same age as Amahli, and her best friend.

Jharav also stood at the top of the steps, a huge smile on his face. At his side was his wife Ustila – a quiet girl much younger than he. Amahli knew, from grown-up talk that she certainly shouldn't have been overhearing, that following Xiang's attack on the settlement Ustila had refused to let any man come near her for more than two years. It had caused a great deal of surprise, therefore, when she had wedded Jharav following the death of his first wife, whom he had brought out from Taibeth in the colony's early days. Amahli liked Ustila – she was gentle and kind. She was glad that the girl had found happiness with dear old Jharav.

The retired warrior bowed low. 'My honoured friends,' he began, 'allow me to be the first to welcome you to your new home.' He drew a deep breath. 'Who would have thought, when first we met as foes in the Tower of Incondor, that we would one day stand here, having achieved so much . . .'

Oh no, Amahli thought. Once Uncle Jharav began in this

351

vein, he could go on without a pause for hours. But as the daughter of the colony's leader, she had been brought up to deal with such dull formal occasions. Composing her features into an attentive expression, she fixed her eyes to the front and let her mind begin to roam.

There was no end to it. Once Jharav had finished, Petrel began to speak. Amahli sighed, and exchanged a long-suffering look with Oriole. It was too much to ask to keep staring in front of her – the girl's mind was already wandering and now her eyes began to follow. She was just gazing up at the pointed turret that contained her room, and wondering what it would be like to wake up every morning and look out of that window at the river, when her attention was caught by a movement in the adjacent sky. At first she thought it was just a wisp of grey cloud coming out of the north; then she realized that it was travelling against the other clouds, counter to the wind. What in the world could it be? A gigantic flock of birds, perhaps? Yet what were those tiny flashes of bright light in their midst? She squinted up into the bright sky, trying to get a better view.

Suddenly a sharp jab in the ribs made the girl gasp. 'What are you doing?' Nereni hissed. 'Pay attention!' Then her eyes widened as she followed the direction of Amahli's gaze up into the sky. 'The Reaper save us!' she gasped. 'Eliizar! Jharav! We're under attack!'

And then the Skyfolk came screaming down from above, the light flashing on their swords and spears, and their faces masked in sinister black.

Pandemonium erupted. The crowd in the gardens broke and ran screaming for cover, leaving a swathe of trampled bodies behind. Nereni grabbed Amahli's hand and dragged her across the terrace towards the house, dodging through a confusion of running figures, while arrows came hissing down around them like a black and deadly rain. From the corner of her eye Amahli saw that Ustila was running with them, and that Eliizar and Jharav had drawn their swords and were flanking the women in a brave but futile attempt to protect them.

Amahli felt herself buffeted by a blast of air as Finch and

352

Petrel took off almost simultaneously. Almost immediately she was drenched and half-blinded by a hot and stinking downpour, and a ball of mangled flesh and bloody feathers that was almost unrecognizable as Finch hit the flagstones right in front of her. Amahli screamed, and took her hands away from her face sticky and glistening with the blood of her friend's father; her father's friend.

Where was her mother? Amahli looked around wildly, but Nereni had vanished. Eliizar and Jharav were nowhere to be seen. The terrace was covered with fighting figures, winged and unwinged, and further skirmishes were being waged in the air above her head, raining down great gouts of blood, and worse. The air shook beneath the burden of curses, groans and screams.

Through a break in the crowd, Amahli saw her friend Oriole kneeling over the body of Finch, one fist pushed into her mouth and her eyes wide and blank with shock, oblivious of the proximity of flashing swords in a confrontation that was being fought right over her head. Amahli grasped at the chance to submerge her own terror in some purposeful deed. Dodging through the mêlée she ran to her friend, dropping down on all fours and ducking beneath the lethal blades of the settler and his winged assailant. Grabbing Oriole's hand, she tried to pull her friend away. 'Ori, come on! You can't stay here – you'll be killed!'

Oriole looked at her, wild-eyed, without the faintest trace of recognition. 'No!' she shrieked. 'Leave me alone!' Hands extended into claws, she lunged at Amahli, and ran right into the gleaming arc of a descending sword. Blood fountained up from her neck as her head lolled drunkenly to one side. To the stricken Amahli, it seemed to take her friend's body for ever to crumple and hit the ground. Her vision seemed to be darkening at the edges. Blessedly, the hideous world was receding, speeding away from her and growing smaller as it went . . .

The cracking blow across her face was hard enough to take her breath away and rock her head back on her shoulders. Dazed, she looked up into the white face of Tiercel. 'Don't faint now, you idiot,' he yelled. Only when she felt the wrenching pain in her shoulder did she realize that he was trying to haul her along by one arm, while he brandished a sword in his other hand with more enthusiasm than skill. Looking up, she realized that the fight had moved a short distance away from her. Suddenly desperate to put the scenes of horror behind her, Amahli scrambled unsteadily to her feet and let him tow her towards the house.

They had almost reached the safety of the building when there was a whine of wings overhead and a shadow swept across the girl's vision. She felt a hand pluck at her shoulder, and cried out in fear. Tiercel whirled, his face set with determination, and thrust his sword upwards. There was a strident shriek of pain, the hand fell away, and a body thudded down almost on top of Amahli. The Skyfolk warrior had been a young woman – with her long, dark hair and dark eyes she could have been Amahli's older sister. For an instant Tiercel stood staring at the body, frozen with shock and horror. This time, it was Amahli's turn to pull him away from the gory scene. Then they were running again, the dripping sword in Tiercel's hand leaving a bloody trail behind them.

The fighting was thick around the door – a small knot of defenders were holding the entrance against a dozen or so Skyfolk. Tiercel dodged round the side of the house, tugging Amahli after him, and broke a window. He laid his cloak over the pieces of shattered crystal in the bottom of the frame and the two of them scrambled inside. From the rooms above them came the sound of more splintering crystal. Tiercel's grip tightened around her fingers. 'Is there anywhere we can hide?' he shouted at Amahli.

'Yes – the cellar. This way.'

Amahli knew every inch of the house. At a run, she led Tiercel to the rear, where the cellar door with its flight of long, dark steps led downwards from the kitchen. They had no light – they simply had to scramble down the stone steps as best they might, pulling the door shut behind them. The cellars seemed to go back a long way. Amahli held tightly to Tiercel with one hand and felt her way along the wall with the other, trying to remember the way the vaults were laid out. At last she found what she was looking for – a narrow alcove that extended back beneath the stairs themselves. 'In here – quick.'

It was a tight squeeze. They huddled there, pressed together, scarcely daring to breathe while they listened to the screams and sounds of destruction coming from above. After a time, the thumping and crashing died away, and everything went horribly silent. After a moment, Tiercel found his voice. 'Maybe it's safe . . .' He got no further. From the house above, the crackle of fire swelled into a roar.

25

Sacrifice

'How many times do I have to tell you – she's sleeping.' Shia was getting more than a little tired of this pestilential human and his endless questions. 'Yes – as far as I know, she's all right, yes – I think that Wolf is with her, and no – I am not going to wake her – in fact I can't.'

'But –'

Shia rounded on Forral with a wrathful snarl, further irritated that several of the Nightrunners who crewed the ship took this as a sign to beat a hasty retreat, leaving herself, Khanu and Forral in sole possession of the bows. 'Wretched human! Would that I had never let you know I could speak with you like this! Now listen.' She walked up to the swordsman and put her forepaws on the ship's rail, so that her golden eyes blazed directly down into his.

'For the last time, Aurian didn't follow us because she had to rescue Chiamh. She did such a stupid thing because the Windeye is her friend. They are now somewhere on the sea in a small boat, and though I can't talk to the Mage unless she wakes, her sleeping thoughts seem not to be unhappy, so I would guess that Wolf is all right and she probably succeeded in what she set out to do. Yes, I'm worried about her too, but no – there's nothing more we can do to find her until daylight comes – SO GO TO SLEEP!'

Smouldering, Forral turned his back on the great cat, and looked out over the rail into the darkness. I almost wish we hadn't found out that the bloody creature could communicate with me like this, he thought, not really caring whether Shia overheard the thought or not. Bad-tempered bugger! I was only asking. You can't blame me for being worried . . . Then a new thought exploded into his mind – a thought so vast, so shocking, so fraught with dangers and possibilities: If I can

356

talk to Shia courtesy of Anvar's Mage blood, can I do the other stuff – the proper magic?

A shiver went through the swordsman that was half-fear, half-excitement. 'Steady,' he told himself. 'Don't get too carried away. Before you go trying anything, this will take a bit of thinking through.' Perhaps he should ask Aurian – but if he could manage on his own, would it not be better to surprise her?

In truth Forral was desperate to impress the Mage, for he felt he had been of little use to her so far – a situation that was not within his normal experience. Since he had arrived back in this strange body, he had been at a constant disadvantage – everyone else seemed to know what was going on, new friendships had been made between old comrades and these strange new folk; Parric and the Xandim being a good example. Though people tried to be kind to him, he knew that his occupancy of Anvar's body made them very uneasy. They had all known Anvar; had all been his friends and companions. Forral could not help feeling like a stranger and an interloper. He sighed. This was not turning out at all the way he had imagined it would – but maybe the magic would make all the difference. It would certainly be worth a try – and in the meantime, he would make himself useful by going below decks to see how poor old Vannor was faring.

The swordsman was halfway across the deck when a new thought struck him. He had never seen Parric since he had come aboard – in fact, he was certain that the cavalry master was not aboard the ship. What the name of all the gods had become of him?

'Did you see it?' Iscalda shuddered. 'Just as we were pulling out of the cavern. That hideous black shape – it was hunting down the soldiers . . .'

'I wonder what it was,' Schiannath mused.

'Better not to know.' Iscalda pulled her cloak around her shoulders. 'It looked a ghastly way to die.'

'At least Chiamh escaped that,' Schiannath said heavily.

'Poor Chiamh – he sacrificed himself to save our lives.' Iscalda leaned on the railing of Yanis's ship, the Nighthawk and looked back the way they had come, though there was nothing to see but dark sky and darker ocean. 'Forral is talking nonsense – I saw Chiamh fall, Schiannath, I saw the soldiers hacking at him, over and over. There was no possible way the Windeye or anyone else could have survived that.'

Schiannath put his arm around her shoulders. 'He was very brave,' he said quietly. 'All those years our people ignored and despised him because he lacked the presence of his grandmother – yet which of them would have possessed the courage for such a deed?' He sighed. 'It is a double tragedy. Chiamh should have taken a mate long ago, had he not been forced into his solitary existence by the mockery of the folk who should have respected and revered him. He had no heirs, Iscalda – his bloodline ended here, tonight, in a foreign land. The Xandim no longer have a Windeye, and never will again. It is as though, at a stroke, we have become blind and deaf to the deeper world around us.'

'Try telling them that,' Iscalda said bitterly. 'They won't care. Most of them don't think beyond fornication and filling their bellies. That's a deep enough world for them. Save for Chiamh and his ilk, we haven't advanced much further than the herd animals from which we were created.'

'Some of us have,' Schiannath told her comfortingly. 'At least we have learned to look to greater heights and wider horizons. And in Chiamh's memory we'll take the others with us – if we have to drag them every inch of the way.'

In the light of the small lantern that hung from the mast, he saw Iscalda's eyes flash as she looked up at him sharply. 'Will you go back and fight to be Herdlord again?' she asked in amazement. 'After you led so many into slavery at the hands of the Phaerie, I would suggest we avoid our brethren at all costs. Why, they'll tear us limb from limb if we try to return!'

'Would you rather live out the rest of your life as an exile?' Schiannath demanded. 'Don't you think we've seen enough of that?'

'I –' Iscalda's reply was snatched from her mouth by a blast of chill air. A great, dark shape loomed over Schiannath and Iscalda, blocking the light from the lantern. They heard shouts, screams and curses as the remaining crew and passengers scattered for cover. There was no time to draw a sword – the Xandim hurled themselves to the deck as the entity swooped down upon them.

Schiannath, protective as always, tried to throw himself in front of his sister – and had the breath knocked out of him as the creature came crashing down on top of him. When a bony and all too human elbow caught him in the face, he scarcely knew whether his eyes were watering from the impact, or he was weeping with relief. He eased himself out from beneath a thrashing wing and helped Linnet right herself, then pulled Iscalda to her feet.

The winged girl was incoherent with fright, and it took Iscalda some time to calm her, while Schiannath, mopping at a bleeding nose, kept back the curious Nightrunners who crowded around – now they had been reassured that it was not a Death-Wraith who'd come hurtling down on their ship. Bit by bit, Iscalda coaxed Linnet's story from her. When the fighting had started, the young girl had been sensible enough to stay well out of danger – she had flown up to the roof of the cavern and had stayed there, clinging to a projection of the rock. She had been paralysed with shock and fear at the sight of the carnage that was taking place below her, and had been too terrified to leave her perch even when the ships departed.

Only the Death-Wraith had finally had the power to move the winged girl – her refuge was no longer safe, not from this terrifying monstrosity who could fly as well as she. When the Wraith had vanished into the tunnels to hunt down the soldiers, Linnet had seized her chance and swooped out of the cavern entrance, heading out to sea, away from the appalling sights she had witnessed. Lost in the darkness as she was, the girl would have perished for sure, had she not caught sight of the faint pinpoint twinkle of the Nighthawk's lantern, far out across the waves. In the dark, she had badly misjudged her landing, but luckily, Schiannath and Iscalda had broken her fall.

Telling her story had calmed the winged girl considerably. Now she could look around with comprehension and with concern for her friends, seeking the comfort of familiar faces. The one face that she truly wanted to see, however, was missing. 'Where's Zanna?' she demanded fearfully of Iscalda. 'Is she all right? She did escape, didn't she?'

'Don't worry,' Iscalda soothed. 'She's down below in the cabin, but –'

'I must see her,' Linnet leapt to her feet.

Forral stepped out of the crowd to block her way. 'Not now, lass,' he said softly, taking her arm. Turning to the assembled Nightrunners, he said, 'that's what I've come up to tell you all. I only wish there was some way I could soften the blow. Valand, Zanna and Tarnal's little boy, has just died of his injuries.'

Cries of grief and dismay went up from the assembled Nightrunners. As one, the crowd stepped back from the swordsman, as though to put a physical distance between themselves and such evil tidings. Valand had not only been a child of great confidence and charm, who had been greatly loved by everyone in the Nightrunner caverns – he had also been Yanis's designated heir, their future leader. For many, it seemed the final blow. The Nightrunners were finished for good.

Hawks did not fly at night. They seldom flew over the sea. It did not occur to the hawk to wonder why he was doing both of these things right now. He only knew that something precious was being taken away from him – something so much a part of him that its absence caused a tearing feeling of pain somewhere deep within him. He only knew it was getting further away from him with each passing minute. He only knew that he must find it – or die.

Though he could not see well in the dark, he knew the direction of that precious, missing thing he sought. He could feel it ahead of him – a warm glow like the sun beating strongly on his face. This good feeling vanished if he veered off track, even by a little. As the hawk drew nearer to his goal, he could see it ahead of him in the darkness – a light that shone, not with a visible glow, but with a glimmer like a single bright star within his mind.

With absolutely confidence, the hawk plunged down through the darkness, landing surely on the side of a rocking boat. He could see it now – the thing that had been calling him. It was strapped to the back of that tall woman who also seemed so important to him. With a self-satisfied flip of his wings, the hawk settled down next to the Harp of Winds, and prepared to sleep until morning.

The wind grew stronger with the grey dawn and the swell on the sea increased. Flurries of sleet came hissing across the water as the Nightrunners gathered on deck. It did not take long to consign the lost ones to the deep. Firstly, the three adults who had all succumbed to their wounds since the ship had embarked were wrapped and weighted and were slid, one by one, into the sea. Last of all came the pitifully small body of Zanna's child.

As Valand's corpse slid down the tilted plank towards the water, Zanna darted forward with a wail, snatching at the blanket that wrapped him, and trying to claw him back from the hungry sea. Tarnal caught her and she fought him like a fury, trying to follow her child. In the end he was forced to pick her up bodily and carry her back down into the cabin, where her cries could still be heard.

All the leaders were incapacitated by grief. Zanna and Tarnal needed time to mourn the loss of their firstborn son. Vannor was prostrated by the double losses of Dulsina and his grandson, while Yanis mourned his beloved Emmie. It soon become clear to Forral that someone would have to take charge, and while he actually knew next to nothing about ships and sailing, it looked as though no one else was volunteering. He called the demoralized Nightrunners together on deck, and was heartened to discover that practically all of them, even the old grandmothers, knew how to sail, and that many of the younger smugglers were regular sailors on the route to the southern lands. He had talked the matter over with Schiannath and Iscalda, and after due consideration, they had decided that despite the risks, they must head south – and as quickly as possible. Forral was adamant that Aurian would be heading that way – and so he was going south, too – supposing he had to swim every inch of the way.

The swordsman was extremely anxious to find the Mage,

and was also concerned about the whereabouts of the other ship; the first vessel that had managed to flee the cavern – not to mention the flotilla of small boats that had escaped, scattering out in all directions on the face of the dark ocean. Luckily, Linnet came to the rescue. After some food and a few hours' rest, the winged girl was feeling greatly recovered, and she volunteered to fly out, hunting back and forth across a wide stretch of ocean, to see whether she could spot any of the other ships from the air, and lead them back to the principal Nightrunner vessel.

Aurian awoke with a cramp in the leg that was tucked beneath her at an impossible angle. She felt tired, cold and bleary, and huddled closer to Chiamh in the well of the small vessel, trying to escape the chill of the strengthening wind. For a moment, she had no idea where she was, until she felt the rocking of the boat and raised her head to look over the side at a grey sky and grey sea. It all came back to her, then. She muttered an oath, wishing she could go back to sleep again and blot out the memories.

Just as she was settling down again, a series of high-pitched, staccato cries exploded in her ear, and the tip of a pointed wing poked her in the eye Aurian shot bolt upright, waking Chiamh; one hand clasped to her watering eye. She gasped with delight to see the hawk. 'How did you get here?' she cried. 'Chiamh, look – it must have followed us! Does that not prove it must be Anvar?'

'You know that I never needed any convincing.' The Windeye studied the hawk gravely. 'The trick will be, to get him back into his rightful body.'

The boat's rocking motion had been increasing, even over the last few moments, and now, as it slid down into a trough, a double spray of water fountained over the bows, drenching Wolf and Grince. Wolf, still half-asleep, jumped up with a sharp yip of panic. He shook a silver shower from his thick grey coat and looked over the side of the boat at the miles of heaving ocean. 'It's a lot bigger than our lake at home, isn't it?' he said in uncertain tones.

'I don't suppose there's anything to eat on this damned

boat?' The thief came in so fast on the tail of her son's complaint that Aurian had to smile at his ruse to distract the wolf – Grince might not have been capable of mental speech, but the growing fear was plainly manifest in the rolling of Wolf's eyes. Then she realized that not only did they have no food on the boat – they had no water, either. And she didn't like the look of the weather at all. There was no way a small craft like this could withstand a heavy sea.

Chiamh caught her eye – and Mage and Windeye entered into an unspoken compact not to frighten the two youngsters further. 'I'm sure we'll find somethi –' Aurian was beginning, when Grince interrupted her. 'I'm sure I remember Emmie saying that all the small boats carried water bottles for emergencies.'

Aurian realized that Grince had also made himself part of the silent agreement – not to panic Wolf. In her mind, Aurian fervently thanked the gods. Aloud, she said, 'well done, Grince. Why don't you and Wolf see if you can find it?'

'All right. But then I think I ought to be trying to row.' Grince frowned at the heaving sea. 'It's getting too rough to keep drifting now – Emmie told me that when the waves get bigger, you have to keep the boat pointing into them, or you get swamped.'

Aurian nodded, looking at the thief with new respect. The lad certainly had his wits about him. Under her breath, she whispered, 'Chiamh – keep Wolf occupied if you can. I'm going to try to contact Shia.'

The Windeye nodded. 'When you've done that, I'll ride the winds, and see how far we are from the other boats – or anywhere else, for that matter.'

Closing her eyes to focus her concentration, Aurian sent her thoughts spiralling out from the central point of the boat, far and wide across the ocean in search of her friend. Initially, her searching mind met only with emptiness. Then suddenly Aurian felt another consciousness pounce upon her thoughts.

'Aurian? Is that you? Are you all right? Well, it's about time you stopped lazing around – this wretched human of yours has been pestering the life out of me. You were asleep so long I thought you planned to hibernate!'

'Shia – it's good to hear you! We're in a small boat . . .'

'Yes, you told me last night. Who is with you?'

'Wolf is here, Grince and that dog of his – and guess what? Chiamh is with me, and he's absolutely fine. Not a scratch on him!'

'Well! That is good news!' Even though Shia was using her mental tones, the Mage was sure she could detect the undercurrent of a happy purr. 'Just wait until Iscalda finds out,' the cat went on. 'She had poor Chiamh dead for sure. According to that human of yours, she saw a bunch of soldiers poke him full of holes. I don't think I'll mention anything until you get here. Let it be a surprise for them – after all the deaths, they need some good tidings to cheer them. Zanna lost her cub this morning.'

'Oh, Shia – no. Poor Zanna. What dreadful news!' Involuntarily, Aurian glanced in the direction of Wolf. 'Shia, we have no food on board and very little water, and the boat is too small to weather a sea like this for any length of time. Do you think the Nightrunners will be able to find us?'

'As luck would have it, I do.' Shia sounded very smug. 'Linnet is searching, Aurian. When she finds you, she'll lead us to you, or you to us. All you have to do is wait.'

Aurian could have collapsed with relief. 'That's the best news I've had in a long time, Shia. I'll see you soon, then.'

'I can't wait. Then you can talk to your dratted human yourself.'

The Mage told the others the good news that rescue was imminent, then took a sip from Grince's water bottle and settle back to wait. 'While we're waiting, do you still want to go out there and look for the ship?' she asked Chiamh.

'You do not have to go, Windeye – and you, my daughter, do not have to wait. I will take you.'

The boat heaved upward on a gigantic swell as a sleek grey back broke the surface of the water nearby.

'Ithalasa!' Aurian cried. 'It is you! But how did you know?'

The Leviathan rolled to regard her with one deep, wise little eye. 'Indeed it is I – and fortunate to have reached you in time. I have swum hard and fast to reach this place. As for how I know: when you took to the sea last night, I felt the power of the Artefacts from afar. Ever since you left this world I have been watching; waiting; always knowing that you would eventually return.'

'But what are you doing here in northern waters?'

Ithalasa sighed mightily, showering the Mage and her companions with a misty veil of droplets from his blowhole. 'Alas, Little One, when last I helped you, my people were displeased, just as I had feared. I have been exiled here – no, do not distress yourself needlessly, Mage. It was my decision, and it was for the best. And see – I have not been alone all this time. My mate came with me, as did my pod, my family of the seas.'

Other sleek shapes breached the surface around the boat. 'I will not ask them to speak with you,' Ithalasa went on. 'Let my crimes – though I do not believe them to be crimes – continue to be on my own head.'

Grince gave a squeak of fright and pulled the oars quickly back on board as the Leviathan set its head against the stern of the boat and began to push the craft effortlessly through the choppy water.

'It's all right,' Aurian told him with a smile. 'This is a friend.'

'A friend? You can call this bloody monster a friend?' Grince shook his head. 'I will say one thing, Lady. Life with you is never dull.'

Though she had not encountered the Mage, Linnet had found several other small craft: rowing boats, skiffs and fishing cobles that had been pressed into service as escape vessels for the terrified Nightrunners. The larger boats, that were lucky enough to have sails, she led back to the Nighthawk by way of the lesser craft, which were being tossed around by the heaving sea. The little boats could then be towed back to safety by the larger, sturdier craft. Soon the lost vessels had begun to arrive, and the wet, frozen, sick and dispirited smugglers were being taken aboard the larger ship, and the decks became crowded with folk in various stages of discomfort and desperation. Forral and the Xandim tried their best to find food and blankets to make folk comfortable, but were at their wits' end to find ways of helping the cold, the hurt and the heartsick refugees.

'This is hopeless,' the swordsman grumbled. 'There just isn't enough room. We need to rig up shelters of some kind, and we need a healer. And what in the name of perdition do those so-called Nightrunner leaders think they're playing at? They aren't the only ones with griefs to bear. They should be out here helping these poor folk, not skulking around in comfort below decks.'

Down in the cabin, Vannor scarcely heard the sounds of distress that filtered down from the decks above. He was sitting beside Zanna, who had mercifully cried herself to sleep at last, and holding her hand. He was far away from this place; lost in memories of Dulsina and wondering, with bitterness, how he had been such a blundering oaf as to miss so many good years with her.

'Dad? Dad?' Martek's voice intruded into Vannor's reverie. The boy, with Emmie's white dog by his side, was standing beside Tarnal who sat slumped over the cabin's narrow table, his head in his hands. The boy was tugging at his father's sleeve, but Tarnal, sunk deep in exhaustion and grief, made no response.

Sympathy for the child prodded Vannor out of his introspection. Poor Martek – he had lost his brother today, and no one had any time for him. He held out his hand to the child. 'What's wrong, Martek? Come and tell your granddad. Are you hungry?'

The boy shook his head. 'Granddad – when is Valand coming back?'

For an instant Vannor turned cold all over. He scooped the child up and sat him in his lap. 'Valand had to go away,' he explained gently. 'He died, Martek. He can't come back.'

'But where? Why? Can't I go too?'

A shiver went through Vannor and he hugged the boy tighter, with a fervent prayer that the gods would not make Martek's wish come true. 'Valand had to go far away, lad, so he could look after granny Dulsina. They went together.'

'And they can't come back? Not ever?' Martek quavered.

366

'That's not fair, granddad! I miss Valand! Why did they have to go away?'

'We all have to go at some time,' Vannor explained. 'Sooner or later, we all make that journey – but not before it's our turn. You were lucky, Martek. You got to stay here with your mother and your dad and me. I know you'll miss your brother, but you'll see him again one day, lad – I'm sure you will.'

'But when?'

'I don't know.'

'Will Valand miss me?'

'Of course he will. Both of you will have to be very brave. Do you think you can?'

'Be brave like Dad?'

A small sound over the table made Vannor look up. Tarnal was sitting up straight, and wiping his face on his sleeve. 'Braver than me, I hope,' he said softly, holding out his arms to the boy.

'Nobody's as brave as you.' Martek scrambled up on to his father's lap. Tarnal hugged his son close and looked across at Vannor. 'Thank you,' he whispered. The white dog, finding itself ignored, began to whine. Somehow, the desolate sound made Vannor's skin crawl uneasily. 'Martek,' he said. 'Why is Snowsilver in here? She'll wake your mother.'

The boy looked down at the dog. 'Oh,' he said. 'I forgot. Uncle Yanis said I could have her. Can I keep her, dad? Is it all right?'

What? Yanis giving away his wife's beloved dog? Vannor's feeling of unease intensified. 'Martek,' he said carefully. 'What did Uncle Yanis say, exactly? And where did this happen?'

The boy frowned with the effort to remember. 'He was sitting in the cargo hold. He was crying. He said would I look after Snowsilver, because he couldn't anymore. He said he was going to find Aunt Emmie . . .'

'Seven bloody demons!' Tarnal tipped the astonished boy off his lap and ran for the door, Vannor a step ahead of him.

Once they reached the hatch, Vannor had the sense to let Tarnal go first, with the lantern. With only one hand, he wasn't much good at climbing. Craning his neck, he peered down past the descending smuggler, into the darkness of the hold. The lantern light gleamed on a dark, wet slick that covered the floor. Tarnal reached the bottom, jumping to one side off the bottom rung, to miss the shining area. He turned away, his mouth twisted in sickness and grief. After a moment, he took a deep breath. 'Don't come down, Vannor. It's too late.'

Tarnal looked up at his wife's father, and Vannor saw an expression of grim resolution settle on his face. 'It looks as though I'm the leader of the Nightrunners now – so I suppose I had better start leading.' With no further hesitation, he took hold of the ladder and began to climb out.

'Fare well, Ithalasa. I hope I'll see you again one day.'

'Fare well, Windeye. When the time is right, we will meet again. In the meantime, take heart. Remember – all those with the powers of magic can live long enough for many possibilities to resolve themselves. Who knows? One day you may get your wish.'

'I don't think so.'

'Well, time will tell. May fortune attend you, my friend.'

I wonder what that was all about? Aurian mused, as Chiamh turned away to climb up the rope ladder to the ship.

'Curb that Magefolk curiosity, Little One – that was no affair of yours.' Ithalasa chuckled. 'Not yet, at any rate,' he added cryptically.

Aurian sighed. 'I wish I could spend more time with you. We always seem to be saying goodbye,' she complained.

'Ah – but what joy in our reunions! I thank you for telling me of your plan to return the Cauldron to Death, should you win it. You give me hope. It may well be that when my people realize that you have done this responsible and selfless thing with the Artefact, they will see that I was right to trust you, and my exile will end.'

'I hope so. I wasn't very responsible with the Staff of Earth,' Aurian replied truthfully. 'And I made an awful mess of the business with the Sword.' On the voyage, she had confessed her mistakes to the Leviathan.

'That may be. But you acknowledged your errors, and did

not compound them. And rest assured, even now you are making atonement. Do not let this setback cause you to falter at the last hurdle. Your instincts are good, Daughter. Only trust them, and all will be well.'

The Leviathan touched her mind gently in farewell, and swam away. His parting words echoed in the Mage's mind long after he had vanished.

When Aurian climbed up on the Nighthawk's deck she found Tarnal helping to settle his people. Before she even had time to utter a word of condolence, he had taken her by the arm and steered her out of earshot of the others. 'Please, Mage – can you help Zanna? I know how much she respects you, and I thought . . .' He broke off, his face contorting with distress. 'She just sits there. Sometimes she cries, but she won't say a word. It's not that she isn't brave, but Dulsina dying and then Valand, and Yanis, just this morning . . . When she was a young girl, you know, she wanted to marry him – before she met me. It's just too many dreadful shocks all at once . . .'

'All right, Tarnal.' Aurian laid a comforting hand on the young man's arm. She could tell that his concern over Zanna was one burden too many. 'Don't worry – Zanna's a strong woman. I'll go and talk to her.'

The cabin was in darkness, its one porthole shrouded to blot out the day. With her Mage's vision, Aurian could see Zanna, sitting upright on the bunk, her hands clasped around her knees, staring into nowhere. The Mage said nothing. She simply pulled up a chair and waited.

'How do you bear it?' Zanna burst out at last. 'Aurian, you must understand what it's like. You lost Forral, then Anvar. In a way, you lost your son to Miathan's curse. What makes you keep on going?'

'When I was a young girl,' Aurian said softly, 'Forral gave me the best advice of my life. When the problem seems too big, just do the first thing first. Take that one initial step along the road, and you'll find the rest of the steps will fall into place.'

'But I can't see that first step. The road is dark in front of me, now.'

The Mage extended her hand, and a sphere of amber

Magelight blossomed softly above her palm, sending the shadows fleeing away from the grieving woman. 'Out there on deck,' she said quietly, 'your people are huddled in the wind and rain. Some are hurt and many are grieving just like you . . .'

'Don't ask me to comfort them! I have nothing to give!'

'You have your cabin, Zanna. You could let others grieve in comfort for a while, and get the wounded into warmth and shelter. You could help.'

'And drown my sorrows in good deeds?' Zanna's voice was thick with bitterness. 'Is that all the advice you have to offer me?'

Aurian shrugged. 'You asked. But let me tell you this from experience – there's no such thing as drowning your sorrows in good deeds, good wine, or anything else. It's just easier to live with them if you keep busy, instead of sitting on your backside in the dark and feeding them with every "if only" you can think of. It's a mistake I've made more than once, and lived to regret, believe me. And remember – Vannor and Tarnal, and especially little Martek, need you right now, just as much as you need them. You can help each other – not just your own loved ones, but the whole Nightrunner family. Your first step is the hardest one, Zanna – but it's right through that door.'

Zanna looked at the Mage, and then at the door. 'All right,' she said after a moment. 'I think I can go that far.'

'Where the bloody blazes are we?' Parric roared at the ship's captain. 'This can't be the Xandim shore – we couldn't have reached it yet. You damned idiot. You've been going the wrong way!'

Jeskin tore his arm free from Parric's angry grasp, and spat over the side. 'I never said anything about going south,' he pointed out truculently. 'These folk have had quite enough trouble without me dragging them off on a three or four day voyage to foreign parts. That's Easthaven over there, mate – and that's where I'm headed. A lot of the folk here have family and friends in the village – I've a niece there myself – and they'll take us in. We'll blend in fine, become crafters and fish-

370

ers – and who's to say we was ever Nightrunners? Not the Easthaven folk, that's for sure. They got no truck with anything that ever came out of Nexis – and it looks to me like they got more sense than some folk I could mention.' He spat again, and glared defiantly at the thunderstruck and fuming cavalry master. 'If you want to go south, mate, you'll find somebody else to take you – and I wish you luck.'

Suddenly a knife appeared in Parric's hand and levelled itself at Jeskin's ample belly. 'Turn this bloody boat around – now!' he barked.

Jeskin looked down at the knife, his expression unaltered. 'No,' he said calmly. 'And if you stick that thing in me, there'll be plenty of others here to take us in – after they've hanged you, of course, and thrown your body in the sea.' Turning his head he spat a third time, within an inch of Parric's boots. 'And it's a ship,' he added, 'not a boat.'

Cursing vilely, Parric put the knife away. He was beaten and he knew it. It had been pure misfortune that he had become separated from the others in the fighting and ended up on the wrong ship, and now there was absolutely nothing that he could do – except make his way back to Nexis, and deal with that bastard Pendral, the cause of all this trouble, once and for all. It wouldn't make much of a difference to Aurian, perhaps, but it would improve the lot of the Nexians at least, and it would make him feel a whole lot better.

26

The Mountain of the Blind God

Two days later, the Nighthawk, with its cluster of smaller boats in tow, approached the Xandim coast. A ragged cheer went up when the dark outline appeared on the horizon, as the thirty-eight Nightrunner survivors looked forward to an end, at last, to their frightful journey. The last days had not been pleasant for anyone. Though the cargo hold had been scrubbed clean following Yanis's sea-burial, and the refugees could be sheltered from the elements at least, the space below decks had not been designed for human habitation. The quarters were cold, damp, cramped and noisome; food had been scarce and water strictly rationed. Aurian had found her healing skills in demand over and over again, and it was only thanks to her that no further lives were lost.

Compared to the horrors they had left behind them, the Nightrunners felt they had little to fear in the southern lands. Following Yanis's initial journey to the southern settlements some ten years ago, to pick up the Mage and her companions, the Xandim and the smugglers had formed a successful trading partnership that had ripened, through time, into ties of friendship. Tarnal knew that, though his people arrived as medicants, they had valuable skills to offer the Horsefolk, including that of building the swift and sturdy Nightrunner ships in which the Xandim took a tremendous interest.

For Aurian and her friends, however, it was a very different matter. They had been responsible, some ten years ago, for tempting over a hundred Xandim from their homes, and leading them into slavery in a foreign land. The welcome that they might expect this time might be a great deal warmer than they would like. The Mage and her companions had discussed the matter with Zanna and Tarnal, and had decided to hide below decks when the ship docked and sneak away after nightfall, with Aurian using the Old Magic of D'arvan's talisman to give the Xandim the power of flight.

To Aurian's surprise, Vannor had insisted on coming too. She had expected that he would have wanted to stay with his daughter and his grandson, but he had insisted that he could be more use to the Mage, and besides, he wanted to escape the painful memories of Dulsina. After talking it over with Forral, Aurian had agreed. To be on the safe side, no one would know of this plan save the Nightrunner leaders, and the rest of the Wyvernesse community had been sworn to secrecy regarding the presence of the additional passengers.

Chiamh had suggested making their way up to his old home on the upper slopes of the Wyndveil. They should be safe enough there, for the Xandim did not venture into the Vale of Death with its ancient tombs. The Windeye wanted particularly to consult with Basileus, the Moldan of the Wyndveil, who was better equipped than anyone to give the companions a clear picture of what had been happening here in these Southern Kingdoms.

As the ship entered the harbour Aurian craned her neck to see out of the small cabin porthole. The Xandim settlement had changed since she was last there. The low stone houses had proliferated around the edge of the cove and had a more permanent aspect and the inlet had been dredged to form a harbour. Long stone piers had been built out on either point to increase the shelter afforded by the bay. A group of Horsefolk crowded the quays, looking slightly puzzled at this unscheduled visit, but waving welcome to the ship none the less.

Izmir, the chief of the settlement, stepped forth as the Nighthawk tied up, and Tarnal leapt ashore and spoke to him softly and urgently for several minutes. Aurian saw the Xandim's expression change from smiling welcome to dismay and sorrow, and guessed that the new smuggler leader had told him of Yanis's death. When he saw the pitiful condition of the refugees, the Xandim leader welcomed them without delay or ceremony into the great communal meeting-lodge of the settlement. The Nightrunners went gratefully, shown the way by members of the Xandim community.

Chiamh looked through the porthole and muttered something that sounded suspiciously like an oath. 'Look at that,' he said. 'The Xandim never welcomed me anywhere in my whole life, and I don't suppose they'll ever start now.'

Zanna was the last to leave the ship – almost. Aurian and Forral, Linnet, and the three Xandim made their sad farewells, and the Mage passed on the thanks of the cats and Wolf. Then she noticed that Grince was lurking in the shadows, in the corner of the cabin.

'I'm going with you,' the thief said firmly.

Aurian glared at him. 'I thought we had already been through this.'

'But you'll need me,' Grince insisted.

'In the name of all the gods, why would I need you?' Aurian snapped at him, thoroughly exasperated. To her surprise, Grince's brash front vanished. 'Lady, please. In my whole life, no one has ever needed me – except Warrior. I don't belong here with these people – not that I'm not very grateful to you,' he added, with a nervous glance at Zanna. 'Lady Aurian, you saved me, back in Nexis. I owe you now. Give me a chance to pay you back, please. I was the best thief in the city – my skills will do me no good here, they'll just get me into trouble. They might be useful to you, though.'

'Take him,' Chiamh said suddenly. 'I don't know why, exactly, but I have a feeling . . .' He shivered. 'Aurian, let him come with us. You won't regret it.'

Aurian looked quizzically at the Xandim seer, then flung up her hands in defeat. 'All right, Grince. You can come – but you can't take that dog with you, I'm afraid. It just wouldn't be practical.'

'That's all right,' Zanna said. 'Martek will look after Frost until Grince returns.' She stepped forward to hug them all. 'Please,' she said, 'take care, all of you – and come back to us when it's all over.'

'We will,' Aurian said. But though no one would mention the possibility aloud, she knew they were all thinking the same thing – that this could be the last time they ever met.

That night, Izmir and his Council of Elders entertained the

Nightrunners to a lavish feast, and for the first time in days, Zanna let herself relax a little – until the chieftain himself actually brought up the subject of the Mage. He had been asking Tarnal if the Nightrunners ever had any contact with the Phaerie.

Tarnal shook his head. 'No – thank all the gods. At least we remained hidden from them. They view Mortals as no more than animals.'

'Then you will understand the position of the Xandim,' Izmir said grimly. 'How we rue the day that our folk were tempted across the sea by wicked traitors among their own kind. Not to mention, of course, the northern Magefolk who were fomenters of the whole sad business.' He looked sharply at the Nightrunner leaders. 'And they never did return?'

The swiftness of the question took Zanna completely by surprise. She inhaled sharply – and choked on a mouthful of food. Instantly the room dissolved into confusion as she was thumped on the back, given a cup of water, and handed a cloth to mop her streaming eyes. By the time she had recovered, Tarnal had gathered his wits. 'It sounds very unlikely that someone could still be lost in time and then return,' he said smoothly.

'But they were your friends?' Izmir pressed.

'Yes,' said Zanna belligerently. 'Why, does that make a difference?'

The chief frowned. 'Not to me, but sadly, I must ask you to forget your former friends – especially if you are speaking to anyone outside this community.' He leaned forward earnestly. 'It is different with us – for many years now we have traded successfully with the Nightrunners, and friendship has grown between our folk,' he looked at Zanna and Tarnal. 'Your people will stay with us, and become part of our settlement. You have skills, such as your shipbuilding, that would benefit us greatly.'

'Are you saying it could make trouble for us if it were widely known that we were friends with Aurian and the others?' Tarnal demanded. 'Why?'

'Please – do not blame me too harshly, and do not let this affair deprive your folk of the sanctuary that they so badly need. Your friends are under a sentence of death, Tarnal, if they ever return here. For many seasons now, a watch has been kept throughout the Xandim lands for your companions. I have the strictest orders concerning the Mage and the others, as does every chief of every settlement along the coast. If they are found in the Xandim lands they must be taken to the Fastness, and from there they will go to the mountain of the Blind God.' He sighed. 'I cannot say for certain – the decision will rest with the will, or the whim, of the God. I fear, however, that they will be sacrificed.'

A lone Xandim herdsman, encamped by his fire on the broad, wind-scoured plains, looked up and saw a cluster of dark dots pass across the face of the moon, flying very high and fast. He frowned. What in the name of the goddess were they? It didn't quite look like Skyfolk, who didn't usually fly by night in any case. Still, what else could it be?

Aurian had forgotten all her earlier fear, and was truly enjoying herself. Combined with the relief of having slipped out of the Xandim settlement unnoticed, there was a nerve-tingling thrill to hurtling through the air in the frosty moonlight, and the night wove a glittering bewitchment all its own to augment the Old Magic which sped her on her way. The Mage crouched low against Chiamh's neck for a moment to get her glowing face out of the icy wind, and buried her hands in the warmth of the Windeye's streaming black mane. With the Othersight that came when she was wearing the talisman, she could see the land below as great fractured plates of topaz and amber that had been piled on top of one another to overlap. The strands of trees that dotted the grasslands were like the crystal growths on a frosty window. The winds were swirling torrents of silver, and the true rivers that meandered through the plains were twisting serpents that glowed with misty radiance.

Grince rode behind the Mage, clasping her around the waist in a grip so tight that it was almost painful, and keeping a wary eye on the hawk, that clung tightly to her shoulder, sheltering from the wind in a fold of her hood. From the corner of her eye, Aurian could see Schiannath and Iscalda

376

speeding along beside her, their life-force linked to the paths of the wind by the talisman's power and the Mage's will. Forral was riding the great grey Schiannath, who was like a storm cloud, driven before the wild wind, and Vannor rode Iscalda, who shimmered like a pearl in the moonlight. Between the two Xandim, in a cat's cradle of rope, a great net was suspended – one of the cargo nets from the Nightrunner ship. Shia, Khanu and Wolf, unhappy passengers all, dangled in the net, and Aurian felt sorry for them. She knew from experience that it was definitely not the most pleasant way to travel. They would be chilled, cramped, and aching before the journey's end. Much happier was Linnet, who flew on the other side of the Mage, effortlessly matching the pace set by the Xandim.

Aurian was pleased with the speed they were making. Even though the Xandim carried extra burdens, she could feel the Old Magic buoying them up, and so far, at least, she was experiencing little fatigue from the maintenance of the spell that made flight possible. If they kept up this pace, she estimated, they could be in Chiamh's Chamber of Winds three nights from now. And then? The Mage wished she knew. When she had looked into the Well of Souls, she had seen Eliseth in Aerillia – but was that any guarantee that the Weather-Mage would still be there?

When she had first reached the Dragon City, not long before sunset, Eliseth had been somewhat dismayed by the extent of the destruction. Anvar's memories of the earthquake had been, of necessity, blurred by panic and the need for a swift escape. By the time the tremors had stopped, he had been safely back underground, and had never had a chance to see the condition of the city as Eliseth was seeing it.

The Magewoman's winged bearers had landed her on the top of the highest tower – the very same place from which Anvar and Aurian had first looked down on Dhiammara. Below her, the great emerald spire in the centre of the city was cracked throughout its length and splintered into a jagged spike, and the valley floor was a network of chasms and cracks, which gave the impression of ruin and decay. When Eliseth looked more closely, however, she saw that most of the low buildings, each one hollowed from a single gem, appeared to have survived more or less intact. She turned to Sunfeather, who stood at her side, his mouth screwed into an expression of distaste. 'It'll do,' she said shortly, daring him with a frosty look to contradict her.

He shrugged, irritating her – deliberately, she knew – by his lack of response to her challenge. 'Very well, Lady. I'll send the men down to check which buildings are safe, and to look for somewhere suitable for us to spend the night.'

By nightfall the Weather-Mage had been installed, if not comfortably, at least adequately, in one of the simple buildings. Bern, whose task was still to carry the well-wrapped Sword of Flame for her, had deposited the Artefact here in her shelter before seeking his own bed in a house nearby. Her failure to master the Sword had been Eliseth's only setback so far – other than that, she had good reason to feel pleased with herself. Her plans were working out beautifully. She had been told by the ever-attentive Sunfeather that the Khazalim would be arriving the following night, in darkness, when it was safe to cross the desert. Tomorrow night also, the first of the slaves would begin to arrive from the settlement in the forest. Eliseth held out her hands to warm them at the flickering fire, and stretched with drowsy contentment. Now, before she curled up to sleep in the pile of thick blankets and luxuriant furs that Sunfeather had brought her, she would reach out to make contact with Vannor's mind, and check on Aurian's progress.

Eliseth filled the grail with water from the leather bottle by her side, and summoned Vannor's image, sinking into his mind like a stone falling into a clear lake. Her concentration faltered as she found herself flying through the air at a tremendous speed, and with a sickening lurch, she found herself back in her own body. With a curse, she collected herself, breathing deeply and sitting perfectly still until the giddiness had passed. Then, cautiously, she tried again. What in the name of perdition was going on? The last time she had entered his mind, Vannor had been on board a ship, and his thoughts were such a confused welter of anger, fear and grief that she

378

had been unable to make sense of them. Now, however, he was calmer, and raking through her victim's latest memories, she was astounded at what she found.

Eliseth discovered, with a flash of annoyance, that she was too late to exact her vengeance upon Zanna – the wretched woman had been left behind in the Xandim settlement on the coast. Zanna's fate was a minor detail, however; soon forgotten when the Mage discovered, to her intense shock and dismay, that Aurian could make the Xandim fly. Eliseth fought against a cold, sinking feeling of unease. This changed everything. She had thought herself secure, with plenty of time to prepare before Aurian could get anywhere near the Jewelled Desert. Now, she would have to hasten her plans along – and, as well she knew, such haste could easily breed mistakes that might cost her, if she did not take the greatest of care.

For the first time, Eliseth wondered whether she had been wise to have left the Horsefolk unconquered; a potential enemy at her back. Then she shrugged. How foolish, to let panic cloud her thinking. After all, since the forest settlement had been taken, she had hostages that the Mage held dear. She made a mental note to discover the identities of Eliizar and Nereni when the slaves arrived.

'So – let Aurian come,' Eliseth muttered venomously. 'I'll be ready.'

By travelling at night, Chiamh and his companions succeeded in completing their journey unseen. Hiding each dawn in one of the sparse stands of timber that dotted the otherwise featureless plains, they kept an uneasy watch in turns throughout the daylight hours, while the others rested. It had been a wearying, cold, and hungry journey. The Xandim were luckier than the humans, cats, and Wolf, for they could graze, at least, but Zanna had been able to furnish little in the way of rations for the others.

As Aurian hoped they arrived on the upper slopes of the Wyndveil on the third night, just before dawn. Though they were almost certain they had not been spotted from the Fastness, Chiamh deemed it wisest to get everyone out of the sky and under cover before the sun came up, so he searched

379

for a current of gleaming air that dipped sharply, and, with Schiannath and Iscalda hard on the Windeye's heels, the horses and riders swooped down like striking hawks into the Vale of Death, where the Chamber of Winds speared the heavens.

Though Chiamh had long ago convinced himself that he and the Xandim were done with each other for good, he was astonished to find himself deeply moved by the first sight, blurred and vague though it was, of his old home. As his hooves touched lightly down on the stretch of short, soft turf in front of the soaring pinnacle of rock, he could scarcely wait for Aurian and Grince to dismount, so that he could change back to his human form. Without waiting for the others he ran into the cavern at the spire's foot.

Within, he found the devastation of ten years' neglect. His blankets and furs had been eaten away by mildew, his scanty belongings had been scattered and gnawed by wild animals, who had decorated the floor with piles of droppings as abundant evidence of their tenancy. Chiamh was suddenly grateful to Parric for teaching him some new curses while they stayed together in the Nightrunner caverns.

'Windeye! I have never heard such language. Do you not know that all wild creatures are the little children of the goddess?'

'Then Iriana should teach them better manners . . .' Chiamh began – then he recognized the voice.

'Basileus!'

'Indeed – and who did you expect? Well met, little Windeye. I have never been so delighted to see any living creature in all the endless ages of my existence. But where have you been? Why did you stay away so long?' Abruptly, all the joy left the Moldan's voice. *'There is much that you should know, my friend. Events of considerable gravity have transpired here, these last few years . . .'*

Not again, Chiamh thought. Lately, life seemed to consist of nothing but evil tidings and dire events. In that moment, he became aware that he was phenomenally hungry, dirty and cold – and so weary that he felt about a thousand years old.

'Rest then,' the Moldan said kindly. *'I forget the frailties of*

you flesh-and-blood folk. My news has waited almost ten years – it will keep a little longer.'

Just then Aurian entered, and viewed the scene with a low whistle of dismay. 'Seven bloody demons!'

'Greetings, Wizard.'

'Oh – greetings, Basileus.' The Mage inclined her head respectfully, though there was no point in looking in any particular direction – not when the Moldan was the entire mountain. 'It's good to be back again. We have a great deal to tell you.'

'And I, you. But settle yourselves first. I will wait.'

Shia entered the cavern and sniffed. 'Squirrels,' she said decisively, wrinkling her nose. 'Rats and a family of foxes.'

Chiamh looked around grimly at the devastation. 'I don't know where to start.'

'I do.' Aurian stuck her head out of the cavern entrance. 'Grince?' she sang sweetly. 'Remember what you said about being useful? Well, how are you at scrubbing?'

'Khanu and I will go hunting,' Shia offered. 'Maybe there are still wild goats on the slopes of Steelclaw . . .'

'WAIT!' Basileus shouted urgently. *'Do not set foot on Steelclaw – it has become an evil place once more. There are rabbits and deer in the woods down this valley – you can hunt there for what you need.'*

Shia who had become increasingly irritable and short-tempered as the journey had progressed, now had a stubborn light in her eyes. 'But there are already cats on Steelclaw,' she argued, 'so whatever it is, it won't harm . . .'

'No,' said the Moldan flatly. *'There are no cats on Steelclaw. Not any longer.'*

Shia and Khanu were too stunned to speak.

'But what happened to them?' Aurian demanded. 'Was it disease? Did something attack them? Are they all dead? If not, where did they go?'

'I do not know what became of them,' Basileus replied, his voice heavy with regret, *'but I do know why it happened. It is all part of what I must tell you, after you have rested. There will be time enough then – but in the meantime, keep away from*

Steelclaw — all of you. Be sure you warn the others, who cannot speak as we speak.'

'My people . . .' Shia murmured. 'All gone.' Head droop-ing low, she left the cavern, Khanu padding close behind her. The Mage started to follow, but Khanu forestalled her. 'Wait a little, Aurian. Later, she will need you. For now, I think she needs another cat. We'll help each other.' He followed Shia out.

Chiamh sighed. 'Well, I suppose the best thing we can do now is make this place habitable.'

Among the Windeye's belongings, Forral found an old cop-per cooking pot and a bucket that did not leak too much, and Aurian lit a fire to heat water. The nearby stand of pines by the pool provided twigs and a sturdy bough to make a broom. Vannor and Chiamh sorted and tidied his belongings, throw-ing out what could not be salvaged. Even with everyone help-ing, the sun was high enough in the sky to be peering over the high, sloping sides of the sheltered vale by the time they had the place straight. Afterwards, they took turns to bathe in the churning pool beneath the waterfall, and dried their shivering bodies on the few blankets that they still possessed.

By sunset, the companions were clean, sheltered, and fed, for Shia and Khanu had returned dragging the carcass of a deer. As darkness fell, they retired to the cavern, and Basileus began to speak, with Aurian and Chiamh translating his words for the others.

'It must have been almost ten years ago when I first realized that Steelclaw was inhabited again. There was a new feeling of tension in the stone — some tentative probing and prying, across the Dragon's Tail ridge. At once, my heart misgave me. "Who is there?" I asked — knowing that there could be but one answer. Ghabal. He was still as mad as ever — he spoke in riddles and mys-teries, saying that he had been freed from his imprisonment when the last of the Magefolk had quit the world — yet it had been a Mage who had brought him home, his consciousness still held in that same piece of rock torn from Steelclaw, in which it had been imprisoned long ago.

'Ghabal's presence made me uneasy at once — such a mad

twisted creature as he would always make a perilous neighbour, and his power seemed as great as it had ever been, making the danger even greater. One of the earliest results of his return was the banishment of the cats. To this day, I have no idea what became of them. I cannot think that Ghabal killed them all – there was no concentration of scavengers around the mountain, and there certainly would have been if that many bodies had been present. It is my belief that the cats, sensing the Moldan's return, left of their own accord – but where they went, who can say? Nevertheless, Shia and Khanu should not despair. Their people may now be living happily in some other place.'

Basileus paused a moment, as if to marshal his thoughts, before continuing. *'I was also worried about the Mage who was roaming at large on Steelclaw's slopes – and on mine, whenever he felt so inclined. I could tell at once he was as mad as the Moldan.'*

Dread had settled like a cold stone in Aurian's belly. She could keep silent no longer. 'A Mage, you say?' she interrupted. 'An old man, with gems for eyes?'

'Indeed, it is just as you say. I had a feeling you would know him. He has no eyes, just shining jewels, which is why the Xandim call him the Blind God, though somehow he still sees . . .'

'Blind God?' Aurian snorted. 'Well, I see his arrogance has not been blunted by the years – nor by what Eliseth did to him. I was hoping she'd finished him for good . . .'

'No you weren't.' Forral looked at her shrewdly. 'I know you better than that, Aurian. You wanted to finish him yourself.'

'And?' the Mage challenged.

'Yes, yes,' Forral grinned. 'You know that I want to finish him, too. You must admit, love – I've a damned good reason.'

'So what is this cult of the Blind God, Basileus?' Chiamh interrupted.

'At the full of the moon, and at the dark of the moon, one of the Xandim – usually a criminal, or one who has earned the displeasure of the Herdlord and the Council of Elders, is brought up to the Field of Stones and sacrificed. The Xandim purportedly earn the favour and protection of the Blind God – not to mention impunity from his wrath – though it seems to me that the Council and the Herdlord perpetuate this brutality to get rid of those against whom

they bear grudges. The God, on the other hand, gains . . .'

'Don't call him a god,' Aurian said tightly. 'His name is Miathan, and I know what he gains. The monster is feeding on the life-force of his victims to increase his powers.'

'Well, he won't be doing it much longer,' Forral said grimly.

The Mage nodded agreement. There would never be another chance like this. It was time to complete their unfinished business with the Archmage.

Forral was awakened by a cold nose poking in his ear. He jumped up, reaching for his sword – and found that his assailant was only Wolf. The swordsman sat down again and took deep breaths to slow his racing heart. 'Ho, Wolf,' he said tentatively in mindspeech. 'What's the matter?'

The wolf whined and stretched out its forelegs, dropping its nose down to its paws and cocking its ears.

'Are you really my father?' it asked.

The question, coming out of nowhere as it did, took Forral completely unawares. 'Yes,' he said firmly. 'As a matter of fact, I am.'

Wolf gave a little whine. 'I don't understand. Grandma Eilin said you had brown hair, and a beard. She said you were dead. Everybody said that – except Shia, and she won't even talk about it.'

'Hasn't your mother told you all about this?' Forral asked in some surprise. 'I should have thought . . .'

'Well, it was my fault, really. I wouldn't talk to her at first, because I thought she didn't want me – then when I got on the ship, there was just no time. She never really had a chance to explain.'

'All right,' he said to his son, 'I'll explain instead. This is what happened . . .'

It took some time to tell the entire tale. Wolf was full of questions, and Forral found himself having to reach back into his memory to relate incidents even as far back as Aurian's childhood, to clarify his relationship with the Mage. When he discovered that the Archmage who had put the curse on him was the same Miathan who had killed his father, Wolf started to growl softly. 'One day,' he said, 'I'm going to kill him.'

You won't have to, my son, Forral thought – because I intend to kill the bastard myself.

The Mage awakened in the night to find Chiamh shaking her shoulder gently. 'What?' she muttered in sleepy irritation. 'What's wrong?'

The Windeye held a finger to his lips for silence. 'Come with me,' he whispered.

The Mage sighed, fastened her clothing, and strapped on her sword.

'Make sure you bring the Staff,' Chiamh whispered. With a shrug, Aurian slipped it through her belt as usual, and slung the Harp on her back for good measure, before flinging her cloak around her shoulders and pulling on her boots. Then, walking softly and carefully so as not to wake the others, she crept out of the cave, following the Windeye and wondering what in the name of perdition was going on.

As they left the cavern, they came across Shia, on guard in the entrance. 'Where do you two think you're going?' she asked.

'Just up to my Chamber of Winds,' Chiamh replied.

'What?' Aurian hissed aloud. 'Oh no we bloody aren't!'

She turned to go back into the cave, but Chiamh caught hold of her arm. 'Truly, this is important,' he insisted. 'Come out here where we can talk.'

The Mage went with him as far as the pool, with its waterfall like a drift of pale smoke and its roiling surface aglimmer with a filigree of moonlight. Here she stopped and swung round to face the Windeye, hands on hips. 'Well?'

'Listen,' Chiamh said urgently, 'I don't know much about this Miathan, but I do know one thing – you shouldn't try to fight him without the Staff of Earth. I've been talking to Basileus about the trouble you were having with the Staff – and he thinks we can put it right.'

For an instant, Aurian wasn't sure she had heard him properly. Then the anger took over. 'You talked to Basileus?' she said in a voice that was deceptively calm and quiet. 'You discussed my private business – my personal shame – with that Moldan?'

'Curse it, what was I supposed to do?' the Windeye flung back at her. 'He knew, Aurian. He asked me. He's an Earth-elemental – he could sense immediately that something had happened to the Staff.'

'Well, if he knew, why the suffering blazes didn't he ask me?'

'Because he wanted to know whether he'd be able to help you before he talked to you,' Chiamh told her patiently. 'He didn't want to get your hopes up for nothing.'

'Get my hopes up?' Aurian blazed. 'I'm not a bloody child!'

'Then stop acting like one, damn it,' Chiamh roared at her. 'Don't you hear what I'm saying? Basileus can help you. Or would you rather throw away this one priceless opportunity to save the Staff through your accursed, stubborn, stiff-necked Magefolk pride?'

The Mage shut her mouth with a snap. She had never heard the Windeye lose his temper before. The shock cooled her anger instantly, as though he had thrown icy water at her, instead of hot words. 'I'm sorry, Chiamh,' she said. 'I'm acting like a fool. It's just that –' her voice caught, and she cleared her throat. 'I'm truly ashamed of what I did.'

The Windeye caught hold of her hands. 'If the Staff's powers return, will you finally believe you can forgive yourself?'

The ghost of a smile crept on to the Mage's face. 'You know what? I think I might.'

'Good. In that case, let's make a start.' Chiamh gestured towards the pinnacle. 'The first thing you must do is climb up to the Chamber of Winds.'

Aurian's face fell. 'Must we? Surely we could fly – it would be a whole lot safer.'

'No,' the Windeye told her firmly. 'That wasn't what Basileus said. He said that if you want to redeem yourself you must meet this challenge, and conquer your own fear. And if you'll notice, I didn't say "we". I'm sorry, Aurian. I'm afraid this is something you must do on your own.'

27

The Pinnacle

After Aurian had left the cavern, Shia found herself becoming more and more unsettled. At first, she told herself that her mood was distress at the mystery of her vanished people – or maybe it was unease for Aurian, who had gone wandering off into the night with the Windeye. What was Chiamh up to, trying to get Aurian up on top of the pinnacle at this hour, in the dark? Full well he knew how the Mage felt about high places!

'If Aurian hurts herself up there . . .' Shia's long black tail switched back and forth, and she growled deep in her throat. Unable to endure another moment sitting still, she rose to her feet and began to pace back and forth across the cavern mouth with long, lithe strides. What was wrong with her? There was an unaccustomed tension in her spine and tail, and she burned all over, as though there was a prickling itch beneath the surface of her skin.

Before she knew what was happening, Shia was on her back on the floor, rolling and writhing in the dust. Suddenly she became aware of a new smell – a rich, heady musk that she had not previously noticed. She looked up to see Khanu, stalking around her stiff-legged, his fur brushed up along his spine and his throat vibrating with a deep, rumbling thunder of his purr. Oh no, she thought. I don't believe this! Of all the inconvenient . . . Then another wave of Khanu's musk rolled over her, and her senses were submerged in the compelling imperatives of the moment.

Uttering seductive little croons, the cat continued to roll, tempting her suitor; daring him to approach. With a bound he was on her – and Shia's paw lashed out, her claws catching him a glancing blow across the nose. Then she was on her feet, eyes blazing; circling, snarling; watching him rub his nose and back away, his face furrowed with puzzlement. But she knew that her own lure was too powerful; that her voluptuous scent would draw him back towards her . . .

Shia darted away from the mouth of the cavern and the sleeping humans within. This was no time to be near the puny two-legged ones! Khanu pursued her, catching up with her in the grove of pines near the pool. Cunningly, the cat turned her back on him, her head and forepaws pressed low to the ground. She sneaked a coy look behind her, to see Khanu stalking closer, his glowing eyes, shining with reflected moon-light, like two smaller moons come down to earth. Just as he came within reach, Shia bounded away with a derisive yowl, and spun to face him, ears flat and fur a-bristle; one forepaw raised, its claws extended.

She spat – he leapt. There was a tussle: a blur of motion so fast that it was over before Shia had time to register what was happening. Then she was free again – speeding up the steep sloping side of the valley, devouring the ground in great, stretching leaps, with Khanu hurtling after her, only a claw's length behind the end of her streaming tail.

Together they went up the mountain like a whirlwind: rac-ing, turning, biting, spinning, whirling, clawing, dodging and tussling – until finally, Shia tempted Khanu once too often – or maybe she was tiring now, and couldn't dodge so fast. She had ducked around a rocky outcrop and was waiting for him on the other side, uttering coy little croons; head down, hindquarters raised, tail waving alluringly. As he rounded the boulder, she whisked to one side – but too late. Khanu's weight came pressing down on her, and his teeth met, gently but firmly, in the loose skin at the back of her neck.

Shia yowled and scuffled with her claws, but she was frozen in position by his hold. With a howl of triumph he entered her, and she braced herself, half-snarling, half-purring, as he began to thrust vigorously. Then it was over – with a squall, he emptied himself into her, and leapt backwards. As they pulled apart, a white-hot pain shot through Shia's vitals and she gave an ear-splitting screech, turning to claw viciously at her mate once more.

For a moment, both cats stood, glaring and bristling, then a

388

languor stole over them, and bit by bit they began to relax, shaking their heads and looking around them in a dazed fashion as the world came back into focus. Khanu, blood dripping from one torn ear, came purring to rub heads with her, but Shia suddenly stiffened beneath his caress. 'Khanu!' she cried in dismay. 'Have you seen where we are?'

Khanu looked around him – and his purr stopped abruptly, as though his throat had been cut. 'Let's get away from here – quick!'

But it was too late. The cats' wild chase had brought them, all unknowing, across the Dragon's Tail. They were on the forbidden slopes of Steelclaw – and something was aware of them.

Aurian stiffened when she first heard the yowling that came faint and far-off on the wind. Shia was in trouble. One hand slipped from its hold, and she scrabbled frantically to regain her balance on the narrow ledge. Once secure, she pressed herself hard against the stone, trembling all over, her heart racing so that her blood sounded like distant surf in her ears. As soon as she had calmed herself sufficiently, she reached out with her mind to the great cat – and met with such a turmoil of raw emotion that she snatched her consciousness back quickly, as though she had been burned.

'Well well!' Despite her precarious position, the Mage chuckled to herself, with relief as much as amusement. So Shia's howls stemmed from passion, not danger. Aurian smiled fondly at the thought of little fuzzy black cubs, though she was aware that it made her mission even more urgent. All too well she remembered her own grim pregnancy in the mountains, and did not want Shia to suffer the same discomforts and dangers.

Recollecting her own current discomfort and danger, Aurian pulled her thoughts away from the cats and returned her attention to the task in hand. Surely she must be nearly there by now? But when she looked across the void at the pinnacle that soared beside her, only three arms' length away from the cliff, she realized that she still had quite some distance to climb. Bitterly, she remembered the last time she had been here, when Ibis and Kestrel had transported Anvar and herself to the top of the spire – and she had watched Chiamh scramble, fly-footed, up this thread of a goat track as though it had been the broadest of highways. 'How did he manage it?' Aurian muttered to herself wrathfully. 'It's just not fair!' With an effort, she pulled herself together. I'm more than halfway now, she thought, trying to boost her sinking courage. That in itself is quite a feat for a Mage who's terrified of heights. Why, I'll be at the top in no time!

Aurian needed every scrap of her courage. She was crawling up the narrow, steeply-sloping ledge, not daring to stand, so her knees were bruised and cut, and her hands torn and bleeding. Despite the cold night, she was drenched in a sweat of terror and exertion that kept trickling down into her eyes, blurring her vision and stinging like perdition. To increase her discomfort, the Staff of Earth was poking into her ribs with every move she made: a painful and perilous distraction when perforce she must keep all her attention on the trail.

Between the cliff and the pinnacle, a chasm yawned, so dark, deep, and narrow that even her Mage's sight could not plumb the bottom. In one sense, it helped not being able to see how far she might fall; yet where her eyesight stopped, her imagination had an unpleasant tendency to take over; furthermore, long stretches of the ledge were also obscured in the deep, deceptive shadow, forcing her to creep slowly along, inch by inch, shaking all over, until the danger had been passed.

Aurian kept her eyes on the narrow trail one step ahead of her bleeding hands, gritted her teeth, and just kept crawling, trying not to stop. Every time she was forced to halt, it grew increasingly difficult to move again . . .

'Keep going, Aurian – you're almost there.' The Windeye's soft voice came out of nowhere.

The Mage raised her head and shook it to flick the straggling, sweat-drenched hair out of her eyes. Just beyond her right hand was a tangled webbing of slender rope that stretched across the chasm, made fast to the cliff by rusted iron spikes driven deep into the rock. Since the pinnacle narrowed towards the top, the distance between it and the cliff had widened now, to a distance of about five yards. Aurian already thought her mouth was very dry. Now, her throat closed up completely, as her mind refused to even consider the possibility of crossing the chasm on those fragile strands.

'Honestly,' Chiamh coaxed, 'it's not as difficult as it looks. You put your feet on the lower ropes, hold on to the upper strands, and just inch your way along. It's practically impossible to fall.'

Luckily for the Windeye, Aurian was well beyond speech at this point, but he was close enough for her to send him, in the mode of mind-speech, an image of an extremely obscene gesture.

Chiamh chuckled wickedly. 'You can't make that one good, without coming over here.'

'And remember, Wizard,' the voice of Basileus added, *'the alternative is to go back down again by the track – in your case, probably backwards all the way.'*

Silently cursing the pair of them, Aurian took a deep breath and knelt in an upright position, reaching above her head for the upper set of ropes. Clasping them so tightly that her hands were knots of bone, she used them to pull herself up to her feet.

Then, carefully, she began to shuffle her feet along the lower strands. Where the makeshift bridge left the cliff, the rope dipped suddenly beneath her weight. Aurian gave a squeak of terror, clinging tightly to the upper strands as her stomach leapt up into her throat, and she bit her tongue. The remainder of the crossing was a blur. Some deeply buried instinct for survival seemed to take over from Aurian's conscious mind, and it decided that she had better get across that gap as fast as possible. She remembered a rapid, lurching scramble, a dreadful instant of frozen horror when she thought she must be slipping – then Chiamh was reaching out for her, and she hurled herself to safety, feeling his arms gather her; both of them collapsing in an entangled heap on the secure and solid floor of the Chamber of Winds. Long shudders passed through Aurian's body as her mind shook itself free of the terror and she began to realize that she was safe at last.

'*Well done, Wizard,*' the voice of Basileus boomed in her mind. '*You have conquered your fear, and have proved yourself courageous and worthy of the Staff. Now, you must make one last, dark journey, to restore both its powers and your own faith in yourself.*'

Aurian sat up and centred herself right in the middle of the Chamber of Winds, well away from the yawning drops on all four sides. She took the dull and lifeless Staff from her belt, and sat cradling it, running her hands along its polished, twisting length. 'But how can I accomplish that?' she asked.

'*Lift yourself free from your body, Wizard. Ride the winds with the Windeye, and see what you will find.*'

Though the Mage couldn't see how that would help, she was certainly willing to give it a try. She looked at Chiamh.

'I'm ready to risk it if you are,' he told her, his brown eyes twinkling.

'All right, Chiamh – I trust you.' Taking a firm grip of the Staff in one hand, she stretched out the other to grasp the hand of the Windeye. As his eyes began to flood with reflective silver, Aurian breathed deeply, letting her body relax as her mind began to drift . . .

And suddenly, as easily as that, she was out and free, drifting like mist above her corporeal form and looking around her at the translucent crystalline structure of the Chamber of Winds, that was also, she thought, the body of Basileus. It gave off a soft, warm glow like sunlight through the petals of a rose. Drifting gently, the Mage let herself revolve until she caught sight of Chiamh, who hovered above his own mortal shell in the form of a swirl of golden incandescence. 'Both of you are extraordinarily beautiful like this,' she told them.

'As are you, my friend,' Chiamh told her. 'You look like a swirl of gems from the Jewelled Desert, or spindrift glittering in the sun.'

'*Instead of drifting around there admiring one another, I advise you to get going,*' Basileus cut in. '*I thought you were here to heal the Staff?*' Though his words were sharp, his voice, while the Mage was in this disembodied form, was like the slow, smooth pouring of honey.

She looked at the Windeye and a sparkle of amusement

chased across his glowing golden surface. 'All right, Basileus,' he said. He extended a long, luminescent tentacle towards Aurian. 'Come on, Mage.' Aurian spun out a shimmering strand of her own and extended it towards him. The two glistening limbs met in a flash of warm brilliance, and Aurian felt waves of pleasure pulse through her, her own exultation mingling with that of the Windeye to amplify the sensation. Chiamh reached out with another tentacle and caught hold of a current of moving air as it flowed past, and the two of them sped away from the pinnacle, like two glowing leaves borne swiftly along on a stream of light.

Swiftly they travelled, heading up towards the very topmost peak of the Wyndveil. The Mage relaxed and let the Windeye take her, simply trusting that he and Basileus knew what they were about. As they neared the summit, Aurian realized, with a shock, that they were no longer alone. Swimming through the air in front of herself and Chiamh, as though leading the way, were the twin serpents from the Staff, the Serpent of Might and the Serpent of Wisdom, moving as easily through the air as they had moved through the mysterious waters of the Well of Souls. It was only then that she realized that she no longer held the Staff of Earth, either in its mundane form or its incorporeal avatar. Dread and dismay coursed through her, causing her to tighten her grip involuntarily on the Windeye's shining limb. Immediately, Chiamh slowed his speed, though he kept them drifting inexorably forward along the river of air. 'Is something wrong?'

'The Staff,' Aurian cried, 'I've lost the Staff!'

Again, the sparkle of amusement shimmered across the swirling golden mist that was the Windeye. 'Don't fret – of course you haven't. You're here to heal and reclaim the Staff, remember – that means you'll have to recreate it all over again.'

Aurian looked at him in some doubt. 'But I . . .'

'Come on,' Chiamh told her. 'You'll do just fine.'

Aurian realized that they were hurtling towards a dark hole; a gaping black maw set in the very apex of the mountain. Instinctively, she tried to shut her eyes, but in this incorporeal state, she could not. The next moment the great mouth seemed to leap forward and swallow them, and as it did so, the Windeye vanished. The Mage was surrounded by a cocoon of thick darkness, and was completely alone.

Aurian stopped moving – or thought she did. With all her senses muffled, there was no way to tell. The blackness pressed down on her; a cloying, muffling weight, that paralysed and imprisoned her, as though she had been buried alive under thick, black loam. Though the Mage was striving to be calm, terror began to rise within her. There was no way out of here – she could neither see, nor struggle, nor call out for help. Has something happened to my body? she thought with increasing panic. Is this what death is like? But she had ventured into Death's realm, and knew that it was not like this. Aurian's scorn against her own fanciful idiocy braced her as nothing else could have done. Remember, she told herself firmly, this was always supposed to be an ordeal. It's a test, a challenge; so stop being stupid, and get on and deal with it.

At first there seemed no way to light up the profound blackness that enmeshed her – until Aurian began to think of Chiamh. Where was the Windeye? What had become of him? Then the words that he had spoken in the Chamber of Winds came back to her: 'You look like a swirl of gems from the Jewelled Desert, or spindrift glittering in the sun.' Of course! the Mage thought. I can use myself. She thought of her coruscating, incandescent form as the Windeye must have seen it, and poured all her energies into the image, trying to make it stronger and brighter.

Gradually, the black feelings of misery and dread that had pressed down on the Mage seemed to be lifting a little. In time, the physical darkness seemed to be less intense. Could it be working? Aurian concentrated on her incorporeal form, and remembered Chiamh's words. She thought of the multi-coloured radiance of the Jewelled Desert; of the glitter of white surf; of sunlight glancing off the ocean in spangles of dazzling light; of stars on a frosty night; of moonlight on a field of virgin snow.

Yes – it was working! Aurian's determined summoning of light was beginning to send the darkness into a retreat. She actually could see it creeping back now: shrinking away from her radiant form.

Then suddenly the darkness was gone – and Aurian cried out in pain as she was pierced through and through by spears and splinters of viridian, emerald and sea-green light. There was no way she could close her eyes – there was no way to escape the brittle radiance that pierced her like a thousand swords. Only when she had pulled her wits together and dimmed her own luminescence, did the light soften, swirling around her like a snowfall of glittering green flakes.

At last the Mage could see herself as Chiamh had seen her – but in the form of myriad green reflections that curved away on all sides to a dizzying infinity. When she had managed to make sense of the many conflicting, splintered reflections, she discovered that she appeared to be floating inside a massive hollow gem. And all this green . . . It was as though she had been trapped inside the crystal that held the Staff of Earth's power – or was she viewing the scene through the eldritch medium of the Othersight, and was this place truly something else entirely?

A flash of scarlet flashed at the edge of Aurian's vision. She spun, trailing sunburst limbs of fire, and saw the red and silver Serpent of Might approaching her, swimming with swift ease through the scintillating green void. From the other side, the Serpent of Wisdom was also approaching, its green and gold markings far less easy to see as it blended into the emerald background. Aurian's heart leapt to see them. At least she had not lost them in the darkness. Even as she was wondering why they should be converging on her, the serpents struck, sinking their fangs into glittering, amorphous plasm that was the Mage. Rivers of fire raced along Aurian's streaming limbs towards the central core of her being. She screamed, shrill and voiceless, as the agony spiralled through her. The serpents struck her again and again, clamping their fanged jaws into the insubstantial gossamer of her discarnate form, and tearing away great mouthfuls like shreds of glistening cloud.

Deep within another mountain, the Archmage was awakened from uneasy dreams.

'Trespassers! Intruders! We are invaded!'

'What in the name of perdition is wrong with you, Ghabal?' Miathan muttered irritably.

'Awake! Awake! We are attacked!'

Not again! Under his breath, the Archmage cursed. Lately, Ghabal's madness had taken this form: every time a bird flew over, or a breeze brushed by his stony flanks, the Moldan was imagining invaders. 'Come now – who could be attacking you?' he soothed. 'The Xandim? That's nonsense. They wouldn't dare. Why, since the cats departed, no one save me has come closer to you than the Field of Stones.'

'Intruders! They set foot on me! They touched me!'

Miathan sighed. 'All right – I'll take a look. Will that satisfy you? Now, where were these so-called invaders?'

'On my western flank – they must have come across the Dragon's Tail.'

'Very well.' The Archmage reached up to a shelf carved into the cavern wall beside his bed, and carefully, using both hands, he took down a large silver casket. Throwing back the lid, he reached inside and lifted out a great black gem, almost as large as his own head. The stone was unfaceted, like a black pearl – except that it lacked a pearl's soft lustre. Instead of reflecting light, the gem seemed to absorb it – indeed, when the Archmage withdrew it from its casket, the room seemed to grow darker, as though swarming shadows were creeping down the walls and out of the corners.

'Do you have to use that accursed stone?' the Moldan asked sharply. *'It is an evil thing, filled with unquiet spirits.'*

'Don't be stupid!' Miathan snapped. The cold gems that were his eyes glittered with an avid light as his gnarled and knotted hands caressed the smooth lightless surface of the stone. 'This is my creation, my treasure,' he crooned. 'It will be my revenge!'

Long ago, Miathan had decided that, since he had no Artefact of his own; nor, as far as he could see, any chance of obtaining one; there was only one solution – he must try to make one.

In all the ten years that Miathan had been here, his defeat by Eliseth had never ceased to rankle. Though to date she had failed to discover his whereabouts, he would not be able to rest, he knew, while she was still at large in the world, for he would be forever looking over his shoulder. Unfortunately, because she held the stolen Cauldron of Rebirth, he still lacked sufficient power to overcome her, but soon that would change.

This audacious plan had the full support of the Moldan. *'Once we wield such power, the world will fall to its knees before us!'* Ghabal had crowed. Miathan had decided not to disillusion him – he needed Ghabal's help in the matter of crystals, and the benefit of the Moldan's experience concerning the storing of power in the lattices of stone. He had been experimenting for several years now, and had perfected a method of storing the accumulated life-energies of his sacrifice victims in this smooth crystal. So far, though, he had failed to achieve the most important factor: the actual character and intelligence, the sentience, that all the original Artefacts possessed – or so he thought. The Moldan disagreed. It had taken an intense dislike to the stone, almost bordering on hysterical fear. Ghabal insisted that the gem was inherently evil, and filled with the vengeful spirits of the dead.

Arrant nonsense! Miathan thought. Clasping the crystal to his chest, he lay back on his couch, thankful that the cold stone was well padded with a thick layer of fragrant hay and herbs brought by the Xandim from the lowlands, then woven bags well-stuffed with feathers and fleece, brightly-dyed woollen blankets, and a generous pile of sheepskins and furs, including the heavy pelts of several great cats who had not left the mountain in time. It wasn't too bad, he conceded, this business of being a god. He might be stuck with living here in this mountain cavern, but at least he had the best of everything, food and wine included. The frequent offerings brought to him by the Xandim were sufficient to satisfy all his needs – save one. Revenge.

'Do you plan to seek out those intruders at any time this year?' Ghabal's acid tones reminded the Mage of what he was supposed to be doing before he had lost himself in thought.

'All right, all right,' snapped Miathan. 'I'm going.'

The Archmage lay back, covering himself carefully with a

pile of furs. These days, his old body simply could not afford to lose too much heat while he was absent. Once settled, he closed his eyes and relaxed, until the interior of the cavern became clearly visible to him through his closed eyelids. Now that his inner form was discrete from its shell, he rose gently above his discarded body, and sailed through the wall of the cave and into the thick, dark layers of rock beyond.

Emerging on the shattered pinnacle of Steelclaw, Miathan pointed himself towards the west and swooped down over the Dragon's Tail, and stopped there: hovering. To his utter astonishment, the Moldan had been right for once. Far below, on the mountainside above the ridge, were two small, familiar black shapes that he had not seen for some considerable time. Well! Miathan thought. So two, at least, of the cats had returned to Steelclaw. How very fortuitous – he could do with some new furs.

Given the unexpected appearance of the felines, the Archmage wondered whether more of the creatures were wandering at large. A cat-hunt might be a useful way to test the powers of his new Artefact – and failing that, it would provide some entertainment, at least. Living up here in isolation, save for his deranged companion, meant that Miathan very rarely had such an opportunity to enjoy himself. Presumably, the animals had come from the Wyndveil, so he set off in that direction, heading roughly towards the Xandim Fastness.

When he reached the high valley with the barrows of the Xandim dead, the Archmage was astounded to see the glow that meant living beings on the top of the strange, high spire that stood at the valley's head. What in the world is going on? he thought. Surely that place is taboo for the Xandim? Suspicious now, he crept closer, keeping his thoughts to a low, almost formless murmur to make sure that his approach was unobserved.

As Miathan came closer, he could see two figures in the airy vantage point that crowned the spire. Once, he realized after a moment was a Xandim. He seemed to be watching over the other who lay immobile on the cold stone, clearly deep in trance. In trance? A quiver of anxiety tinged with rare anticipation ran through the Archmage. None of the Xandim possessed the powers of magic! Then Miathan drew near enough to recognize the distant form. *Aurian?* He intended to return to his body, but the shock of seeing her was so intense that he never got there.

Bit by bit the serpents tore away Aurian's inner form, ignoring her struggles. The Mage thrashed and struggled, but there was no escape from her attackers – nor from the agony they inflicted as they tore her asunder. Gradually she found her consciousness drifting and fading, as her memories were torn away one by one, along with every scrap of pride, of stubbornness and belligerence: all the good things and all the bad. Somehow, though, she never lost consciousness completely. No matter what was taken, she always retained a last, deep spark of awareness – and that was how she knew when the serpents had reached the core of her at last. She watched, detached now and at peace, as though from a tremendous distance, as they tore away the last tattered remnants of her old self – to reveal at the centre of her being a sparkling green crystal, just large enough to fit into a Mage's palm.

Then, with tails entwined and jaws interlinking around the gem, the serpents formed a circle and began to spin, creating a whirlpool of magic whose core was in the exact centre of the spherical chamber, within the ring formed by their bodies. Bit by bit, the tatters of the Mage's incorporeal form, that had been drifting around the chamber like slips of cloud, began to gather and converge once more, whirling and spinning and conjoining – until Aurian suddenly found herself back together, glistening and newborn and beautiful – renewed and remade by the serpents of the High Magic, that still encircled her glowing form like a diadem, holding the crystal of the Staff in their jaws.

'Very impressive, my dear.' Aurian spun at the sound of the dry, sardonic voice. There, in the form of a roiling black cloud shot through with bolts of crimson lightning, was the Archmage Miathan.

Having delivered the Mage to her fate, Chiamh returned to the Chamber of Winds, where he slipped back into his corporeal form. Even though his own neglected body was shivering with the night's bitter cold, he took off his cloak and covered the still, pale form of Aurian where she lay. 'I feel dreadful about this,' he told Basileus. 'I can't believe I let you talk me into it. Poor Aurian! She's going to suffer dreadfully. Maybe I should just go back and see . . .'

'No, Windeye! You were told how it must be. This is a trial that Aurian must face alone.'

'But . . .'

'Do you want her to fail? Because that is what will happen if you go back there and intervene. And you would intervene, my friend. Having seen the intensity of her suffering, you would not be able to help yourself. Leave it now,' Basileus added in kindly tones. 'So long as she has the courage and the strength and the purity of purpose, she will survive, and emerge triumphant.'

Reluctantly, Chiamh was forced to accede to the wisdom of the Moldan – but he simply couldn't leave the poor Mage to her fate without at least bearing witness – and there was one way he could do that, at least. As the familiar, melting coldness of his Othersight sank through his body, he turned to gather a silvery skein of wind between his fingers, and began to stretch and mould it into a gleaming mirror. Then, kindling the disc to life with his Othersight, he bent his will upon Aurian, and peered into the depths.

The Windeye cried out in horror and dismay. 'This isn't what you said! You said she could remake the Staff! Instead it's killing her!' So intense was Chiamh's distress that he lost control of the mirror, and it dissolved to formless mist between his fingers.

'Patience, Windeye. Let us hope Aurian will prevail. Instead of the Mage remaking the Staff, the Staff is remaking her. I did warn you – you should not have watched.'

Too distraught to form another mirror, Chiamh sat down beside the Mage's still body and stroked the tangled hair away from her forehead. What have I done? he thought desperately. What have I done? Then the Windeye stopped breathing. Beneath the cloak, bright enough to glow even through the thick woven fabric, he saw a brilliant green light, pale and flickering at first, then growing strong and steady.

400

'Thanks be to the goddess . . .' Chiamh lifted the cloak gently aside. There, still clasped tightly to the Mage's breast, was the Staff of Earth – and the great green stone between the jaws of the snakes was gleaming brighter than it had ever done before.

Forgetting to breathe, the Windeye leaned forward, expecting Aurian to open her eyes and return to him at any moment. He waited and waited – but nothing happened. The Mage made no movement, and her pale face might just as well have been carved from stone.

28

A Long-Awaited Meeting

Forral awoke to the alarming realization that half his companions were missing. Where were the two cats? Where were Aurian and the Windeye? He leapt to his feet.

'*Hush – do not wake everyone! Your friends are all quite safe.*'

'What? Who in the name of all creation is that?' But Forral already had a good idea, thanks to his previous experience of mental communication with Shia. 'Are you this Basileus that the Windeye was talking about?'

'*Indeed. You would have heard me earlier, when we were all talking, if you had tried a little harder.*'

'I suppose so,' Forral admitted. 'I just can't get used to this business of mind-speech. The power seems so much a part of Anvar – it belongs to him, not me. I don't really like to use it. It feels like going into his house while he's out, and using his belongings.' He hesitated for an instant. 'Basileus – did you know Anvar?'

'*Of course. He was very brave. Though he did not believe himself to be especially courageous he . . .*'

'Where is everybody?' The last thing Forral needed right now was to hear a whole list of Anvar's virtues.

'*The Windeye and Aurian are on top of this pinnacle, in Chiamh's Chamber of Winds.*' There was a stiff hint of reproof in the Moldan's voice. '*They are restoring the Staff of Earth. It would not be wise to disturb them, but they should be returning soon. The two cats are . . .*' The Moldan's low-pitched mental tones turned shrill with horror. '*They are gone, they are gone! It is too late to stop them! In their folly they have gone to Steelclaw!*'

'What? What does that mean?' Forral demanded.

'*It means that your presence here will be – or already has been – discovered by the Blind God!*'

402

'Miathan, eh?' the swordsman growled. 'Good. He can come here as quick as he likes.'

'*You fail to understand, human. It is unlikely that he will strike at the Mage here, in this mundane world where she has the assistance of her companions. At present she is in the Elsewhere Beyond the World, the realm of the mind and the spirit, where once the Phaerie were exiled. She has just been through a tremendous ordeal to recover the Staff – it is likely that she will be wearied and disorientated. If he moves quickly, and catches her now, in this vulnerable state, she will not stand a chance. Oh, if only Anvar were here!*' the Moldan cried. '*Another Mage might tilt the balance . . .*'

'Bugger Anvar,' Forral growled. 'He isn't here but I am – and in his body I surely must have access to his powers, or I wouldn't be talking to you now. What must I do, Basileus? Tell me how I can get to Aurian and help her.'

'*Lie back, relax, let your mind drift . . . Think of Aurian. Think of going to her, to help her . . . Let yourself drift away, away from your body, towards Aurian . . .*'

Forral let himself be lulled by the Moldan's words. He thrust all thoughts of panic and danger, of Aurian in trouble and needing him, out of his mind. He simply concentrated on the image of the Mage's beloved face, and let the words of Basileus lull him and teach him . . .

It didn't happen the way he had imagined it would. With an abruptness that shocked him, Forral was somewhere else entirely – in a weird, unearthly world that rippled with a scintillating green light.

Back in the cavern, Wolf opened one eye and looked at Forral's still body. 'I expect I could do that,' he said.

'*I expect you could,*' replied Basileus. '*Do you want to try?*'

Aurian looked at the writhing knot of darkness that was the Archmage. Good, she thought. Let's finish this at last.

Without warning, the twin forms of the Serpents of the High Magic swam between Aurian and the Archmage. No longer small enough to fit on Aurian's staff, they loomed gigantically over the two Mages.

'The Rules of Gramarye apply here, Beyond the Worlds,' the Serpent of Might said in a clear voice. 'The indiscriminate loosing of magic is forbidden in this higher sphere of existence. No magical weapons or implements may be used to boost your powers – this contest must be judged by your own innate skills, and more important, the strength of your will. If you fight, your battle must be structured. You must take the form of creatures from your own corporeal world, and focus your powers through what would be their natural weapons: fangs, spines or claws. The arena in which you fight, and the corresponding physical forms you must take, will correspond to the elements of Air, Fire, Water, and Earth. A Challenge must be one to one, and no one else may interfere. Do you Challenge?'

Aurian looked at the Archmage. 'Well?' she demanded. 'Do you Challenge?'

Miathan's reply was the last thing she had expected. 'Aurian, I never wanted it to be like this. It's all my fault – together we could have achieved such greatness as would have been told in legend for a thousand years – had I not ruined everything. But surely, my dear, even you must see that Eliseth is the enemy now? Already she has the Cauldron and she has captured the Sword, even though she cannot use it. You are well matched, the two of you – there is no guarantee that you can defeat her. Lately, it seems, the skirmishes have all gone to her. But together, Aurian, we could wipe her threat forever from the face of the world. My dear, I have always loved you, right from the beginning. Please, will you not reconsider? Will you not join me, even now?'

Aurian thought of Anvar, sold into drudgery and his powers stolen. She thought of the day she had given birth to her long-awaited child, and found a wolf instead. She thought about Forral, so pale and still and cold in death, and her heart turned over within her.

'Do you Challenge?' she repeated, her voice like stone and steel and the endless void between the stars.

The cloud of darkness seemed to shrink in upon itself. 'Is there no forgiveness?' Miathan whispered.

The silence stretched out; a deepening chasm between the

Mage and the one who had been her mentor, her protector – and her betrayer.

Aurian felt no hate for him – she was far beyond that now. She had no feelings for him save a steely resolution to be rid of him for good. Miathan was simply vermin, a rat, only using this whining remorse when he was cornered. As long as he was allowed to continue in the world, then there would be no end to the damage and mischief he would do – but like all cornered rats, he would be at his most dangerous now. She knew that if Miathan refused to Challenge, then she must – and in the battle of magic that would follow, that would give him first blow, and his choice of ground. Also there were other matters to be considered. 'What about the curse on my son?' she asked him.

'If you'll join me, I will take it off – I promise.' Miathan leapt eagerly on her words – a little too eagerly.

'But don't you need the grail for that?' Aurian asked suspiciously.

'I – oh, yes – of course. Yes, you see? We must join forces. If we don't get the grail from Eliseth, then how am I to lift the curse from the poor . . .'

'You can't do it, can you? You actually cursed my child, and you don't know how to undo what you did.' Aurian could hear her voice rising in anger.

'Why do you waste time on this? Kill her now!' Suddenly, Miathan had been joined by another black shape – but this one was vast, like a gigantic sea creature with a nest of grasping tentacles, a single pale eye, and a gaping maw in the centre, bristling with ranks of pointed teeth.

'Stay out of this, Ghabal – ere I make you wish you had stayed where you belong – walled up in a Magefolk tomb!' Aurian turned – and gasped. This must be Basileus – but she had never imagined him looking like this! He was wearing a similar shape to Ghabal's hideous form – but the Moldan of the Wyndveil was glorious and resplendent; his bright golden eye sparkling, and his many limbs a mass of iridescent colour that was patterned with spots and streaks of moving light that seemed to move about independently beneath the surface of his glistening skin.

Even as Aurian watched, the two titans converged with

405

ponderous but savage force, their writing tentacles grasping and groping as they grappled for a hold. Then all at once, her view of the struggle was obscured by a wall of malevolent darkness. Miathan, without crying Challenge, had taken advantage of her moment of distraction and attacked.

Responding to her anger, Aurian's incorporeal form crackled with a sheet of searing fire. With a cry, Miathan loosed his hold and dropped away.

'Wait! Archmage! I Challenge you, you misbegotten bag of offal! *I* Challenge!'

The black cloud that was Miathan thinned and turned almost transparent with shock. 'You! But . . .' Then suddenly he burst out laughing. 'You haven't the wit to know when you're beaten, do you? You fool!'

With a cry of anger, Aurian spun round to see who had stolen her prey – and her anger turned to shock.

'Forral! You can't . . .'

'He has.' The Serpent of Wisdom's voice was quiet but inexorable. 'The Challenge has been made and accepted.'

Instead of the amorphous forms that the others had chosen for their foray into this Elsewhere, the swordsman was wearing his old, true shape. Aurian found herself glowing gently, with love remembered and love renewed. Which was all very well, but . . .

'What in the name of all the gods do you think you're doing, you idiot?' she demanded. 'How in perdition do you think you can defeat Miathan in a magical battle?'

'Because I have Anvar's body, I also have his powers,' Forral explained. 'Basileus explained what to do. In my mind, I just think of it as a normal fight with swords – the sort I was always so good at – and the physical form I assume in this place will take care of itself.'

Before the Mage could say another word, the Serpent of Might intervened once more. 'Ignore the Moldai – other rules apply to them. Proceed with the Challenge.'

In an instant, the light within the sphere flashed from green to translucent blue. In that same instant, Forral vanished and a golden eagle hovered in his place. Where Miathan had been, the dark and massive form of a condor vaned the air. With a harsh cry, the huge black raptor swooped down on its smaller prey. The eagle, slighter and more manoeuvrable, banked to one side and sideslipped, losing height but avoiding the clutching talons of its foe. With an angry shriek the condor tried to turn, but underestimated its weight and size, and stalled in the air, plunging downward, out of control. Then the great wings snapped open with a gargantuan effort, pulling the great bird out of its dive – but it was too late. The swift eagle cut lightly through the air and intersected the condor's path, lashing out at the condor's eyes with its scimitar-curved talons. Screaming horribly, the condor fell, one eye leaking a trail of gore, and . . .

Abruptly, everything altered. The light seemed to thicken with acrid, smoky fumes, and the air pulsed in blasts of heat like the beating of a gigantic heart. Its colour had changed to an uneasy, flickering red. In the place of the condor and the eagle two huge firedrakes, like sinuous dragons but lacking the great wings, faced one another across a shifting surface of burning embers. One, of a burnished copper hue, had a ragged void that leaked glowing blood, where one jewelled eye should have been. The other, its scaly skin a pure gold, exhaled a gout of sizzling flame and raked at the embers with one immense clawed foot.

This time, the sinuous red lizard was considerably more cautious. Aurian, looking on, suspected that Miathan, not understanding how Forral had come by his magic, had under-estimated the swordsman badly. It was a mistake he would not make a second time.

Without warning, another jet of flame shot out of the golden dragon's maw. The red beast, unnerved by its failure to conquer its foe in the air, had hesitated an instant too long. Caught off guard, it leapt to one side – and the uncertain surface of embers shifted and gave beneath its unwary feet. The red lizard staggered, floundering, one thick foreleg deeply mired in the fiery morass. The more it floundered, the deeper the panic-stricken firedrake began to sink.

Forral crept forward with exaggerated care, distributing his weight as widely as possible on spread toes. The red dragon spat great, untidy gouts of flame in his direction, but it was too

407

busy trying to extricate itself to concentrate on its foe. Forral's jaws gaped wide to deliver a killing blow and . . .

His shape shimmered and changed – became solid, and streamlined: sleekly-muscled and beautifully marked in elegant curves of black and white. Aurian remembered the time, long ago, when Ithalasa had been telling her the history of the Cataclysm by feeding a series of images into her mind. He had told her of the race of Leviathan warriors, the Orca, who had been created to save the Seafolk from the aggressive Mages of the land and air – and clearly, this was such a creature.

The water around Forral shimmered with light and shadow, in gold and soft sea-green. The Orca champed the fierce set of teeth in a mouth that seemed curved into a permanent smile. With a swirl of his tail, he turned towards the Archmage and charged . . .

. . . To meet the razor jaws and the flat, dead gaze of an enormous shark.

The instincts inherent in Forral's new shape took over. He swerved down to one side with a twist of his muscular body, and came at the shark from an oblique angle, and from below.

He was taken completely unawares by how fast the shark could move. Even as he came up and rammed it with all his force, the shark writhed round, bending back on itself like a bow, and caught his flank with its wicked teeth as he curved away. Forral whistled shrilly with pain as a long slash was scored along his side. A thread of blood went spiralling away from the wound in a glowing stream, and Aurian guessed that in actuality, it must be his life-force that he was losing. Miathan, however, had not escaped unscathed. He seemed to be sinking; dropping away, writhing and curling himself about the telling injury that had been inflicted when Forral rammed him.

'I hope that hurt, you bastard,' Aurian muttered grimly.

Forral plunged down after him, clearly hoping to finish it quickly, but the Archmage recovered himself, and the swordsman was met by vicious snapping teeth that forced him into a hasty retreat. He pretended to dodge, feinted, and came in from the other side, his teeth scoring into the thick abrasive leather of Miathan's hide before he twisted away again, out of reach of those lethal jaws.

Now it was Miathan's turn to bleed – and the gore in the water, both that of himself and Forral, seemed to send him into a frenzy. He came straight at the swordsman, jaws gaping, eyes blank with mindless hate.

To Forral, it seemed that there was no escape this time. He fled, trying to put some distance between himself and the shark so that he could turn and attack it obliquely once more. He had underestimated the speed of the creature, however. Already it was right behind him, its teeth snatching at his tail and slicing chunks of flesh from the broad, flat surface . . .

When Wolf arrived he soon realized that he and the others were not literally beneath the sea, but that they had taken these shapes to suit the infinitely changeable otherworld in which this confrontation was being played out. Once he had worked that out he found that he too could take on a similar form to the others. Though unskilled in magic, he had found the image of a giant eel simple enough to create. Once transformed to his satisfaction he raced towards Forral and the Archmage – but a glowing tentacle suddenly looped around his body and hauled him back.

Wolf recognized his mother – and even in the shape of a glittering cloud, she looked very angry. 'What the blazes do you think you're doing?' Even in his thoughts, he heard the snap to her voice. 'Stay there,' she ordered. 'We can only watch.'

'Is that the one who cursed me?' Wolf demanded hotly.

'Yes. But your dad will deal with him – I hope.'

With an appalling tearing sound, Forral ripped his tail from the jaws of the shark. He turned, toothed jaws agape, to confront the creature . . .

. . . And suddenly he was standing on a broad grassy plain with a low grey sky above him. He was back in his old, much-missed body, and in his hand was the familiar, comforting shape of his old sword. Forral wanted to laugh out loud. Here in the element of earth, the weapons chosen were very much more to his taste than fang and claw and flame.

409

It was his only comfort, however. Blood leaked from a shallow tear in his side, and one leg was gnawed and savaged, and would barely take his weight. His opponent, however, was on no better case. Blood was seeping through Miathan's robe, and he held himself awkwardly, his breath whistling and short. Forral suspected that his ramming of the shark had produced a broken rib in Miathan's human form. He held his sword in an awkward grip, for one hand was blackened and burned – and one of the gems was missing from its socket, leaving him with a one-eyed gaze.

'So – it ends at last,' the Archmage hissed. Warily, he began to circle the swordsman, his glittering one-eyed gaze hypnotic and unrelenting as that of a snake. The swordsman noted with surprise and grudging respect his opponent's concentration and stance, and wondered whether Miathan had possessed this skill in his corporeal form. Forral kept turning to face him, but otherwise refused to overstrain his damaged leg. They were both wounded and exhausted from their previous struggles – let Miathan do the work!

The Archmage lunged forward, testing his opponent, his thrust clumsy due to the seared hand. Forral parried easily, trying to hide his wince as he flexed the injured leg. Miathan pressed him – again, their swords impacted with a resounding clang. Forral brought his blade around, sweeping deftly under Miathan's guard. As the Archmage jumped back like a startled rabbit, Forral found himself beginning to smile.

Miathan circled, his blade darting in and out, seeking a rare opening and trying to betray the swordsman into taking a false step. Forral kept him moving, kept harrying him, always conserving his own strength. Soon, Miathan began to tire. Forral moved in now like a striking snake, low and deadly – and far more mobile than he had pretended to be. Step by step, he began to drive the Archmage backwards.

Though Miathan had begun by giving a good account of himself he was foundering now. His breathing was laboured, and his movements growing jerky with fatigue. Forral noted with keen interest that the injured rib made it difficult for his opponent to lift his arms above the level of his shoulders. There was the rasp of ripping cloth as the tip of Forral's sword caught the robe over Miathan's breast. Damn – that was close!

Miathan's face had turned pasty grey with fear, and Forral grinned wolfishly. 'I'll wager you're wondering where these powers of mine came from?' he said, the grin never leaving his face.

The Archmage merely grunted and swung across his opponent's sword. Forral used Miathan's own momentum to flick his blade contemptuously away. 'Well, it's Anvar's magic, as a matter of fact,' the swordsman went on, parrying a hacking stroke with a roll of his wrists. 'I like to think I'm doing this for the both of us.' His blade flicked out and again cloth tore with a shearing sound. A red stain spread across the gaping rent on Miathan's left sleeve. 'That was for Aurian,' Forral told him.

'And this is for Wolf.' Again, the swordsman lunged in, and slashed across the Archmage's ribs. Miathan screamed with pain, but kept his head and thrust his sword into Forral's good thigh. The swordsman staggered back and his injured leg collapsed beneath him. He fell heavily backwards and rolled as Miathan's sword came flashing down, missing him by a hair's breadth – but the Archmage, with a broken rib and a slash across his chest was slower to recover. Before he could straighten, Forral scrambled up on to one knee and thrust his blade through Miathan's heart.

As the Archmage crumpled, the swordsman gripped his sword hilt tightly and used Miathan's weight to drive the point in further. 'And that was for me,' he said grimly.

29

High Lord of Nexis

D'arvan's first view of the Phaerie city was, Maya excepted, the most beautiful thing he had ever seen in his life. Apart from a single night spent in the Vale with Eilin, and occasional pauses along the route to snatch a little sleep and rest the horses, he had been travelling continuously since the horrific attack on the Nightrunner stronghold. D'arvan simply could not get back fast enough. Ever since that dreadful night, the carnage had haunted the Mage's memory and disturbed his dreams. After the atrocities he had witnessed: the agony and bloodshed inflicted by human upon human – it was difficult to blame his father and the Phaerie so harshly as he once had done. Now, each day that Pendral continued to live and rejoice in the authority of the High Lordship, was an affront to the Mage. D'arvan would never have believed that such aggression was in his nature – but now that he had discovered it, he welcomed it. Maya and her friends at the garrison had been right all along. There were some things existing in the world that only violence could put right.

D'arvan glanced across at Hargorn. Despite his grief over his old friend Dulsina and his concern for his companions who were missing, the veteran seemed to have stood the gruelling ride surprisingly well. It had been his idea to round up a couple of the swift and sturdy Nightrunner ponies – otherwise, the Mage acknowledged, they might still have been walking this time next month.

Hargorn was gazing at the Phaerie city on its hill, his face wearing the same expression it had worn since leaving Wyvernesse – a sour, twisted mouth and the blackest of scowls. 'Bloody daft idea,' he muttered. 'If you ask me, it's criminal.'

D'arvan smiled to himself. All the interminable length of

the journey, the veteran had never hesitated to make his feelings clear on the idea of D'arvan using the Phaerie to attack
Nexis and take over the city in the name of his father. His
arguments all started with: that's the most ridiculous idea I've
ever heard, went on to: what kind of a feeble excuse is that?
and: don't expect the Nexians to thank you for it, and ended,
glumly with: well, I only hope Maya will be able to talk some
bloody sense into you.

D'arvan had been content to let him grumble: Hargorn's
grousing was the most normal thing that had happened to him
since – he could scarcely remember when. Since he had first
left Nexis with Maya, he supposed – about the time that
Forral had been slain and this whole insane business had
started.

The Mage's wits snapped back to attention as the veteran's
usual litany of complaint broke off abruptly with: 'Thara's titties! What the bloody blazes is that?'

'You know perfectly well what it is, Hargorn,' the Mage
said. 'You saw Aurian flying with the Xandim back at
Wyvernesse. My father has seen me approaching, that's all,
and sent an escort. You can ride back to the city in style.'

'I'd rather keep my fragging feet on the ground, thank you,'
Hargorn muttered sourly. 'But I don't suppose your bloody
Phaerie will give me a choice.'

D'arvan shrugged. 'You can ride all the way up that hill on
your fat Nightrunner pony if you want to – I don't suppose
anyone will stop you.'

'No, not at all,' Hargorn said quickly. 'I'd hate to think I
was holding up your plans for the conquest of us mere
Mortals.'

D'arvan was gratified to see Hargorn's face light up, however, when the Phaerie steeds landed and Maya leapt to the
ground from her perch behind the Forest Lord. He can't possibly be as glad to see her as I am, D'arvan thought. That one
glimpse of her had soothed so much of the pain he had carried
with him since Pendral's attack. He couldn't wait until they
were alone – if only the news he had to impart to her had not
been so tragic.

Maya scowled at him fiercely. 'What the bloody blazes are

413

you doing back here? I thought you were supposed to be helping Aurian!'

D'arvan found himself grinning. Oh, how he had been looking forward to surprising her! 'Hellorin and I worked something out between us before I left,' he told her. 'He found a way to gift Aurian with the Old Magic so that she could get the Xandim to fly without me. It worked tremendously well – so I came back to you.'

The frown didn't leave Maya's face. 'But what if she needs you? What if she needs the help of another Mage?'

'She has Chiamh,' D'arvan said firmly. 'Maya, there was no way I ever intended to go off and abandon you here to carry our child alone. Now, I've done what I can for Aurian, and she's more than happy that I come back to you – in fact she insisted.' He held out his hands to her. 'In fact, if you'll let me get into the palace, I have a whole collection of messages for you . . .'

'And what about me?' Hargorn demanded belligerently. 'I haven't seen the bloody woman for ten years, and I can't get as much as a hello out of her.'

Maya made him an obscene gesture. 'I see you haven't changed much in ten years – you're still as twist-faced and grouchy as ever.' With a laugh, she let go of D'arvan and ran to hug her old friend.

Hellorin looked on indulgently as Hargorn and Maya embraced. 'Mortals,' he said, shaking his head.

D'arvan looked at his father coldly. 'Speaking of Mortals,' he said, 'how soon will we be ready to attack the city of Nexis?'

Hellorin shrugged. 'Whenever you like. I have been making our preparations in your absence.'

'Good,' said D'arvan. 'Let's do it tomorrow night.'

Even on a stolen horse, it had taken Parric several cold, hungry, miserable days to travel overland from the coastal village of Easthaven to Nexis. He had amused himself along the way by imagining himself in the taproom of the Invisible Unicorn, and planning exactly what he was going to eat and drink when he finally found himself there. He only hoped that old hen Hebba would remember him – because he had no means of paying for anything.

Since the old river road from the east was blocked nowadays, Parric was forced to circle north and go round into the hills to reach the city. It was dusk when he finally turned on to the northern highway and looked down from the ridge at the smoking chimneys of Nexis.

The black-liveried guards at the gate almost made him wish he hadn't bothered coming back at all. They were surly, suspicious – and clearly on the lookout for a bribe. Well, that was their hard luck. Parric explained to them, graphically and in no uncertain terms that they were sadly mistaken if they thought he had money. He also informed them that, if they refused to let him in, he was going to camp right where he was outside the gates, and cook and eat his horse. By this time, he had worked himself into such a thoroughly bad temper that he meant every word of it. The guards took one look at his grim expression and admitted him at once.

There was a roaring fire in the taproom of the Unicorn, and Hebba and Sallana, the serving maid, were working at full stretch. The place was packed tight with a mass of bodies, and the heat and the noise were overwhelming. To the cavalry master, it was absolutely wonderful. Parric had to elbow his way determinedly through the throng of early evening drinkers, labourers mostly, who tended to call in for a glass or two of ale before going home for supper.

'Hebba!' he cried, when he finally managed to get within sight of her. 'It's me!'

Hebba's expression turned glacial. 'I remember you,' she said. 'The vulgar one.'

As a joyous welcome it left a lot to be desired, but Parric was determined not to let it spoil his night. Years, it had been, since he had tasted a proper pint of ale in a genuine tavern, and he deserved it after everything he had been through: first the years of slavery in Hellorin's city, then the dreadful massacre of the Nightrunners . . .

Only at that moment did Parric realize he had no idea whether this woman's business partner was alive or dead. He was on the verge of blurting out the news of the bloodbath, when common sense prevailed. The Nightrunners were viewed by the authorities here as criminals. If it was seen that he knew what had happened, there would be awkward questions asked at the very least, and his most likely prospect was a quiet arrest and an unofficial execution. No – difficult though it would be, he must keep his mouth shut – until Pendral was dead, at the very least. At that moment, the cavalry master had no idea how he could accomplish the High Lord's death, but he decided to wait until tomorrow to come up with a plan – just as soon as he had recovered from the headache he intended to earn himself tonight.

The evening went very much as the cavalry master had planned. The hours flew by in a blur of good food, good ale, and later, when a few drinks had made him mellow, good company. Indeed, it seemed no time at all before everyone was going home. 'Don't leave,' said Parric, clutching the sleeve of a burly mason. 'Don't everybody leave yet. Why, it's still early. We've time for another . . .'

'You most certainly do not.' Parric's new friend had somehow turned into Hebba, who was standing in front of him with a broom in her hand and a truculent expression on her round, red face.

'But I'm old Hargorn's old friend,' the cavalry master protested. 'Old old friend . . .'

'Hargorn would befriend any piece of human refuse that gave him a hard-luck tale – and besides, he isn't here. You have me to deal with now. Go on, you – get you gone. Haven't you got no home to go to?'

Parric made a valiant effort to stand up. 'Actually,' he said, 'I don't –' and fell flat on his face.

The cavalry master awakened with his tongue stuck to the roof of his mouth and a herd of wild horses stampeding through his head. Though it was pitch dark, he conceded, after a moment, that the horse part could be right, at any rate – judging from the smell and his bed of prickly straw, he seemed to be in a stable somewhere.

How did I get here? Parric wondered. Great portions of the latter part of the evening had vanished from his memory. He still felt light-headed from the ale, so he judged that it was probably nowhere near morning yet. He staggered to his feet, driven by two urgent needs. The first was managed quite easily – he simply relieved himself in the opposite corner of the stable. The second was a little more complicated, but if he didn't get a drink of water soon, he would perish.

Feeling his way along the rough, cobwebbed wall, Parric groped his way out of the building. He realized at once that Hebba was not as harsh as she had pretended to be – though she could well have thrown him out into the gutter, she had let him shelter, instead, in the stable of the inn. Once outside he could see quite clearly: the moon was high and almost full, cloaking the city in cold blue light. The cavalry master was glad of it – it showed him the revolting slick of dark slime around the inside of the horse-trough. Luckily, there was also a pump nearby, so he could have his drink fresh and clear.

Parric rose from his haunches and wiped chilled hands on his tunic and his dripping face on his sleeve. Gods, but it was good to be back in Nexis! When he had been a captive of the Phaerie, he had honestly believed he would never see this place again. His breath smoking in the frosty midnight air, he turned to look out across the city. It was a view worth savouring. The Unicorn was situated on the same plateau as the garrison, high on the north side of the valley. From here, he could look down and see practically the whole of Nexis laid out before him, including the gracious colonnades of the Grand Arcade, the squat rotunda of the Guildhall, and the high promontory, once the home of the Magefolk, that cast a long shadow like a dark shrouded figure stretching right across the city.

At first Parric thought it was a result of all the drink. Spots before my eyes, he thought, rubbing them hard. Then he looked again, at the swirling skein of dark specks that rose like a swarm of bees above the Academy. There was something familiar about them.

Then he remembered, and his blood turned to pure ice in his veins. Someone had removed the time spells from the horrors imprisoned down in those black vaults, and the Nihilim were swarming over Nexis.

Parric was not the only one who looked on, aghast, at the

Death-Wraiths. High over the northern moors, about a league out of Nexis, the glittering throng of Phaerie warriors faltered in their flight, and halted, hovering in mid-air, to witness, with magically-augmented vision, the dreadful sight of the Nihilim whirling in their mad dance of death above the city, then plunging down into the unprotected streets in search of their prey.

Hellorin pulled up his mount beside D'arvan's Xandim steed. 'Do you know anything about this?' he demanded. 'You were the last one to talk to that Mage, the Lady Eilin's daughter – and she was the last one to venture beneath the Academy where the Wraiths were imprisoned. What has the wretched woman loosed upon us now?'

D'arvan clenched his fists tightly in the Xandim's mane. 'I can't think how this can have happened. Aurian only freed that single Wraith – the one that shared poor Finbarr's body. Mind you, it had certainly escaped from Wyvernesse when I left the place, so it might have found some way to free the others.'

'Folly! Pure folly!' Hellorin snorted. 'Where was her brain when she set a Wraith free to inflict death and horror upon the world? I never heard of anything so ridiculous. Trust a meddling Mage to stir up trouble!'

'She had her reasons,' said D'arvan, 'though I agree with you – in the light of this new development, it may have been a mistake. In any case, our chief concern is how this will affect our plans. I don't really think that Nexis is a very healthy place to be tonight.'

'I think we should wait here for a while, and see what they do.' Maya spoke up from her place at D'arvan's other side. 'After all, we're far enough away to see them coming and beat a hasty retreat if they start heading in this direction.'

'Who asked you, Mortal?'

'Sounds a good idea to me.' Hellorin and D'arvan spoke simultaneously, and turned to glare at one another.

'You forget, my Lord,' Maya said coldly to Hellorin, 'that I'm not one of your empty-headed little chattels to be filled with Phaerie seed. I'm a warrior, and I used to be second-in-command of the Nexis garrison. I know what I'm talking about.'

418

'Maya is right,' said D'arvan. 'It would be folly to reject her advice just because she's a Mortal.'

'Very well,' the Forest Lord answered offhandedly. 'I daresay it would do no harm.'

Time passed, and the moon dipped down towards the horizon. Even at this distance, they could hear the screams from the beleaguered city. Maya turned to D'arvan. 'I'm not sure this was a good idea after all,' she said quietly. 'It's awful to have to stay here and listen to those poor folk . . .'

'Look! Maya – look at that!'

The Death-Wraiths were leaving Nexis. The great black swarm of them, like a whirlwind of autumn leaves, rose above the city and darkened the setting moon. The swarm amassed itself into a tight knot above the Academy, and darted away at a tremendous speed towards the south.

'Seven bloody demons!' Maya breathed. 'Do you think that was all of them? And where could they be going?'

'Yes, I think it was all of them,' D'arvan said. 'They looked so purposeful . . . Somehow I get the feeling we won't be seeing them back in Nexis . . .'

'It looked as though they only stopped to feed,' Hellorin put in.

'That's what I thought,' D'arvan mused. 'And they've gone south . . . You know what I think? I think they've gone in search of Aurian.'

'If that's true, then may the gods help her when those creatures find her,' said Maya sombrely.

Hebba awakened to find the window open and a dark figure at the bottom of her bed. Before she could scream, the black silhouette swooped down on her.

'Shut up! Don't scream!' A hand clamped itself firmly over her mouth, and her assailant began to talk very rapidly in a tense, hissing whisper. 'It's me, Parric. The Wraiths are back – we're in dreadful danger. Don't make a sound. Pick up those blankets and come down with me to the cellar right now. Try to stay calm, for both our sakes. I'm going to take my hand away now – all right?'

Hebba nodded. As Parric took his hand away she took a

419

deep breath to scream – and instantly the hand clamped back down again, tighter than before. 'Look here, you brainless old biddy – I'm not doing this for the good of my health. I'd have been long gone by now, had it not been for climbing all the way up here to save your neck. If you scream this time, I'll be gone before you can take another breath – and you can fight off the Wraiths as best you can.'

This time, when the little man removed his hand, Hebba clenched her teeth tight to bottle up the scream that she could feel building inside her. With shaking hands she gathered up the blankets in a trailing bundle and followed Parric downstairs. He had his sword in his hand, but frankly, she didn't think there was much point. She had seen the Wraiths at their deadly work the last time they had hit Nexis, and frankly, there was little good that swords, or anything else for that matter, could do against such creatures.

It was a nightmare getting down the steep, uneven cellar steps without a light, but Hebba knew better than to strike any kind of spark. Parric pulled the trapdoor shut behind them, and bolted it from the inside. 'They may not think to look here,' he whispered. 'They'll have plenty of other prey outside.'

Hebba shuddered.

'Do you think I could have one of those blankets?' the cavalry master asked plaintively. 'We may as well make ourselves comfortable – it looks as though we're going to be here all night.'

'Quick,' D'arvan cried, urging his Xandim steed into the air. 'Ride now, while the Nihilim are still departing! Forward!' Following his gesture and his example, the ranks of the Phaerie surged upward, streaming out behind him like a glittering comet tail. Massing in the air, they went hurtling down towards the city.

Hellorin caught up, and drew his mount abreast of the Mage. 'What in perdition do you think you're doing?' he shouted. 'I know I said that this is your campaign, but shouldn't we wait until the Nihilim have gone?'

D'arvan shook his head. 'They won't be interested in us.

Whatever they want, it's in the south. If we're quick, though, the Nexians will think we've driven them away!'

The Mage looked across at Maya. With her long black hair escaping its braid and streaming out behind her, and her eyes sparkling from the exhilaration of this wild ride, she looked like one of the battle-maids out of ancient legend. When he caught her eye, however, her doubt was plain. 'It'll be all right, love,' he called to her. 'We'll make this as easy as we can, and in the end, the Nexians will come to see that it's better us than . . .' He gave his father a sidelong glance.

'I suppose so,' Maya replied. 'Well, if I'm to be the most hated woman in Nexis, I don't see any sense in putting it off.'

'You won't be,' D'arvan tried to reassure her. Then, they were above the city, and his words were drowned in the silvery clamour of Phaerie horns.

Even from the depths of the cellar, Parric could hear the pandemonium and panic in the streets outside. He shuddered, trying not to imagine what was going on out there. Hebba gave a wavering cry and hid her head beneath the blankets, attempting not to hear. For some time, the cavalry master listened, bleak-faced, to the jarring, whining buzz that the Nihilim emitted as they struck; to the sounds of running feet, and the dreadful screams of those who had not run fast enough. Then the harrowing noises stopped completely – and that, in its own way, was worse. What was happening up there? Was it safe to come out? Or had the Death-Wraiths slaughtered everyone on the streets, and were they now waiting to pick off the survivors one by one, as they emerged from hiding? Perhaps it would be safer to wait a while . . .

Then Parric heard another sound – the high, clear, vibrant notes of Phaerie horns, drawing rapidly closer. Parric's curses were loud and inventive enough to bring Hebba out from under her blankets, bristling with indignation. In all the excitement and tragedies since he'd returned to Wyvernesse, he had forgotten D'arvan's threat to attack the city. The Mage had not forgotten though – why, the bastard was already here!

'Stay here,' Parric ordered the astonished Hebba. 'When I'm gone, bolt the trapdoor behind you again – and don't open it for anyone unless you're sure you know them and you'd trust them with your virtue, your money and your life.'

And then he was gone, dashing up the cellar steps and leaving Hebba – luckily, speechless for once with indignation – behind him.

Lord Pendral was shaken from his wine-sodden slumbers by a timid servant. 'Lord, Lord, wake up! The Death-Wraiths are back!'

'What? How?' Pendral scrambled over the top of the skinny young girl, her breasts barely budding, who shared his bed that night. His feet had never touched the floor so fast in years. Roughly, he pushed the servant aside. 'Get out of my way, you. I've got to hide!' He threw a furred cloak over his bed-gown, and whisked, with a speed that belied his ponderous bulk, into his strongroom. The door of thick wood reinforced with iron bars slammed shut behind him. The servant and the girl were left looking at each other as there came a series of snicks, clicks and squeaks from behind the door – the sound of keys turning in locks and bolts shooting into their sockets.

Suddenly the braying of horns swirled out across the night sky. The servant started, and rushed to peer out of the window, his hand pressed to his mouth in horror. The waif was scrambling into her clothes as fast as she could, her face astonishingly calm. The servant guessed that, having put up with Pendral's more perverted entertainments for a night, the Phaerie would hold little fear for her. He looked at the thick, locked door of Pendral's strongroom – he won't be able to hear a thing in there, he thought – and then looked back at the girl. 'Think we should tell him?'

She pulled a thin blouse across the bruises that covered her breasts and throat. 'Nah.' For a moment, she looked as if she was about to spit. 'Let the bastard find out for himself.'

The Phaerie spiralled down into what appeared to be an empty town. 'Now remember,' D'arvan ordered his forces, reinforcing the message by mind-speech, 'this time, we want as little violence and bloodshed as possible.'

He had an uneasy feeling that he was talking to himself.

D'arvan chose what he judged to be the most central spot, the roof of the grand Arcade, and spoke to the Nexians, amplifying his voice by magic, so that everyone would be able to hear. 'Citizens of Nexis – you may leave your houses. You are safe now. The Phaerie have driven the Wraiths away, and as long as we are here, they will trouble you no more. This is not a raid such as happened previously – we are simply taking over the rule of this city from the corrupt High Lord. We hope that Mortal and Phaerie will work together for the common good, and so long as you co-operate, no one will be hurt. With your goodwill, we can undo the damage inflicted by the Archmage, and make this city great once more.'

D'arvan finished his speech to a deathly silence. Then Hargorn, standing at Maya's side, burst out into derisive laughter. 'You expect them to believe that?' he hooted. It seemed that he was right. The streets remained dark and silent. No one came out to rejoice and proclaim D'arvan the saviour of Nexis.

'There,' said Hellorin. 'You were wrong – this proves it. We tried it your way – now we'll give the Mortals the firm hand they need.' He turned to his assembled forces. 'Very well – you all know the plan. Secure the garrison, and the Academy, institute patrols, fit collars to any troublemakers and we'll transport them north. Meet any resistance with force. Go to it!'

'No!' D'arvan cried in horror. No one was listening. On the rooftop, he and Maya wept as they were forced to watch the subjugation of their city by flame and sword.

Eventually, the red sun rose through a heavy pall of smoke, illuminating the ravaged remains of the city. Groups of Phaerie were clearing out the last nests of resistors by the simple expedient of torching the buildings in which they hid.

'There.' Hellorin mounted his steed and turned to his son with a feral smile. 'Farewell, my son – I give you your city. Now that it has been conquered, it is yours to deal with as you please.' Without waiting for a reply, he spurred his horse skywards and headed back towards the north.

'That bastard,' Maya muttered thickly. 'He meant to do this all the time.'

'And now we've got to deal with the wrack and ruin he's left behind,' said D'arvan bitterly. 'I've a good mind just to leave – head south, find Aurian.'

'No. No, D'arvan, we can't. Not now.' Maya's face was set with grim determination. 'If we run away from this, the Nexians will get Hellorin as overlord. We can't do that to them. No, somehow we'll have to stay here and try as best we can to put things right – preferably without getting torn to pieces along the way by the very folk we're trying to protect.'

As the flames licked greedily at the walls and roof of Vannor's old mansion, Parric turned his back on the conflagration, and walked away whistling, following the fleeing servants down the hill to the old river road. Almost as an afterthought, he flicked the burning stump of a torch away from him into the bushes. 'Well, Pendral,' he said cheerfully, 'I'd rather have had your head on a pole, but since you refused to come out . . .' He shrugged. 'Ah well – in the end, I don't suppose it makes a lot of difference – and at least I got to you before the Phaerie did.'

The streets of Nexis proved too much for his grimly cheerful mood. Parric darted from cover to cover, avoiding patrols of steel-eyed Phaerie and trying not to see the burnt-out shells of houses and the corpses that littered the streets. D'arvan's promises hadn't lasted very long, he thought bitterly.

At last he reached his goal – the Unicorn. In all conscience he knew he had better go and rescue Hebba out of the cellar, or the timid woman would be there until the sun turned cold. He was greatly surprised, therefore, to walk into the place and not only find it unscathed, but also to find Hebba sitting at one of the tables, making inroads into a large glass of brandy.

Having come all this way to rescue her, Parric was ablaze with indignation. 'Hey!' he said. 'I thought I told you not to come out until you found –'

'Found someone I trusted, yes,' Hebba put in. 'And there he is . . .'

Out of the back room, carrying another bottle of spirits, came Hargorn. Parric let out a whoop of delight. 'I thought you were dead!' he cried.

'Not me.' Hargorn's smile was thin and strained. 'Though after what I've just witnessed, it would be a lot more restful.'

'Don't you worry,' Parric told him. 'We won't let them get away with it. We've resisted tyrants before, you and me. Why, we can . . .'

'No we can't,' Hargorn said flatly. 'The city is under Phaerie rule now, Parric – and there's not a damned thing we can do about it. We have one choice – between D'arvan's offer of co-operation and Hellorin's brutality. Most Nexians don't understand that yet – and I'm afraid we're going to have to help convince them.'

Parric stared at him, aghast. 'What? This time we support the tyrant?'

'Come on, Parric. D'arvan didn't order the killing – you should know better. That was Hellorin. D'arvan isn't a tyrant really – and don't forget that our Maya will be – I don't know – queen, or something.' Hargorn shrugged. 'Maybe you'll feel better if you just call D'arvan a conqueror. But whatever you want to call him, it makes no difference – we no longer have a choice.'

30

The Watcher on the Wind

Grince awakened to find that he lay on an uneasy bed. Not sure at first whether he was half-asleep or imagining things, he laid his hand down flat on the floor of the cavern. No – it was no dream. There was motion in the stone: a faint vibration that was growing with every moment. Around him, some of the others were beginning to stir. In their corner, Schiannath and Iscalda were waking. Vannor, asleep on one of the stone benches that ran along the wall of the cavern, rolled over, muttering. 'No, no. I won't go back.' One last twist of his body sent him tumbling to the floor, where he sat up with a curse, half-dazed by his rough awakening.

Linnet uncurled herself, the tip of one great wing sweeping through the ashes that had spilled from the edge of the fire. She yawned delicately, and rubbed her bleary eyes with the back of one hand. 'What's happening?' Then her expression changed. 'Yinze's mercy! It's an earthquake! Quick – get out of the cave!'

Grince remembered the Nexis earthquake and understood the panic in her voice. In a trice he was on his feet, and heading for the exit. Only when he fell over Wolf in the dim firelight did it occur to him that some of his companions were simply not waking up.

'Where's Chiamh?' Iscalda shouted, adding to the confusion. 'And Aurian?'

Grince realized that the two great cats were also missing.

'I can't wake him!' Vannor was shaking the unmoving body of the one they called Forral. 'And he's hurt – look at all this blood!' His voice was rising in panic.

'Here,' Schiannath ran across and put his hands under Forral's arms. 'You take his feet.'

Vannor tucked Forral's feet clumsily under his arm and

held them in place with his one hand. Together, staggering under the weight, they lifted the supine body out of the cave, while Grince and Iscalda did the same for the motionless form of Wolf. Linnet darted here and there, gathering weapons, blankets, and the leftover food. The ground was shaking and shuddering so hard now that it was difficult to stay on their feet.

Outside, the water in the pool had flooded its banks, and in the grove of pines, the trees were thrashing wildly. Two went down with the agonizing groan of falling timber, dragging their stronger brethren with them. By now, the entire mountain was vibrating. A massive boulder came crashing down the steep side of the valley and buried itself deep in the turf not ten feet from where Grince was emerging from the cavern.

'Get away from the pinnacle,' screamed Iscalda as they burst out into the open. 'Fly, Linnet! We'll take the others.' She and Schiannath changed into horse-form faster than Grince had ever seen.

'Help me, Grince,' Vannor, even with two hands, would have had difficulty hoisting Forral's dead weight up on to Schiannath's high back. Between them, however, he and Grince managed to hang the limp body over the Xandim's withers, and Vannor leapt up behind. The thief ran back and hoisted Wolf into position, and vaulted up behind him. Then the Xandim were off, racing down the valley, trying to get as far away from the shaking pinnacle as they could.

Forral blinked as the body of the Archmage turned transparent, and vanished into the misty haze that was the disintegrating field of conflict. In the eldritch realm Beyond the World, clearly nothing remained in the same form for very long. Even as he watched, the landscape, which at least had seemed familiar, faded back into the vast, shimmering green sphere in which he had found himself when he'd arrived. A cold spear of alarm pierced the swordsman. Just how real had this titanic conflict been? When he returned to the normal world, would he still bear these wounds? And what of Miathan? 'Oh gods,' Forral groaned. 'Don't tell me I'll have to kill the bastard all over again.'

427

'You won't. Wherever his body lies, he's dead all right. You've seen to that.'

Forral turned to find Aurian and Wolf at his side. The Mage still wore her normal, earthly shape, but Wolf – the swordsman felt a fierce glow of joy and pride. At the Mage's side was a sturdy young lad of about ten years, with brown eyes and dark, curling hair.

'Looks like his father, doesn't he?' said Aurian softly.

'He has his mother's magic, though – or he wouldn't be here,' Forral replied proudly. 'And what's more,' he added with mock fierceness, 'he shows the same talent for being where he shouldn't be that *you* had at that age.' Smiling, he held out his arms and embraced both Aurian and his son. In this place it felt strange – there was no sensation of physical touch, but instead there was a mingling – an exchange of energies and joy that felt just as good, in its own way, as a fleshly embrace.

Aurian touched his face lightly. 'I never thought I'd see that dear face again,' she said. 'And Wolf, too – he got the opportunity to meet his father after all these years. I'm so glad you had the chance to come back, my love. This moment is worth everything.'

'Is it over?' Forral asked her, when he found his voice. 'Now that Miathan's dead, is his curse on Wolf removed?'

'No, father,' the lad said – and Forral was pleased that he could answer for himself. 'The curse is only partly off. Now that the Archmage is dead I can wear my human shape in this place, but until my mother finds the grail I'll still be a wolf in the normal world.' He looked down at himself wonderingly. 'Weird, isn't it? It's not very efficient. You must use an awful lot of energy just to stay up . . .'

He was interrupted by the voice of Basileus. *'You must leave here at once! Not only do you face grave danger from my struggle with Ghabal, but your bodies are in grave peril in your own world!'*

Forral swore. So involved had his family become with their own affairs – the death of Miathan and the reunion with Wolf in his human form at last – that the struggle between the two Moldai, taking place on the far side of this immense green space, had been the last thing on their minds.

'Don't wait!' Basileus urged. *'You have no time. Get back to your bodies now!'*

With an appalling tearing sound, the two Moldai pulled apart, their tentacles inflicting dreadful injuries even as they let go of one another. With their spirits locked in this deadly battle Beyond the World, they had no idea that their titanic struggle was wreaking such havoc in its mundane counterpart. Basileus was in a pitiful condition, with great chunks of his body being torn away, and many of his limbs bitten down to bleeding stumps. Ghabal, however, was in a far worse state, with most of his tentacles missing and his being mauled beyond recognition. The death of his Mage companion had seemed to drive away the last shred of sanity that the Moldan possessed, and he had attacked Basileus with reckless ferocity, not caring what damage he might sustain in the process.

All down the aeons, even before Ghabal's madness had struck, he and Basileus, though forced into such close proximity, had never been in accord. Now, with an intense shock, Basileus realized that he could finish their agelong enmity once and for all. Though part of him cried out in disbelieving protest against killing another Moldan, he knew that in this case, there was nothing left to be done. The flight of the cats from Steelclaw had proved that. If Ghabal could not be stopped, then his evil influence would continue to pervade and pollute the mountains, and he would never rest until Basileus had been destroyed.

The Moldan braced himself to close with his injured enemy – and then remembered. The humans must be warned, lest their helpless bodies be injured in Ghabal's death throes. He flung out a few swift words of warning to them to return to the mundane world – and then struck at his foe one last time.

As the struggle continued, however, he soon realized that it was hopeless – the two Moldai were just too evenly matched. Basileus could inflict any amount of peripheral damage on his opponent, but simply could not get close enough to finish the fight without risking mortal injury to himself.

'Take him now, Basileus! I'll hold him for you!'

The voice took the Moldan completely by surprise. *'Chiamh! You should not be here!'*

'Never mind that. Perhaps I can repay you for all your help. Let's finish this business.' Another vast, tentacled creature, its canopy patterned in vibrant purples and blues, drifted into position above the struggling Moldai. The slender, attenuated filaments of its limbs shot out and wrapped themselves around Ghabal, effectively trapping him so that he could not escape.

Too fast to be seen, Basileus whipped his own tentacles around his enemy's body, reeling the helpless Ghabal in towards his vast maw with its rows of sword-sharp teeth. Ghabal, already badly wounded, struggled fitfully, but lacked the strength to escape. Snarling, the demented creature heaped curses down on the heads of Basileus and the Windeye, but as he realized the hopelessness of his case, the curses turned to screeches of alarm interspersed with pitiful pleas for mercy. At the last moment, Chiamh let go of the mad Moldan, and the screeching increased to an agonized crescendo as Basileus tore him limb from limb.

The entire mountain range was shaken by the death-throes of the Moldan. Forral came back into his body, and felt the earth bucking and heaving beneath him as though the very mountains were writhing from a mortal wound. Wolf, with the resilience of youth – coupled with the fact that *he* had not fought in a formidable battle – had recovered first and was standing over the swordsman, whining anxiously and poking a cold nose into his face.

Already it was grey daylight. Forral found himself on the broad plateau that he had seen from the air on the approach to Chiamh's vale – and of course, he had not returned as himself, but was lodged, once more, in Anvar's body. The transition was a wrenching disappointment. For a little while, he had experienced the joy of being himself again, whole and complete – but that was over now.

Iscalda was trying to elbow the wolf out of the way so that she could try to bandage the swordsman's leg, and his other injuries, with strips of cloth that she had apparently torn from the clothing of everyone present.

'Aurian,' Forral gasped. 'Where's Aurian?'

'We don't know,' Iscalda said tersely. 'Linnet has flown back up the valley to look for her and Chiamh. The cats are missing too.'

Forral swore and tried to rise.

'You stay exactly where you are.' Iscalda pressed him down again with one hand on his chest, and Forral was dismayed to find that she could do it without effort. 'There's nothing you or any of us can do until Linnet finds them.'

'Chiamh! Chiamh – come back! Wake up, damn you!' Aurian clutched at the Windeye's sleeve and shook him as hard as she could, without any response whatsoever. She swore. What in perdition had happened to him? If she couldn't wake him soon, it was likely that they both would die.

Aurian tried another tack. 'Basileus? What's happening? Can't you stop this?' There was no answer. Not a flicker of response from either Moldan or Windeye.

The Mage had returned to her body on the pinnacle, to find that the Chamber of Winds had turned into a very perilous place. The whole chamber was shaking and swaying, and every now and again her heart would almost stop as another sharp cracking sound accompanied yet another section of fractured stone. The slender spire of rock might well collapse at any moment – and the spider's web bridge had been completely torn away. Chiamh possessed the only way to get down – and she could not bring him out of his trance.

Aurian pressed herself flat, trying desperately but without success to find some kind of purchase on the smooth stone floor. 'Oh blast you, Chiamh, wake up,' she muttered. 'Wake up, *please*.'

'What's wrong? What's ha – oh, goddess! I didn't think this would happen!' The Windeye tried to sit up, and managed it on the third attempt. By clinging to one another, he and the Mage managed to stay more or less upright, though actually standing up was out of the question. His mental call to the Moldan was so loud that Aurian could pick it up quite clearly. 'Basileus? Are you all right?'

'I cannot stop the shaking, Windeye. These are Ghabal's death throes – they must run their course.'

The Windeye cursed softly. 'All right, Aurian,' he said. 'I'm going to have to change to my horse-form in this position and then stand up. As soon as I'm on my feet, get up on my back as quickly as possible, and we'll make our escape. You have got your amulet, haven't you?' As she nodded, he gave her a smile that was pure relief. 'Well, that's a blessing. Don't forget, it takes both of us to make me fly. Once I've changed, don't waste any time.' Before Aurian had time to answer, his outline began to shimmer, and in the next moment, the stocky, black-maned bay horse lay on the stone beside her.

It was a nightmare time as Chiamh struggled to his feet on that unsteady surface. At last, after several bruising falls that brought Aurian's heart into her mouth with the thought of broken legs, he managed to get himself more or less vertical, standing straddle-legged like a newborn colt. Then it happened. Just as Aurian was braced ready to hoist herself on to his back, the stone underfoot gave a particularly violent lurch. The Mage's legs went out from underneath her and she fell flat on her face. Chiamh stumbled, slid – and was gone over the edge.

'Chiamh!' Aurian shrieked. She hid her face in her hands, unable to look down into the chasm. The dire peril of her own position was lost in overwhelming grief for her friend.

A shrill, demanding whinny broke into the dark well of her sorrow. Astounded, the Mage looked up – and knew that she had gone completely mad. There before her, hovering in midair with no help at all, was Chiamh.

Another lurch of the pinnacle brought Aurian out of her shock with a jolt. She could work out the whys and wherefores later – when she had her feet back on solid ground. The Windeye manoeuvred delicately into the Chamber of Winds and landed lightly, barely touching the vibrating floor. Somehow, Aurian managed to scramble on to his back, then they were away. The Mage had no need of her talisman – the Windeye was managing the entire business himself. As they left the crumbling pinnacle, Chiamh gave an exultant whinny, and carried a very puzzled Mage away to safety down the valley.

It seemed an eternity before Forral saw a black speck in the sky. Then he recognized Aurian on Chiamh's back. 'She's here, Wolf,' he cried. 'Your mother's coming!'

The Mage was looking very pale as she dismounted and ran to the side of Forral and her son. She took in the swordsman's bandages at a glance. 'I thought you'd carry your injuries over to this world,' she said. 'I should have warned you. Thank the gods they've fixed you up.' She hugged them both, first Forral, then Wolf.

'Are *you* all right?' Forral took her hand. 'You look bloody awful, love.'

Aurian grimaced. 'It *was* bloody awful. I hope I never have to go through anything like that again.'

'I doubt you will,' the swordsman reassured her. 'After all, Miathan is dead, and . . .'

'I don't mean *that*,' Aurian cried. 'I mean being stuck up on top of that accursed spire in the middle of an earthquake!' She got to her feet and turned to the Windeye, who had changed back to his human shape and was grinning all over his face. 'I'm extremely glad you did what you did,' she said, 'but how the bloody blue blazes did you manage it? I thought the Xandim couldn't fly without the aid of the Old Magic.'

Chiamh shrugged modestly. 'No more they can – the normal Xandim. But my powers as Windeye stem from the Old Magic. I thought as much when you demonstrated your own Othersight, the first time you used the talisman. Ever since then I've wondered whether or not I could fly on my own – but I never had the nerve to try until today.' He grimaced. 'It wasn't the best way to find out, believe me. Now I understand exactly what it is you hate about high places, Aurian.'

Eventually the tremors died away completely, much to everyone's relief, although the Windeye spoke to Basileus, who recommended that they wait a while before returning to the cavern, in case of aftershocks. The Mage spent the intervening time healing Forral's hurts and looking out anxiously for

Linnet bringing any news of Shia and Khanu. To her dismay, the winged girl returned towards noon, having failed completely to find the cats. It was close to sunset before Shia and Khanu came slinking back – from an entirely unexpected direction. 'Where in the name of perdition have you two been?' the Mage demanded.

'We were on Steelclaw,' Shia said wearily. 'The Dragon's Tail was fractured in the earthquake. We've had to come round the long way – practically the entire distance down that mountain and back up this one. And I should warn you folk – this is no longer a safe place to stay. We crept past the Fastness unseen, but the Xandim were mustering outside. I think they plan to come up here and see what has become of their accursed Blind God.'

Aurian looked at Chiamh. He nodded. 'Let's get back to the cave at once,' he said, 'and prepare our belongings. If the Xandim are coming here, then we don't want to waste any time getting away.'

Though the companions were too weary to travel all night, they managed to get deep into the mountains to the south of the Wyndveil, where the Xandim could not follow. Chiamh and Aurian had said a sad farewell to Basileus, who made them promise to return as soon as they could. 'He seems very confident that we *will* return,' Aurian said to the Windeye afterwards. 'It's good to know that someone has so much faith in us.'

'I have faith in us too,' Chiamh replied. 'We'll accomplish what we set out to do, you'll see. *And* we'll come home to tell our grandchildren about it.'

'*Grandchildren*? Please, Chiamh – one trial at a time!'

At least it had sent them on their way laughing.

When the night was growing old they stopped to rest at last, though it was a cold and comfortless camp without a fire. Though the Skyfolk rarely ventured this far east, they didn't think it wise to risk drawing attention to themselves. Aurian, who had offered to take the first watch, was surprised to see Chiamh get up after a little while. 'Can't you sleep?' she whispered.

'It's not that,' he replied. 'I was just thinking that we no longer know the whereabouts of your enemy – not for sure, at any rate. With these Winged Folk to support her, she could be anywhere by now. I think I'd better ride the winds and see if I can find her.'

Aurian was truly grateful to him. 'What would I ever do without you, Chiamh?' she whispered.

'You'll never have to find out,' the Windeye said mysteriously – and was gone before she could ask him what he meant.

Chiamh walked a little way away; out of sight of the camp but within call in case there should be some need. A cold sensation like a drench of icy water flooded over his body as he switched to his Othersight. Choosing one of the fluid paths of silver air, he launched himself off on the winds and headed for Aerillia.

Eliseth was no longer in the city of the Skyfolk. Chiamh was busy conducting a painstaking search when he had a stroke of good fortune, and overheard two winged sentries discussing the expedition to Dhiammara, and how much they would have liked to be included. The Windeye, following the night breeze, drifted away. He was about to return and tell Aurian what he had discovered when he had an idea. Why not go on, instead, all the way to Dhiammara? Riding the winds, the trip would take no time, and it would be useful for Aurian if he could find out what was really happening there.

Eliseth's home in the dragon city was much more tolerable now. In the handful of days since she had arrived, she had worked incredibly hard, ordering her new slaves from the forest colony to clear the fallen masonry that clogged the corridors of the emerald tower, and having them make the place habitable again. The Magewoman had had every necessity flown in from the ransacked forest colony, with additional luxuries coming in daily from Aerillia.

Today she had finally been able to move into the tower, and the timing was perfect. Her winged watchers had told her that the visitor she had been expecting was about to arrive that night. Eliseth walked over to the large red crystal that stood on an ornate metal tripod in a corner, its glow providing the room with light and heat. As she warmed her hands, she reflected that it hadn't taken her long to master the crystal magic of the late and unlamented Dragonfolk. Absently, she straightened the golden goblets on the table and stroked the sumptuous fur that covered her carven chair. She was glad her new quarters had been made ready in time to impress her guest, for it was not every day she had the opportunity to entertain a queen – even if the queen in question was nothing but a little Mortal slut with delusions of grandeur.

The drumming of wings could be heard outside. Ah – the Khisihn was here at last. The Weather-Mage stepped to the door of her chambers to greet her guest, who had been escorted along the curving green corridors by Sunfeather and an honour guard of two winged warriors, resplendent in full regalia.

'Her Majesty, Queen Sara,' Sunfeather announced.

The guest had thrown back the deep hood of her travelling cloak, and the welcoming smile froze on Eliseth's face as she realized that this woman was northern-fair, and not of the Khazalim at all! What was going on? If this was a deception or a joke on someone's part, they would suffer for it, by the gods!

The fair little queen forbore to curtsey. Instead, she inclined her head regally, a gesture between equals. Outwardly, the bright smile stayed on Eliseth's face. Inwardly, she seethed. 'Your Majesty,' she said, with a corresponding nod.

'Please,' said the queen, 'let us have no such formality between us. I am sure that women of our high station can be friends. After all, we have so much in common – even the fact that we both come from Nexis – and the fact that Aurian is also my enemy.'

The smile vanished from Eliseth's face as her jaw dropped open.

Hearing Aurian's name, Chiamh, who had been hovering, invisible, near the ceiling in a corner of the room, drew a little closer so as to be sure he didn't miss anything the two women were saying. He had come in on the draught as the visitor entered, curious to have another look at Aurian's enemy,

436

whom he had not seen since her attack on the Mage in the Vale, when she had stolen the Sword of Flame. The visitor was a mystery, however. She might only be a Mortal – but *Queen* Sara? The queen of what country? And when and how had she come from Nexis? Though one was a Mage and one a Mortal, he could see exactly what the two women had in common: their golden beauty, their naked ambition – and their relentless hatred of Aurian.

At Eliseth's invitation the queen seated herself, arranged her skirts with elegant grace, and accepted a cup of wine. 'Now,' she said, 'if I might get directly to business, Lady – the troops I promised you are on their way now and will be here at Dhiammara before morning. As arranged, I have told them to use the ground level entrance. They will make their quarters in the lower caverns, and guard that means of ingress at the same time. In return for my assistance, you will give me your backing, once Aurian is disposed of, to take over the rule of the Khazalim in my own right, instead of as a mere Regent.'

'Indeed,' Eliseth agreed smoothly. 'Since my conquest of the Forest Kingdom succeeded so well, I now have a good number of slaves to maintain this place, and a secure supply base beyond the desert. Aurian should present us with few problems. My winged watchers are ever vigilant, and unknown to her, I have a spy in her camp. No matter when she comes, or how she chooses to come, we will have fair warning – and we will be ready.' Her eyes glittered avidly. 'Once that bitch is out of the way, we can divide these Southern Lands neatly between us and bring them under our rule.' She smiled coldly. 'All will benefit from the new state of affairs . . .'

'Especially us,' Sara finished with a chiming laugh, and the two women lifted their glasses to one another.

After what Chiamh had just heard, the remainder of the two women's conversation was fairly inconsequential. He learned that Sara would be staying in Dhiammara for some days, but heard little else that was of use. Unseen in his high corner, he fidgeted impatiently, waiting for someone to open the door and give him a breeze on which he could escape, and return to Aurian with his news.

31

A Matter of Trust

The sky was growing light in the east by the time the Windeye
returned across the mountains to Aurian's camp. As he slid
down the shining paths of air towards his abandoned body, he
noticed that the knot of pine and spruce in which he had concealed himself was no longer deserted. Shia was watching over
him in his absence. As he settled himself with a groan into his
cold, cramped form, the cat cocked her head and peered into
his face. 'About time,' she said grouchily. 'Aurian thought it
wasn't safe to leave you alone and helpless out of sight of
camp, so I said I'd keep an eye on you for her. It was high time
she got some sleep.'

'Is she sleeping now?' Chiamh asked. 'I'm sorry to have to
wake her, but I must speak with her urgently.'

'Can't it wait?' Shia snapped, her tail twitching. 'The poor
thing has to rest sometime, you know.'

'Who's watching the camp? Khanu?'

The great cat's fur bristled up on the back of her neck, and
her tail lashed back and forth like a whip. 'Look,' she said
defensively, 'some of us can't help these things. It's the way
we're made – unlike *some* folk, we can't choose our times and
places. It wasn't my idea.'

Chiamh frowned. 'Shia, what you were doing last night is
your business entirely. I wish you and Khanu all the luck in
the world.' He smiled wryly. 'For what it's worth, I may be
just a little envious, but I didn't mean to pry.'

Shia growled under her breath. 'I just feel so *stupid*. I
wouldn't have felt so bad, had we not ended up on Steelclaw.
When I think of the risk and the danger – not just to ourselves,
but to everyone!' She shuddered. 'It's an alarming and
uncomfortable feeling, to know that your wits can just desert
you like that.'

'Well,' Chiamh comforted her, 'it may have been the proximity to your home territory that set you off. You know, like salmon swimming home to spawn.'

'Is that what they do?' Shia asked with interest. 'All I know about them is that they make good eating.'

'Stop trying to change the subject,' the Windeye chuckled. 'When will your cubs be due?'

'Do you mind?' the cat protested. 'I'm trying not to think about it. About two moons and a half,' she added after a moment. 'Didn't you need to talk to Aurian?'

'Whether I did or I didn't, I can certainly recognize a change of subject when I hear one. No, you've convinced me to let Aurian sleep on. We won't be going anywhere while it's daylight, in any case. I think I'll get some rest myself.'

But Chiamh had overheard enough in Dhiammara to make his sleep uneasy, and to fill his dreams with images of bloodshed and war.

'I never thought I would see this place again,' Eliizar said bitterly. He looked out from between the bars of the hastily-constructed slave stockade at the gigantic, ground-level cavern that was hollowed out of Dhiammara's mountain. 'I curse the day I last set eyes on it,' he went on, 'and I curse the Mage who brought me here.'

Nereni took his hand. 'My love, it's scarcely fair to blame Aurian. How could it be her fault that her enemies attacked our home? Why, were it not for her, we would never have *had* a colony.'

'And were it not for her, we would never have had a child – and look what happened.' Eliizar's voice thickened with grief. '*Why*, Nereni? How, after all these barren years of longing, could the Reaper see fit to bless us with a child, and then be so cruel as to snatch her away again? I'll tell you why . . .' He turned on Nereni, his one eye blazing fiercely. 'Because the Reaper never meant us to have her, that's why. That Mage interfered with nature, and made us go against the god's divine will. Amahli was an abomination in his sight. She was taken from us as a punishment . . .'

Nereni leapt angrily to her feet. 'I will *not* sit here and listen to you saying such things!' she spat. 'And if you ever call our daughter an abomination again, I swear I'll kill you with my own bare hands!' She stormed off across the cramped pen, barely noticing as the other slaves scrambled quickly out of her way. Finding the furthest corner away from Eliizar, she sat facing the wall so that she would not have to look at him – and so no one could see her cry.

After a time, Nereni felt a hand on her shoulder. She spun round angrily. 'Eliizar, go – oh, it's you, Jharav. Well, go away. I don't want to talk to anybody.'

Ignoring the hostile shoulder that she turned towards him, the fat old warrior sat down with a grunt beside her. 'Be patient with him, Nereni! It is grief that makes him say these things. You know how he worshipped Amahli . . .'

'And I did not, I suppose?' Nereni snapped.

'You know I didn't mean that – we all have our grief to bear,' Jharav sighed.

'Yes – exactly. You lost poor Ustila, but I never hear you talking like Eliizar, about gods and punishment and suchlike nonsense. Is the world not a bad enough place without bringing the gods into it?'

Jharav laughed sourly. 'I doubt that the priests would agree with you there, but for us ordinary folk, it might not be such a bad thing. Nay, but truly, Nereni, you cannot throw out the good with the bad. Why, I gain a great deal of comfort from thinking of my Ustila safe and happy in the Reaper's care.'

'Yes, but your god is a kindly god,' Nereni argued. 'Eliizar's Reaper seems all spite and vengeance – surely a god would be above such petty things?'

The warrior shook his head. 'Give him time, Nereni. Give him time.'

'I need scarcely bother,' Nereni retorted bitterly. 'What would be the point, Jharav? It won't be long before that evil woman works us all to death. What can she be planning to do with this city that we seem to be reconstructing with our bare hands? And what will she do with us – those that survive at least – when it's finished?'

'As to that, I scarcely dare imagine. But I suspect that the

440

Evil One intends to reign over the entire South from here,' Jharav told her gravely. 'This place would make an ideal stronghold. And if she already controls the Aerillian Skyfolk – cursed be their name – then it can only be a matter of time before the other lands and races will fall into her hands.'

'In that case,' Nereni said with quiet dignity, 'I would rather be dead, and with my daughter.'

Just at that moment, Lanneret, Raven's three-year-old son, came toddling up. 'Reni,' he quavered, tugging at her sleeve, 'Mother's crying again.'

Nereni sighed, and gathered him into her arms. She was horrified to see that even his little legs had been weighed down with shackles and heavy chains – a precaution that had been taken with all the captive Skyfolk, to prevent them escaping from Dhiammara by air. 'All right, little one,' she told him. 'I'll come right now.'

As she got to her feet, she turned back to Jharav. 'You know,' she said, 'before I met Aurian, I was always too nervous and afraid to be any use in an emergency or a crisis. Now look at me – I shoulder not only my own burdens but everyone else's, too.' She gave a short, sour laugh. 'Sometimes I'm not sure whether I am grateful to the Mage or not. It was far easier to be helpless.'

Raven was sitting beside her consort's unmoving body, her tears dripping down on to the winged man's bruised and swollen face. On the ground beside her, her baby was screaming, but Raven did not even spare a glance for the tiny girl. 'Oh, Nereni,' she whispered. 'I think he's going to die.'

Aguila had been severely beaten and kicked while trying to protect his queen and children from the brutality of Sunfeather and the guards. For over a day now, he had been unconscious, his breathing shallow and his body cold. To Nereni, there were all bad signs, but for Raven's sake, she tried to keep her fears to herself. In a way, Aguila's lack of consciousness had been the very thing that had so far protected the queen from Sunfeather's advances. There was a whole history of spite and hatred between the two warriors – Sunfeather had always believed that he should have been Royal Consort instead of Aguila with his lowly background.

Nereni knew that he would use this chance to take Raven, to make her pay for rejecting him – but Sunfeather wanted Aguila to witness his victory. Until it could be seen whether her consort would live or die, Raven was fairly safe – as long as Sunfeather's patience held out.

Nereni concealed the flash of rage she felt at Raven's disregard for her babe. Doesn't she realize how lucky she is to have little Elster? the Khazalim woman thought. Some of us will never see our daughters again – we would give anything to have what Raven has. Nevertheless, she took the winged woman in her arms, and let her weep for a time – before she took her to task. 'Raven, you must face facts,' she said firmly. 'We have no medicines for Aguila, nor a physician to help him. All we can do is try to keep him warm, and pray that his own strength will suffice to bring him through. In the meantime, however,' she added sternly, 'you *can* take care of your children – and you must. Lanneret gets frightened when he sees you crying like that. You must be brave for him. And you must feed your daughter, Raven, and hold her to keep her warm. She needs you more than Aguila does at the moment. What would Elster say if she could see you neglecting her little namesake thus?'

At the mention of Elster's name, Raven flinched as though Nereni had hit her. 'That's not fair!' she protested. 'How could you bring Elster into this when I'm so afraid Aguila will die?' The last word was muffled with a sob.

Nereni turned away in disgust. 'You're a queen,' she said shortly. 'Act like one. Feed your daughter. Comfort your son. Set your people an example. And never, never lose hope that one day we will get out of here.'

Aurian barely had time to wake up properly and choke down a leathery mouthful of two-day-old venison before Chiamh was trying to drag her off somewhere. As usual, she was not in the best of moods on first awakening. 'What *is* the matter with you,' she said testily, as he grabbed her hand and led her away from the others. 'What's all the mystery? Whatever it is, can't you just tell me?'

Since they could have no fire, they had camped just below

the treeline of the mountain for concealment and shelter. The Windeye led the baffled and irritated Mage on a twisting path through the woods, and the Mage's hawk, who had stuck firmly by her throughout the entire journey, followed them, swerving and banking between the trees.

'I don't want any of the others to know I went to Dhiammara last night,' Chiamh explained quietly, as they went along. 'I was afraid you'd let it slip.'

'But I didn't know you went there. You told me you were going to Aerillia.'

'Whatever – I definitely don't want the others to remember that I can ride the winds and spy on Eliseth.' Chiamh guided the Mage down a steep rocky defile to a tree-shaded mossy bank where a turbulent little mountain stream swirled and seethed over its bed of rocks, making such a noise on its downward journey that no one within a dozen yards of it could possibly be overheard.

The Mage forgot her irritation and listened, with growing dismay, to what the Windeye had to tell her. He did not get far.

'She's in *Dhiammara*?' Aurian interrupted. 'But that place is a natural fortress. And how in the name of all the gods did she find out about it – not to mention Aerillia . . .' She fell silent as the dreadful realization dawned on her. 'What with everything that happened at the Well of Souls and afterwards, I never thought to ask myself how she could have ended up in Aerillia. Chiamh – how could Eliseth have known? Until lately, she'd never been out of the north in her life!'

Chiamh took her hand. 'Aurian, I'm sorry. That's why I had to get you out of the camp and talk to you in private. In future, we must guard every word we say. One of our companions is Eliseth's spy.'

'I don't believe it!' Instantly, Aurian was furious with the Windeye. 'How dare you say such a thing?'

Chiamh said nothing – he simply waited until the initial shock had receded.

Aurian bit her lip. 'I'm sorry,' she said. 'Are you absolutely certain of this?'

'I'm certain. That's what she told the Queen of the Khazalim.'

'*Sara*? What the bloody blazes was that backstabbing bitch doing there?'

Chiamh grimaced. 'She's supplying Eliseth with warriors. I see there's no love lost between the two of you,' he added drily. 'But how do you know her?'

'Know her? I've known the little whore for years. She started life as a fortune-hunting guttersnipe in Nexis – in fact she and Anvar were childhood sweethearts, if you can believe it. Then she married Vannor for his money.'

'*What?*' Chiamh looked absolutely stunned. 'This *is* the Queen of the Khazalim we're talking about?'

'Believe me. When the Wraiths struck, Vannor asked Anvar and me to take her with us, out of the city. Then when we got shipwrecked and ended up in Taibeth, she was sold as a concubine to Xiang, and decided he was a much better proposition than a mere merchant.'

The Windeye shook his head. 'Goddess save us,' he muttered. 'It will be interesting when we get to Dhiammara and she and Vannor meet.'

Aurian put her face into her hands. 'Don't even think about it.' Then she looked up sharply. 'Never mind that. Sara is small fry compared to Eliseth. You were saying that one of us is a *spy*? Chiamh, it can't be true, can it? This is appalling news. Which of us could it be? And how long has it been going on?' She jumped to her feet, as though she wanted to get physically away from the unwelcome news. 'Chiamh, would you mind leaving me for a little while? I need to think this through. Tell the others – oh, I don't know. Tell them I'm thinking. It's true enough.'

'All right.' As he turned to go, Chiamh hesitated. 'But I'm going to send Shia to watch over you,' he told her firmly. 'I know you can trust the cats, at least. If one of our companions is really Eliseth's spy, then he's also her agent, and the rest of us are in grave danger – especially you, Aurian. As soon as your enemy realizes you know her location and you're on your way there, I'm sure we can expect some kind of attempt on your life.'

Once the Windeye had gone, Aurian sat down again. She took a handful of pebbles from the bank of the stream and began to flick them, one by one into the water. '*I know you can*

444

trust the cats, at least,' Chiamh had said. Did that mean that she couldn't even trust him? Or that she shouldn't? No, surely that's nonsense, the Mage thought. How could Chiamh be Eliseth's spy? He wouldn't have told me . . .

'Not unless he wanted to sow suspicion and dissent between you and your other companions,' said her inner voice.

'That's rubbish,' Aurian told herself firmly. 'Chiamh came with me through time, as did Iscalda and Schiannath. Eliseth never had a chance to get at them. It's far more likely to be one of the others, who were in Nexis while Eliseth was there – or Aerillia for that matter. It could even be Linnet – or Grince. He was certainly determined enough to come along on this trip . . .'

Aurian knew, though, in her heart, that it was most likely to be someone who'd had an encounter with the grail. Could the traitor be Vannor? Or Forral? 'Dear gods,' Aurian whispered to herself. 'Not Forral – surely? And what can I do now?' One thing was for certain. There was no way she could get to Dhiammara to face Eliseth without the Magewoman knowing. Any possibility of surprising her enemy had just been wiped out completely.

'What *is* the matter?' Shia appeared through the trees, her voice sharp with anxiety. 'Chiamh wouldn't tell me – he just sent me to guard you. You're shielding your thoughts, my friend, but I could feel your distress all the way here. What has happened?'

'We're in a real mess, Shia.' Quickly, Aurian told the cat what had happened.

Shia thought for a while, absently licking at a huge black paw. 'You know, there's one thing you haven't considered,' she said at last. 'If this spy has been among us all the time, then Eliseth could have had you slain long ago, without you coming anywhere near her and certainly while we were completely unprepared for treachery. It would have been the easiest thing in the world just to stick a sword or a knife into you as you slept – and certainly a lot more safe and sure from her point of view. So why has she not ordered your death? It seems to me that there can only be one answer – she *wants* you to come to her. But why?'

Aurian looked at her friend as though she had never seen her before. 'Dear gods,' she said slowly. 'You're absolutely right – and there can only be one reason. Shia, I was a fool not to think of it before. Eliseth wants the remaining Artefacts! She's going to lure me to Dhiammara, the most defensible place in the South, so that I can deliver the Harp and the Staff right into her hands before she finishes me.'

'So she thinks,' Shia snarled. 'If she wants to finish you, she'll have to go through me to reach you.'

Aurian reached out and touched the cat's broad, sleek head. 'No, Shia. I've lost enough friends since this business started. I'm not going to sacrifice the rest of you now. There must be some other way . . .'

'As far as I can see,' Shia said, 'there's no point in letting Eliseth know you've discovered that she has a spy, because that will mean she'll find out that you can spy on her. There's only one thing we can do. We must head for Aerillia now, as quickly as possible, and hope to catch your enemy unprepared.'

'We couldn't make it quickly enough,' Aurian argued. 'She's already prepared. We need some way to get close without her knowing . . .'

'You could always shield,' said Chiamh.

'*What?*' Aurian turned white. She looked frantically around, but could see nothing – yet the voice had come from somewhere close to her left ear.

Shia let out a threatening growl, rushed past Aurian – and pounced. There was a muffled shout – and suddenly Chiamh appeared, sprawled on the ground underneath the great cat, who had her forepaws on his chest. Her fangs were bared and her fierce golden eyes blazed down into his. Aurian's hawk dived around them, uttering shrill, angry cries and swooping dangerously close to Chiamh's eyes. With difficulty, Aurian quieted the furious creature, though she was quite happy for Shia to stay just where she was. Once the Mage had calmed her hawk, she stood, hands on hips, glaring down at Chiamh. 'Now,' she said coldly. 'Perhaps you'd like to explain why you were spying on me.'

'Aurian, be sensible,' the Windeye gasped. 'If I had wanted

to spy on you, would I have spoken up as I did? Had I felt the need to eavesdrop, I could have left my poor abused body safely behind, and watched you from the winds . . .'

Shia looked around at the Mage. 'When you think about it, that does make sense,' she said dubiously.

Aurian nodded. 'I suppose so . : .'

'Please – just get this accursed cat off me and let me explain. She's breaking my ribs,' Chiamh protested in strangled tones.

'All right,' said Aurian with sudden decision. 'Let him up, Shia. But Chiamh – this had better be good. I've got into the habit of trusting you, and I'd hate to have to stop now.'

The Windeye struggled to his feet, gingerly feeling his ribs. 'Oh, it's good all right. I think I've just found a way to get us into Dhiammara. I was just practising on you – and you've got to admit, it worked. You never even knew I was there.' He looked at the Mage and grinned. 'Trust me, Aurian – you're simply going to love this.'

32
City of Dragons

Skua stood up on a high balcony that encircled one of the multiple spires of Yinze's Temple, watching the sun set and listening to the wind shrilling through the grotesque structure to produce the eerie keening known as Incondor's Lament. The nerve-twisting sound was music to the High Priest's ears. The Lament belongs to me, he thought. This sound is a part of Aerillia and now it is *mine* – along with all the rest of the city.

The last of the low autumn sun slid behind the mountains, and the gold light dimmed from the bristling turrets, the soaring towers and the slender, twisted spires of Aerillia. Skua turned one last time to survey his domain. Now that the Magewoman had gone, he could truly call it his. The city of the Winged Folk was of little concern to her: now that she and Sunfeather had taken Dhiammara, they would be surely be content to leave this place to him.

Skua sighed happily. All his life he had been a devout and faithful servant to Yinze, and at last his god had given him his due and proper reward. He had waited years for this moment, serving patiently as a disciple to the corrupt and power-crazed Blacktalon, then dealing with the tantrums, the vacillation and the mistrust of the inexperienced child who had assumed the throne. Though from time to time he experienced a pang of guilt at betraying his queen, he always comforted himself with the thought that he was leading the lost and godless denizens of Aerillia back to the true ways of Yinze. Already he was formulating a stringent new set of laws to protect his flock from sin – for was it not better to punish their bodies in order to save their souls?

Skua shivered, as a raw and icy wind came out of the north. Odd, he thought. The weather must be changing. Perhaps he should go inside now . . . As he walked around the curve of the balcony, he noticed, in the far distance, a great black cloud that seemed to be sweeping down with uncanny speed out of the north. Well, he thought, that would certainly explain this chill – it looks as though we're in for a rare storm. The approaching tempest, however, could do little to dampen his exhilaration. Aerillia has seen storms before, he thought. I'm sure the city can weather it.

The wind came again, fetid and dank like the exhalation from an open tomb. A shiver of unease passed through the High Priest's frame, but he told himself firmly that he was imagining things. What could go wrong now? Yinze would never allow any harm to befall his favoured servant. From the city below came the thunder of many wings as people began to panic, leaving the city in droves and heading south. Fools, Skua thought. That storm will catch them right out in the open . . .

The vast black cloud stretched across the sky now, growing larger by the moment. Though Skua knew now that this could be no natural phenomenon, he stayed where he was, paralysed with horror like a bird fascinated by the glittering gaze of a snake; aghast with the knowledge that Yinze had betrayed him after all, just as Skua had betrayed his queen. He was still standing there when the Nihilim covered Aerillia like a great black cloak, and began to feed.

It took Aurian and her companions two hard nights' flying to reach the forest on the edge of the Jewelled Desert, sparing little time to hunt and forage on the way. Though Aurian was wearied by the gruelling journey, as were Linnet and the Xandim, the Mage couldn't help but thinking wryly of the length of time it had taken her to cross these very mountains on foot when she was heading north, with Eliizar, Nereni, and the others. As she flew over the forest, seeking the remains of the settlement, the fate of her poor friends made Aurian's thoughts turn grim. Chiamh had told her what he'd overheard about Eliseth's attack on the forest community. If Nereni and Eliizar were still alive, they would now be slaves in Aerillia – and what had happened to the Mage's last, secret gift to them? She had used her healing skill to help her friends conceive their longed-for child at last – but what had happened to it? Had it been safely born? Had it survived Eliseth's treacherous onslaught? If anything had happened to them . . . Aurian gritted her teeth and clenched her fingers so tightly in Chiamh's long black mane that he whinnied in protest.

If Eliseth was using the remains of the colony as a supply post, it was certain to be guarded. The Mage's companions settled down in hiding at the north-eastern edge of the forest, well away from both the human colony of Zithra and the Skyfolk settlement of Eyrie up in the hills to the north-west. Aurian and the Windeye left their bodies and flew in low and silent on the winds, in the darkest hour of the night, to find out just what was taking place. As the sun rose, they found the broad cleared areas in the forest, and saw buildings and cultivated fields in clusters below. Aurian muttered a curse. The whole area was swarming with Skyfolk.

'Good,' said Chiamh determinedly. Even though they were out of their bodies and using mind-speech, he still spoke in a low voice. 'This will give us a chance to practise our shielding before we actually get to Dhiammara.'

'Look on the bright side, eh?' Aurian said wryly. 'Well, I suppose you're right. I don't like leaving an enemy at my back, but what else can we do?'

'If you cut off the head, the rest of the snake will die,' Chiamh reassured the Mage. 'Eliseth has the rightful Queen of the Winged Folk in captivity, remember? Once we can free Raven and remove her enemies, these Skyfolk here will change sides pretty quickly – I hope. In the meantime, we may as well take a good look while we're here,' he added. 'Just in case these warriors decide not to co-operate later on, let's see exactly what we're up against.'

For a time, they watched the Winged Folk working busily; sorting, stacking and packing the contents of the colony's storerooms into sacks and nets for transport. Eliizar's folk had enjoyed a good harvest this year and Aurian and Chiamh looked wistfully at the piles of fruit, vegetables, grain and dried meat that were all being paraded before them. Aurian sighed. 'I wish it were possible to actually steal stuff in this incorporeal form.'

'Ah well,' said Chiamh, 'it won't be too much longer before we're feasting in Dhiammara.'

'I know you can fly tremendously fast in your equine form, but we can't go as fast as when we ride the winds,' Aurian argued. 'It's bound to take more than a night to get across the desert. We'll be pushing it to get there in three.'

'Don't worry, we'll make it,' Chiamh comforted her.

'We'd be a lot more sure of arriving if we could get some food from down there, and some extra cloaks and blankets to shelter us from the glare of the desert days.'

When Aurian and the Windeye returned to the others and made their report, however, Linnet spoke up immediately. 'We don't have to go without that stuff. I can go down and get what we need. I'll say I've just been transferred from Aerillia – they'll never know.'

The Mage found herself beginning to smile. 'What – you just plan to walk in, take the food and walk out again? As easily as that?'

'No.' Linnet shook her head. 'No, I'm not quite that innocent, lady. I doubt it will really be that simple. I think it *is* possible, though.'

Aurian nodded thoughtfully. 'I believe you're right.'

'Let me go too,' Wolf broke in eagerly. 'No-one would suspect a wolf . . .'

'You're right, they wouldn't,' Forral said flatly. 'They'd just put an arrow through him. This isn't Eilin's valley now, Wolf. You'll stay right here.'

Wolf subsided with a sulky whine.

'Don't even think about it,' Forral told him firmly. 'I'm going to be watching you like a hawk, my boy. You aren't going anywhere.'

Later that day, after she had rested, Linnet bathed in a freezing mountain stream with the usual disregard that the Winged Folk displayed towards cold, and tried to make herself as presentable as possible. Then she set off flying towards Zithra, taking with her the hopes and good wishes of all her companions.

The winged girl's stomach was taut with a mixture of

nerves and excitement. She was well aware how much depended on her – and just how much danger was involved. She must be very careful not to let them catch her out.

As she reached the outskirts of the settlement, Linnet was hailed in midair.

'Ho! You! Where are you going? Identify yourself!'

The winged girl looked round to see two armed sentries arrowing up at her from the trees on the hillside. Wary of the crossbows that they carried, she descended at once to land in a clearing. As soon as she touched the ground, the sentinels closed in on her. 'Where are you from?' one of them demanded. 'I haven't seen you before.'

'Haven't you?' Linnet retorted pertly. 'You haven't been looking then. I've been up in Eyrie, clearing buildings. They sent me down here to help out.'

'Where's your uniform?' the other guard demanded. 'You look like the contents of a ragbag.'

Linnet laughed. 'That's just what I'm wearing. I had an accident yesterday when a bag of rotten fruit burst all over me. They had to kit me out from what they could find in Eyrie while my gear was cleaned – the smell was unbelievable.'

One of the sentries laughed. 'I can well imagine,' he said. 'All right, girl. Off you go down to the settlement – they'll soon find enough work for you down there. Don't burst any more bags of fruit now, will you?' he called after her as she left.

Limp with relief, Linnet glided down to the main settlement in the valley, where she found a winged captain in charge of the foodstuffs and told her story again. The captain, busy and harassed, didn't even bother to ask any questions – she was only too glad of an extra pair of hands. Soon the winged girl found herself in a line of workers packing food into sacks for transportation to Dhiammara.

It was a simple enough matter to appropriate two of the sacks; one of cheeses, and one of dried meat, plus a pair of large waxed skins for carrying water. Linnet simply 'lost' the bags and left them in a dark out of the way corner in a lean-to porch on one of the houses. Along with a bundle of old blankets filched from one of the houses, that was all she could carry. It was more difficult to sneak away from the work team, but Linnet chose her moment. Slipping back between the houses she returned to her precious loot, arranging her burdens as best she could about her person and slinging them in position with rope. Looking carefully around her to make sure she was not being watched, she headed off, flying low between the trees rather than taking to the open skies where she could be spotted.

It had to happen, of course, in a place where the tree cover was thin, but at least the sound of wings overhead served as a warning. Linnet looked up to see a patrol of winged warriors in the distance, heading towards her. Her heart leapt into her throat. Her pilfering had been discovered and they were coming for her! Then she realized that they were coming from Eyrie – entirely the wrong direction. 'Idiot!' she told herself. Nonetheless, if she couldn't get herself under cover, there would be some very awkward questions asked. Linnet looked around wildly – then through the trees to the right of her, she noted the glint of grey stone. A building? Here, so far beyond the settlement? Thank Yinze for a miracle!

The house was a burnt-out ruin, but plenty of hiding-places could still be found among the rubble. Linnet slipped into a niche beneath a cluster of beams that had fallen like a child's jackstraws, somehow supporting each other without falling down. Crouching there in the sooty, smoke-reeking darkness, she listened hard until the sound of wings had completely cleared from the skies.

Dusk was falling as Linnet struggled out from her cramped refuge, straightening her filthy wings with a sigh of relief.

'Don't move or I'll shoot!'

The winged girl stiffened, cursing under her breath. Not *now*, when she was so close . . .

'Put those bags down and step away from them!'

Suddenly it occurred to Linnet that the voice sounded terribly young . . . Stooping as if to slip the bags from her shoulders, she reached down swiftly and picked up a stone from the rubble, turning and throwing in one fluid motion. There was a cry of pain, a crossbow bolt whizzed harmlessly past her left ear to go clattering off a piece of broken wall – and Linnet turned fully, to see two children in the shadows.

Aurian looked at the pair of youngsters, still unable to believe that this lovely young girl was the child she had helped Nereni conceive. 'I'm amazed that you survived,' she said to them. 'You were incredibly lucky not to suffocate in that cellar when the rest of the house burned above you.'

'It was the wine cellar,' the winged lad explained. 'It was ventilated. There was air coming in from the outside all the time.'

Aurian was scarcely listening. She was remembering Tiercel's father, Petrel, and wondering whether he had survived the attack.

'We had an awful time getting food, though,' Amahli added. 'We could only go out at night and forage in the woods . . .'

'I'm glad you came.' Abruptly Tiercel's cloak of assumed maturity fell away from him. 'We couldn't have stayed there forever, but I just didn't know what else to do or where to go.'

The Mage wished that she could so easily hand on the responsibility to others. Sadly, that had not happened for years, and probably never would again.

'Lady,' Linnet reminded her urgently. 'They're bound to miss me soon, down at the settlement. We should go now, before they start combing the forest. And we can't leave these two here to be caught.'

'You'd rather take them into the midst of a battle?' Aurian asked her waspishly – but she knew that the winged girl was right. 'Very well,' she said. 'It's dark enough to take on the desert now, so let's get moving. Amahli – you ride behind Forral on Schiannath's back. Tiercel – can you manage to fly the distance?'

The dark-haired lad grinned. 'Don't worry, Lady. After these last cramped days of hiding, I'm looking forward to stretching my wings.'

When everyone was mounted and assembled with all their burdens, Aurian leapt up on Chiamh's back and helped Grince up behind her. 'Right, my friend,' she murmured to the Windeye. 'Let's do it – now!'

454

The Mage felt Chiamh's mind join with hers as, together they meshed their shields into an amalgam of two different types of magic. Aurian was using the High Magic of the Staff to protect them from magical view through scrying and also to shield them so that the spy, whoever he was, could not pass on any messages to Eliseth as to their whereabouts and progress. Chiamh, on the other hand, was protecting the companions from physical view by a variation of his illusion spell. He was simply projecting an illusion, in fact, that there was no-one there at all. It took a great deal of concentration to keep it up, but it certainly seemed to work very well, as Aurian had discovered that day in the forest.

As they took off into the darkening sky and headed for the desert, the Mage realized that talisman or no talisman, she was now feeling the pressure of their additional burdens of water, food and Amahli, plus the different kind of stress involving the maintenance of her magical shield. She knew that Chiamh too must be in a similar predicament, and only hoped that their strength would hold out long enough for them to get to Dhiammara and do what they had to do. The next few days would be crucial.

'Hey – two of the horses have got loose!' The Khazalim sentry on watch at the cavern mouth could not believe his eyes, though he was glad of a diversion to break the monotony of this pointless duty. 'Come and help me,' he yelled at his fellow-guard. Between them they managed to round up the horses who were milling about near the entrance to the cavern. The creatures, quite docile, allowed themselves to be led back inside to the picket-lines. The guards, preoccupied, had their backs turned towards the opening, and did not notice the lithe, shadowy figures of the two great cats who slipped on silent feet into the vast, sparsely torchlit cave.

'Reaper's curse on these troopers,' the sentry grumbled as he fastened the animals up again. 'Some of them are so careless. These creatures might still have been wandering about outside when the sun came up, and that would have been the end of them – and such handsome animals, too,' he added, smoothing the neck of the white mare as she nosed in his pocket for titbits. 'Why, if I had such a beast as this, I'd take better care of her.'

'Hurry up,' grumbled his partner, clearly less of a lover of horseflesh. 'We'll be skinned alive if the captain finds us away from our posts.'

'I can't for the life of me think why. The prisoners are all locked up, and who's going to risk their life crossing that accursed desert to get to this place? The arse-end of nowhere – that's where we are . . .' The men's voices faded into the distance as they walked away. Once they were safely gone, the white mare spat out a bunch of keys on to the sand. Then the outlines of both beasts blurred and shimmered, and Iscalda and Schiannath stood in their place. Using the lines of genuine horses as cover, they picked up the keys that Iscalda had lifted from the guard's pocket and melted into the shadows at the far end of the cavern, keeping well away from the soldiers bivouacked around the upper pool. Near the slave stockade, built around the pool on the lower level, they were joined by two great cats.

Eliizar didn't sleep any more. No matter how hard the slaves were worked through the day, either clearing and repairing the jewelled buildings in the city above or exploring and opening up the chambers that honeycombed the mountain, he would return to the stockade at night, pick at his supper, and spend what should have been his hours of rest leaning against the bars that caged him, staring into space and thinking about his daughter. He scarcely even talked to Nereni these days. At first she had been sympathetic, then she had grown worried, and finally angry, but nothing she said made any difference to Eliizar any more. The present was so unbearable to him that he preferred to spend all his time walking in the sunlit afternoons of the past.

'Eliizar? Eliizar!' The swordmaster came out of his reverie to hear someone calling his name in a hissing whisper. As his vision came back into focus, the blurred pattern of light and shade on the other side of the bars resolved itself into a familiar face.

'Schiannath?'

456

'Shhh! Listen, Eliizar – and for the sake of the goddess, keep quiet. Aurian is here. We need to free you folk and create a diversion in these lower caverns. Here are the keys –' He passed the bunch, warm from his hand and for some reason somewhat wet and sticky, to Eliizar. 'Now,' he went on, 'I want you to creep around and unlock all the shackles on the Skyfolk before we do anything else. And whatever you do, keep them from getting excited. If we wake the guards at this point, we're lost.'

Eliizar nodded, his heart beating fast with excitement. Just as he was turning to go, the Xandim warrior reached through the bars and caught his sleeve. 'Oh – and I almost forgot,' he whispered. 'We found your daughter in the settlement. She's alive!' He faded back into the shadows, leaving the speechless swordmaster alone. As the import of Schiannath's words gradually came home to him, Eliizar felt his heart, which had been closed and clenched so long in grief, opening up like a flower. Tears of joy and gratitude blurred the sight in his one good eye. 'Thank you,' he whispered. 'Oh, thank you!' In that moment, he had no idea to whom he was speaking, but the words were no less heartfelt for that.

Raven sat with her son on her lap and her little daughter in her arms, rocking both children absently as they slept. She was glad of them now, just as she was glad of the support and companionship of Nereni, who stayed with her constantly. Aguila, by some miracle, still lived, but as he had sunk deeper and deeper into a torpid state, Raven had gradually given up hope that he would ever wake again. Now he seemed to exist between two worlds: barely clinging to life, but somehow, with a stubborn determination that was so much a part of his waking nature, refusing to accept the finality of death.

As she kept vigil, Raven found herself thinking more and more often of their early days – of how he had cheered her first lonely days as Queen, and how, when they had first met, she had treated him as a coarse and common soldier until dear Elster had put her right, and told her to marry him. Raven recalled the ridiculous look of shocked incredulity on his face when she had asked him to wed her, and smiled fondly through a glimmer of tears. 'Oh, Aguila – get well, you idiot. Come back to me, please . . .' So lost was she in her prayers and memories, that she did not notice the stealthy movement and the buzz of subdued excitement that was taking place around her. The first thing she saw was Eliizar, with an enormous smile on his face, holding out a bunch of keys. He was looking right through her, however – he only had eyes for his wife. 'Nereni, Nereni,' he whispered joyously. 'Amahli is alive!'

Eliizar returned to Schiannath. 'Now what?' he whispered. Schiannath's grin flashed white in the darkness. 'Now we turn the tables on your guards,' he whispered. 'Dead or imprisoned, I don't care – but none, absolutely none of the enemy must be permitted to escape to warn the folk above. Pass the word. I'm going to open these gates now. Tell them to wait for my signal – and come out fighting.'

As the thick band of storm clouds blotted out the last of the moonlight across the Dragon City, Eliseth paced the lofty observation platform on top of Dhiammara's highest tower, unable to contain her restlessness. 'Where *is* she?' she muttered. 'Aurian must come soon.'

It was completely unnerving. For three days now, the Magewoman had been blind and deaf as to Aurian's whereabouts. Just when the wretched woman had been heading south towards the desert, and Eliseth really needed to keep a close eye on her enemy's progress, she had lost contact with her spy. Each time she had tried to insinuate herself into Vannor's mind, she had come across a hard, blank, reflective surface that would not yield to her probing will. 'That bitch is coming, though,' Eliseth said to herself. 'I just know it.' Already she had doubled her patrols in the skies around the mountain, and put the Khazalim troops who manned the lower corridors on full alert. The grail and the Sword were safely hidden, and she had just completed her last defence – the build-up of a storm above the city that she could unleash at will. Surely that would be enough?

'It's been a long time, Eliseth – I've been looking forward to this meeting!'

With an inarticulate cry, the Magewoman spun round, looking frantically for the source of her enemy's voice. There was no one on the rooftop, but there – down there among the city's scattered buildings – was that not a tall, familiar figure with flaming hair? Curse her – she was heading for the emerald tower.

Frantically, Eliseth waved her arms, trying to attract the attention of the guards she had stationed round the rim of the crater. 'There,' she cried. 'Are you blind, you fools? Aurian is here! Why did you let her through?' She ran to the edge of the roof and began a headlong descent of the spiral track that led down to the ground, but her pace was slowed by the need for care, for there was no rail or guard to prevent her from plunging to her death should she miss her footing. Down in the city, the Mage had disappeared. Instead, Eliseth reached for Vannor – and found him nearby.

The fight in the great cavern was brief but bloody. The settlers of both races, winged and human, were savagely glad of a chance to avenge their dead and repay the ruin of all their dreams. The Khazalim woke to find their sentries gone, their weapons stolen, and the exits to the cavern blocked: the cave mouth to the outside being guarded by two Black demons of unmatched ferocity. The access that had been hewn into the bowels of the mountain as an alternative to the Dragonfolk's peculiar crystalline means of transport up to the city, was blocked by two strange northern warriors – a man and a woman – who were soon joined by the slave who had been the leader of the rebels – the man who, rumour said, had killed the great swordsman Xiang himself. No one dared face him now that he was free.

A good half of the southern warriors survived: mainly those with the intelligence to realize that their cause was lost from the start. They were locked in the same stockades that they had previously been guarding, with the bitter knowledge that their own laziness and laxity had put them there.

When the cavern had been secured, Aguila and the rest of the wounded settlers were gently lifted or helped from the stockade before the enemy were locked inside. They were made comfortable in the encampment near the upper pool and the leaders gathered there to make their plans.

'What now?' Petrel asked Schiannath. Like Eliizar and Nereni, the winged man and his mate Firecrest were ablaze with excitement at the news of their son's miraculous survival.

'Now we get up to the city,' the Xandim said. 'Aurian said there was a secret way up, something I couldn't make out about a crystal, but if Eliseth had brought the Khazalim in to guard this cavern, she must know about it . . .'

'I don't think she does,' Nereni put in. 'From what we could overhear, she discovered the cavern separately from the chambers in the mountain – she got into those from above. That's why she made us dig a way into the lower levels of the chambers – she thought that failing all else, she'd make her own entrance. There were two transporting crystals,' she added brightly, ignoring Eliizar, whose smile was vanishing rapidly. 'We didn't go in them, but Shia did.' The little woman frowned, trying to remember. 'There was one by the pool,' she chattered brightly – 'don't poke me like that, Eliizar, you know how I bruise – but that one didn't go all the way, and they had an awful time, Aurian said, with chasms and invisible bridges and all sorts. And then there was another one – the one they came *down* by. That one was in the back of the cavern, over there . . .'

Shia went to the back wall, her whiskers bristling, and sniffed at the stone. Suddenly she halted with a low growl, all the hair on her spine standing on end. Though they had no Mage to interpret for them, it was quite clear that the cat had found the place.

Schiannath leapt to his feet. 'Right, let's get moving,' he said briskly. 'Skyfolk, you can fly up the outside of the mountain. You'll know what to do when you get up there – your task is to deal with the airborne threat. We'll have to go up in shifts – how many folk do you think this contraption will take, Nereni?'

The woman shrugged. 'About six or eight, I would think. Not many.'

'Well, the cats can be first,' Schiannath decided. 'They can do the fighting of about ten! Iscalda, you had better go with them to get things organized at the top – and what about you, Eliizar? Do you want to go in the first load?'

Eliizar stepped back hastily. His face had gone a ghastly greenish shade. 'I don't –' he began. Nereni narrowed her eyes at him. 'Your daughter is up there,' she said.

The swordmaster swallowed, and stepped forward. 'All right – let's get this over with.'

Nereni hugged him. 'I'm very proud of you,' she said softly, and stepped back to join Raven, who was staying behind with Jharav to take care of the wounded and the children.

Since Nereni couldn't use a weapon, she knew there was no sense in her trying to take a warrior's place. Nevertheless, as she watched the warriors departing in small groups, as though they had been sucked into nothingness by the wall, she wished vehemently that at some time in her life, she'd had a chance to learn to fight.

'But you can't just go off like that and leave us all alone,' Amahli protested to the man with one hand. 'The Lady Aurian said you were supposed to stay here in this building and guard us. What if someone comes?'

'No one will come,' Vannor said impatiently. 'And I don't see why I should have to stay here and miss all the action playing nursemaid. You'll have to manage. You've got the wolf, after all.' With that, he was gone.

A moment later, when Amahli and Tiercel looked around for the wolf, he was gone too.

'All right, Grince – let's see how good a thief you really are,' Aurian whispered.

Since the entrance to the emerald tower had been destroyed in the earthquake, Eliseth's slaves had repaired it with stone from the mountain, and hung a great, heavy iron door with a series of complex locks.

'Where in the name of all creation did she get *that* from?' Forral muttered.

Aurian shrugged. 'There were a whole lot of chambers down inside the mountain with doors like this. We never did find out what was behind them – we couldn't get inside.'

'I'll get inside the bugger,' Grince muttered, sliding a slender dagger into one of the latches. 'I never saw a lock that could beat me yet.'

'Well hurry up,' Forral told him. 'We want to be in there before Eliseth thinks to come back this way . . .'

Suddenly Aurian's hawk took off from her shoulder and flew round her head in circles, screeching with excitement. 'Look,' the Mage pointed upwards. 'They did it! The cats and the Xandim have freed the slaves.' In the sky above, the air was full of winged figures, swooping and swerving through the low storm clouds as they fought with savage ferocity. Behind her, from Grince, came the sounds of clicking, scraping and swearing. She realized that now the slaves had been freed, Shia would be bringing folk up in the crystal contrivance that emerged within the emerald tower – and the tower had better be open. 'Grince,' she said, 'do you think you'll be . . .'

'Got it!' the thief grunted. There was one last click, and the door swung open.

'Good man!' Aurian clapped him on the back.

Grince grinned up at her. 'Told you you'd need me, didn't I?' he said.

The spiral corridor within the tower still glowed with its faint green light, and Aurian was assailed by a powerful memory. She turned back to Forral and took his hand. 'Do you remember this place?' she said softly. 'You came back to me and led me here . . .'

'Of course I remember,' the swordsman said with a catch in his voice. 'Gods, but it was good to see you again! Death almost obliterated me over that escapade –' he squeezed her hand. 'It was worth it, though.'

They rounded a curve of the spiral to discover that the crystal contrivance had already disgorged the cats, Iscalda and Eliizar. With a whoop of delight, Aurian hugged Eliizar. 'Where's my daughter?' the swordmaster asked her urgently.

'She's safe, don't worry. She's in one of the buildings, and she's guarded.' She turned to Iscalda. 'Just keep them coming while we search this building.'

'We can't.' Shia looked glum. 'It's jammed. I remember, it was never the same after the earthquake – well this is all of us you're going to get.'

'Well, we'll have to manage,' Aurian said. 'We'd better start by searching the building in any case.' The Mage was absolutely certain that Eliseth would have locked up the Sword and the grail in this place – but after a fruitless search of the emerald tower, she was forced to admit she was wrong. Standing in the midst of the sunburst chamber, the heart of the tower, Aurian gave herself up to some serious swearing. If the Artefacts were not here, then where were they? And more to the point – where was Eliseth?

33

Resurrection

Eliseth ran through the streets of Dhiammara, seeking the elusive figure of her enemy. It was difficult to concentrate – she was viewing the scene through multiple vision as she switched from one of her puppets to the other, and back to her own sight once more. To her relief, she had found Vannor at last, and what was more, had found her access to his mind unblocked. She had sent him out into the city in search of Aurian too.

After a long and fruitless search, she grew weary and impatient. Furthermore, a glance up at the skies showed her that Sunfeather's Skyfolk were finding themselves no match for the ferocity of Petrel and the colonists of Eyrie. It was time to bring matters to a head before she lost the advantage – if she could not find her enemy, it was time to lure Aurian to her. Reaching out with her mind, she contacted Bern, who was safely hidden in a nearby building. Manipulating him deftly, she planted orders in his mind to bring the Artefacts to the platform on top of the city's highest tower.

'Aurian!' Eliseth cried, augmenting her voice with magic so that it echoed throughout the whole of the dragon city. 'I'm tired of this game of cat-and-mouse! If you wish to challenge me, you will find me on top of the highest tower.' There was no answer – not that she had really expected one. Hurrying, the Magewoman turned her steps towards the tower.

When Eliseth reached the top, she found Bern already there, his chest heaving from the climb. The grail and the Sword lay on the stone at his feet. Good – that was fine. Now what was Vannor up to . . .

Even as she slid into his mind, he found the Mage.

Vannor rushed through the streets, baffled and bewildered.

His mind kept fading in and out and there were alarming gaps in his memory. Every so often he would blink, it seemed, and find himself in a different street entirely. There was only one imperative in his mind that overrode all his confusion. Find Aurian – that was all he knew. He made for the sparkling green tower – and suddenly there she was.

'Vannor?' Aurian stepped forward. She was frowning. 'What are you doing here? You're supposed to be looking after those children . . .'

And then Eliseth slid into Vannor's mind, and she drew his sword and struck at the Mage. The blade bit into Aurian's neck and she went down in a pool of blood. There came an anguished cry, and Eliseth looked up through Vannor's eyes and saw Aurian coming round the corner, sword in hand, her eyes ablaze with rage and grief. The Weather-Mage looked down again, and bleeding in the street was the Xandim creature that Vannor knew as the Windeye. Then Aurian's sword flashed down, and Vannor saw no more.

Aurian stared in horror at the two men. Then she flung herself down beside Chiamh's body, taking in the mortal wound at a glance. Eliseth's clumsy blow had meant to behead him, but instead had hacked a great gash where his neck joined his shoulder, through which his lifeblood pumped with each beat of his faltering heart. There was no time to heal such a dreadful wound – he would be dead long before she could finish, and besides, she had to find Eliseth. Drawing on the power of the Staff, she took the Windeye out of time – and Vannor too, though she was fairly sure she had killed him. So he had been the spy all along – but it had been Eliseth who had looked out of his eyes when he struck the death blow. Aurian had struck him down in anger and the need to be rid of Eliseth's puppet, but Vannor had been her friend. Now, it was imperative she find the grail – for the sake of both Chiamh and his killer.

Aurian's companions stood around her, stunned and horrified at what had just happened. 'Chiamh was my decoy – he projected an illusion of himself as me,' she explained quickly. 'I told the idiot it was dangerous . . .' Her voice caught, and she swallowed hard. 'Somehow, Eliseth was controlling

465

Vannor . . .' She shrugged. There was no time for this. 'And now I'm going to have it out with her.' She headed off towards the tower, leaving them to follow as best they might, then paused. 'The rest of you stay here,' she said. 'And I mean it.'

Shia looked at Forral. 'Do you think she means us?'

'No, she couldn't possibly.'

'That's what I thought.' Together, they set off after the Mage.

'All right, you two.' Aurian spoke without even glancing backwards. 'I knew you wouldn't take any notice.'

Around her head, the hawk still swooped and hovered, plainly not taking any notice either.

'Wait, wait!' Iscalda came running up behind the Mage. 'This is madness! Why climb all the way up there when Eliseth is expecting that? I'll take you, Aurian. We'll fly.'

Quickly, Iscalda changed to her equine shape of a white mare. The Mage scrambled up on to her back, drawing on the powers of the talisman to find the paths upon the wind. Up they went, climbing towards the spiral tower and the tall, silver-haired figure that stood on top.

Aurian never had the slightest inkling that the attack was about to happen. She heard a rending scream, and saw a flash of silver as a swordblade clove the air close to her ear. She collected herself in time to see the flailing figure of Sunfeather plunge towards the ground, with her hawk still clinging to his face, gouging at his eyes with its long, curved beak. The bird only broke away before the winged man hit the ground.

Aurian remembered her suspicion, never quite forgotten, that the hawk might contain Anvar's spirit, and began to wonder anew.

Eliseth gave a shrill cry of horror when she saw Sunfeather go down. 'Damn you!' she shrieked. 'Curse you for all eternity!'

Stirred by the Magewoman, the wind began to swirl and scream around the tower, trying to pluck the Mage from Iscalda's back. Using the Staff to boost her powers, Aurian formed a shield around herself and her companions, including the hawk, who had soared back up to her shoulder, and was sheltered, like the mare, in the protective bubble of the energy barrier.

466

Eliseth's first bolt of lightning hit them, and glanced off the shield in a shower of sparks. It was followed by further bolts, and a shower of hail that also rattled harmlessly off the barrier.

Aurian dropped her shield for an instant, and struck at the tower with a bolt of energy from the Staff of Earth. For an instant, the soaring building was enveloped in a haze of vibrant green force, and Aurian heard the boom as it shook all the way down to its foundations. A network of cracks snaked up the stonework, but still the tower held. Eliseth's servant, who had been trying to shelter behind her, was knocked off his feet by Aurian's bolt, and rolled helplessly over the edge. His long, drawn-out wail was cut off sharply as he hit the ground, and Aurian shuddered. Eliseth, secure behind her own shields, simply laughed at the Mage.

Then, for the first time, Aurian noticed that Eliseth had made a mistake. The Sword of Flame was still lying on the tower roof – outside the Magewoman's shield – and Forral had climbed the spiral path, with Shia a step behind them. They crept across the roof behind Eliseth's back, and Aurian sent Iscalda hurtling downwards as she saw Forral make a dive for the Artefact.

The Mage suddenly remembered that she had told him why she had failed to win the Sword the first time, and her blood turned to ice in her veins. 'No . . .' she thought. As Forral's hand grasped the hilt of the Sword, he looked up at her with such love and longing in his eyes, that Aurian knew in an instant what he was about to do. 'No,' she screamed inwardly. 'No no no . . .'

Everything seemed to happen very slowly. Forral turned the hilt of the Sword in his hands and hurled Anvar's body down upon the blade. Eliseth began to turn round, her mouth open in a shriek of protest as Aurian, still some three feet above the level of the roof, leapt down from Iscalda's back and rushed to the swordsman's side.

Forral pressed the hilt of the Sword, slippery with his lifeblood, Anvar's lifeblood, into the Mage's hands. 'Yours,' he whispered.

'*Yours,*' sang the Sword. A tongue of red fire ran down the dripping blade, and Aurian felt the power shudder through her. *'Yours. Bonded with lifeblood, with a sacrifice, as was promised. Claimed and joined at last . . .'*

Aurian felt sick. This filthy thing! But she wouldn't let weak sentiment undo Forral's sacrifice. Half-blinded by tears, she leapt to her feet and swung the fiery Sword in a great, shearing arc that cut right through Eliseth's shield in a massive shower of sparks. Turning her hands as Forral had taught her when she was a little girl in her mother's Vale, the Mage brought the Sword round in the return stroke, and locked eyes with Eliseth, the fire of Aurian's anger meeting the ice of the Magewoman's hatred. Then the Sword of Flame bit down through Eliseth's skull, down through her flawless face and buried itself deep in the Magewoman's body before coming to a halt at last.

Aurian slumped, exhausted and wretched, over the body of her vanquished foe. Am I dying too? she thought dispassionately. The light seemed to be growing brighter and brighter through her closed eyelids, and that unearthly, plangeant singing . . . Singing? Who in the name of all creation could be singing? No living creature made a sound like that, yet it seemed so familiar . . . Wearily, Aurian raised her head and opened her eyes. The sun was rising – and there were Dragons everywhere; some red, some gold, some green – all blinking their huge eyes of slumbering fire and stretching out their ribbed, translucent wings to catch the early sun.

A huge gold creature reclined next to the Mage on the bloodstained roof of the tower. He looked familiar, somehow. 'But . . .' said Aurian, 'but . . .'

The morning came alive with light and music as the dragon began to speak. 'But I perished in the earthquake when the treasure-chamber collapsed?' A fall of shimmering colour laced the air as it began to laugh. 'Illusion, Mage – all illusion. The Sword was designed to bring us back into time when it was claimed and evil defeated, for we did not wish to live in the world until it was a better place . . .' The dragon tilted its head and looked at her critically. 'I must say, you took your time about it.'

Aurian's temper flashed. 'And I must say I'm surprised that you invented such a filthy thing as this.' She looked down in disgust at the bloodstained Sword, which was still humming its fierce song of bloodshed and slaughter. 'Furthermore, you can have the foul thing back!' With all her strength she drove the blade point-down into the stone of the tower roof. To her surprise, the Sword sank in easily for over half its length, and stuck there. The dragon looked at her, its eyes open very wide with surprise – and a good deal of respect. 'Temeritous Mage,' it sang. 'Another legend born!'

'A pox on your legends,' Aurian snapped – and then relented. It was absolutely impossible to stay angry for long with something so magnificent and so beautiful. She thought it must probably be a survival characteristic, since the Dragonfolk were such an irritating race in general.

'I'm glad you're back,' she told the Dragon softly – 'but I hope you appreciate the sacrifices that have been made for you.' With that, she turned to Forral – and came face to face with the vast and looming figure of Death. 'Well, you've got both of them now,' she said bitterly. 'Are you happy at last?'

'On the contrary, Mage,' said the Spectre. From the tone of its voice, it almost sounded as though it was smiling within the dark depths of its cowl. 'I may not have both – not yet. I have come for the grail, however. Are you still prepared to keep your promise?'

'May – may I borrow it for a few minutes first?' Aurian asked quickly.

This time, the Spectre laughed out loud. 'As the Dragons say, no one ever beat a Mage for gall. Yes, you may borrow it – on condition that you promise never to trespass in my realm again – until I invite you, that is.'

'I think I can safely promise *that*,' Aurian told him.

'See, then, I can even help you.'

The Mage heard the drumming of wings, and saw Petrel's Skyfolk approaching, bearing the bodies of Chiamh and Vannor. Gently, they laid them down beside the Mage.

'One belongs to you,' Death's voice came again, 'and one to me. The Windeye you may have, but the other was snatched from my realm, and must return.'

Aurian nodded wordlessly. She would miss dear Vannor.

Death Himself picked up the grail from a sheltered corner of the rooftop, and Aurian watched astonished as the black discoloration cleared in his hands to a bright, unsullied gold once more. Inclining his head, he handed it back to her. It seemed to be filled to the brim with blue-white light. Kneeling over Chiamh's mutilated corpse, she sprinkled some of the liquid radiance on his dreadful wounds. His eyes opened and he smiled up at her. 'I thought I was dead,' he said softly. 'I'm glad I'm not. I would have missed you.'

'What about me?' said an impatient voice in mindspeech. Aurian turned to see Wolf. For an instant she wondered what to do – and then she knew. 'Here, my son,' she put the grail down in front of the shaggy grey form. 'Drink.'

As Wolf lapped at the luminescent contents of the grail, the radiance seemed to seep into him, spreading throughout his body, growing stronger and stronger until the glow was too bright to look at. When Aurian could look again, the sturdy, dark-haired lad that she had seen Beyond the Worlds stood there, clad in a shaggy grey cloak.

Aurian leapt up to embrace him, only to feel him stiffen in her arms. 'Dad,' he cried out in anguish. 'He's dead!'

Before Aurian could answer, the air turned chill, and a dark shadow blotted out the early sun. The Winged Folk scattered with cries of dismay and even the Dragons flapped their great wings and hissed uneasily. Aurian, fearless, strode to the edge of the roof, the grail held in her outstretched hands. 'Here it is,' she called. 'I have kept my promise to you, too.'

In a dark, thin stream like smoke, the Nihilim poured into the grail – and emerged again, radiant and resplendent, with translucent silver wings. Death bowed low to the Mage. 'Indeed, Lady,' he said in deepest respect, 'of all your feats, this may truly be the greatest. You have my gratitude – and the gratitude of all Mortal creatures everywhere.'

As the seraphs vanished, a misty figure began to form beside the Spectre, growing more solid by the moment. 'Forral!' Aurian cried.

The swordsman, in his true form, held out his arms to her, and Aurian was amazed to find that she could touch him as though he were made of solid flesh.

470

'My gift to you,' Death said softly. 'A chance to say farewell.'

'I can't,' Aurian cried. 'I can't lose you again!'

'Yes you can, love,' the swordsman said firmly. 'I'm dead anyway, remember? I'm not supposed to be here. Death was right – it's time I went on now. Vannor and I will go together. I got to see you one last time, and I got to meet my son, and that's all I really wanted. You'll be safe now, and happy . . .' He took the grail from her hands, and poured the last of the radiance over the bloodstained form of Anvar. Before Aurian's eyes, the body began to heal.

Forral bowed to Death, and handed him the grail. As the Spectre vanished, the swordsman embraced his son, and took the Mage in his arms. 'Anvar is my last gift to you,' he whispered. 'Be happy. Safe journey, love – until we meet again.' He vanished like smoke, and Aurian's arms were empty – but at her feet, Anvar stirred, and opened his blue eyes, and smiled, while unregarded, the body of a hawk fell to the ground nearby. 'My love,' Anvar whispered. The minds of the soulmates touched and brimmed over with joy as Aurian embraced him, welcoming him home at last.

Zanna was standing on the promontory beyond the fishing settlement, looking out as the rising sun painted a path of rose and gold across a sleek green ocean. She had wakened early, from the strangest dream. Vannor had been standing before her, wreathed in a nimbus of effulgent gold. 'I'm just off now, lass,' he'd said, 'so I thought I had better come and say good-bye. Forral and I are going together. We're taking the grail back to Death – but you don't want to hear about all that. Everything turned out all right in the end. Eliseth is dead, and Aurian and Anvar have been reunited – oh, and Wolf has turned into a boy at last. Anyway, I'd best be off, love – I'll miss you. Take care of yourself and my little granddaughter, won't you? Keep me in your heart, and I'll never be far away.' Zanna had felt the ghostly imprint of a kiss on her forehead – and then she had awakened. Vannor had gone, but the kiss somehow remained.

The Nightrunner wiped the tears from her face and looked

471

out across the ocean. It had been real – of that she was absolutely certain. 'Goodbye, dad,' she whispered. 'Take care of yourself.' She wondered how he had known about his granddaughter – at this point, she had not been sure herself that she carried a child. I wonder if I should break the news to Tarnal yet? she thought.

Out to sea, her eye was caught by the sparkle of sunlight on fountaining spray. Zanna caught her breath. There were whales out there! More whales than she could ever have imagined! Then, coming down from the north, she saw another cluster of the sleek dark shapes – only four or five – with one whale, the biggest, far outstripping the others. The two groups converged in a glorious display, leaping joyfully from the water with tremendous grace; flinging the sea from their great bodies in glittering diamond arcs. Even as Zanna watched, the small group of Leviathan were absorbed into the greater family of their comrades – and then all of them were gone together, vanishing into the golden blaze of sunrise like a dream emerging into morning.

Some days later, Aurian and several of her companions prepared to depart from Dhiammara for good. Most, including the captured Khazalim, were returning to their homes. Eliizar and Nereni were looking forward to returning to their settlement to start the work of rebuilding their lives. To everyone's surprise, Raven and Aguila, who had been healed by Aurian, were going back there too. 'I never had any luck in Aerillia,' Raven insisted. 'Let the priests keep it, if they're so keen. Besides, I would miss Nereni.' She gave her old friend a dazzling smile.

'And we're going back to the Xandim – Chiamh, Iscalda and I,' said Schiannath. 'It's about time someone knocked them into shape. We'll be near enough to Aurian and Anvar to visit, though.'

Eliizar was standing with his arm around his daughter. 'And where will you go?' he asked the Mages. 'Surely not back to the north?'

Anvar shook his head. 'No – we've talked about it, and while there's still a great deal to be done in the north – the

472

missing cats and the business with the Phaerie for instance –
we've decided D'arvan will have to handle that for a while – a
good, long while.'

'We may still wield the Staff and the Harp, but we want a
rest,' said Aurian with a smile, 'and we want a chance to be a
family. Anvar was telling me about a wonderful bay he found
once, where the sea is warm and blue, and there's a lush forest
behind, full of fruit and game . . . We plan to settle down there
and let someone else take on the troubles of the world for a
time. There are even hills just inland with some caves for Shia
to rear her cubs.' She smiled at her friend, who was sitting
rubbing heads with Khanu.

'Indeed – you can help me look after them, if you're so
keen,' the cat said privately to the Mage.

Aurian smiled. 'What will you do?' she asked Grince.

The thief chuckled. 'Oh, I think I'll get by,' he said.
Rummaging in the inner pocket of his tunic and pulling out a
little leather bag, he poured the contents into his hand in a
sparkling stream.

Aurian gasped – and burst out laughing. 'Pendral's jewels!
Why, you little wretch,' she chuckled. 'You've carried them
around with you all this time?'

'Too bloody right I did,' Grince snorted. 'After all I went
through to get them, did you think I'd leave them behind?'